Waking Up Gray

Please Return To Betty

Other R.E. Bradshaw titles:

OUT ON THE SOUND
(Adventures of Decky and Charlie, # 1)

SWEET CAROLINA GIRLS

THE GIRL BACK HOME

RAINEY DAYS
Finalist Lesbian Fiction Readers Choice Awards
Golden Crown Literary Society Awards Finalist
Suspense/Thriller
(Rainey Bell Series, #1)

COMING SUMMER 2011

RAINEY NIGHTS
(Rainey Bell Series, #2)

WAKING UP GRAY

R. E. BRADSHAW

PUBLISHED BY

R. E. BRADSHAW BOOKS

US

Waking Up Gray

R. E. Bradshaw

R. E. Bradshaw Books/May 2011

ISBN 13: 978-0-98357-200-8

http://www.rebradshawbooks.com

Rebecca Elizabeth Bradshaw on Facebook

For information contact rebradshawbooks@gmail.com

Acknowledgements

The very first acknowledgement I need to make is to the North Carolina Language and Life Project (NCLLP) at North Carolina State University and to the public television stations of UNC TV. It was while watching the NCLLP production of "The Carolina Brogue" that the idea for this novel began. Growing up on the Outer Banks of North Carolina, I was immersed in the Brogue for most of my life. It is a charming and unique feature of the area and I encourage anyone who hasn't visited the Outer Banks to do so, but if you cannot, at least take a listen to the brogue in it's purest form. Information about the NCLLP can be found on the website: http://ncsu.edu/linguistics/ncllp/index.php

To the readers who took a chance on an unknown independent author, I am eternally grateful. It is your words of encouragement that keep me at the keyboard. I would be remiss if I did not mention the wonderful women in the Facebook group, Readers of Author R. E. Bradshaw. Thank you for many hours of laughter and inspiration.

To all the authors and readers in the Virtual Living Room, who have offered much needed advice and help, God bless you.

Kaycee, thank you for being patient while working with this newbie. Editing my manuscript could not have been easy. I promise to work on the comma situation.

Catherine, you have no idea how much I appreciated handing the formatting over to you.

Patty Henderson, you are a Godsend. Thank you, thank you.

Chris, Linda, Dawn – Thank you for keeping me laughing and sane.

Lynne, you have been my best friend for twenty-five years. Your constant love and encouragement have been a blessing. I am so lucky to have you in my life.

Mom, thank you for reading to me and beginning my life long love affair with books.

Dad, thank you for your undying faith in me.

Jonathon, you are the best son in the world and we are so proud of you. Thank you and Kendra for handing out my books to all your lesbian friends.

And lastly, but definitely not least, Deb, you are and have been the wind beneath my wings for twenty-four years. This is just one in a long line of dreams you have made come true. I love you and thank you for believing in me.

"Only that day dawns to which we are awake."
Henry David Thoreau

Chapter One

The Hatteras Class ferry, drafting at only four feet through the shallow inlet, was packed with tourists trying to hang on to the last vestiges of summer before school and jobs beckoned them home. The floating behemoth rumbled and roared its way through the Pamlico Sound, carrying a full load of cars and campers, followed by a chorus of seagulls. The larger black-backed scavengers squawked and screeched, with the gray Laughing Gulls adding their trills to the mix. Children and adults alike giggled and squealed while tossing pieces of bread above their heads as the large birds swooped and dove to within inches of their faces. Some of the more brave souls held the bread aloft until a bold gull would dive in and take it from an outstretched hand. Those passengers still spooked by the movie, 'The Birds,' remained at the bow of the boat, far away from the action at the rear.

On this, the last Friday in August, the sun blasted its rays down from a beautiful clear blue sky. Off the coast, a tropical storm was heading straight for the Outer Banks of North Carolina, spurring the current influx of tourists to enjoy the weather while it lasted. Next weekend would be the Labor Day holiday, one of the busiest times of the year, but the weather reports were ominous. It was, at the least, going to be a wet weekend. Today there were no signs of the offshore disturbance. The ferry pushed the clear green water aside as it made its way across to Ocracoke Island. The deck began to sway with the waves, when the vessel broke out from behind the protection of Hatteras Island, and moved out into the ocean waves pouring into the Sound through the inlet.

Mary Elizabeth Jackson Moore, Lizbeth to family and friends, studied the name on the side of the ferry, "Chicamacomico," from her perch on the hood of her car. She knew the name from the historic life-saving station in Rodanthe. She passed through the tiny village, at the north end of Hatteras Island, an hour and a half ago. Lizbeth was on the last legs of a long journey, both figuratively and literally. She started this trip from her home, in Durham, that morning, but the voyage began many years ago. Now, she was crossing from Hatteras to Ocracoke Island on a ferry named Chicamacomico, and the word mesmerized her. She knew it was an old Native American place name, previously designating the area around the present day village of Rodanthe. It wasn't what it meant, as much as how it felt in her mouth when she said it. It was something about the rhythm of the syllables that made her smile.

Lizbeth loved words, old and new words, words naming things and places no longer in existence; all words fascinated her. From her first memories, she had been in love with the dictionary. She studied words for the fun of it and then found out someone would give her a degree for that. She was currently in her final semester of study in Linguistic Anthropology at Duke University. By taking classes through the summers, she would graduate with a Master's Degree in only five years. She was headed to Ocracoke to complete the final assignment, her thesis paper.

Lizbeth intended to spend the next three and a half months studying the Carolina Brogue, unique to the Outer Banks of North Carolina. She needed to collect evidence to support her theory that the almost Cockney accent and word usage were a product of many years of isolation on the barrier islands. This isolation protected some parts of the original speech, brought to this country by the islanders' English and Irish ancestors. It was a dream project for Lizbeth. She had been coming to Ocracoke all of her life. As a child, she had fallen in love with listening to the "hoi toide" accent. It was a pure pleasure to study it, in hopes of preserving the quickly disappearing brogue of old. The sound of a native islander speaking was part of the charm of the quaint village community on the south end of the small island.

Lizbeth Jackson - she dropped the Moore after the divorce - was not the typical college student. She began her first undergraduate courses at age thirty-five. She turned forty in July and found her first gray strand of hair this morning. Lizbeth started her education at Duke after raising a daughter and while divorcing a husband. Years of seeing to everyone else's needs and wants had left her tired and unfulfilled. After the divorce, Lizbeth decided to take care of her own desires for a while. The results had been astounding and the woman she had been destined to be, before life got in the way, began to emerge. She was happy and satisfied with her current path.

A young man took his shirt off in front of her and threw it into the back of his Jeep Wrangler. He reached in the Jeep and started a Jimmy Buffet CD, turning it up to overcome the growling ferry engines. From behind her dark sunglasses, Lizbeth watched his tanned muscles ripple. She was beginning to think it was true that women reached their sexual peak at forty. She had started to pay more attention to the men around her, finding the ones her own age uninteresting, but those young hot studs all over the Duke campus were becoming increasingly attractive. She smiled at her inner cougar. The young man by the Jeep looked to be in his early twenties, around her daughter's age. Well, it never hurt to look. After all, she was forty, not ancient.

Lizbeth's arms began to tingle under the glaring sun. She reached into the canvas bag beside her, pulling out sunscreen, and applying it to any exposed areas. She had a beautifully rare combination of fair skin, dark hair, and piercing blue eyes. At five foot six, she was equipped with long lean muscle, and could still wear the same size jeans she wore at twenty-one. She was blessed with a fast metabolism and maintained an exercise regimen since the birth of her only child. Lizbeth Jackson might have been forty, but she wore forty very well, so well in fact, much younger men frequently asked her out. She hadn't accepted any of their offers, but the idea of a twenty-something suitor was starting to appeal to her.

She leaned back against the windshield of her car and bathed in the warm sunlight while the ferry started the wide turn toward the Ocracoke docks. She was going to live on an island, a magical place treasured since childhood, until mid December. Then she would graduate, beginning the New Year with a Master's degree and a job in the state library system; it was all arranged. Lizbeth smiled to herself. Her future held the greatest of possibilities. No more looking back at what might have been.

Jimmy Buffet crooned from the Jeep stereo. The song was 'A Pirate Looks at Forty.' Lizbeth sang along to herself. The ferry rocked through a wave set and life was good.

#

Lizbeth disembarked the ferry with a smile and a nod from the khaki clad ferryman, as her car bumped up the ramp. She turned the sixty-five Mustang, a prize from the divorce, to the right and onto NC Highway 12, joining the line of cars making its way slowly toward the village at the far end of the island. There were only thirteen and a half miles from the Hatteras Ferry dock on the north end to the Swan Quarter and Cedar Island Ferry docks on the south end of the island, but with the traffic, it took Lizbeth nearly thirty minutes to drive it.

Ocracoke was one of the barrier island strips of sand along the coast that kept the ocean from reaching the mainland. It bore the brunt of the angry sea and would soon serve that purpose again, according to the weather broadcast coming over her radio. Lizbeth didn't care. Today the sun was shining and the skies were clear. Memories of her previous trips to Ocracoke flooded her mind as she drove past the waving sea oats on top of the dunes lining the ocean side of the road.

Lizbeth had been a regular visitor, with her family, every summer as far back as she could remember, until she turned sixteen. That was the summer she met James and begged to stay in Durham with a friend. Maybe things would have worked out differently if she had joined her family, but then she wouldn't have her daughter. She thought about the first summer she brought Mazie down to Ocracoke. Laughing and kicking at the surf when it washed across her toes, at only six months old, she took to the water like a duck. That was back when she and James, though faced with the stress of being very young, new parents, were still happy and in love. Lizbeth tried to remember the pleasant times when she could, but the bad still outweighed the good.

Sea oats and twisted live oaks sprung up along the highway. Six miles into the drive, Lizbeth passed the Banker Pony pens, on the Sound side, where the National Park Service maintained a herd of about thirty formerly wild ponies. The ponies roamed freely for two hundred years, at times in herds as large as five hundred head. Depending on the story one chose to believe, the Banker Ponies were the descendents of animals left by Sir Walter Raleigh's expedition, Spanish ponies brought by DeSoto, or shipwreck survivors of vessels that lost the battle with the Diamond Shoals. The infamous shoals off the coast of North Carolina earned the nickname, "The Graveyard of the Atlantic," now host to countless souls.

The island, a slender splinter in the Atlantic, grew broader then thinner again, as Lizbeth watched the Pamlico Sound come in and out of view. From an aerial map, Lizbeth thought the island looked like a fishing rod with the village resembling the reel, attached on the Sound side and protected from the ocean waves. She slowed the Mustang down to a crawl on the outskirts of civilization, represented by the first manmade structures looming up out of the marsh on the right. The charm of Ocracoke Village, like its speed limits, brought the hurried world to a creeping pace. The meandering speed prevented Lizbeth from running over several tourists, who were trying to share the skinny road with the vehicular traffic. She couldn't wait to park her car.

Highway 12 turned into Harbor Road as it snaked to the right around Silver Lake Harbor. The sign at the turnoff for Howard Street read, "Drive Real, Real Slow," another reminder of the slow pace of island life. Howard Street had never been modernized. It was merely a lane used by the residents to reach their houses, some of them standing since the early 1700's. The street was paved with only crushed oyster shells, hard packed in the sandy loam. Moss-covered picket fences lined Howard Street, shaded by a live oak canopy entangled with cedar trees. With so few vehicles passing through, the road took visitors back in time, engulfing them in the quaint old cottages interspersed with aged family cemeteries.

Lizbeth pulled into the driveway of the familiar cottage. It was a classic "story and a jump" style, prevalent in the original homes. The "jump" consisted of the two bedrooms upstairs, shaped by the steeply slanting roof, having only half windows and low, cramped ceilings. Downstairs, at the front of the cottage, a narrow hallway leading to the dining area and kitchen at the rear intersected a small parlor and another bedroom. The wooden, slat-sided exterior was painted white, with blue trim. A sitting porch wrapped its way around the front and right sides of the house. The porch was screened-in, top to bottom. Two old rocking chairs and a small table sat next to the front door. A day bed called to Lizbeth from the side porch for her to come and take a nap. She dearly wished she could.

After an already long day of travel, she was anxious to unpack the car. Lizbeth pulled in slowly, passing the red brick chimney, and stopped at the end of the driveway. She fished around in her purse and finally located the keys to the cottage. Her great-aunt, Minnie, had lived in the cottage all her life. She played hostess to Lizbeth's family and all the other members of the Jackson clan that had a notion to spend time on the island every summer. Aunt Minnie was a true "O'coker," always welcoming her guests with a smile and a bear hug. She would forever hold a special place in the Jackson family. She passed several years ago, leaving the cottage to Lizbeth's cousins, who graciously agreed to let Lizbeth rent it this Fall at a discounted price. Still, this little sabbatical was costing Lizbeth nearly ten thousand dollars. She could afford it. Her ex-husband was paying dearly for his unfaithfulness.

Lizbeth got out of the car, stretching up to the sky, taking in a huge breath of the fresh island air. She opened the trunk and began the task of unloading the car. Using the key, she let herself in through the front door while balancing a box of papers on one hip. The cottage was spotlessly clean. Lizbeth knew her cousin Sharon had someone come in and make the place ready for her. She would have to remember to send her a thank you note.

She put the box down on the end of the couch and took a tour of what would be her home for the next fourteen weeks. The cottage, built in the late 1800's, had few alterations over the years. With good maintenance, the cottage had survived hurricanes, tropical storms, and nor'easters for more than a century. White bead board covered the walls of the small rooms and low ceilings. A fireplace dominated one wall in the parlor and was bookended by windows made of antique panes of glass, the bubbles and swirls giving away their age. A few panes had been replaced over the years and were easily distinguished from the originals by their lack of imperfections.

The floors were old wood planking, worn smooth from years of sandy feet. The cousins had recently had the floors resurfaced, the final coat still glistening from its recent polish. The bedroom, across from the parlor, had two sets of twin beds stuffed into the tiny space. There was barely room to move in between the four beds. Now that it was a rental property, Lizbeth assumed they were trying to get as many beds in the small cottage as possible. Down the hall, on the same side as the parlor, was the only bathroom, with a tub, toilet, and sink all crammed into the tiny room. The recently repaneled walls enveloped her in the aroma of cedar.

At the end of the hall, the kitchen, a long narrow room, ran the entire width of the cottage with a breakfast nook at one end. Lizbeth found a bottle of wine on the top shelf of the otherwise empty refrigerator. A note and a bow were attached to the neck of the bottle. The note was from her cousin, telling her to enjoy her stay. Lizbeth intended to do just that as soon as she finished unloading the car. She opened the back door, stepping onto the little porch, where someone had left a few fishing rods, a tackle box, and a bicycle. She wasn't sure she would do much fishing, but the bike would come in handy. No one who lived on the island drove around the village. Everyone walked or rode a bike. It was part of the charm of Ocracoke, to leave modern conveniences to the mainlanders.

A few modern conveniences were a blessing though. The old cistern, beside the house, was no longer needed to collect fresh water, but remained as an ode to the days before the island had a municipal water system. Thank goodness the outhouse was no longer necessary. Central heat and air had been added to the cottage in the nineties; until then the only air conditioning was the breeze from outside. The temperature today was in the upper eighties, with not much wind. Houses and trees sheltered shady Howard Street from the light breeze. Lizbeth began to sweat in the heavy humidity. She turned the air-conditioning on after a few trips up to the stuffy second floor. The cottage had been unoccupied for a few days and with the recent temperatures, it needed a good airing out. Lizbeth would open all the windows later, after dark, to freshen the air, but right now, she needed to cool the place down.

She chose the bedroom upstairs that looked out over Howard Street. She noticed an old woman sitting on the porch of the cottage across from her. The woman was working intently on a large bowl of snap beans, breaking off the ends and snapping the beans in two. She did this while watching the people walking up and down the street, stopping her snapping to wave or smile occasionally at a passerby. The woman was a local and vaguely familiar to Lizbeth. She knew she was a friend of her Aunt and remembered meeting her many years ago, although she could not, at the moment, recall her name.

At last, she shut all the doors on the car and locked it. Lizbeth hoped not to have to get back in it for a very long time. Now all she needed to do was make the walk down to the Community Store for supplies. It would take several trips over the next few days to get everything she would need, because she could only buy what she could carry. Lizbeth had packed a cooler with some meat, a few dry goods, and fresh vegetables, but she needed bread and milk. She'd have to check the bathroom for toilet paper. This wasn't the sort of place where she could just pop off to the Seven-Eleven if she ran out in the middle of the night.

Lizbeth grabbed the canvas shopping bags hanging in the kitchen and headed out the front door. She had just stepped into the street when the lady on the porch called out to her.

"Howdy, neighbor."

Lizbeth smiled, walking across the lane to the picket fence in front of the other woman's home. She could see the woman clearly now through the screen guarding her porch from the ever-present mosquitoes. She had the worn leathery skin of someone who had spent many years outside. Her long hair was gray and pulled back in a ponytail. She looked to be in her seventies, but her blue eyes sparkled like a child's.

Lizbeth answered, "Howdy to you, too."

"You must be one of those Jackson girls. Y'all look so much alike."

"Yes ma'am. I'm Lizbeth Jackson. My daddy is Aunt Minnie's sister Olive's grandson, David." Lizbeth knew it was important to get the genealogy lined out for older folks. It helped them put things in perspective.

"Yes, Lizbeth, I 'member you. You ain't been to these parts in a while now."

"No, ma'am. I haven't been down to the cottage in fifteen years. My ex-husband's family has a cottage in Atlantic Beach, so I spent my vacations there. I missed the island though. I can't believe how much it's grown."

"Yep, they keep building more places to put those dingbatters. They'll sink this island one day, with all their commercializin'."

Dingbatter was a reference to the off-islander, or tourist, and usually not a bright one. A dingbatter might ask, "What time does the two o'clock ferry leave?" This and other unique words and unusual ways of using existing words, found on Ocracoke, had driven Lizbeth to study the locals' distinctive way of speaking. She was happy to have such a perfect subject for her study right across the street. Lizbeth listened as all the long "i" sounds became "oi" in the older woman's brogue. Island became oiland, like became loike, tide became toide, and so on. It was music to a Linguistic Anthropologist's ears.

"Well, at least Howard Street is the same," Lizbeth said. "I'm so sorry, but I cannot remember your name."

"Darlin', I'd forget it myself if they didn't call me by it at least onc't a day. It's Fanny O'Neal."

"Oh, yes, Miss Fanny, now I remember. It's so good to see you again." Lizbeth added the appropriate Miss, in the classic southern show of respect for one's elders.

Fanny smiled broadly, her leather skin creasing into deep dimples on both cheeks. Fanny had smiled often in her lifetime. She asked Lizbeth, "How long you here for?"

"I'll be here until mid December. I hope we can become great friends."

"Well, Lizbeth, I don't see that as bein' no hard task." Fanny flicked a bean tip off her lap, and added, "Where you off to?"

Lizbeth could have stood there listening to Fanny talk for hours and had forgotten about the canvas bags in her hand. Suddenly reminded, she answered, "I have to go to the Community Store for a few things."

"First thing I'll tell ya' is buy your groceries off island. They charge a right lot for their wares down here," Fanny offered.

"I brought most of what I need for this coming week. Later I'll have to make a trip to Avon for bulk shopping, but for now it's the Community Store for me," Lizbeth said, smiling, holding up the bags.

Fanny seemed to be enjoying having someone with whom to talk. She continued, "My granddaughter, Gray, takes me up the beach 'bout onc't a month to get supplies. You'll meet her. She lives here with me. You might remember her. Y'all are 'bout the same age."

"Maybe, I don't remember much, just flashes. I was so young all those years ago. In any case, I look forward to meeting her," Lizbeth said, then looked up at the sky. "It's getting late. I better get moving. It was so nice to see you again, Miss Fanny."

"If you're out later, come on over and sit on the pizer and we'll visit some more," Fanny said, with a wave and a smile.

Pizer, pronounced with a long "i," was the Ocracoke word for porch. Lizbeth suspected it was a bastardization of the word piazza. She smiled, saying, "Thank you for the invitation. I'll take you up on it, if not tonight, sometime very soon," before walking away.

As she walked toward the store, Lizbeth reveled in the feeling that she had done the right thing in coming here. Her work would be rewarding and her life was finally on a positive track. She was so happy she couldn't hold it in. She felt wonderful and even skipped a few steps, before she thought about what she must look like, a grown woman skipping down the road with a grin on her face. Then, changing her mind, she smiled even more broadly and began to skip once again.

#

Lizbeth didn't make it to Fanny's pizer for that chat. After hauling her groceries back to the cottage, she made a salad from the fresh vegetables she bought that morning at a roadside stand outside of Plymouth. She sat down at the breakfast nook table, bringing along the bottle of wine and a glass. While she ate, she read over the very rough draft of her thesis paper for the hundredth time. Finished with her meal, Lizbeth went into the parlor, where she began to go through files and boxes of paper, organizing for the task at hand. Namely, making years of research make sense.

After several hours and a few glasses of wine, the activities of the day caught up with her. She yawned and looked up at the clock. It was after ten and she was exhausted. Lizbeth had turned the air-conditioning off earlier and opened all the windows when the temperature outside dropped to just below seventy. She didn't bother with closing the ones downstairs before going up to bed. This was Ocracoke; she could leave her doors and windows unlocked, if she wanted to, and still rest peacefully.

Lizbeth could hear the bugs and frogs outside in full voice this evening, as she ascended the stairs. She undressed quickly and threw on an old nightgown. When she climbed into the cool crisp sheets, her body relaxed. She was asleep almost before she turned off the lamp on the bedside table. Shortly, Lizbeth was aroused from her slumber by the sound of a motorized moped pulling up to the house across the street. She glanced at the clock. It was eleven fifty.

Now awake, she got up. Her housecoat was draped over the wing-backed chair near the window. Lizbeth reached for the coat and looked out at the street. In front of Fanny's house, a woman sat on a moped, the engine now silenced. The female moped driver was talking to a tall woman with short blond hair standing beside the gate to Fanny's yard. The voices carried in the still night air.

The driver was saying, "Come on, Gray. Just one more."

Lizbeth realized this must be Fanny's granddaughter, Gray. She heard Gray answer, with a chuckle, "No, now you go on back to the campground, before your husband comes looking for you."

"Oh hell, he's passed out by now. Please, just one more."

Due to the darkness and shadows, Lizbeth could not make out any of the women's features. The only reason she was sure the tall one was a blonde was because her hair caught the light from the nearly full moon when a breeze blew the leaves out of the way for a moment. Lizbeth had not turned the light on by the bed, so she was sure they could not see her, either. She watched as the tall blonde took a step toward the driver.

Lizbeth heard Gray say, "Okay, one more, but then you have to go. I have to get up in the morning. Got a full load, first thing."

What happened next made Lizbeth take another step back, further into the shadows. Gray leaned down, tenderly taking the other woman's face into her hands, and then she kissed her. Lizbeth couldn't take her eyes away. The kiss was not a long one, but it had been long enough for Lizbeth to know it wasn't an innocent kiss, to say the least. The driver reached for Gray as she backed away toward her house, but she was out of reach.

"Now, go on back up the beach and thanks for the ride."

The driver came back quickly with, "No, honey, thank you. I enjoyed the ride very much." The woman cranked the moped, while at the same time laying her head back in a laugh. She said, "I hope to take you for another spin the next time I come down." Then she put-putted away.

Lizbeth watched as Gray waved goodbye and then disappeared into her house. It wasn't until Gray vanished that Lizbeth realized she had been holding her breath since the kiss. She questioned the feeling in the pit of her stomach and why she had not turned away. There was something very exciting about what she had just seen. She examined the information she had, surmised that Gray must be a lesbian, and she had just had her way with some tourist's wife. From the sounds of things, Gray must have rocked that woman's world. She certainly didn't want to let Gray go into the house.

Lizbeth went downstairs, got a bottle of water out of the refrigerator, and went out to sit on the porch. She sat in one of the old rockers, drinking her water, listening to the sound of no traffic, no sirens, no noise at all except the sounds of nature all around. The house across the street had the same architectural design. When the light came on in the room that mirrored her own upstairs, she figured that was Gray's bedroom. The light was only on for a few minutes and then the room fell dark again. Gray must have gone to bed.

Lizbeth thought again about the kiss she had witnessed. It had excited her sexually. She knew her body was going through some kind of awakening, because she was thinking more and more about sex these days. Lizbeth had only been with one man, her husband, until after the divorce. Since then she had slept with a couple of old acquaintances out of boredom and horniness, but these feelings she was having now portended something unusual was happening to her body. Lizbeth had never kissed a woman and certainly not had sex with one, but in her current state of newfound heightened sexuality, even that kiss had excited her libido. Maybe she should take a page out of Gray's book and have a hot affair with a tourist. No complications, just sex.

Lizbeth finished her water and headed back to bed. She laughed at herself for thinking of bedding complete strangers. She might think about it, but Lizbeth knew she wouldn't. Casual sex just didn't hold that much appeal for her. It was probably because she had been the victim of the cheating husband, who said in his defense, "It was just sex."

She crawled back into bed. The kiss played over in her mind just before she drifted back to sleep.

Chapter Two

The next morning, while in the kitchen making breakfast, Lizbeth turned on the little portable radio on the counter. A young woman with a heavy southern accent read the weather report.

"Earl, Earl, Earl. That is a lot of what we will continue to hear through this week. There hasn't been a huge change in the track, but the storm remains a dangerous category four. The storm is still expected to come within a couple hundred miles of the coast. This means we could see a few showers, a heavy bout or two not out of the question, winds breezy and lots of wave action for the next few days."

Earl was huge. It had formed as a low-pressure cell off the west coast of Africa and moved into the Atlantic on August twenty-second. It now had six days to build in strength. On August twenty-fifth, the storm had been designated the fifth tropical storm of the season, and given the name Earl. Earl had continued to intensify as it made its way across the ocean, feeding off the warm sea temperatures. The forecast was for at least heavy winds and rain for Ocracoke if the storm continued on its current path, and brushed past the Outer Banks of North Carolina. All eyes were on this track and what affect the warmer Caribbean waters would have on the building monster. Ocracoke and most of the eastern United States seaboard was now on hurricane watch.

Lizbeth listened as the reporter went on to say the beaches along the outer islands were now under a rip tide alert. Rip tides formed by the meeting of strong currents flowing out from the shoreline and the current rushing in from the sea. The turbulent water beneath the surface drowned many an inexperienced ocean swimmer. Lizbeth decided she would not be getting in the ocean today.

Instead, after arranging a make do office in the corner of the other upstairs bedroom, she sent emails to some friends and family, letting them know she had arrived safely. When she was finished, she shut down the laptop. The day was already beginning to turn balmy. She closed all the windows in the house and started the air-conditioning again.

Lizbeth felt like being a tourist today. She went upstairs, undressed and slipped into her black one-piece bathing suit. She threw on a pair of gray cotton shorts over the suit and rolled them down at the waist. Before leaving the bedroom, she coated her fair skin in sunscreen and then deciding she might need it, threw the bottle into a canvas bag that she planned to take with her. She also added an over-shirt, just in case the sun became too intense. She found her straw sunhat, retrieved her sunglasses and wallet from her purse, and stepped into her flip-flops. She stopped to look in the mirror. Not bad for forty, she thought, and smiled at her reflection.

Lizbeth took the bike off the back porch and checked the tires. Satisfied they were sufficiently full of air, she dropped her bag in the front basket and rode off down Howard Street. At once the happy tourist, Lizbeth stopped along the way at several shops run out of cottages. There were quilts, candles, handcrafted pottery pieces, jewelry, paintings, so much in fact, that Lizbeth had to tell herself she didn't need to try to see it all in one day. She had months to take it all in.

She left the shelter of the shady lane and ventured out into bumper-to-bumper traffic around Silver Lake Harbor. She peddled unhurriedly, not bothered by the cars around her. When people came to Ocracoke, they needed to slow down. Even if the driver wanted to go faster, it was impossible because the road was jammed with pedestrians, bikes, scooters, and motor vehicles, all on a narrow strip of asphalt.

Lizbeth cycled over to Lighthouse Road, following it to the white squatty tower. The Ocracoke lighthouse, the second oldest operating lighthouse in North Carolina, was built in 1822. It replaced an earlier lighthouse built in 1798 in the shape of a wooden pyramid, which lightning burned down in 1818. The present day lighthouse, standing at a height of seventy-five feet, shone a stationary beam visible for fourteen miles. Lizbeth found the lighthouse and keepers quarters captivating, as she always had. It fascinated her that the exterior of the lighthouse had originally been coated in a formula of lime, salt, ground rice, whiting, and clear glue, which had been mixed with boiling water and applied to the bricks underneath while still hot. It gave the structure an adobe like appearance.

The white painted surface of the lighthouse glowed in the mid-morning sun, as Lizbeth reached out to touch it. Objects like this lighthouse held time still for Lizbeth. It represented happy memories of family and friends. Even as everything else had changed, this lighthouse stood timelessly unaffected, holding her memories. She spent a few minutes letting her thoughts wander back through the past. It seemed all of her happy memories were from before she found out about James' infidelity. After that, she had only gone through the motions of life, never really feeling happy again, until now.

If a brain injury was severe enough, a doctor placed the patient in a drug-induced coma. Lizbeth put herself in an emotional coma, just so she could function through her injuries. Her wounds may not have been physical, but she was battered nonetheless. She was just emerging from more than a decade-long sleep. Like a butterfly, she was spreading her wings after lying dormant for too long.

Lizbeth peddled back out onto the highway. She headed north, stopping to buy a sandwich and some water at Jason's Deli to take to the beach. Her destination was the beach near the airport. She could not ride the bike to the beach through the thick sand of the Point Trail, and it was quite a walk to the water through marshlands on the other trail. She pedaled another half a mile up Highway 12, left the bike at the airport, and walked the remaining quarter mile to the beach. The surf was choppy with waves swelling to six feet at times. The wind gusted occasionally, but overall, it was a beautiful day on this stretch of sand, once named "Best Beach in the U.S." by Dr. Beach. Lizbeth spent the entire afternoon alternately walking the beach, lounging in the sun, and watching the waves. She ventured in only deep enough to splash water on her body when she grew hot, because the sea did not look welcoming, as predicted.

Lizbeth returned home around six o'clock, spent and a bit sunburned, even with the sunscreen. She took a shower, applied lotion to her reddened skin, and climbed the stairs to dress. She put on her loose fitting gray Duke tee shirt, to avoid much contact between clothing and skin, and added a pair of blue cotton shorts. She combed the tangles from the wind out of her dark hair and let it hang down around her shoulders to dry. She peered in the mirror at the single strand of gray hair she discovered yesterday, grabbed it between two fingers, and promptly yanked it out of her scalp. She didn't feel like being gray, yet.

She ate another salad for supper. Soon the weather would turn and the fresh vegetables, handpicked from local farms, would be gone until next summer. She couldn't seem to get enough of them, as she crunched a cucumber slice drenched in ranch dressing. Store bought vegetables in winter just didn't have the same taste. After supper, she poured the remainder of the wine from last night into a glass and went to sit on the porch. She took a book with her, but never opened it. She became enchanted with the people walking in front of the cottage. Tourists wearily dragged toward their cars after a hard day of sightseeing. Locals walked toward home at the end of their workday or headed toward the docks to begin the evening shift.

Smells of frying seafood and grilling beef mingled in the air. A breeze blew steadily through the trees, bringing the aromas of suppertime from the restaurants where it mingled with home cooking in the village. Lizbeth sat listening to the different accents as the people passed her house. Two French Canadians' elegant flowing romance language drifted in the air, before being drowned out by a young woman. Most likely from the Jersey Shore, she complained loudly in her sharp accent that there weren't any hot nightclubs on the island. Lizbeth was most fond of the southern drawl in all its varieties. Southerners expressed themselves not so much with the words they used, but with the cadence and inflection of how they said them. Once again mesmerized by language, she did not notice Fanny had also come out on her porch until she heard her voice calling out to her from across the street.

"Lizbeth, come on over, sit a spell."

"Thank you, Miss Fanny. I believe I will," Lizbeth said, standing up and setting the still unopened book aside. She carried her wine glass with her as she crossed the street to sit with the older woman.

"You got a might bit a sun today, there girl," Fanny said.

Lizbeth looked at her lobster pink legs. "Yeah, I guess I'm going to have to go up a few notches on the sunscreen."

"Nothin' like the beach sun, I tell ya'."

"Oh, but it was worth it. It was a gorgeous day. I enjoyed myself, being a tourist, sightseeing, and playing on the beach," Lizbeth said with such enthusiasm it made the old woman smile.

"Well, I hope so," Fanny said -- an islander way of applauding someone's statement -- followed by a hearty laugh.

"Granfanny, who you up there cacklin' with?" The voice snapped the old woman's head around.

"Well, look what the cat drug in," Fanny said, smiling at the blonde approaching the porch steps.

Lizbeth immediately recognized the blond head. It was Gray, Fanny's granddaughter. Now, in the fading light of day, Lizbeth was face to face with the woman she had seen plant the kiss that Lizbeth had not forgotten. In fact, she thought about how it made her feel several times today. That feeling seized her again when she looked into Gray's crystal blue eyes, the very same sparkling blue as the grandmother's.

Gray was tall, probably five nine or ten. She was muscular, but not overly so. Gray had the athletically toned body of a tri-athlete. Even though she possessed the androgynous good looks of a teenage boy, she had not lost her femininity. Her grandmother had told Lizbeth that she and Gray were about the same age. Lizbeth thought Fanny must have believed Lizbeth to be much younger than she was. Gray's blond hair was really a darker color underneath; maybe a dark blond, but the sun had bleached nearly all the color from the top of her head. Her perfect white teeth shined out at Lizbeth, in stark contrast to her darkly tanned skin.

Lizbeth could tell that this woman lived outside, yet her skin looked healthy and smooth, unlike her grandmother's weathered face. There were a few wrinkles around the eyes, squint lines from years on the water, easily recognized in the locals who made their living from the sea. She was wearing long, brightly colored swim shorts and a white tank top over a sport bathing suit top. Gray moved with long easy strides up the walk, entering the porch, a small cooler clutched in her left hand. She extended her right hand toward Lizbeth as she closed the distance between them, smiling brightly at her grandmother's guest.

"Hi, I'm Gray O'Neal. Hope this old woman hasn't been feeding you too much bull. She likes to do that to tourists."

Lizbeth could hear the O'coker accent in Gray's speech, but there was something else catching her ear. It could be southwestern, Texas maybe. Lizbeth shook Gray's hand, but didn't have time to answer her, as Fanny jumped in.

"She's not no dingbatter, that's Lizbeth Jackson, Minnie's great niece, David's girl."

Gray chuckled, releasing Lizbeth's hand, turning to her grandmother. "I told you, I don't remember people like you do. Hell, I didn't remember half my own family when I moved back, can't expect me to keep up with Minnie's, too." Turning back to Lizbeth, she said, "It's a pleasure to meet you Elizabeth."

Lizbeth corrected her. "It's Lizbeth. My sister is only a year older than I am. When she started talking, she left a couple of syllables out of my name and it stuck. Just say Liz and Beth and put them together."

Fanny wasn't finished with the genealogy lesson. She interrupted the introductions with, "You ought to know who you kin to on this island. It can make for strange bedfellas if'n you don't."

Gray responded, "I 'magine," another bit of island slang, meaning to agree with a statement.

"Well, I don't think we have to worry about that," Lizbeth said, joking, and then added, "It's nice to meet you Gray."

Fanny continued, "No, Minnie and me didn't share no kin, we just grew up like sisters."

Gray looked at Lizbeth with a grin that should have belonged to a mischievous boy. She said, "Well, I guess that clears us to sleep together, Granfanny says we're no kin."

The shock must have shown on Lizbeth's face. Gray laughed at her expression. "Easy there, I was just kidding."

Lizbeth let out a weak laugh to cover her embarrassment. Fanny saved her from having to speak.

"Gray, supper's on the table. Wash up and eat, then come visit with us, before you go out a cattin' tonight."

Lizbeth thought ol' Fanny knew her granddaughter well, because if Lizbeth understood the meaning of cattin', that's exactly what Gray had been doing last night. Gray excused herself and went into the house, leaving Lizbeth and Fanny on the porch.

"Miss Fanny, how old do you think I am? You said you thought Gray and I are about the same age, but she looks much younger to me."

"Gray's forty-four. I 'member you being a few years younger, but not by much," Fanny answered.

Lizbeth was shocked. "I just turned forty in July. Wow, she looks so much younger. I would have said early thirties at the most. Must be this healthy salt air." She thought for a minute, then added, "Has she always lived with you, here in this house?"

Fanny, it turned out, loved to tell a story, and she was out of the gate on Gray's history. "Gray and her momma lived with me when she was growing up. Gray's daddy, my son, was killed when his fishin' boat sank, caught in a sudden storm. She was three. She was the first of my kin to leave here and get a college degree. Then she moved to Texas, worked at Sea World in San Antonio for seventeen years. She came back in 2004 for a while, when her momma got the cancer. After her momma died, she came home the next year and been here ever since."

Texas. Lizbeth had been right. She prided herself in recognizing dialects and accents from around the country. Gray had been off the island for a long time and now the two regional dialects were fighting for dominance in her speech. Although, it appeared the banker brogue was winning the battle. It would have to, listening to Fanny speak every day.

Part of Lizbeth's brain was trying to grasp on to anything, the speech patterns, grammar, and pronunciation. She concentrated on the language to distract her from what the other part of her brain was screaming. When Gray shook Lizbeth's hand and smiled at her, Lizbeth felt her heart pitter-patter the same way it did when a handsome man paid her attention. It had nearly shocked the breath out of her when the sensation of Gray's hand in hers sent tingles up her arm. This was all highly disconcerting. The only way she could maintain focus was to continue to study Fanny's speech and keep her talking.

"I should probably remember Gray, since she lived here when we came to visit, but we were so busy being vacationers, I guess I never got to meet her."

"Oh, you met her. You were probably three or four at the time." Fanny had begun another story. "That would make Gray seven or eight. She was runnin' 'round underfoot, trying to get people to pay her for chores. She had recently discovered the love of money. Gray ran pretty wild back then, since her momma and me both worked down at Mr. Sam's hotel. The village raised her. Times were dif'rent. You couldn't let a young'un run loose like that now."

Lizbeth remembered that her parents had only two rules while on Ocracoke. No swimming alone and be home by dark. It was a charming period where no one considered the thought of someone kidnapping children.

Fanny went on. "Gray pestered your momma until she said she'd pay Gray to watch you and your sister playin' in the yard while she went inside to make supper. Her job was to keep y'all in the yard." Fanny started to chuckle at the memory. "Well, ol Gray there wasn't much for babysittin'. She wrangled the two of ya' till it stopped being fun and then her mind went to work. She found some rope on the back porch, told y'all you were playin' pirates and tied you to a tree. She told y'all if you made noise the pirates would come and cut off your heads, and ride them around stuck on the bow of their boats."

By now, Lizbeth was laughing, too. She did not remember the incident, but she could picture it in her mind. Lizbeth said between giggles, "I guess she'd heard too many Blackbeard stories."

Fanny nodded. "That child has always been fascinated with ol' Edward. For years she told everyone she was gonna be a pirate when she grew up."

"How long did she leave us tied up?"

"Well, your momma came out of the house, because it got so quiet. She found Gray sitting on the porch steps, alone. When she asked where you kids was, Gray stood up and said, 'Miss Jackson, I don't know how you do it. Them young'uns is a handful. I had to tie 'em up just to take a minute's rest.'"

Lizbeth joined Fanny in hoots of laughter. Gray stuck her head out the door, a biscuit still in her hand.

She asked, "What are you two going on about out here?"

"Your grandmother is regaling me with stories from your pirate past," Lizbeth said, as the giggles subsided.

"I told you that old woman is full of bull. Don't believe half of what she says. She's senile," Gray said, poking fun at Fanny.

"Drime," Fanny said, which in island parlance was about the same as calling someone a liar. Lizbeth figured it was like saying, "You're dreaming, if you think that's true."

"She was telling me that this was not the first time we met," Lizbeth said. "Seems you tied me to a tree when I was a preschooler and told me if I made any noise the pirates would cut off my head."

Gray stepped out the door, finishing the biscuit, clutching a glass of iced tea in her other hand. She swallowed and said, "Oh, that story. I had forgotten that, but I get reminded periodically when Fog Horn here gets to tellin' stories." Gray paused, and then winked, saying, "So, you're one of those little girls. You're all grown now. Come back for revenge?"

Lizbeth, embarrassed by Gray's obvious flirting, covered it by asking Fanny, "So what did my momma do? Did she pay her?"

"Yep, she did. Said she wished she'd thought of it herself."

The three women laughed while Gray pulled up a chair to join them.

Gray asked Lizbeth, "How long are you here for?"

"I've rented the cottage through mid December. I'm working on my Master's thesis. It's the last thing I have to do, before I can graduate."

"You're in grad school?" Gray asked.

"Yes, but it's a five year program and I actually just got my Bachelor's last year. I kind of got a late start," Lizbeth answered.

True to the Ocracoke way, Gray did not ask why Lizbeth had started school so late in life. Most folks on the island felt that if you wanted them to know something personal, you'd tell them.

Gray continued, "What's your thesis about?"

"I'm getting a Master's in Linguistic Anthropology from Duke. My paper is on preservation of the Carolina Brogue."

"Well, you've come to the right place. Fanny there is an expert on the brogue," Gray said, pointing at Fanny. "You'll have to pick her brain."

"There's been a mess of folk through here, recording how we talk," Fanny said. "I always tell 'em, if'n they had lived on this here island, they'd know how funny we think all the woodsers sound."

A woodser was a person who grew up on the mainland. Lizbeth was a woodser. She commented, "Yes, Miss Fanny, I imagine we do sound funny to you island folk."

Fanny indicated Gray with a nod of the head. "That one there come back here from Texas with more twang than brogue. She's 'bout got it out of her system, but it took years."

"That's right. I came back with a shit kicker accent. Natives couldn't understand me half the time, till I started picking the brogue back up," Gray added.

Lizbeth studied Gray's smile. It was so contagious that she found herself smiling back at her. When she realized she had been staring, she quickly said, "It's funny, most people say the bankers are hard to understand."

Gray chuckled. "You should see it when a foreigner, like a German, tries to talk to an O'coker. They might both be speaking English, but one can't understand the other."

The three women talked for an hour or more about the island and how much it had changed since Lizbeth's childhood. At one point, Fanny turned to Gray, saying, "I thought you were going to Gaffer's tonight."

Gray shrugged, saying simply, "I reckon they can get along without me."

Lizbeth was inexplicably elated at that pronouncement. She didn't want Gray to go. She was having too much fun talking to her. Gray was charming, not to mention easy on the eyes. Lizbeth found herself watching Gray's full lips when she spoke. Her blue eyes appeared to twinkle in the moonlight.

Lizbeth had never felt attracted to a woman in her life, but she knew that was what it was; she recognized the symptoms. Her palms were sweaty and her heart began to beat faster whenever Gray moved closer. When Gray leaned over her to place her tea glass on the table, Lizbeth felt her heart jump into her throat. Once again, she played the game with her brain of trying to concentrate on the conversation, while her inner monologue was questioning her very sexuality. She struggled like this for another hour and then stood up.

"I really have to go home. The sun today took my energy," Lizbeth said.

Gray laughed. "You city girls need to work up to a whole day in the island sun."

"Yeah, I guess I over did it on my first day."

Fanny, who appeared to have dozed off, woke up when the other two started moving around.

"Well, I reckon I need to go on in to bed myself," Fanny said. "Lizbeth, would you like to go with Gray and me to church in the mornin'?"

Lizbeth's heart leapt at the thought of seeing Gray tomorrow. She was beginning to think an alien had invaded her body overnight. She could no more control this attraction than she could the tides.

She answered Fanny, "I would love to attend church with you. What time should I be ready?"

"We go to the 'leven o'clock service," Fanny said.

Gray added, "The dress code is strictly casual. I wear shorts and my flip-flops."

"Sounds like my kind of church," Lizbeth said. "Just come across the street when you're ready. I'll be waiting. Good night, Miss Fanny. Thank you for the hospitality." Lizbeth went out the screen door.

Gray followed. "It was good to meet you again, Lizbeth."

"I'm glad you didn't feel the need to tie me up, this time," Lizbeth joked.

"I'll only do that if your momma pays me again," Gray countered.

"See you tomorrow morning, Gray. I had a wonderful time."

Gray beamed that perfect smile at Lizbeth. "I had a good time, too. Goodnight, Lizbeth."

"Goodnight," Lizbeth said, and then moved away to her own home.

When Lizbeth closed her eyes that night, she saw the kiss again, playing out in her mind. Only, Gray wasn't kissing the other woman this time. She was planting that sweet kiss right on Lizbeth's waiting lips. Lizbeth's eyes flew open. What in the hell was going on with her? She lay there mulling her attraction to Gray over, afraid to close her eyes, in the off chance that she would see Gray kiss her again. The exhaustion finally shut her eyes for her. She spent the night dreaming of more than a kiss with Gray. Evidently, her mind was enjoying itself, while Lizbeth's ability to stop it slept soundly unaware.

Chapter Three

Gray came over at ten thirty to get Lizbeth for church. They joined Fanny on the street, becoming part of the promenade of locals down to the Methodist Church. Gray, true to her word, wore khaki shorts, a white linen button up shirt, and her orange flip-flops. Fanny wore a more traditional Sunday dress, but had Reebok tennis shoes on her feet. Lizbeth, not sure about Gray's casual dress statement, had put on a yellow sundress and sandals.

Lizbeth tried to concentrate on the old church. As she walked up the red brick steps and into the white clapboard-sided United Methodist Church, she remembered the story of the hand-made wooden cross resting on the altar. An islander and his wife constructed and painted the cross, made from salvage of a ship on which an island native served and lost his life. A German U-boat torpedoed and sunk the ship, "Caribsea," on March 11, 1942. The war department did not inform the family of the man's death; they learned a few days later when one of the lost man's cousins found his framed engineering license washed up on the beach. Later, the ship's nameplate and other debris floated up at his family's dock. The story always brought chills to Lizbeth.

Gray was even more attractive in the bright light of day. The white shirt set off her deep tan. Her eyes were not visible behind dark sunglasses, but when she took the glasses off inside the church, the clear crystal beauty of Gray's irises again took Lizbeth aback. Lizbeth could not keep her eyes or mind off Gray as they sat through the service. Today, it wasn't the story of the cross giving Lizbeth chills. Sitting close enough to feel the heat from Gray's body, Lizbeth grew more and more uncomfortable as the service droned on in her ears. She heard not a word. She mechanically rose with the congregation and tried to sing the hymns when prompted. Yet, she remained lost in her own battle to save her soul from its infatuation with the gorgeous woman beside her in the pew. Gray did not seem to notice, which was a good thing because Lizbeth was, by now, convinced that her own body might just grab Gray and kiss her, whether Lizbeth's brain consented or not.

Lizbeth considered forty years old a little late to be switching teams, but then, she had only known one team, and most of that with one man. Could she have missed something in her sexual awakening because she got pregnant and married just before her eighteenth birthday? What if she never gave herself the chance to grow into the person she was really meant to be? Had she been gay and turned that part of her off when she married James? Maybe sexuality wasn't as cut and dried as the world would like her to believe. Instead of black and white, sexuality might be painted in shades of gray. She tried to think of girl crushes she may have had in adolescence. She had practiced kissing on the lips in sixth grade with her best friend, Sherry, but didn't all little girls do that? She had no idea what was happening, and was pondering the answers to her questions when the congregation stood to exit the church. She was so lost in thought that Gray had to touch her to get her attention.

Lizbeth looked up to see both Fanny and Gray staring down at her. She panicked, afraid they would somehow know what she had been thinking. She quickly looked back at the front of the church, crossed herself, and said, "Amen," as if she had been in deep prayer. She felt stupid for doing it. She wasn't even Catholic. It didn't seem to bother Gray or Fanny one way or another. They must have bought the prayer bit because they said nothing about her non-attentiveness at the end of the service as they left the church together.

Once outside, the locals gathered to visit with one another before going home for Sunday dinner. Lizbeth hung to the side, listening, glad to have the brogue she was hearing take her mind off the tall blonde. Gray stood under the tree in deep conversation with some older gentlemen. Lizbeth grew closer to hear what they were saying. In the purest brogue she had heard so far, two of the gentlemen debated the coming of Earl.

"Hit's fixin' to blow a gale, for shore," one of them said. He was white haired and sea worn, the years on the water etched in the wrinkles on his brown face. Correct English would have read, "It is going to blow a gale, for sure."

The other man, gray headed, with the same wrinkled squint lines, spoke next. "We'll be mommicked for shore, if'n she takes a turn." He used the female pronoun, even though this hurricane possessed a male name. Just like boats, hurricanes had been traditionally referred to as female, until recent history. The O'cokers had a hard time dropping tradition.

Lizbeth noted the use of the word mommick, meaning to beat up or rough up, and the sound of the word sure, pronounced like shore. On occasion, she would glance at Gray, watching her as she absorbed what the old men were saying.

"They'll be sendin' the tourons off island and back to the country, should she track to land," the white haired man said.

Lizbeth made more mental notes. Tourons was just another word for tourists and country in this instance meant the mainland. She was surprised at the number of truly Ocracoke words she knew. She had studied hard and researched the Carolina Brogue for the last twelve months. It seemed the preparation was paying off. Lizbeth noticed Gray was looking at her and she smiled back reflexively.

Gray flashed that million-dollar smile, and Lizbeth's insides did a flip. Instantly, although she wanted to listen to the men converse, Lizbeth felt the need to run away. She knew if she made a sudden move to distance herself from Gray, it might look awkward, giving away her infatuation. She fought the urge to flee when Gray started towards her.

"Are you quamished?" Gray asked, her brow wrinkled with concern.

Lizbeth knew Gray was asking if she felt okay, another O'coker word.

"I'm beginning to get hungry," Lizbeth answered. Lightheadedness starting to overtake her functions, the words came out thickly and sounded strange to her.

"Come on," Gray said and grabbed Lizbeth's elbow, leading her toward where Fanny was holding court with a few women, who appeared to be her contemporaries.

The electricity from Gray's fingers on her bare skin was burning up Lizbeth's arm. She was too shaken to do anything but follow the taller woman. She wondered if Gray could feel it too. If she did, Gray bore no outward signs of it. When Gray finally dropped her elbow, Lizbeth rubbed it, attempting to stop the tingling. Gray saw her.

"I'm sorry; did I hurt your sunburn?" Gray asked, a look of concern on her face.

Lizbeth stuttered out, "No... no, I just felt an itch, that's all. Can't scratch because it will sting." Lizbeth couldn't look at Gray. Eye contact might send her over the edge.

"You should come by the house and I'll cut you some fresh aloe. It will help," Gray offered.

"Thank you, that would be great," Lizbeth said. A kind of wa-wa echo bounced between her ears, accompanying her words.

She was no more thinking about the sunburn than the man on the moon. All of her thoughts were focused on this seemingly uncontrollable crush she was developing for Gray. It had now reached a critical stage. She was having trouble standing this close to Gray without staring. Her heart was racing. She must have been losing color in her face, because Gray was looking at her with a worried brow.

"Are you sure you're okay?" Gray asked.

Hell no, she was not okay. She was having palpitations and her head was spinning. She could feel the beads of moisture forming on her upper lip. Gray took a step toward her, which only made it worse. Lizbeth's entire body broke out in a cold sweat. She took a step, wobbled a little, and tried again. She had lost the ability to speak. She began to develop tunnel vision, then the tunnel folded in on itself and everything faded to black. Lizbeth felt strong arms catch her just before she completely lost consciousness.

#

Lizbeth's eyes fluttered open. Not six inches from her face were Gray's blue eyes. Lizbeth tried to grasp the situation, but couldn't seem to get it together. Was she dreaming?

Gray whispered in a soft, calm voice, "Lizbeth... Lizbeth... Hey there."

Suddenly Lizbeth's world came back in focus. She was in Gray's arms, as Gray cradled her while kneeling in the sand. Lizbeth tried to sit up.

"Hey, whoa. Give yourself a minute," Gray said, gripping Lizbeth a little tighter, preventing the struggling woman from leaving her grasp.

Lizbeth had only fainted two other times in her life. The first time was in the middle of telling her parents she was pregnant. Next had been when she found out her husband was cheating on her the first time. Lizbeth was borderline hypoglycemic. In times of great stress, her blood sugar would plummet. Most of the time, she didn't notice the hypoglycemia at all. She ate small meals interspersed with light snacks, which is what her doctor had recommended. This morning, however, she had been so anxious about seeing Gray, Lizbeth completely forgot to eat. She had hustled around making sure her makeup was perfect and spent extra time on her hair. She had just finished when Gray knocked on her door.

"Sugar," Lizbeth finally was able to mumble.

Gray asked, "Are you diabetic?"

Lizbeth shook her head, no. She tried again. "No breakfast."

Gray understood. She turned to someone and said, "We need juice or a Coke." Gray looked back at Lizbeth. "We'll get you on your feet in just a minute."

Lizbeth remained in Gray's arms. She continued to look up into Gray's face, studying it up close for the first time. Gray had a strong jaw line and high cheekbones. She wore no makeup. She was a natural beauty. The words handsome woman came to Lizbeth's mind. Gray was handsome. She by no means looked like a man, but she did have that unique androgynous quality that turned the heads of men and women alike.

Gray frequently looked down at Lizbeth, but she was focused on the church doors, awaiting Lizbeth's drink. She didn't seem to notice Lizbeth staring at her. When the Coke can was finally produced, she helped Lizbeth sit up and placed it in her hands.

"Here ya' go. That'll fix you up. There's enough sugar in there to wake up a classroom full of kindergarteners."

Lizbeth turned the can up and chugged half of it before she came up for air. She could feel the cold liquid traveling through her body. Her limbs began to tingle as the sugar hit its mark. The fog from her brain subsided and she was finally able to sit up on her own. Gray remained on her knees beside her. Lizbeth finished the entire can before she looked back at Gray. She handed the empty can back to her.

"Thank you," Lizbeth said and took Gray's extended hand. Gray stood up and pulled Lizbeth to her feet. Lizbeth was still a bit shaky and swayed into Gray's chest.

Gray caught her and held on until she was sure Lizbeth could stand on her own. Lizbeth looked up into Gray's eyes. This time Gray was looking back. Time froze for Lizbeth. She didn't know how long she held Gray's gaze, but it was long enough. A sly grin formed on Gray's lips.

"There you are," Gray said. "You left us for a minute. I'm glad I was close enough to catch you."

Lizbeth, almost in control now, became aware that concerned onlookers surrounded them. It looked like the entire congregation had witnessed the event. Fanny came over and put her arm around Lizbeth's waist.

"Darlin', you need to come on to the house," Fanny said. "Let's get some food in you."

"I'm so stupid. I know I should not go without a meal, but I just forgot to eat this morning," Lizbeth offered. "I'm sorry if I scared you," she said to the now dispersing crowd.

"Well, I know you Catholics like to go to services early. You just weren't used to our schedule," Fanny said.

Lizbeth started to say she wasn't Catholic and then remembered the sign of the cross she made at the end of the service. She just nodded in agreement.

Fanny continued, "I guess that was the Lord's way of sayin' you need sumtin' good t'eat. You're too skinny."

Gray fell in to step with them as they turned towards home. She chuckled, adding, "Yep, the Lord works in mysterious ways." She winked at Lizbeth.

Lizbeth leaned into the older woman and said with a sigh, "Yes, yes he does."

\#

The Lord may not have worked a miracle, but Fanny's fried chicken, mashed potatoes, sliced garden tomatoes, and corn on the cob did. Lizbeth ate until her stomach felt completely full. It always hit her like that if she let her sugar levels drop. Now, her body demanded food and as much as it could hold. The whole thing still embarrassed Lizbeth. Fainting like that in front of the congregation would ensure she would be the talk of the village before Sunday dinner had been digested.

"I still can't believe I fainted. I mean, I know that it's a distinct possibility if I don't eat, but I haven't just dropped like that in years," Lizbeth said and then took another swig of sweet iced tea.

"Maybe all that sun yesterday made you weaker," Gray said. "Speaking of that, don't go home without some aloe plant. I'll just give you a pot of your very own and you can keep it growing."

Lizbeth was able to smile at Gray now, without thinking the fainting spell would return. The food had fortified her. She said, "Thank you. I could definitely use it." Lizbeth stood up to take her plate to the sink, saying, "And thank you so much, Miss Fanny, for this fine dinner. How on earth did you manage all this and attend church, too? I couldn't even remember to eat breakfast."

Gray stood and took the plate from Lizbeth. "Sit back down, you are a guest. After this visit, you are no longer a visitor and will be expected to fend for yourself, so enjoy it." She poured more tea in Lizbeth's glass.

Fanny chuckled. "I've been gettin' up afore the birds my whole life, so I cook our Sunday meal in the mornin' and leave it in the oven to stay warm."

Gray was emptying the table of dishes and bowls. She chimed in, "I've been trying to tell her to use the microwave to warm the food, before we come home from church and have to ask God for a new house, 'cause she's burned this one down to the foundation with Sunday dinner."

"I been doin' that longer than you been alive and this house is still here and so are you," Fanny shot back.

Gray teased the old woman, "Drime. You were cooking on a woodstove when I came along. You didn't have an oven to leave the food in."

Fanny scoffed, "Some folks sure can say a word."

Lizbeth was enjoying the banter between the two other women. Fanny had just told Gray she had a big mouth and talked too much. Lizbeth was so glad she studied the idioms and understood the conversation. If she hadn't she wouldn't know half of what they were saying. Fanny and Lizbeth remained at the table while Gray did the dishes. Lizbeth used the time that Gray's back was to her to examine her thoroughly without being seen.

Gray's haircut matched the one worn by Jethro Gibbs, Mark Harmon's character on 'NCIS.' Not the strictly marine buzz, but the one with the longer hair on the top, short on the sides. In fact, Lizbeth thought, if Mark Harmon had a beautiful twin sister she would look exactly like Gray. Maybe that was it. Lizbeth had always found Mark to be exceedingly sexy. She was transferring the lust for People Magazine's former sexiest man of the year to this woman who reminded her of him. That's all it was, she decided, and congratulated herself on solving the problem.

The celebration didn't last long. She listened only enough to keep up with the story Fanny was telling, but continued to look at Gray whenever the other two women were distracted. Her eyes traveled down Gray's back and locked on Gray's butt. She had a nice tight, rounded one. Her tanned legs were smooth, with tight muscles, and Lizbeth flashed on those legs wrapped around her. "Oh God," Lizbeth thought, "I've become a sex maniac overnight." She felt the blood rush to her face.

Fanny's voice broke her from her terror. "Good, I see some color comin' back in your cheeks. You must be feelin' better."

Lizbeth smiled, glad to be distracted from her thoughts of Gray. "Yes, I do feel so much better, but I think I need a nap. When I let my sugar get low like that, it makes me tired." She needed an excuse to go home. Lizbeth didn't want to be in this tiny room with Gray anymore. She was afraid of what her mind might think of next. She clearly had no control over it.

Gray turned around, drying her hands on a towel. "Are you sure you're okay now? I've got to go run a tour in a minute, but I'm sure Fanny wouldn't mind the company."

"Of course I would rather stay here and chat with you, Fanny, but I really do need a nap. I'll be good as new in a couple of hours. Maybe I'll come back later."

"Come on back and let me know how you made out," Fanny said.

Lizbeth thanked the O'Neal women again for their hospitality and the fantastic food. Gray walked Lizbeth to the front porch, carrying a small pot containing an aloe plant. It was the first time they had ever really been alone together. It made Lizbeth nervous. She made small talk to cover her anxiety.

"What kind of tours do you do?" Lizbeth asked.

"I run tourists to Portsmouth Island, show 'em Teach's Hole, Beacon Island, tell a few stories. It pays the bills."

"That sounds like a wonderful job."

Gray smiled. Her entire face lit up when she said, "Yes, I guess it is."

The smile was holding Lizbeth hostage. She couldn't leave Gray's presence so she kept talking. "What do you do when the tourists leave?"

"I run a couple of pound nets and some crab pots so I can stay busy year round."

"Now, that sounds like hard work," Lizbeth commented.

Gray's eyes sparkled. "It is, but then I get to be on the water every day. It's worth it."

The combination of her eyes and the smile on Gray's face was more than Lizbeth could take at the moment. She took the potted plant from Gray, smiling back at her.

"Well, I don't want to make you late." Lizbeth paused, then added, "Thanks for catching me."

Gray grinned. That mischievous little boy look took over her face. She leaned in close to Lizbeth. It became apparent to Lizbeth that Gray was fully aware of the predicament in which Lizbeth found herself. Gray was flirting with her.

"I didn't so much catch you as help you down to the ground," Gray said, and then added in a whisper, "I think maybe the catching will come later."

Lizbeth was stunned for a moment. Gray knew Lizbeth was developing a crush on her. Was she that obvious? Was she sending signals she was unaware of? On the other hand, Gray flirting with her had sent Lizbeth's heart into overdrive. It made Lizbeth feel things she had not felt in years. It appeared Gray was attracted to her as well. It had been a long time since Lizbeth felt wanted by someone, especially someone she wanted as well. Her brain kicked back into gear as she thought of what to say next. Lizbeth pushed the screen door open and stepped down on the first step. She paused and looked back up at Gray.

Lizbeth smiled flirtatiously, even though part of her brain was screaming, "Are you out of your mind?" She asked Gray, "What makes you think you can catch me?"

Gray grinned wider. "'Cause I caught you before."

"Yes, and I ended up tied to a tree," Lizbeth said.

Gray laughed. "Works for me."

Lizbeth winked at Gray and said, in her best pirate imitation, "Aye matey, but you might be needin' a bit more rope, this time."

Gray's laughter followed her across the street.

#

Lizbeth needed someone to talk to, but there was no one she would trust with this. Lizbeth and her daughter were extremely close. Although they shared everything about each of their lives, calling her daughter to tell her, "Your mother might be a big ol' lesbian," wasn't something Lizbeth was willing to do. Mazie was the last person about whom Lizbeth wanted to think. With Mazie on her mind, Lizbeth began to reflect on the consequences of any kind of a sexual relationship with Gray.

Lizbeth knew lesbians. She wasn't that sheltered. The ones she was friendly with were professional women, whose private lives were not the topic of dinner conversation. Molly Kincaid, a very successful Durham attorney and well-known lesbian, remained one of her closest friends, but they never really talked about Molly's love life. Molly was a very private person. Lizbeth met several of Molly's girlfriends, but knew next to nothing about her relationships. Lizbeth felt sorry now that she had never asked Molly if she was in love, or if her heart had been broken.

What would Molly say if Lizbeth called her? Would she be able to help, or would she laugh and say, "You're on your own?" Molly was a lesbian and Lizbeth was afraid to talk to her. How was Lizbeth supposed to handle being a lesbian if she couldn't talk to one? Then again, being attracted to one woman did not make her a lesbian, did it? Lizbeth hadn't even kissed Gray, although she had felt the strong pull to do so.

Maybe the kiss would immediately turn her off and she would never look at another woman in her life. Somehow, she doubted that Gray O'Neal would turn her off.

Lizbeth made up her mind, found her cell phone, and called Molly at home.

Molly answered after only one ring. "Lizbeth, good to hear from you."

"Hi Molly, I hope I'm not disturbing you. Are you busy?"

"Not too busy for you. What's up?"

"First of all Molly, I owe you an apology. In all the years we've been friends I never once asked you if you were happy, if you were in love, and I am very sorry."

Molly was intrigued. "Wow, what's going on? I can hear it in your voice. Something's happened."

Lizbeth's throat began to tighten as she fought back tears that seemed to come out of nowhere. "I know this is going to sound crazy, but I really need to know, are you happy being a lesbian?"

Molly laughed, relieving some of Lizbeth's stress.

"Good Lord, Lizbeth, have you been drinking?"

"No, I swear, I am stone cold sober. I wish I was drunk, though."

"Okay, strange as that question was, I'll bite. Yes, I am happy being a lesbian and yes I've been in love, just not at the moment. What's going on with you? Aren't you supposed to be on Ocracoke?"

Lizbeth walked to the kitchen for a bottle of water. Her throat was so dry she could barely speak. "Yes, I'm on Ocracoke finishing my thesis."

Molly waited during the pause and when no more information was forthcoming, she asked, "Did you change your major to Women's Studies? What's with the lesbian question? No dodging, spill."

"No, I didn't change my major." Lizbeth took another drink of water, trying to get up the courage to say the words aloud. "I met a woman."

Molly stifled a laugh when she said, "Oh my God, to whom do I owe the toaster?"

Lizbeth laughed, too. "I saw Ellen. I know what you're saying. No one is owed any toaster."

Molly snickered. "Not yet."

"Be serious, I need help here," Lizbeth pleaded, although she thought Molly was probably right.

Lizbeth could hear that Molly was trying not to laugh when she said, "Okay, what can I help you with?"

"Molly, you can't breathe a word of this."

"I'm a lawyer. I keep people's darkest secrets," Molly responded.

"Well, here goes." Lizbeth paused and took in a deep breath, before continuing, "Like I said, I met this woman and I... I don't know...I can't..."

Molly jumped in. "Let me make this easier for you. You met this woman and suddenly out of nowhere, you felt an unexplainable attraction to her. You can't get her out of your mind. Every time she walks in a room, your heart beats faster and you can't keep your eyes off her. She makes you go weak in the knees."

"I fainted."

"Lizbeth, you did not. Did you?"

Lizbeth laughed at Molly's reaction, adding, "Yep, fainted right into her arms, in front of the entire Ocracoke United Methodist Church congregation."

Molly couldn't believe it. "You fainted in her arms. That's hilarious. What made you faint?"

"She touched me. Well, that and I hadn't eaten breakfast."

Molly was whipping herself with laughter. It took a minute before she could say anything. "Lizbeth, I hate to tell you this darlin', but you have a mad crush on a woman. I hope she's a lesbian. Straight girls can be so bothersome."

"Oh, she's gay all right. I saw her kissing this woman the other night and…"

Molly stopped laughing. "Whoa, she's with another woman? That might not be the best place to start your lesbian career. That can get ugly."

"Gray - that's her name - is somewhat of a Casanova from what I can tell. That was just some tourist she picked up in the bar, a married one, I might add."

Molly didn't like the sound of that. "Lizbeth, don't get hooked up with one of those love 'em and leave 'em types. Unless you're just experimenting, then go for it. I gotta say though, I don't think you would have fainted if you were not already head over heels with this one."

"Molly, she's beautiful, and funny, and smart, and… God, yes, I have a crush the size of Texas on her, and it's scaring the hell out of me."

Molly giggled again. "It's too late to turn back. She's hooked you, now it's just a matter of reeling you in."

"But Molly, I…" Lizbeth stuttered.

Molly instinctively knew what Lizbeth wanted to hear. She said, in a calm serious tone, "Lizbeth, I have never regretted being a lesbian, not one day, not one minute. Yes, I have some social barriers to overcome, but when you're really true to yourself, those negatives are minor in comparison to what you've gained. I'm not going to tell you it's easy, but it's worth it to love the one you're meant to."

Lizbeth sighed. "There are so many people who will be disappointed in me and…"

Molly didn't want to hear that. She interrupted, "Who would you rather disappoint, them, or you? Besides, I think you'll be surprised at the reactions you get. You can never predict how someone will take the news. I will tell you this, if you care more about what people think of you than being who you really are, then pack now, leave, and never look back."

Lizbeth knew Molly was right. "I put everyone's needs before my own for so long, I don't know if I can put me first. I need to rewire my brain."

Molly said, encouraging Lizbeth, "Be selfish for a change. You never sowed your wild oats. Go out there and live life. You have been given a second chance. Take advantage of it. You have plenty of money. I've seen your divorce papers, remember. Have some fucking fun!"

Lizbeth felt her face and neck flush at what she said next. "Speaking of that, I'm not sure what... I mean I've never..."

Molly returned to her soft tone. "When it's the right time, you'll know. When you're ready, it will be the most natural thing you've ever done. You don't need anyone to tell you what to do. Fall in love, Lizbeth. You deserve it."

"Molly, you are a wise woman. I'm so glad I called you."

"That's what friends are for," Molly said, "And I may very soon be able to call you family. I'll keep my fingers crossed."

"You're a good friend, Molly. Thank you. I guess I better let you go."

"Call me and let me know how it's going," Molly said, then added quickly, "Lizbeth, if you go through with this, I promise you one thing..." She had to pause to keep from laughing. "You'll be kicking yourself in the ass when you realize what you've been missing."

Lizbeth could still hear Molly laughing when she hung up the phone.

#

Lizbeth didn't go back to visit Fanny that afternoon. She lay on the couch, staring at the ceiling until almost six, and then she snuck across the street. She left a small basket of fresh vegetables from her stash, and a thank you note, explaining she was turning in early. She didn't have the strength to handle seeing Gray again today.

She made sure to eat a little extra before going to bed and swore to herself she would not make the low sugar mistake again. Lizbeth climbed the stairs, weary and panged, before the sun was down. She hadn't felt this run down in years and yet she was alive with anticipation. She closed her eyes and immediately the image of Gray at the church appeared. Gray hovered over her, holding Lizbeth in her strong arms, wearing that raffish grin, her crystal blue eyes locked on Lizbeth's. This time Lizbeth didn't try to make it go away.

Chapter Four

The lullaby of the peepers and cicadas, through the open bedroom windows, had helped a ragged Lizbeth get a greatly needed restorative sleep. She woke early, fixed her breakfast, and was having coffee on the front porch, reading emails on her laptop, when Gray's voice broke the morning silence.

"You're up early."

Lizbeth couldn't contain the smile that was enveloping her face. Gray was wearing Ray Bans, board shorts, and a tank top over her sport bathing suit top, which Lizbeth was coming to recognize as Gray's signature look. She carried the little cooler in one hand. She was grinning back at Lizbeth like the Cheshire cat.

Lizbeth found herself flirting shamelessly. "Yes, I feel so much better this morning. I slept like a baby. No mopeds woke me or anything."

Gray cocked her head and raised an eyebrow in question. "Oh, have the mopeds been keeping you awake at night?"

"You could say that," Lizbeth answered coyly. "Would you like some coffee?"

Gray looked at her watch. "I wish I could stay, but I have a full schedule today. Got to make money while they're here. With the storm coming, it looks like it's going to be a short week anyway. As it is, with the swell, I can only take a half a load. Might be a short day, anyway, if it gets worse."

"How bad does it have to get for you to cancel?" Lizbeth asked.

Gray chuckled. "When the tourons start throwing up on my boat, I pretty much call it quits."

"I guess you know what you're doing. Be careful. I don't think I've had the full Gray experience and I'd hate to miss out now."

Lizbeth couldn't believe how blatantly she was hitting on this woman, but it was exhilarating. She was having fun, just as Molly said. Lizbeth had made up her mind to throw caution to the wind, to hell with what people might think. She was going to take this ride, come hell or high water. From the sounds of things the high water might be coming.

Gray seemed to enjoy Lizbeth's newfound confidence. She gamely played along. "Well, I'd hate to disappoint you, so I'll be extra careful."

Lizbeth winked. "You do that."

Gray seemed torn. She looked at her watch again. "I really have to go." She started to turn toward the dock and then stopped. "Hey, you want to go for a walk after supper?"

Lizbeth's heart leapt with joy. She tried not to give away her excitement when she answered, "Yes, I think I'd like that very much."

Gray smiled broadly. "Okay, around seven thirty." She winked, adding, "I'll pick you up."

Lizbeth couldn't help how she felt and she knew she was letting the cat out of the bag, but she was unable to resist Gray's charms. "I'll be here," she said.

Gray's raffish smile returned and just before she walked away, she shivered and said, "Hum, kinda chilly this morning." She dropped her gaze and peered over the top of her glasses at the front of Lizbeth's tee shirt. "See you later," she said and left with her laughter trailing behind her.

Lizbeth looked down at her shirt. She had thrown on an old, worn out, white tee shirt, not thinking about what it looked like. She was horrified. Her nipples were at full attention, poking at the thin fabric. She looked down the street after Gray. That's when Lizbeth realized Gray was walking backwards, watching her. Gray let out a cackle, smiled and waved, then turned back toward the docks and was gone.

\#

For the remainder of the morning, Lizbeth spread her research out in her little make-do office upstairs. She immersed herself in the work and emerged at lunchtime surer than ever that coming here was going to make writing the paper so much easier. Surrounded by her subject matter and real live experts, she had an entire resource library out her front door.

Throughout the morning, thoughts of Gray filtered in and out between diphthongs and idioms. Lizbeth considered what Molly had said to her. If Gray was a player, then Lizbeth was about to be played. At this point, it didn't matter. Gray was slowly reeling Lizbeth in and she had stopped putting up a fight. She might end up being another trophy for Gray's wall, but she didn't care.

After lunch, she put away the papers, organized now in appropriate stacks. All of her research was on her laptop, but she liked to hold the sheets of paper, physically placing them in the order she needed. It helped her see the big picture. Tomorrow she would work some more, but for the rest of the afternoon she was a free woman.

Lizbeth listened to the forecast on the little radio in the kitchen. Earl was becoming more of a threat. Beaches south of

Ocracoke were closing and there was talk of evacuation. Lizbeth saw no need to worry, but she did want to be prepared. She checked around the cottage for supplies. She decided to take a walk to the Community Store to pick up some more candles, batteries, and fuel for the hurricane lamps, before the tourists panicked and bought it all. She also needed a few more food items.

Lizbeth changed out of the thin white tee shirt to a more appropriate one for going out of the house. Still, she left her bra out of her outfit because her shoulders were still a bit red and sore from the sunburn. She looked over at Gray's cottage to see if Fanny was on the porch. She would've offered to pick up something for her at the store, but Fanny was not in her customary rocker. Lizbeth carried her canvas bags happily down Howard Street, following the same path Gray had taken that morning.

It did cross her mind that she might see Gray, because the Community Store was down at the docks. A Community Store had stood on the same site for many years, back into the 1800's. The current building had been there since the 1950's, offering everything a person on the island could need from fresh produce to fuel for your boat. It wasn't Wal-Mart, but it had enough of what folks needed to stay in business.

Lizbeth didn't see Gray around the docks. She did see a sign on one of the slips that said, "Austin's Portsmouth Island Tours." Down a few slips, on the other side of Kitty Hawk Kites, there was another sign, this one for O'Neal's Portsmouth Island Tours. Lizbeth was sure there was plenty of business to go around. Ocracoke was a very popular vacation spot, although there didn't seem to be as many people today as on Saturday. Of course, schools were starting back up, accounting for most of the absence of tourists, and the visitors today appeared past child rearing years.

Lizbeth was glad she came when she did. Almost all the batteries were sold out, but she did manage to get one set of fresh ones for the radio and flashlight. Grabbing a few essentials, two bottles of wine, toilet paper, some fresh peaches, and canned non-perishables, she paid for her purchases and walked back out into the bright sunshine. To look at it, one would never know there was a hurricane brewing in the Atlantic. The sky was crystal blue, much like the color of Gray's eyes. There she was again, invading Lizbeth's thoughts.

Lizbeth walked back behind the Kitty Hawk Kite building, peeking at the dock on the other side, where she had seen Gray's sign. Still no boat tied to the dock. She had not realized how much she wanted to see Gray, until she didn't, and then she was flooded with disappointment. "Oh girl, you got it bad," she said under her breath.

On the way back home, she bought a couple of handmade candles from a woman selling them in her front yard. They were the kind Lizbeth made as a child. Her father would take them out to the beach where he would melt big hunks of wax, collected from the bottoms of burnt candles, in an old pot hung over a camp fire. The kids would dig holes and pack the damp sandy walls tight and the bottoms flat. Tying a wick to a piece of driftwood, they would lay the stick over the hole, suspending the wick in the space. Then her father would pour the hot wax in the holes. They would wait until the wax set, then dig up the sand covered candle. It was a fond memory.

She carried her wares home, unpacked everything and put it away, then made herself a snack of some of the fresh peaches she just purchased. No way was Lizbeth fainting again. She had taken the warning very seriously. Lizbeth also went through her workout routine, which consisted mainly of stretches, but included crunches, lunges and her standard twenty-five pushups. She had been remiss the last couple of days, not exercising, but she thought the bike ride Saturday had been quite a work out, so she didn't feel too bad.

Lizbeth had to keep busy or she would spend her time engrossed in thoughts of Gray O'Neal. She checked across the street, still no Fanny. She finally pulled a novel off the bookshelf in the parlor. Previous renters had left a wide assortment of reading materials behind. She chose a Sneaky Pie Mystery by Rita Mae Brown and took it out on the porch with a bottle of water. She crawled up on the day bed and began to read. It wasn't long before she fell asleep.

During her nap, she dreamed of Gray. There was nothing sexual about the dream. She was talking to Gray and wandering the streets of the village. Then Gray was in the boat, waving at Lizbeth on shore. Suddenly a large wave rose up out of the harbor, taking the boat down and Gray with it. Lizbeth woke with a start, bolting to a sitting position, momentarily unable to fully wake. It wasn't exactly a nightmare; it didn't last that long. It was more like those dreams she had that made her jump right before she fell into deep sleep. It did unsettle Lizbeth, but she shook it off and went inside to fix supper.

She cooked a steak on the grill and had a salad for the side dish. It was after six when Lizbeth got into the shower. She took her time, shaving her legs and pits, and conditioning her hair. Lizbeth wasn't planning to sleep with Gray on their first...well, date. Then again, she had not planned to have a crush on her either, so better prepared than not, she thought. She finished in the bathroom and went upstairs to dress.

Lizbeth combed through her hair. If she didn't style it, it would form natural waves. It hung down just a little below her shoulders. Lizbeth thought her hair was her best asset. Most people told her it was the combination of all that dark thick hair and her piercing Elizabeth Taylor blue eyes. She stood in front of the mirror naked, having closed the blinds, just in case Gray was already home and upstairs. Lizbeth had discovered this morning that if Gray left her blinds open, she could see right into her room. She had not seen Gray, but she could clearly see the painting of a schooner on her wall.

Lizbeth had worked hard to stay trim and firm. She liked the way she looked at forty. Today forty didn't feel so damn old. Lizbeth felt younger than she had at thirty, but back then, she was living with a man she had grown to despise and raising a daughter. Her life was much better now. Lizbeth's marriage had ceased to feel like wasted time, and felt more like a learning experience to take forward into this second chance she had been given. It had taken four years to get here, but she was pleased with the results.

Lizbeth coated her skin with body butter that smelled like fresh coconut. She took her time with her makeup, not wanting to wear too much, just enough to enhance her natural looks. She put on the sexiest bra and panties she brought with her. She hadn't packed for a sexual encounter, as this was supposed to be a working sabbatical. She added her black Bermuda shorts and a white cotton tank top. Lizbeth didn't want to dress up too much. They were just going for a walk, Gray had said. She added a little perfume and called it good.

Lizbeth made it downstairs at seven fifteen. She drank a glass of wine to calm her nerves and waited. It was the longest fifteen minutes of her life, but promptly at seven thirty, there was a knock at her front door. She was back in the kitchen, about to pour another glass of wine, when the tapping on the screen door startled her.

Lizbeth left the wine glass on the counter and headed up the hallway. She could see Gray smiling on the other side of the door. From the look on her face, Gray liked what she saw. Lizbeth did too. Gray looked fresh, like she'd just stepped out of the shower. Her hair was still a little damp on top. She was wearing khaki cargo shorts and a white tank top, with a lightweight, short sleeved, white cotton over-shirt, unbuttoned.

The ribbed tank top contoured to her body. Lizbeth could see the faint ripples of Gray's ab muscles through the fabric. A shiver shot down her spine.

"Good evening, Miss Jackson," Gray said.

"Good evening to you, Miss O'Neal." Lizbeth stepped out on the porch, pulling the front door closed behind her.

Gray opened the screen door for Lizbeth. "You ready to take a stroll?" She asked.

Lizbeth stepped down the steps and looked up at the sky. "It's a beautiful evening for one."

Gray let the screen door shut. She reached down, lifting a small soft-sided cooler from the ground at her feet, sliding its long strap over her shoulder. She held out her hand, indicating the way to Lizbeth. Lizbeth smiled and started walking in the direction Gray pointed.

"What's in the cooler? You're not planning on getting me drunk are you?" Lizbeth teased.

Gray smiled, saying, "It's just a little something, in case you forgot to eat. Wouldn't want to have to carry you back to the house."

Lizbeth laughed. "Oh, I ate. If I keep swooning into your arms, people will talk."

Gray grinned. "People are already talking. That was the most exciting thing to happen at church in awhile."

"Where are we going?" Lizbeth asked.

Gray just smiled and said, "You'll see."

They proceeded down Howard Street to Fig Tree Lane and headed toward the Back Road. Lizbeth's body was on high alert. It could sense Gray's close proximity and the prospects excited every nerve. Gray smelled like fresh soap and linen sheets that had been hung in the sun to dry. A hint of fresh fruit caught the air, probably from Gray's shampoo. Lizbeth got close enough to feel Gray's body heat once, but quickly put more distance between them, because the thrill took her breath a bit.

Gray was easy to talk with. They spent the first part of the trip talking about the weather and the coming storm. Gray didn't seem too worried. She thought it might rain and get windy, but she wasn't concerned. She told Lizbeth that Fanny, who was eighty-five, had never left the island in a hurricane, not even during the storm of '44, which did a real number on the Outer Banks.

"They estimated the winds were over a hundred miles an hour here in the village, and the tide ran high at over fourteen feet. The entire island was underwater," Gray was saying.

Lizbeth was astounded, looking around, imagining the water over her head where they were walking. "Did anybody die?"

"Nope, there has never been a single death caused by a hurricane on Ocracoke Island. Some drunks drowned in a boat just off shore, in the Sound, but they would have been all right if they'd just come on land, instead of partying out on the water."

"What about the houses? What about your house? Fanny said it's been there since 1809." Lizbeth was fascinated.

"The water washed through and left it standing," Gray said, and then added, "Even with all that water, the island only lost six houses and a couple of businesses. The boats were a different story. Quite a few ended up on dry land, up in the village. Took a while to find them all. Never did locate some of them. They just washed away."

Lizbeth loved these island people. She said, "It's so amazing how the folks down here just clean up and go on. You never hear them complaining."

"There's a price to pay to live in such a beautiful place," Gray said. "Every now and then we have to pay the sea back for what it has given us, at least that's what Grandpa always said."

They were now on the Back Road. It too was a narrow street, but it was paved with asphalt and had clearly marked lanes. The winds had calmed to a light breeze. It was still warm, probably in the mid seventies. The few clouds there were earlier had blown away, exposing a clear beautiful blue sky fading to lavender above. On the horizon, ahead of Lizbeth, she could see the faint glow of the reddening sunset through the trees. It was a perfect evening. There were still no indications of the coming storm off shore.

"So, how'd you end up a forty year old college senior?" Gray asked.

"Life," Lizbeth answered, not offering anymore.

Gray took the hint and changed the subject. "I can't believe I don't remember you, except for the rope incident. We must have crossed paths more than once."

"We were always so busy being on vacation, I guess we just didn't run into each other, and if we did, you wouldn't have been hanging out with dingbatters like us."

Gray laughed. "No, I stayed out on the water pretty much. Didn't have too much time for foreigners, I guess."

"How did you ever leave this place?" Lizbeth couldn't understand why someone would leave a paradise like this.

"Fanny insisted I go to college. I wanted to anyway. I loved school."

Lizbeth interrupted. "I'm a little surprised. You don't strike me as the structured education type."

Gray grinned. She knew what Lizbeth was saying. "Structured no, but reading and learning, yes. I made good grades, got a scholarship, and went off to East Carolina."

"What's your degree in?"

Gray showed a little pride when she said, "Marine biology. That's why I got the job at Sea World. Not much of a marine biologist job market here."

"No, I guess not," Lizbeth commented. She paused and then asked, "Were you homesick?"

Gray looked reflective as she thought for a moment, and then answered, "A little, sometimes, but I was young and seeing the outside world, really for the first time. My time in San Antonio was full of so much life. I didn't have time to be homesick until just before I came back. By then I was overwhelmed with the need to come back here."

"How long have you been back?" Lizbeth asked.

"Five years, in December."

Lizbeth saw the first flicker of something in Gray's eyes, pain maybe. Something had happened to Gray five years ago.

Gray shook off whatever it was and continued, "I started working at Sea World the first year they opened in Texas, as a lowly hired hand. I had just graduated. That fall I got to see the first killer whale born there, Kayla. I fell in love with her and my job that day. Seventeen years later, I had worked my way up to Aquarium Curator."

Lizbeth was intrigued. "And you just decided to come home?"

"Yeah, something like that," Gray said, softly.

Lizbeth wanted to know more, but she let it drop. It appeared they both had pasts neither really wanted to talk about.

They reached British Cemetery Road and turned toward North Point. The sky above was darkening, turning more lavender than blue, a pink cast toward the horizon. As they approached the British Cemetery, Lizbeth grew quiet. She had always felt this simple plot of land, donated by the people of the island to England, was a place owed respect. A German U-boat torpedoed a British ship on May 11, 1942, and the tiny plot was the final resting place of four of her seamen. All hands were lost. These four men washed ashore on Ocracoke and the villagers gave them a Christian burial. It was a reminder of how close the Germans actually were to America's eastern coastline.

Respects paid, and continuing on their walk, the lightheartedness returned along with the twinkle in Gray's eyes.

"Fanny tells me you have a daughter," Gray said.

"Yes, Mazie. She turns twenty-two January first," Lizbeth said. "She graduated from UNC last May and got married in June. They live just outside of Durham, near Fearrington. She starts law school in January at Duke and soon will join her father at his firm." Lizbeth heard her own tone change when she mentioned James. It was still hard not to hate him.

"Sounds like a smart girl," Gray said.

Lizbeth brightened. "She is. She's brilliant. So much smarter than me."

Gray looked down at Lizbeth. "Don't sell yourself short. She had to get it from somewhere. Doesn't sound like it came from your husband."

Lizbeth laughed. "What makes you say that?"

"Whatever he did to piss you off must have been incredibly stupid," Gray said, grinning

Lizbeth smiled back. "How do you know?"

Gray didn't hesitate in her smoothness. She was seductive without even trying. She lowered her voice. "You're here alone, aren't you? I don't see a ring. I'm assuming there was a divorce. He had to be stupid to let you go."

Lizbeth flushed warm all over. She was glad for the fading twilight. They were approaching the Sound. Lizbeth could just see it around the bend in the road. The blue sky faded from lavender to pink, as they neared the water. Where was Gray taking her? Moreover, what was in the cooler?

Lizbeth had not said anything since Gray's last comment. Gray's presence overwhelmed her, and the seductive tone in Gray's voice had hit its mark. Lizbeth was blushing like a little girl. When Gray put her hand in the middle of Lizbeth's back, to get her to move to the other side of the road, Lizbeth heard her breath catch in her throat. She hoped Gray had not heard her. She felt utter disappointment when Gray removed her hand after they successfully made the crossing.

Gray stepped in front of Lizbeth and pulled a low hanging cedar limb out of the way. She stood there looking at Lizbeth, as if Lizbeth was supposed to walk into the woods behind the tree. Lizbeth stopped and raised her eyebrows in question.

"Gray O'Neal, you are not taking me into the woods to tie me up are you?"

Gray let out a laugh. "No. Come on. I want to show you something."

As Lizbeth passed under Gray's arm, which was holding the branch aside, she said, "I hope there's no rope in that cooler."

Lizbeth heard Gray's mischievous laughter behind her. "Guess you'll have to wait and see."

Lizbeth kept her head down, walking ahead of Gray, trying to avoid the low hanging, twisted limbs of the live oak in which they maneuvered. In a few minutes, they emerged from the woods onto a small sandy beach. It was isolated, with no houses or other people in sight. A large piece of driftwood waited like a park bench for someone to sit and watch the sunset. It appeared that's what Gray had planned.

It was an incredibly romantic scene. The Pamlico Sound spread out in front of them, as far as the eye could see. The water was calm and sparkled with the reflection of reds and pinks mingled in the sky above. The little ripples of waves lapped rhythmically at the edge of the water. The sun, now a giant red ball, was just beginning to dip below the horizon, casting a long glowing image across the surface of the water. A few ducks swam just off shore. Pelicans and sea gulls flew overhead, looking for a place to nest for the night.

Lizbeth followed Gray over to the driftwood bench. They sat down and just stared out over the water for a few hushed minutes.

Lizbeth broke the silence. "This is magical."

Gray didn't take her gaze from the water, but responded, "Yes, it is."

A few more minutes passed before Gray opened the cooler, producing a bottle of white wine, two wine glasses, and containers of cheese and crackers. Lizbeth watched silently as Gray's strong hands removed the wine cork with ease. She poured Lizbeth a glass and then one for herself. Lizbeth thought at that moment, with the way the light was shining on her, Gray was the most beautiful human being, man or woman, she had ever seen. Gray smiled and Lizbeth felt a shock of electricity throughout her entire body.

Gray held out her glass for a toast, saying, "To magical places."

Lizbeth touched her glass to Gray's and said, "Amen."

They watched the sun setting for a few more minutes before Gray spoke. "Now that I've been back here a while, I know I could never leave again."

Lizbeth looked over at Gray. "It must be thrilling to wake up surrounded by this every day."

Gray continued to survey the horizon. "Some folks are just born where they should stay. Wandering around out there in the world won't make them happy. This is all I need to make me happy," she said, but there was a melancholy in her voice.

Lizbeth commented, "Ah, a pirate married to the sea."

Gray laughed. She put some cheese on a cracker and handed it to Lizbeth. "Here, try this. One of my clients from Wisconsin sent it to me."

Lizbeth felt playful and teased Gray. "One of those married women clients you're so fond of?"

Gray grinned at Lizbeth and cocked her head to one side. "Wow, I need to be careful what I discuss on the street when your windows are open."

"I wasn't trying to listen, if that's what you're implying," Lizbeth shot back playfully.

"Guess I had my beer ears on. Didn't realize how loud we were talking."

Lizbeth had a large glass of wine at the house and she was almost finished with the one Gray had given her. The wine gave her courage to begin her own seduction game, and to her dismay, she did. She lowered her eyes over the top of her wine glass. "Do you do that often? Pick up married women, I mean."

The question caught Gray a bit off guard, but then her raffish charm returned. "Just doing my part to keep the tourists happy."

Lizbeth snickered. "Well, that particular tourist seemed happy enough when she drove off on her moped."

"Were you watching me, too?" Gray asked, still grinning.

"I got up to see what the noise was and I became intrigued, you might say," Lizbeth said, holding out her glass for more wine.

Gray poured the wine and studied Lizbeth. She could feel Gray's eyes on her. Gray was sizing her up. Lizbeth could almost see the wheels turning behind her eyes. Gray was trying to decide what to do next. Lizbeth's body was screaming, "Kiss me." Her brain was trying to talk rationally, but only sounded like a mumbling old woman in the corner. Lizbeth had stopped listening to her. She sipped her wine and watched Gray.

Gray put more cheese on a cracker and put it in her mouth. She stared out at the water, slowly chewing, and then washed it down with wine, before turning back to Lizbeth, apparently having resolved whatever she had been mulling over. The seductive grin returned to her face.

"Intrigued? Exactly how intrigued are you?" Gray asked.

Lizbeth was losing all her inhibitions. She was having an almost out of body experience. She felt as if she was watching herself with no control over her actions. Some unseen force was pushing her to behave in a way that seemed inconceivable to Lizbeth, but she could not resist it. She looked Gray straight in the eyes when she said, softly, "Very."

Gray took a sip of wine and turned her body so she was facing Lizbeth. "Lizbeth, I may have misread you, but I didn't think you were gay."

Lizbeth was not a big drinker and the wine was giving her the giggles. She said, "My friend, Molly, says all women are straight until they're not." She laughed.

Gray chuckled at Lizbeth. "I guess she's got a point there."

Lizbeth was nervous, causing the giggles to worsen. She knew exactly where this conversation was going. It frightened her and exhilarated her at the same time. With every sip of wine, her courage was building. It was false courage, but courage nonetheless. She wanted this woman to kiss her. She wasn't sure what else she wanted, but the awakening between her thighs was a good indication. Lizbeth turned up the wine glass and downed its contents.

Gray watched, but didn't say anything, as Lizbeth poured more wine into her glass and then refilled Gray's with the remainder of the bottle. The sun had disappeared below the horizon now. Only the glow of the day remained. Above them stars began to twinkle in the indigo sky. The moon wasn't up yet, but the ambient twilight still bathed them in a soft blue light. Gray was obviously waiting to see what Lizbeth would say next.

Lizbeth smiled down at the sand and then looked over at the beautiful woman beside her. At that moment Lizbeth made the decision to follow her heart and damn the consequences. "You make me nervous, Gray."

Gray grinned. She knew what Lizbeth was saying, but she toyed with her. "Why? What am I doing that makes you nervous?"

"You don't have to do anything, you're just being you. I've never met anyone like you," Lizbeth answered.

"I hope that was a compliment."

"It was… Gray, you have no idea how attractive you are, do you?"

Now it was Gray's turn to flush red. Even in this dim light, Lizbeth could see the compliment embarrassed Gray. "Thank you. I'm glad you think so."

Lizbeth said with much enthusiasm, "Oh, I do," and then tried to reel it back in, but it was too late. She attempted to cover with, "I'm sorry, it's just I've never… I've never been interested in a woman before. It's quite unsettling."

Okay, it was out. She'd said it aloud. Lizbeth waited for Gray's reaction.

Gray tried to get Lizbeth to relax. "I'm honored to be your first girl crush."

Lizbeth had never been the type of person to question things. She spent her life doing what was expected. Never asking anyone why she felt this way or that, Lizbeth had gone along pretending she was happy with the way things were. Then after the divorce, she gained self-confidence and a voice. She would never have had this conversation with Gray four years ago, even if she had found her attractive. She would have been afraid to say the things she wanted to say, but she had learned not to miss chances when they came along. This felt like a chance.

She gazed into Gray's smiling face. Their eyes studied one another. Lizbeth let out the breath she realized she had been holding and said, "So what happens next?"

"What do you want to happen?" Gray asked slyly.

"I don't know. You're the experienced one here. What do you usually do when a woman tells you she's attracted to you?"

Gray chuckled again. "Probably kiss her, unless she's unattractive, but that's not a problem in your case."

Lizbeth's body flushed again at the compliment. She smiled at Gray and said, "What's the problem, then?"

"Well, the last time I touched you, you fainted."

"I won't faint this time… I don't think I will anyway. Will I?"

Gray laughed and kicked off her flip-flops. She stood up and stuck her hand out for Lizbeth to take. "Let's just try holding hands first."

Lizbeth took Gray's hand and let Gray help her stand. Gray was strong and lifted Lizbeth to her feet with ease. Lizbeth kicked off her sandals and followed Gray, who was leading her toward the water. Gray stopped to pick up a skinny stick of driftwood and walked into the Sound. Lizbeth didn't know what Gray had in mind, but she felt so safe with her, she'd probably follow her into hell. She had never felt so absolutely secure with another person. Just holding Gray's hand made her feel protected and cared for. It was an overwhelming sense of peace that had engulfed her the moment Gray took control.

They waded out a little where the water was about two feet deep. Neither woman had said a word. Lizbeth was engrossed in the warmth of Gray's hand and didn't feel the need to speak. She quietly observed as Gray looked down in the water, as if she were looking for something. The little stick Gray had picked up had tiny twisted twigs clumped at one end. Gray put that end of the stick in the water and then turned to Lizbeth, still holding her hand. She pulled Lizbeth closer.

"Watch this."

Gray frothed the water with the stick. The water she disturbed filled with blue-green phosphorescent sparkles. It was beautiful.

Lizbeth gasped. "That's delightful. What is it?"

Gray continued to froth the water. "It's microscopic phosphorescent plankton. They emit a glow when the water is disturbed."

Lizbeth squeezed Gray's hand. "That's amazing. Thank you for showing it to me."

Gray stopped frothing and let the stick fall into the water. She turned to Lizbeth, smiling. "There are a million amazing things in this water. If you're interested, I'll show you some of them. At least the ones you can see from a boat."

Lizbeth would have let Gray show her how to fold towels, if that's what she wanted to do. Her growing awe and infatuation with Gray seemed to know no bounds. "I'd like that very much."

Gray squeezed Lizbeth's hand tighter. Lizbeth thought Gray might kiss her for a second, but she didn't. Instead, she pulled Lizbeth toward the shore. When they reached the beach, Gray let go of Lizbeth's hand and repacked the cooler, leaving nothing behind. Just before they left the seclusion of the isolated beach, Lizbeth grabbed Gray's hand again, turning Gray to her.

"Gray, this was beautiful. Thank you for bringing me here. I had a great time."

Gray smiled down at her. "It's my special place and it was my pleasure."

Lizbeth flirted. "Do you bring all your women here?"

Gray winked. "You're the first."

The magnitude of that statement hit Lizbeth like a ton of bricks. Gray had brought her to her special place. She didn't bring other women here. Gray must feel some of what Lizbeth was feeling. Lizbeth knew Gray was feeling it when she looked into her eyes. That moment of recognition seemed to happen to both of them at the same time. They stayed frozen there for an instant, before Gray leaned down and kissed Lizbeth ever so softly on the lips. It was a sweet tender kiss and was over too quickly for Lizbeth. There was no parting of lips and hungry tongues, just the soft brush of Gray's lips on hers, and it had been the most powerful kiss Lizbeth had ever experienced.

Gray seemed pleased with the affect the kiss had on Lizbeth. She didn't say anything, just pulled the stunned Lizbeth by the hand, guiding her through the patch of trees and back onto the street. The walk home was quiet. Both women were lost in thought on the way. Lizbeth was simply staggered by the way Gray's kiss had made her feel. The village was going to bed by the time they reached Lizbeth's doorstep.

Gray opened the door to Lizbeth's porch for her, but didn't attempt to follow her in. Lizbeth turned back and asked nervously, "Do you want to come in? We could have coffee."

Gray, smiling broadly, said, "Miss Jackson, you have absolutely no idea how much I'd love to come in there with you, but I'd better leave you here and say goodnight."

Lizbeth was being left at the door. This wasn't what she had expected from a Casanova like Gray. She had thoroughly expected to have to fight her off, which Lizbeth knew by now wouldn't have been much of a fight, but here Gray was trying to be a Southern gentleman, for lack of a better term. After the initial shock, Lizbeth realized how incredibly sweet the gesture was. Gray was not going to let Lizbeth rush into anything. She was giving Lizbeth time to process what was happening. Gray was being kind.

Lizbeth stepped back on the top step and extended her hand to Gray. Gray took it, but remained on the ground. Lizbeth squeezed Gray's hand and said, "This evening was magical. Thank you."

Gray grinned. "Are you available tomorrow? I'm sure I can find something else to show you." She winked.

Lizbeth assumed her Scarlet O'Hara accent. "Gray O'Neal, I do believe you're trying to court me."

The charm oozed from Gray when she said, "Why yes, Miss Jackson, I believe I am. May I call on you tomorrow?"

Lizbeth, grinning broadly by now as well, said, "I look forward to seeing you," followed by a wink.

Lizbeth let go of Gray's hand. She moved up onto the porch and Gray let the door swing shut. They took one more moment to look at each other, and then turned at the same time, Lizbeth opening her front door and Gray crossing the street. Lizbeth looked across the street before shutting the door. On the top step to her porch, Gray stopped and turned back to Lizbeth. Her face erupted in a smile when she saw Lizbeth watching her.

She called out, "Good night, Lizbeth," and then laughing, disappeared into her house.

Lizbeth closed the door and then leaned her back against it. She said aloud to the empty room, "My god, she might be right. If I react like that to just her lips brushing mine, I might faint if she really kisses me."

Chapter Five

When Lizbeth's eyes opened in the morning, she saw Gray sitting on the edge of her bed looking down at her.

"Hey, sleepy head," Gray said, grinning from ear to ear.

Lizbeth wasn't sure if she was awake or not. She looked around and realized she was on the little day bed on the porch. She checked to make sure she was clothed and discovered she was wearing only a spaghetti strapped, short nightgown with a thin blanket pulled over her. It all began to flood back to her at once.

Lizbeth had been so wound up by the events of the previous evening she could not sleep. She tried reading a book. She even attempted to work on her paper, but couldn't concentrate. She laid in bed, staring at the ceiling for hours, her mind spinning with thoughts of Gray. It was almost three when she came out on the porch and sprawled on the day bed. Listening to the chorus of nature had finally lulled her to sleep. It appeared Gray had come looking for her and found her there.

Gray tried again. "Lizbeth, are you awake?"

"I am now." Lizbeth sat up, pulling the blanket up to cover the thin material of her nightgown. The move wasn't lost on Gray.

"Now you get bashful, after laying out here for all to see," Gray teased.

Lizbeth was embarrassed, but more amused by Gray than shamed. "I couldn't sleep. I came out here to get some air and I must have dozed off."

"Yeah, I saw you this morning when I went to work."

Lizbeth rubbed her eyes. "What time is it?"

Gray stood up and looked at her watch. "Quarter after eight."

Lizbeth squinted up at Gray and said, "Oh my God, I've only been asleep for five hours," and with that, she fell back on the pillow and closed her eyes.

Laughing, Gray said, "Get up. I want to show you something. Meet me at the dock at nine o'clock."

Lizbeth didn't move. "Okay, I can sleep longer though. It's not that far."

Gray yanked the blanket off Lizbeth. "No, you can't. You need to eat. No fainting, remember. And besides, if you come down there with your hair like that you'll scare the tourists."

Lizbeth's eyes popped open. Suddenly seized with what she must look like, her hands flew to the top of her head. Her hair was sticking out in all directions. She had slept hard after she finally passed out. She probably looked like hell. Now she was truly embarrassed. She snatched the blanket back from Gray and covered her head.

Gray chuckled. "Too late. I've already seen it. The image is burned into my brain."

From under the blanket, Lizbeth said, "Go away."

Gray pulled the blanket from the top of Lizbeth's head, so she could see her face. She leaned down and was inches from

Lizbeth when she said, "No. Not until you get up. Come on, you have to see this."

Lizbeth caved. She had to. Gray's eyes were dancing with delight. She evidently thought it was important to share something with Lizbeth. Lizbeth couldn't resist her.

"Okay, I'm up. Just go away while I get dressed."

Gray was excited. She started toward the front of the porch. "Okay, meet me at the dock, just before nine."

Lizbeth stood up, self consciously wrapping the blanket around her. She called after Gray, "Wait. What should I wear? Where are you taking me?"

"I'm taking you on the boat. Wear whatever you want." She stopped at the corner of the porch, just before disappearing out of sight. "Glad we got that out of the way."

Lizbeth, confused, asked, "Got what out of the way?"

Gray's infectious grin returned. "I already know what you look like when you wake up in the morning." Then she disappeared around the corner, her laughter staying behind, ringing in Lizbeth's ears.

#

Lizbeth rushed around making a bowl of microwave oatmeal and eating it standing at the counter. She quickly showered and dressed. She pulled her hair back in a ponytail, and then covered her body in sunscreen before putting on her two-piece, tropical colored bathing suit. It wasn't a tiny bikini, but it was sexy enough for her age, she thought. She slipped a pair of blue Russell workout shorts over the bottom of the suit and grabbed her oversized white oxford to put on over the top. She rolled down the top of the shorts and rolled up the sleeves of the oxford, leaving the front unbuttoned, exposing her flat stomach. Lizbeth had decided to play hardball with Gray. She was trying to look as sexy as possible, while looking very casual about it. The straw hat and sunglasses made her appear mysterious. Just the effect she was going for.

With a couple of water bottles, sunscreen, and a towel in her canvas bag, she met Gray at the dock at five till nine. Eight very excited Asian tourists, ranging in ages from toddlers to grandparents, surrounded Gray. It appeared to be one family. One of the parents, with a toddler in her arms, was translating for the group, and not doing so too successfully. Gray was trying to explain something, using her hands to demonstrate and speaking loudly, as Americans tended to do when attempting to have a non-English speaker understand them. Lizbeth thought it would be a miracle if the Asian woman could understand Gray through her thick Carolina brogue, especially with that Texas accent thrown in the mix.

When Gray saw Lizbeth, she stopped talking in mid-sentence. She froze there, her mouth hanging open, staring at Lizbeth as she approached. The outfit had had the desired effect. One of the tourists turned around and saw Lizbeth.

The middle-aged man got very excited and quickly grabbed his camera. He aimed it at Lizbeth and started snapping wildly, while repeatedly shouting, "Ashrie Judd! Ashrie Judd!"

Gray started laughing. She doubled over and grabbed her knees. Lizbeth couldn't help but laugh, too. She approached the man and was finally able to convince him, through the interpreter, that she was not, in fact, Ashley Judd. Gray gradually stopped laughing, but an occasional giggle still seized her while loading passengers on the boat. She placed Lizbeth on the double bench seat at the console, while she made sure the kids were safely in life vests, comfortable, and ready to go.

Gray cranked the dual Yamaha engines and then went to the front and untied the dock line from the bow. She returned to the stern, untying its dock line and then sat down beside Lizbeth behind the wheel. Gray backed the boat away from the dock and then turned the bow toward the channel leading out of the harbor. As they slowly crept across the slick surface of the sheltered harbor, Gray turned to Lizbeth, still giggling.

"You do kinda have that Ya Ya Sisterhood, Ashley Judd thing going."

Lizbeth, who had developed quite a skill mimicking accents, said in her best Louisiana drawl, "I'll take that as a compliment, suga'."

This cracked Gray up again. She was still laughing when they cleared the harbor and she stood up to navigate the channel. Gray gradually fed gas to the throttle until they were skipping across the chop on the surface of the Sound, heading for Ocracoke Inlet. Lizbeth had to keep her hand on top of her hat to keep it from blowing away. Gray occasionally smiled down at Lizbeth, but mostly kept her eyes scanning the top of the water.

From her vantage point, Lizbeth had a perfect view and even though the beauty of the shoreline and sea surrounded her, she couldn't keep from looking at Gray. Gray was in her element. The love of what she was doing radiated from her pores. Lizbeth thought Gray had been correct when she said some people were just born where they should be. Gray O'Neal was born to be on this water.

As they neared Portsmouth Island, Gray banked the boat to the left, slowing to a crawl when she reached the middle of the smallest stretch of water between Ocracoke and Portsmouth. Gray was focused on the water, searching for something. In a moment, she saw them and gave the boat some gas. Soon the boat was in the middle of a pod of bottlenose dolphins.

Lizbeth saw them about the same time the tourists did. One of the tourists stood up to film with his digital camera, but Gray made him sit down using hand signals. She shook her head and smiled at Lizbeth. Lizbeth knew what Gray was thinking and mouthed the word dingbatter to her. Gray started laughing again. Gray was finding Lizbeth exceedingly funny this morning.

The dolphins jumped and played around the boat. Gray sat down on the seat with Lizbeth, but she was still looking around at the water. Then suddenly she grabbed Lizbeth's arm and pointing with the other hand said, "Look."

There in the pod were two tiny dolphin calves. They were more than four feet long, but still babies in comparison with the adults in the pod. Both seemingly identical calves swam close to and in unison with one adult.

"That's extremely rare," Gray said, leaning in to Lizbeth so she could hear her over the engine and the wind.

"What is?"

Gray explained, "I think they're twins. Most dolphins give birth to only one calf at a time. If they have multiple births, the calves usually die, but these two look extremely healthy. She must be a good mother or the other mothers are helping her feed them. You are witnessing one of those amazing things I was telling you about."

"I'm glad you came to get me. I wouldn't have wanted to miss this."

"I think they are coming in to catch fish. The swells out there are driving schools of fish into the Sound."

Lizbeth looked beyond the surface of the Sound to the ocean waves crashing through the shallow inlet. The water was beginning to get choppier the longer they stayed where they were. Gray headed the boat back to the leeward side of Portsmouth Island, leaving the dolphins behind. The island offered relief from the steadily building wave action. Gray pulled the boat up to a long pier with a ladder leading down to the water. The pier was built way up out of the water and the ladder had to be used to exit the boat.

Gray had tried to explain to her passengers before they left the docks that she didn't think the old man or the toddlers would be able to climb the ladder. The interpreter finally understood and nodded at Gray. In broken English she said, "We go to beach."

Gray turned the boat around and headed for the Sound side beach on the north end of the island, explaining to Lizbeth it was the most sheltered area she could drop these people, so the water wouldn't be too deep and the undertow was minimal. The tourists had not come prepared to spend very long on the beach. They were all in shorts and shirts, wearing socks and tennis shoes. Gray raised the engines so the propellers were barely in the water and then ran the bow of the flat bottom boat up onto the beach. She killed the engines, jumped over the bow with the anchor line, and set it hard in the sand. She did all this with the grace of an athlete.

Gray was able to make the passengers understand they needed to take their shoes and socks off, then stood by the bow and helped them off one by one. She helped Lizbeth down, by lifting her off the boat and plopping her down in the sand. Lizbeth was beginning to understand how Gray stayed so fit. She lifted tourists for a living. She had picked Lizbeth up by the waist as if she was a feather.

Gray led Lizbeth away from the tourists who were now excitedly chatting among each other. When they got about two hundred yards from them, Gray plopped down. She patted the sand beside her and Lizbeth sat down.

"Is this what you do all day?" Lizbeth asked.

"No, I usually just drop them off either on the beach or at the pier and then come back for them four hours later. I run back and forth all day picking up and dropping off. Some days there are more trips than others."

"This is the perfect job for you. You really shine out here on the water."

"Yeah, I guess I'm lucky to get to do what I love."

"Why are you staying this time? Is it because of me?"

"I wish I could say it was, but no. This is my only group today. Heard through the grapevine they're going to do a mandatory evacuation later today. The water's going to be too rough here in a little bit, so I cancelled the rest of the tours. I need time to get my boat out of the water and tied down before nightfall."

"I didn't listen to the radio this morning. Is Earl going to hit here?"

"I still don't think it will come to shore, but it's so huge the outside bands will hit us. If it turns closer, it could get pretty hairy."

"When will it get here?"

"They're saying Thursday night, but they'll start evacuations this evening I'll bet."

"If it's mandatory, do I have to leave?" Lizbeth asked.

"No, they can't make the people who live here leave; just the tourists have to go. If anybody asks, tell them you just moved here and you're one of the Jackson's that owns the house. I mean, if you want to stay that is."

"I'm staying if you're staying," Lizbeth said, without hesitation.

Gray grinned. "I guess you're staying then."

Lizbeth smiled at her. "You'll keep me safe, won't you?"

Gray looked over the top of her sunglasses at Lizbeth. "Yeah, I'll look out for you. Fanny'd have my hide if I didn't."

Lizbeth played coy again. "Oh, so you don't care what happens to me, just that Fanny might get after you."

"It's not that I don't care, it's just I'm more afraid of Fanny than I am of you, at the moment," Gray answered.

Lizbeth threw her head back and laughed. "Gray, I can't imagine you being afraid of anything." She paused, then looked at Gray. "Wait a minute. You said, 'more afraid.' Does that mean you're afraid of me?"

Gray grinned. "A little."

Lizbeth was going to have fun with this tidbit of information. "And what, pray tell, makes a big strong girl like you afraid of a little old gal like me?"

"That outfit for one," Gray said, laughing. Suddenly a look of seriousness took over her smiling face. She looked at Lizbeth for a second, and then said, softly, "I'm afraid I might like you too much."

Lizbeth got serious too. "And that's a bad thing?"

"Wouldn't do to get attached to someone who won't be around very long."

Lizbeth hadn't thought that part of this through. She would be leaving the island in December. What would happen if she did get too attached to Gray? Gray would never leave this place and Lizbeth couldn't stay here. What would she do here with no job and no place to live? No, Gray and Lizbeth were on two different life paths. They just happened to have crossed those paths by a twist of fate. If Lizbeth hadn't come here to work on her thesis, they would never have met, but they had and Lizbeth was totally smitten with this woman. She had to say something. Gray was waiting for a response.

Lizbeth took a deep breath and let it out slowly. She dug nervously into the sand with her fingers and said, "Gray, I don't know where this is going. It's so new and exciting. I know I'm not thinking straight, pardon the pun."

Gray chuckled and Lizbeth went on. "Let's just take it slow, one day at a time, because to tell you the truth you scare the hell out of me."

Gray reached down, retrieving one of Lizbeth's hands from the sand. She squeezed it lightly and smiled at her. "All right then," she said, and stood up. She helped Lizbeth to her feet. Gray looked into Lizbeth's face and then let her eyes wander down to Lizbeth's chest. She pulled her eyes away and started laughing. She said, "Okay, but I don't know how slow it'll go, if you keep wearing things like that."

#

Gray and Lizbeth killed an hour on the beach looking for shells and then loaded the tourists back in the boat. Gray took the boat back to the docks and the passengers disembarked. Lizbeth found it amusing when the tall Gray exchanged bows with her much shorter guests as they were leaving. The man who had taken Lizbeth's picture was the last to go.

He pointed at Lizbeth and said to Gray, in very broken English, "Very pretty."

Gray grinned. "Yes, she is."

Lizbeth was sitting on a short piling at the end of the dock smiling at Gray when she walked up. She stood up and fell in step with Gray toward home. Lizbeth was giggling when she said, "I think that's the first thing either one of you said all day that you both understood."

They burst out laughing and continued to do so every time they looked at each other, all the way home.

#

Gray dropped Lizbeth at her cottage and then pulled a Jeep Wrangler out of a raised garage behind Fanny's house. Lizbeth stood on her porch and waved goodbye as Gray slowly rolled down Howard Street. Lizbeth went into the cottage, showered the salt water and sand from her body, and changed her clothes. After making a sandwich for lunch, Lizbeth settled in for an afternoon of studying.

Lizbeth listened to the radio while she worked. At one p.m., the Hyde County Emergency Services Department released a public advisory. According to the National Weather Service, Earl, now a category four hurricane, was making a northeastern turn off the coast and was forecasted to collide with the Outer Banks. Hyde County was expected to receive significant wind, rain, and storm surges that could flood the low-lying areas, both on the mainland and Ocracoke. Presently, they anticipated a mandatory evacuation for

Ocracoke Island on Wednesday, September first, beginning at five a.m. for all residents and visitors.

Gray's grapevine had been on the money. Lizbeth thought about leaving. After all, a category four hurricane was nothing to take lightly. A storm of that magnitude carried sustained winds of 131 to 155 miles per hour and a storm surge of 13 to 18 feet. Lizbeth looked at the ceiling and thought about the whole room being underwater. She began to wonder if she was crazy for even thinking about staying.

If she was going to leave, she should pack up now and go, but she'd never leave without saying goodbye to Gray. The wait in the ferry line was going to be long, with the hundreds of tourists all attempting to flee at the same time, and then she would have to drive another two hours to get inland. She looked at months of research spread around her. Lizbeth could lose it all if the house flooded. She immediately stopped what she was doing and refreshed the upload of all her files to her online backup. Lizbeth knew she wasn't leaving, but she wasn't taking a chance on her research.

While she was waiting for the upload to finish, her cell phone rang. It was Mazie.

Lizbeth answered, "Hey, sweetheart."

"Well, you sound chipper. Island life must be agreeing with you," Mazie said.

Lizbeth grinned to herself, saying, "Yes, I have to say it is exhilarating."

Mazie got to the point of the call. "I assume you are packing the car. When should you be home?" Mazie must have heard about the mandatory evacuation order, too.

"I'm not leaving."

Mazie registered her shock with a high pitched, "What!"

"Gray says we'll be fine, so I'm not leaving," Lizbeth explained calmly.

"They said everyone has to leave Mother, that's what mandatory means. And who the hell is Gray?"

"You don't have to leave if you own property and this is the Jackson house, so I can stay. Gray and her grandmother, Fanny, live across the street. Fanny is eighty-five and has never left the island during a hurricane and their house has been standing longer than this one. I think I'm safe."

Mazie wasn't buying it. "Have they ever been through a storm as big as this one?"

"Yes, as a matter of fact, in 1944 they endured a storm surge of 14 feet."

Mazie backed off a little. "Well, I see you've done your research."

"I'll be fine, Mazie. Don't worry."

"I'll worry till it's over, but if you really want to stay, I guess I can't make you leave if the state can't."

"No, you can't," Lizbeth said, and laughed.

"Mom, you sound different, almost giddy. What's up with you?"

Mazie was very intuitive. She always had been. Even as a small child, she could discern Lizbeth's moods. Although Lizbeth had tried to shelter Mazie from the pain in her marriage, Mazie always knew when her mother needed time alone or a simple hug. Their closeness made the rest of life more bearable, but right now Lizbeth wished Mazie wasn't so perceptive.

"It's the sea air, I guess," Lizbeth answered, trying to sound convincing.

"I don't believe it, but if you don't want to talk about it, I'll wait. You won't be able to keep it from me long though. You'll tell eventually." Mazie's laughter reminded Lizbeth of her own.

People said the two looked alike. They had the same hair and eyes, but Mazie was tall like her father, which, Lizbeth thought, made her daughter look like a model. Lizbeth was so proud of Mazie. She was happily married to a wonderful man and she had achieved every goal she had ever set for herself. At least Lizbeth had done one thing right. She had raised an incredible young woman.

No matter how much she admired her daughter, Lizbeth was not ready to share Gray with Mazie. She responded to Mazie's last comment, trying to sound innocent, "There's nothing to tell. I've had five wonderful days here and I'm just happy, that's all." She tried to change the subject. "I saw twin dolphin calves this morning. It was amazing."

"I wish I could have been there." Mazie paused and Lizbeth heard someone else speaking. "Mom, I have to go, my car's ready. Promise me you'll be safe."

"I'm in good hands. These O'cokers won't let anything happen to me, I promise."

"I love you, Mom."

"I love you too, sweet girl. Bye, bye."

"Bye, Mom," Mazie said, and then added with a giggle, "I hope he's good-looking." Then she was gone.

Lizbeth hung up the phone. She said to the folded phone in her hand, "Yes, Mazie, she's very good looking, not he."

Oh, if she only had the guts to really say that. She had no idea how Mazie would react, but for some reason she wasn't really afraid of it. Mazie was wise beyond her years. Somehow, Lizbeth knew Mazie would stand beside her no matter what. It was the rest of the world of which she wasn't so sure. What was it Molly had said? "If you care more about what people think of you than being who you really are, then pack now, leave, and never look back."

"One thing at a time, Lizbeth," she said aloud.

After a few hours of studying, the five hours of sleep began to catch up with her. Lizbeth crawled in the bed in her room and took a nap. She dreamed of dolphins, and waves, and sunsets. She woke refreshed and was surprised to see that the digital readout on the microwave said seven fifteen when she walked into the kitchen. Gray must be home by now.

Lizbeth was afraid Gray might have come over while she was sleeping and she had not heard her. She quickly made a salad of the remaining vegetables, forcing herself to eat it, even though she was anxious and really didn't want any food. She went back upstairs, brushed her hair, and checked herself in the mirror. She changed to a fresh tee shirt, because her sleep wrinkled the one she was wearing. Satisfied that the white scooped neck tee and blue shorts looked good enough, she went out on the porch to look for Gray.

Fanny was in her customary rocker. Lizbeth called out to her, "Good evening, Miss Fanny."

"Come on over, young'un, and sit a spell."

Lizbeth crossed the street and bounded up onto the porch. She took the adjacent rocker and fell into rhythm, rocking with the older woman.

"Gray tells me yer stayin' through the storm."

"She seems to think we're safe, don't you?" Lizbeth asked.

"Lord honey," Fanny said, chuckling. "When it's my time, I'm a goin'. Runnin' to the mainland won't stop that."

This pronouncement did not reassure Lizbeth. "But you don't think I'm making a mistake staying here?"

"No, I think we'll be fine. Don't feel like a bad one coming."

Lizbeth was risking being caught in a nasty hurricane, because this old woman didn't feel a "bad one coming," but she thought she could trust Fanny and Gray. Where was Gray? It was almost eight o'clock.

Trying not to be too obvious, Lizbeth asked, "Did Gray get her boat out of the water?"

"She come back 'bout an hour ago, dropped off the boat on the trailer and parked the Jeep. She went back to hope out some more folks." Fanny used the word hope to mean help, another idiom. "She's tied down the skiff, but she'll leave it in the harbor staked out."

"Skiff? Is that what she does her crab pots and nets with?"

"Gray's granddaddy left it to her. She lets Cora Mae use it and Gray fishes on it some in the cold months." Fanny winked. "Haulin' tourons pays better than haulin' fish."

Lizbeth smiled at the memory of Gray on the water this morning. "She sure is in her element out there on the water."

"Gray is as kin to a dolphin as you can be with two legs. She ain't happy unless she's in or on the water," Fanny said.

"I don't know how she stayed away so long in Texas. She just seems to belong here."

Fanny scoffed, "She weren't happy, I'll tell you that. She drug back up here looking mommicked to death. The sea is life's blood to her. She needs it. Gray wouldn't survive out there in the world."

Lizbeth thought about Fanny's comment. She knew the old woman was right. Gray wouldn't survive, at least not happily, off this island. She'd be like the killer whales whose dorsal fins collapse in captivity. It was a visual clue to the great loss the animal felt. Gray could never swim in a circle; she would have to be free. A pain shot across Lizbeth's chest.

The women rocked silently for a few minutes, waving and speaking to all who passed on the street, most of them locals calling out Fanny's name in greeting. The village was quiet, as most of the tourists had started leaving that afternoon. The sun had set on a clear sky, the calm before the storm.

Lizbeth spent the quiet time mulling over what Gray said about being attached to something you knew was going away. Was it better to leave now, before anything happened? Would she be better off not knowing if Gray was the thing she'd been looking for, or would she spend the rest of her days and nights wondering what might have been? If Gray began to mean more to Lizbeth, would she be able to walk away, go back to Durham, and leave her here? Because that's what it would come down to, leaving Gray behind. There was no way this ended any differently.

What about how Gray felt? What if Gray fell in love with Lizbeth? Could she be hurting Gray as well? Lizbeth felt the tears begin to well up in her eyes. The emotional highs and lows of the past two days were beginning to get to her. She was trying to think of a way to get off the porch without appearing rude, when Gray's voice took her from her thoughts.

"Well, this is a nice surprise." Gray was coming through the gate. She smiled brightly at Lizbeth. She was dirty and sweaty and it looked hot and sexy.

Lizbeth blushed and smiled back. It was automatic every time she saw Gray. The flush would come and a grin she could not control would seize her face. "We were just visiting," she said, while watching Gray enter the porch, the tempo of her heartbeat increasing with each step Gray took toward her.

"How's it to the creek?" Fanny asked. Lizbeth thought she was asking about the harbor since it used to be called Cockle Creek.

"Everything's tied down. A lot of folks got their boats out this afternoon. Nobody's panicked. It's kind of a wait and see attitude at the Community Store."

"It's so quiet," Lizbeth said. "It's peaceful."

"The tourists have left for the most part. The announcement came through at eight thirty. The mandatory evacuation begins at five a.m." Gray raised her eyebrows, looking at Lizbeth. "Sure you want to stay?"

"Yes, I'm sure," Lizbeth said, before she had a chance to stop herself. All that thinking about not getting involved with Gray flew out the window.

"Well then, while you and the old woman there finish chewing the fat, I'll excuse myself to take a shower." Gray started into the house, stopped, turned around, and asked Lizbeth, "Will you be here when I get back?"

Fanny couldn't see Lizbeth's face as Lizbeth turned toward Gray. She smiled seductively up at Gray, and raising one eyebrow, said, "I don't know. Are you worth waiting for?"

Gray answered, through laughter, "Guess you'll have to wait and see, won't you?"

Fanny chuckled, but didn't say anything. Gray went in the house. The anticipation of her return held Lizbeth, and she must have been lost in thought, because Fanny's voice startled her.

"You got your hands full with that one."

Lizbeth stopped rocking and looked over at Fanny. "Who? Gray?"

"The very same," Fanny answered, nodding her gray head in agreement.

Lizbeth wasn't sure what Fanny thought was going on, but she was Gray's grandmother, and they lived in the same house. Gray didn't seem to hide her sexuality. In fact, she was so comfortable with it, her being a lesbian didn't seem to bother anybody. Lizbeth knew that the islanders had a 'live and let live' and 'take care of their own' attitude toward each other. It may have begun as a fishing village, but it was now an artists' enclave as well. Eccentricity abounded down these sandy lanes. A Greek goddess, Casanova lesbian, would not stand out in this crowd.

"What do you mean?" Lizbeth asked, half-afraid of the answer.

"Gray's been a wild child since birth. She took on the world when her feet hit the ground. 'Bout drove me and her momma crazy. Only person she'd pay any attention to was her granddaddy. She got that love of the water and all things in it from Laurence. That was my husband. He died ten years back. Gray was stuck to his leg from the time she could walk. If he hadn't kept her out on that boat most of the time, there ain't no tellin' what all she'd a got into."

"I think that's part of her charm, her willingness to live life to its fullest, no holds barred." Lizbeth was smiling, seeing Gray in her mind, the wind blowing through that thick blond hair, as she piloted the boat.

"She's stubborn, too, like a crab with a chicken bone. Once she's made her mind up about something, she cain't be swayed no which a way. Take her name. That ain't what we called her when she was born."

"Her name isn't really Gray?" Lizbeth asked.

"She's named after me. Fanny Gray O'Neal is her given name. I'm named for my grandmother, and her grandmother, and so on back to 1849, when the schooner Fanny Gray sank off the beach here. That day a little girl was born and she was the original Fanny Gray. Been a woman called Fanny in this family every other generation, till ol' Gray there. Some tourist told her a fanny was a hiney when she was four years old, and she threw a fit and fell in it. Wouldn't answer to her name no more. We had to start calling her somethin', so she settled on Gray. Hard headedest young'un I ever had dealin's with."

Lizbeth giggled. She could tell Fanny was a little offended that Gray had chosen not to honor her namesake. She tried to smooth the rumpled feathers of the old woman. "She's not a Fanny. Gray suits her unconventional approach to life."

Fanny chuckled. "I s'pose that's right."

"What happened to her mother?"

Fanny's face darkened. "Mona died six years ago. Got the cancer. She went real fast."

Lizbeth was sorry she brought it up. How much she cared for Gray's mother was etched on Fanny's face. "I'm so sorry to hear that," she offered in condolence.

"That's where Gray gets her looks. Her momma was a handsome woman."

"Those eyes are just like yours, quite stunning," Lizbeth said dreamily, and then suddenly realizing how that must have sounded, tried to redeem herself. In a non- "I'm so infatuated with your granddaughter I want to sleep with her," voice, she added, "Her mother must have been beautiful."

"That she was."

Since Fanny was being so forth coming with information, Lizbeth decided to pry a little. "Did Gray come back from Texas because of her mother?"

"No, Mona'd been gone about a year before Gray moved home. Course Gray was here for the last month Mona was with us, but she went on back to Texas. Came home a year later, the dog beat out of 'er. Been a wampus cat ever since."

That was a new one on Lizbeth. She wasn't sure what a "wampus cat" was. Now, if something was "catawampus" it meant it wasn't straight or plum. Lizbeth would have to look up the phrase "wampus cat" when she got home. The "wampus cat" herself, freshly showered and dressed, interrupted her thoughts.

Gray was wearing white, wide legged, thin cotton pants with a drawstring waist. She had on another ribbed tank top, this one navy blue. The blue from the shirt intensified the crystal blue of her eyes. She was barefooted and carrying three glasses of sweat iced tea when she backed out of the door. She turned and presented the tea to Lizbeth and Fanny, then pulled a chair up close to Lizbeth.

"Okay, now tell me, what kind of lies has this old woman been telling you?" Gray asked, winking at Lizbeth.

"I found out how you got your name," Lizbeth said.

"Is she still going on about that? I can't believe she's still mad because I told her I didn't want to go around being called a not so flattering name for a body part."

Fanny shot back, "We should'a just started callin' ya' 'hiney,' that's what you acted like."

Gray laughed. "Missed your chance old woman. You're stuck with Gray now."

Fanny surprised Lizbeth by saying, "Smartass," but Fanny was laughing, too.

Lizbeth joined in. One thing about the two O'Neal women, they loved to laugh and it was infectious. Maybe that's how Fanny got to be eighty-five and still so vibrant. They both had a wicked sense of humor and a quick wit. Lizbeth imagined it must have been a joy to grow up in a house ringing with laughter. Her own family had fun, but there was a seriousness that didn't exist here in this cottage.

Gray propped her feet on one of the screen porch cross beams. She stretched her long legs out and slid down in the seat of her rocker, getting comfortable. The thin material of Gray's pants fit tightly to her hips. Lizbeth caught sight of tight butt muscles and rock hard thighs through the fabric. The tingling between her legs returned.

"Well, I'm gonna leave you young'uns to it," Fanny said, standing and taking her tea glass with her. "I'm gonna go on to bed. Y'all have a good night." Fanny crossed behind the chairs, so Gray didn't have to move her legs.

Lizbeth touched the old woman's arm as she passed. "I've enjoyed our evening. Have a good night Miss Fanny."

"You too, darlin," Fanny said, patting Lizbeth's hand.

When they were alone, Lizbeth turned to Gray. "Gray, what's a wampus cat?"

Gray answered lazily, "The village rogue, a tom cat that gets around."

"Oh," was Lizbeth's reply.

"Where'd you hear that? I haven't heard that phrase in years," Gray asked, casually.

"Fanny said you've been a 'wampus cat' since you came back from Texas."

Gray's feet fell off their perch. She sat up in the chair and looked at Lizbeth. "What did she tell you?"

"Nothing. That's all she said, that you drug up here with 'the dog beat out of you' and then you became the village rogue, if I translate that right." Lizbeth paused. "She didn't mean you were beaten up literally, did she? I mean you weren't physically attacked were you?"

Gray sat back against the rocker and stared out into the street. Lizbeth waited for her response. Gray finally spoke.

"I'm not as roguish as she thinks. I don't sleep with every woman who throws herself at me."

Lizbeth snickered. "I would imagine there have been quite a few, throwing themselves at you, that is."

Gray turned back to Lizbeth. "I have my standards."

It had not been lost on Lizbeth that Gray dodged the beaten up subject. She tried again. "Gray, I'm not interested in how many women you've slept with. What I want to know is why you came back from Texas? What happened?"

Gray dropped her chin to her chest. All the happiness seemed to drain from her body. She pierced Lizbeth with a cold stare. "I could have asked you what happened in your marriage, but I didn't. I think I deserve the same courtesy, don't you?"

Lizbeth had not seen this Gray before. She wasn't hostile. She was hurt. Whatever happened to her had wounded her to the core of her being. Lizbeth knew that pain. The one that grips you so hard you can't breathe. It tears apart your world as you knew it, and nothing, nothing will ever be the same, because you know that agony exists. Lizbeth had spent every night since it finally subsided praying that pain would never come back. She had promised herself that no one would ever get close enough to hurt her like that again. That was before she met Gray.

"I'm sorry, Gray. I'm sorry someone hurt you like that. I won't ask you about it again."

"I'd appreciate that," Gray said quietly, then turned her gaze back to the street.

They sat there in silence, both lost in thought. She didn't know where Gray's mind was, but all Lizbeth could think about was how wounded Gray seemed. Someone hurt Gray back in Texas. That's why Gray didn't want to get attached to Lizbeth. That's why she had affairs with strangers. Gray, like Lizbeth, had vowed not to let that happen again.

They eventually started talking, but it was about the weather and the dolphins they saw. Gray's mood brightened briefly when she talked about the calves, but she sank back into silence fairly quickly. After a few more awkward moments of quiet, Lizbeth stood.

"I'd better go on home so you can get to bed," she said, through a fake yawn.

Gray stood and moved her chair back to its original position. She opened the screen door and held it there for Lizbeth to pass. Gray seemed to be trying to overcome the mood in which she found herself. She attempted a smile, but it couldn't cover the pain she was obviously feeling. Lizbeth had stirred bad memories and Gray was having trouble putting the lid back on them.

Lizbeth stepped down on the first step, turned back to Gray, and without thinking placed her open palm on Gray's abdomen. She felt Gray stiffen, the muscles under Lizbeth's hand becoming hard. Lizbeth looked at her hand, because she couldn't believe how just this one hand on Gray's tight stomach could send shockwaves through her own body.

When Lizbeth looked up, she saw Gray's face was flushed. Gray's eyes were locked on Lizbeth's. Lizbeth watched desire returning to the eyes that a minute ago were lost in painful memories. Lizbeth smiled and Gray followed suit. The life seemed to flood back in to Gray's countenance. The sparkle came back to her eyes and she cocked her head, enchanting Lizbeth with her charm.

"Why Miss Jackson, you are being quite forward."

Lizbeth moved her hand, sliding it down just a few inches, stopping just above Gray's hipbone. She felt Gray's sharp intake of breath and saw Gray's intentions clearly in those crystal eyes. Lizbeth hoped Gray could see the same thing in hers.

Lizbeth said, "I'm sorry. Is this making you uncomfortable?" but she didn't remove her hand. She saw Gray bite her bottom lip. "I was wondering if I would see more of you tomorrow."

Gray laughed. "You're going to see more of me a whole lot sooner if you keep that hand where it is."

Lizbeth was enjoying her newfound power over Gray. She remained exactly as she was. "I'll take that as a yes." Then without another word, she slid her hand across Gray's ripped abs, turned and walked away, knowing Gray was watching.

Gray called after her, "You know there's a word for women like you, it rhymes with please."

Lizbeth didn't turn around. She gave Gray a hip pop to think about and disappeared into her cottage. She could still hear Gray's laughter when she closed the door.

Chapter Six

Wednesday, September first, Governor Beverly Perdue declared North Carolina under a state of emergency. The Coast Guard issued a warning for all vessels to proceed to port. If Lizbeth had not known about the pending hurricane, she would have never guessed one was coming by looking outside. At eight fifteen, it was already in the mid seventies. The sky was clear and bright with the sun shining, as if the category four monster was not lurking off the coast of the Outer Banks.

Earl was not the only thing lurking around. Lizbeth, who was standing in her parlor drinking her first cup of coffee, dressed in a thin nightgown, was watching Gray, who was also drinking coffee, but pacing up and down Fanny's front porch. When Lizbeth awoke this morning, she had gone to close the bedroom windows against the heat of the day. She noticed Gray was already dressed and sitting in Fanny's chair across the street. It had now been twenty minutes and Gray was still on the porch, checking her watch frequently, and constantly checking Lizbeth's house for signs of life.

Playing hardball was working on Gray O'Neal. Lizbeth could tell that something had changed last night. She remembered her hand on Gray's stomach and how Gray had almost trembled under her touch. Lizbeth wasn't the only one swooning around here. Now, Gray was prowling her porch, just waiting to pounce on any sign that Lizbeth was receiving guests.

Lizbeth, who had suffered all night through tumultuous dreams of the village rogue, decided to play her own version of reel 'em in. She turned the handle on the front door and let it swing open on its own. She didn't let Gray see her and went upstairs to dress. She left the door open, silently beckoning Gray across the street. As she crossed the floor to climb the stairs, she counted, "One thousand one, one thousand two, one thousand three, one thousand four..."

"Hey, Lizbeth, can I come in?" A breathless Gray was at Lizbeth's front door in less than five seconds.

Lizbeth smiled to herself and disappeared up the stairs, yelling down to Gray, "Come on in. Coffee's ready in the kitchen."

She heard Gray go down the hallway to the rear of the house. Lizbeth dressed quickly. She had a lot of work to do to ready for the storm, so she threw on an old tee shirt and her gray shorts. She brushed her hair, pulling it up in a ponytail, put lotion on her face, legs, and arms, and then waited. Pretty soon, she heard Gray coming back down the hall. Lizbeth sat very still on the edge of the bed, listening. She heard Gray pacing in the parlor below. Finally, Gray could be patient no longer.

"Hey, are you ever coming down from..."

Lizbeth timed it perfectly, appearing in the middle of Gray's lament. "Good morning," she said, nonchalantly.

Gray grinned broadly. Lizbeth could almost see the hook peeking out of the corner of Gray's mouth. Lizbeth was trying not to laugh and turned her back on Gray, going to the kitchen for a second cup of coffee. Gray followed right behind her.

"Good morning to you, too," she said. "I was wondering if you wanted me to help you get everything secure, before the storm."

Lizbeth poured another cup of coffee. She leaned against the counter while Gray stood in the doorway. Gray had the hopeful look of a child trying to talk a friend in to coming outside to play. She was so adorable this morning. The dark shadow that had crossed her face last night was gone. Lizbeth couldn't help grinning at her.

"What about your house?" Lizbeth asked.

"Already done. Only thing left is to close the storm shutters and that can wait till later."

"My God, Gray, how long have you been up?"

Gray, who was glowing with excitement, said enthusiastically, "Since five."

Lizbeth tried out her best seductive smile. She raised one eyebrow in question. "Couldn't sleep, huh?"

Gray blushed, grinning. "Something like that."

Gray came toward Lizbeth and the game changed quickly. Gray spit the hook. She stopped just in front of Lizbeth and leaned around her to retrieve the coffee cup she left there. When she did, she got as close to Lizbeth as she could without touching her, then straightened and took a drink from her cup, while looking at Lizbeth over the rim. Oh God, she was smooth. Lizbeth's heart was pounding in her chest. She was at once relieved and crestfallen when Gray took her cup and sat down at the little table by the back door. Only then did Lizbeth remember to breathe.

Gray watched, wearing a self-satisfied grin as Lizbeth followed her to the table and sat down, just like the pied piper leading the mice. Lizbeth no longer held the upper hand; she was back to swooning in Gray's presence. With all the palpitations, breathlessness, and fainting, Lizbeth felt lightheaded most of the time and it wasn't getting any easier. She wasn't hiding it very well, either. Gray probably saw something that triggered her next comment.

"Have you eaten breakfast yet?"

"No, I just got up," Lizbeth said. "I haven't had time to fix anything. I had company pacing outside my door, remember?"

"Do you want me to fix you something?" Gray asked, looking a little concerned.

Lizbeth thought she must be pale. All the blood had flushed from her brain when Gray leaned across her at the counter. Sitting down had helped. She was regaining her senses and her heart was slowing down. Forget fainting, if Gray ever kissed her, she was probably going to have a heart attack.

"No, I'll fix some oatmeal in a minute," Lizbeth answered, now that she was feeling better. "So what do I need to do to get ready for the storm?"

Gray hesitated, not fully believing she had recovered, but decided to go ahead with her plan. "Okay, we need to cut two branches back, so they won't slap the cottage. The rest are okay. All the loose stuff has to be tied down or put away and..."

"Do I have storm shutters?" Lizbeth interrupted.

"No, but Minnie had plywood pieces cut to size. I just have to screw them on. We'll need a ladder for the top windows."

"Do you really think the wind is going to get that strong?" Lizbeth didn't want to climb on the roof and put plywood over the windows.

"It's not the wind, so much as the crap in it," Gray answered.

"What if I wasn't here? Would my cousins have asked you to do it?" It had just dawned on her how lucky her cousins were that she was there and Gray was willing to help.

Gray answered, but she looked like she'd been caught with her hand in the cookie jar. "No, I imagine Bob would've done it. He takes care of the property, now that Minnie's gone."

Lizbeth, who had regained much of her strength, leaned across the table. She smiled at Gray, studying her face. "Gray? What did you do, tell ol' Bob you would take care of it?"

"Something like that." Gray grinned.

"Okay, then you have to go on the roof. I can't believe you turned away a perfectly good man willing to do it."

Gray laughed. "You obviously don't know ol' Bob."

Lizbeth laughed with Gray for a moment, and then said, "So what do we do first?"

Gray stood up. "You, eat. I'll be back in a minute with the ladder and the saw."

"Don't you need help?" Lizbeth said, standing with her.

"No, I got it," Gray said, backing away. She stopped in the threshold to the hallway, an inquisitive look on her still grinning face. "How long did you make me wait before you opened the front door?"

Lizbeth was the one now caught with her hand in the jar. "How do you know I made you wait?"

"Because you said I was pacing outside your door."

Lizbeth saw a way out. "But, I could have just seen you when I opened it."

Gray narrowed her eyes, smiling knowingly. "How long?"

Lizbeth let out a sigh. She was caught. No way around it. She said meekly, "Twenty minutes."

Gray clapped her hands. "I knew it!" Then she hooked her index finger in the corner of her mouth and pulled herself down the hallway and out of sight, still laughing when she closed the front door behind her.

#

Lizbeth and Gray worked side by side all morning. Gray kept Lizbeth in stitches. She was just naturally funny. By lunchtime the plywood was on the windows upstairs, the back of Gray's Jeep had been loaded with limbs and branches from both their yards, and all the loose items had been put away. Gray had also stopped about ten o'clock, claiming to need a snack, but Lizbeth knew she was just looking out for her helper. They ate the last of the peaches and cream, because if the power went out, the cream would spoil anyway.

"When I was a kid, I couldn't wait for the power to go out because it was the only time I could eat all the ice cream I wanted," Gray told Lizbeth.

"You sound almost excited that a hurricane is coming," Lizbeth said.

"There is something energizing about a hurricane. Maybe it's all that raw natural power, and then there's all the cool stuff that blows up on the beach after a big storm." Gray thought for a second, then said, "I think some of my fondest memories are riding out storms in that cottage across the street."

After they ate lunch with Fanny, consisting of sliced fresh tomato sandwiches and big glasses of milk - because the milk wouldn't last, either - they hung the remaining plywood pieces, leaving only the windows on the screened-in porch uncovered. They were both tired and dirty when they finished. They sat on Gray's porch, drinking iced water, and admiring their handy work. Lizbeth was exhausted, but the sweating and hard labor had eased the tension she'd been carrying in her body, and somehow energized her at the same time. Watching Gray's muscles ripple under her tanned skin, glistening with sweat, might have had something to do with it, also.

They had been sitting quietly, slumped in two of the big rocking chairs, when Gray said she needed to take a shower. Lizbeth needed one too, so they parted and agreed to meet back at Gray's at five o'clock. Gray had something else to show Lizbeth.

"Bring a jacket, or a sweatshirt, and some pants. You might get cold," Gray said at the screen door, once again standing, holding the door open for Lizbeth. "And hey, do you drink beer?"

"Yes, I've been known to drink a beer or two," Lizbeth said, smiling as the grin spread across Gray's face.

"Any particular kind?" Gray asked.

"No, I'm easy," Lizbeth answered, and then registered how that must have sounded.

Gray didn't miss a beat. "Oh really? I hadn't heard that about you."

Lizbeth giggled. "Yeah, but I heard it about you."

"That's not true," Gray said, in mock defense. "You heard I was a rogue. I think that means I'm on the lookout for easy women."

"Well, I guess you found one," Lizbeth teased.

Gray laughed, adding, "We'll see."

#

Gray was waiting beside the Jeep, parked in front of her cottage, when Lizbeth emerged from her front door. The wood they had collected was still in the back, joined by a cooler and a blanket. Gray beamed at Lizbeth as soon as she saw her. Gray's childlike excitement twinkled in her eyes. She wore a pair of very faded, old jeans, holes in the knees, slung down on her hips, a plain white tee shirt tucked in at the waist, and no shoes. Gray did casual very well.

Lizbeth was running out of clothes that she had not already worn. She hadn't expected to do a lot of socializing, so she brought only two suitcases, one with summer things and one with things to wear when the weather turned colder. She debated for a while and chose function over glamour, picking her white clam diggers and a comfortable teal, cotton, sleeveless tee to wear. The teal made her eyes an even deeper shade of blue. She threw her windbreaker and a pair of sweat pants in the canvas bag, as Gray had suggested.

They left Howard Street and found a spot on the beach down at the point, south of the village. The sky was still clear, with just a few swirling clouds, and the wind on the beach wasn't too bad. They had the entire area to themselves. Occasionally someone would come by and yell, "Gray!" out a vehicle window, to which Gray would throw her hand up in the air and wave, but no one stopped.

Gray brought Lizbeth to a spot where someone had dug a wide deep hole. The remains of a once roaring fire lay in the bottom. Gray unloaded all the pieces of wood from her jeep into the pit, arranging it so it would catch fast, but she didn't light it.

When she finished stacking the wood, Gray climbed out of the pit. She opened the cooler, grabbed two cans of beer, and placed them in neoprene coozies, designed to keep the beer cold and their hands dry. She handed Lizbeth one of the beers and held out her free hand for Lizbeth to take.

"Come on, let's go for a walk," Gray said.

Lizbeth took Gray's hand and they strolled down by the water's edge, looking to see if the ocean had departed with any of her treasures yet. Gray rolled her pants legs up so they could walk in the edge of the surf, occasionally having to scamper away from a particularly fast approaching wave. Gray would pick up shells and tell Lizbeth their scientific name and then the name by which most people knew them. They laughed and giggled up and down the beach. Lizbeth never let go of Gray's hand. They were comfortable together. Well, except for the enormous sexual tension in the air.

The sun was nearing the horizon. Golden amber burst from the glowing ball and streaked into the heavens. The building clouds, twisted like large meringue wisps dotting the sky, were now tinted with the pinks of fading day and the deeper blues of coming night. The sea was angry. Large waves crested over eight feet high at the sandbars, sending frothy swells crashing toward the shore. Foam gathered at the waterline, moving with each successive series of waves, and blew in clumps caught in gusts of wind across the wide beach.

Gray led Lizbeth back to the fire pit. She started the fire and soon the flames bathed them in a dancing glow. The sand berm around the edges of the pit prevented the wind from blowing the sparks too badly. Gray unfolded the blanket and smoothed it out over the sand. Lizbeth sat down with her next to the fire, where they could watch the waves and the flames at the same time. Gray got them both a cold beer from the cooler, being careful to put the empty cans in a bag she tied to the cooler handle. Gray explained that she adhered to the rule of not leaving anything but footprints behind.

Gray was propped up on her elbows, her legs stretched out in front of her. Lizbeth was leaning back on her hands. Their positions put them at eye level with each other. They sat close together, but not touching. Still Lizbeth could feel electricity jumping from her body to Gray's and back. She was sure, with the right kind of lens, she would be able to see the little blue lightning bolts emanating from their skin. She half expected her clothing to burst into flames any minute. Even the all-consuming crush she had on James when they first met had not been this intense. Lizbeth could swear she could feel the air move with every breath Gray took beside her. One of the most beautiful beaches in the world surrounded her and all Lizbeth could see was Gray.

Gray looked away from the fire and back at Lizbeth. She smiled. They hadn't said anything to each other for a few minutes. Gray said, "I like that we don't have to talk all the time. I mean, you don't ask me what's wrong if I get quiet."

Lizbeth understood. "Sometimes I need to stop talking so I can hear myself think."

"I know what you mean."

"That's all I seem to be doing lately, thinking. My mind is so jumbled with questions. I can't seem to settle on the answers."

Gray asked, "What kind of questions? Maybe I can help."

Lizbeth searched Gray's eyes for something. Was it trust? She was honest when she answered, "I don't know if I want you poking around in my head just now."

Gray chuckled. "What, afraid I might find out your darkest secrets, your deepest desires?"

"Yes, as a matter of fact. A girl has to have some mystery."

Gray sat up, looking down at Lizbeth. "Oh, you're plenty mysterious."

"I could say the same about you," Lizbeth said.

"Like you said, a little mystery never hurt anybody." Gray paused, and then clearly feeling strongly about the subject, she said, "Why do some people feel the need to share their worst tragedies and heartbreaks with the world?"

"I don't know, Gray. Maybe it helps them deal with their grief."

Gray stared into the fire. "The best thing they could do with that shit is put it to rest and never wake it up again. Take whatever lessons you can from it and walk away."

"Damn, Gray, that's harsh."

Gray was on a roll and didn't pay much attention to Lizbeth's comment. She continued, "And you know what gets me, those drunks on the barstool, lamenting their broken hearts, while you watch them make the same mistakes over and over again. They never learn."

"And what lessons have you learned, Gray? Whatever they were they don't sound pleasant."

Gray hesitated. Lizbeth had promised not to ask about what happened in Texas, but Gray had opened the door. She waited to see what Gray would say. Lizbeth hoped the pall that ruined last evening did not return. To her relief it didn't. Gray took in a deep breath and let it out slowly, appearing to have decided to answer Lizbeth's question.

"I learned that trusting someone doesn't make them infallible. I learned not to trust like that again. Isn't that what you learned, too?"

Lizbeth thought about it, and then said, "Yes, at one time I felt that way, but I think it's passed. I don't want to go the rest of my life without falling in love again. Just because I chose poorly the first time, doesn't mean there isn't somebody out there I can trust with my heart and soul. I have to say, it's a pretty depressing future, if I don't think like that."

Gray let out a faint laugh. "I'm more a once burned, twice shy kind of person."

"Wow, somebody did a number on you."

Gray sighed. "Yeah, something like that."

Lizbeth shivered. The sun was sinking over the dunes. The sky above them had gone dark. Twilight had descended over the island. Gray saw that Lizbeth was cold. She got up, went to the jeep, and returned with Lizbeth's canvas bag. Lizbeth thanked her, took out the jacket, and slipped it on. They were both quiet again for a few minutes. Finally, Lizbeth had to say something.

"I met James, my ex-husband, when I was sixteen years old. He was two years older, a senior, and the star quarterback. He was from the right family, had a bright future, and was the handsome All-American boy. I fell madly in love with him and he fell for me. We were the perfect couple."

Gray was listening, while she got two more beers out of the cooler, exchanged them for the empties, and returned a cold one to Lizbeth. Lizbeth took a couple of swallows, watching the sparks from the fire carried off by the wind, wondering if she should continue. Lizbeth had never really told anyone, except her divorce lawyer, exactly what happened to her marriage. Most people assumed correctly that she had caught James cheating, but there was so much more than that. She sighed loudly.

Gray reached for Lizbeth's hand. She squeezed it, saying, "You don't have to tell me this."

"I want to tell you," Lizbeth said. "I need to tell you."

Gray seemed to understand, but looked away, as if she couldn't bear to watch while Lizbeth finished her story.

Lizbeth began again. "I got pregnant in the spring of my senior year, got married right after graduation, and had Mazie at age eighteen. Now, that could have been a devastating blow to a young couple, but it wasn't. We were happy. James comes from money, so that wasn't a problem. Mazie was the love of both our lives. James went to college, I kept house and played mother and wife, and we were happy, still madly in love."

Lizbeth drank some more beer, and then continued, with no comment from Gray. "James finished law school and started working in his father's firm. My life was a dream come true. The handsome prince, the beautiful daughter, the big house, everything I had ever wanted was within my grasp. The one thing I knew that separated me from so many of my friends was I loved my husband and he loved me, unconditionally. That was a fact I knew like I know the sky is blue. My life was perfect."

Lizbeth felt the tears coming, but she didn't try to stop them. Although this was painful, she felt the uncontrollable need to say it aloud, set it free, and watch it float away on the island winds. Gray remained silent, still holding Lizbeth's hand, but not looking at her.

"When Mazie was eight, James and I were asked to be in the wedding of a couple we knew. We were all in this one hotel at Hilton Head. I ate something that made me very sick and I was left in our hotel room, throwing up, during the after rehearsal party. I started feeling better, cleaned myself up, and went looking for my husband."

Lizbeth took in a shuddering breath, the tears coming freely now, not in sobs, just gently falling, trailing down her cheeks. Gray squeezed Lizbeth's hand again.

"I found him on the beach with one of the other bridesmaids. I came over the dune and there he was, fucking another woman. I swear Gray, until that very second, the thought of James cheating on me had never crossed my mind. I trusted him with every ounce of my being. To say I was devastated would be an understatement. I fell completely to pieces."

Lizbeth sniffled and wiped the tears with her jacket sleeve, but she kept going, unable to stop. A faint sarcastic laugh escaped her throat as she said, "I forgave him. I believed him when he said it was a mistake, that he was drunk, that he would give anything if I would just forgive him. Eventually, I was able to let it go, but it nagged at the back of my mind on occasion. James was even more attentive after that. My friends were jealous of how he showered me with gifts and affection, especially my best friend Chelsea."

Gray suddenly dropped Lizbeth's hand. She ran the fingers of both hands through her hair and then held them up in a sign for Lizbeth to stop. Still she had not looked at Lizbeth. "Stop, just stop," she said.

"No, Gray, I want you to know."

"I know where this is going. I don't need the details."

"Yes, Gray, you do. Just let me finish," Lizbeth pleaded softly.

Gray took a deep breath, let it out slowly, and then whispered, "Okay."

"As you may have surmised, James and Chelsea were having an affair and had been for some time. I soon discovered how naïve I really was, when James' true nature was exposed.

He had been cheating on me, on quite a regular basis, the entire time I had known him, all the way back to high school. Now, this man was the basis for my existence. I loved my daughter, but she too was a part of him. He was my world."

Lizbeth drank more beer. The next part was easier. "He, of course, begged me not to leave him. I was the only woman he would ever love and all that bullshit. I tell you Gray, part of me died that day. I couldn't leave. Where would I go? I had not gone to college. Mazie was almost twelve by then. James was still building his career. So I let my heart go dormant. I went through the motions of perfect wife and mother. I devoted all my attention to Mazie and kept James blissfully unaware of what I was planning. The day Mazie graduated from high school, I presented him with divorce papers detailing every sordid affair he had for the past ten years. By then he was worth a whole lot more money and Mazie was grown. Ten years, Gray, ten years worth of feeling dead inside. I took him for everything I could get and then some."

Gray chuckled a little, saying, "Ah, revenge. A dish best served cold."

Lizbeth smiled for the first time since she had begun her tale. "Yes, and it was delicious, but it didn't heal my heart. That has taken awhile." She paused. "Gray, I told you this because you need to know. Whatever happened to you, it will get better. It just takes time. I let that part of me go to sleep, as you say, but then it woke up all on its own, with no help from me, and I'm finding that I do think I could love someone again."

Gray finally turned around to look at Lizbeth. She had tears in her eyes, one having fallen over her eyelid, dripping onto her cheek. She whispered, "But aren't you scared?"

Lizbeth smiled. "Yes, but I'm more alive than I've been in years and I feel like being crazy and throwing caution to the wind."

Gray touched her fingertips to Lizbeth's cheek. Gray's eyes danced back and forth, as if searching Lizbeth's face for some kind of sign. She whispered, "What am I going to do with you?"

The distance between their lips closed slowly. Gray's hand slipped from Lizbeth's cheek into her thick hair, sliding to the back of her head, and gently pulling Lizbeth to her. Lizbeth felt her heart stop. She gasped just before Gray's mouth closed on hers. Every fiber of her being exploded, as a short distance away, the waves crashed loudly into the shore. If Lizbeth hadn't already been sitting down she would have swooned, and all of that was just when Gray's lips first touched hers. When Lizbeth's lips parted, she melted into the sweetest, most intense, absolutely breath-taking kiss she had ever experienced. Now if only Lizbeth could remember how to breathe.

Gray released Lizbeth's lips, but hovered there inches from her face, her crystal blue eyes registering something that looked to Lizbeth like astonishment. Gray had felt it too. That had been an earth-shattering kiss. Lizbeth chest was now heaving, as her burning lungs sucked for air. She had fallen back against Gray's hand and it was the only thing keeping her head from impacting the sand below. Lizbeth had done the very thing she swore she wouldn't do again. She had not eaten since lunch, she was drinking, and she had touched Gray, a lethal combination.

Gray finally smiled and the look of confusion faded from her face. She began to study Lizbeth's expression. "Are you okay?" Gray asked.

Lizbeth said weakly, "I think I need to lie down."

It suddenly dawned on Gray what had happened. She helped Lizbeth down on the blanket and jumped up, running to the Jeep, all the while talking fast. "Oh my God, I forgot to feed you. I brought hot dogs to cook, but I just blanked it out."

She returned with two coat hangers. She reached into the cooler, grabbed two dogs and stuck them on the ends of the hangers. Holding them out over the fire, she continued to talk. Lizbeth just listened. Her body was still tingling and she wasn't sure if it was her blood sugar levels or the fact that Gray had kissed her.

Gray hadn't just kissed her. She had changed Lizbeth's whole perspective on what a kiss was supposed to feel like. True, Lizbeth wasn't that experienced. There had only been James and a few others to compare it to, but Lizbeth knew that a kiss like that didn't come along very often. That kiss had rocked her in to her current trembling state.

Gray was chattering away about how sorry she was for not feeding Lizbeth and turning the wieners in the flames. Lizbeth, who was just holding on to reality by a thread, stared above her at the now deep black sky, peeking out from between the whirling clouds. It was hard to believe Earl was out there in the ocean, churning toward them. Gray babbled on, but Lizbeth wasn't listening. She tried to focus but drifted through the clouds in the sky full of stars. Here on the island, the stars twinkled unimpeded by city lights. A shooting star arched its way across the heavens. Lizbeth closed her eyes, but didn't make a wish. Instead, she thanked the powers that be for that kiss and prayed for clarity.

When Lizbeth opened her eyes, Gray was over her again, grinning down at her. "Hey, ya' gonna make it there, Miss Throw Caution to the Wind?"

Lizbeth smiled back, feeling better. "Yeah. You gotta Coke in that cooler?"

Gray dug in the cooler, pulling out a can. She handed it to Lizbeth, who had pulled herself up onto her elbows. Lizbeth took the soda and chugged until she had to stop and catch her breath. Once again, the southern champagne coursed through her body, restoring her senses. After a few more sips, she was able to sit up.

Gray was holding two hotdogs in dry buns in one hand. "What do you want on your hotdog?" she asked.

Lizbeth was never picky when she had gone too long without eating. She took one of the dry dogs, saying, "Just like this is fine." She immediately bit the end off the hot dog and began to chew heartily.

Gray laughed at her. "You know, you should have said something. I had no idea you were starving."

Lizbeth swallowed and took another swig of Coke. "I meant to eat something before I left the house. I get around you and I forget to eat. I forget to think."

The corner of Gray's smile crept higher on one side, when she said, "I got a little of that going on myself."

They had eaten in silence for a few moments, when Lizbeth blew out a breath of air, signifying the world had come back into sharp focus. She looked at Gray, who was watching Lizbeth's resurrection unfold before her.

Lizbeth exhaled heavily. "Wow! That was intense."

Gray chuckled. "Yes, it was."

Lizbeth waited a few seconds, then asked, "Are you going to do it again?"

"What, not feed you?" Gray teased her.

"Gray, are you going to kiss me again?"

Gray answered quickly, "Not until I've seen you eat a full meal. I'm afraid you might have a heart attack and then what would Fanny say?"

#

As soon as Lizbeth finished eating, Gray packed up the Jeep, doused the fire, and took them home. The National Park Service closed the beaches at night now, which was a total surprise to Lizbeth. So much had changed about the island since she was a child. Lizbeth wanted their time on the beach together to go on, but approaching Park Service SUV's headlights forced then to move along.

Gray filled the ride home with complaints about the park service and the Audubon Society. There was an ongoing fight between the natives of the Outer Banks and the government over the plight of a little bird called the Piping Plover. Gray believed it was all based on bad science and mismanagement that would eventually kill the economy, while the bird moved to another habitat, as was its nature. Gray had been very animated in her argument. Gray's passion, when she spoke, mesmerized Lizbeth. Gray loved this island and these people.

Gray pulled the Jeep to a stop in front of Lizbeth's cottage and killed the engine. She got out and walked Lizbeth to her door. The village was completely quiet except for the occasional blue grass music, coming through the trees on the wind. On a porch somewhere in the tiny village, musicians gathered, as was often the case among the talented population. Repeating the same positions as at the end of their Monday date, Lizbeth stood on the porch with Gray remaining on the ground, holding the door open, grinning. Lizbeth wasn't sure what to do next. She didn't want the night to end, but it appeared she was being left once again at her doorstep.

Lizbeth asked, "Do you want to come in, have some coffee?"

A single chuckle left Gray's throat, before she said, "I don't think that's such a good idea."

"One step at a time, huh?" Lizbeth said, trying to hide her disappointment.

Gray's grin widened. "Yeah, something like that."

"Gray, I had a wonderful time. Thank you for another amazing evening."

"It was my pleasure," Gray said.

A grin seized Lizbeth, surely matching Gray's. "Well, tomorrow then," she said, dripping with southern drawl.

Gray winked. "Yes ma'am. Good night, Lizbeth. See you tomorrow," she said, letting the door close slowly.

She was walking to her Jeep when Lizbeth called after her. "Eight o'clock."

Gray turned around, her brow knitted, questioning, "What happens at eight o'clock?"

Lizbeth tried not to crack up when she said, "That's when I usually get up. Just thought you should know, so you don't have to pace outside my door for hours."

Lizbeth left Gray standing in the yard grinning. This time, Lizbeth's laughter trailed into the night.

Chapter Seven

Lizbeth woke Thursday morning to someone knocking on the front door. Her eyes popped open and when she saw the time on the digital clock, she smiled. It read, "8:00 a.m." on the dot. Instantly energized, she leapt from the bed, ran a brush through her hair, grabbed her housecoat, and tore off down the stairs. She ran into the bathroom, emerging hurriedly when another knock, a few moments later, spurred her toward the front door.

Through the glass in the door, Lizbeth could see a beaming Gray, watching as she approached the door. Lizbeth was as excited as a giddy schoolgirl. When she opened the door, Gray held out a platter covered by a cotton dishtowel.

"Compliments of Fanny," Gray said, grinning.

Lizbeth didn't take the platter. She pulled the towel back and saw scrambled eggs, bacon, fried country potatoes, and two fluffy homemade biscuits, oozing butter.

"Yum. That looks delicious," Lizbeth said and then winked at Gray. "Gonna make sure I've eaten, I take it."

"Something like that," Gray said, following Lizbeth down the hall, still carrying the platter.

"Well, I'll give you one thing... You're punctual," Lizbeth said, reaching for the coffee pot. Gray laughed very close behind her, in the small cramped kitchen. Gray then leaned against Lizbeth's back, while reaching around to set the platter on the counter in front of her. Lizbeth's sharp intake of air was audible. She could feel Gray's breath on her neck. Gray stayed there just a little longer than necessary, and then walked to the table, sitting down.

Lizbeth began to wonder if she would survive this little sexual dance she and Gray were doing. Lizbeth gripped the counter for support. Her knees grew weak and her head would spin, just like now, every time Gray touched her. When she had steadied herself, she continued with the coffee preparations. She still had her back to Gray. Both women remained quiet. To cover the silence, Lizbeth turned on the radio.

The voice of Governor Beverly Perdue rang out clear in the small space. "Those evacuations are serious. You know, I live on the coast. And when they tell you to get out, you really have to think of...take that message seriously. The tourists are taking it seriously. The residents are not mandatorily required to evacuate, but many of them are in the process of evacuating, too... People left behind are on their own."

Lizbeth turned down the radio and faced Gray. That's when she saw Gray staring out the window, a cloud of seriousness on her face.

"Gray, are you worried about the storm?"

Gray's attention snapped back into the room. "I'm sorry, what?"

"What the Governor said, does that worry you?" Lizbeth asked.

"I'm sorry, I wasn't listening. What did she say?"

"She said we're on our own."

Gray didn't seem concerned. "Oh, that just means they won't try to rescue anyone until the danger has passed. Relieves the state of responsibility. It's the standard cover your ass speech."

Lizbeth poured them both a cup of coffee and brought it to the table. She brought a fork and a napkin with her, intending to eat every bit of Fanny's breakfast. If this is how the day was going to start, already weak kneed, she needed her strength. Lizbeth studied Gray's demeanor as she sat down. The cloud of worry had lifted some, but Lizbeth could still see it behind Gray's eyes.

Lizbeth decided not to pry anymore, having quickly learned that Gray didn't like to talk about what she was feeling. She picked up a piece of bacon and took a bite. It was scrumptious manna from heaven. Gray smiled, pleased with the look of pleasure on Lizbeth's face.

Lizbeth swallowed and gathered a forkful of eggs. She asked, before taking a bite, "So what's in store for us, how bad will it get?"

Gray didn't seem worried at all about the storm. She talked about it as if it were a normal everyday occurrence. "I expect we'll see sixty to seventy mile an hour sustained winds. Maybe two to four feet of storm surge."

If the storm wasn't bothering Gray, then Lizbeth suspected she knew what was. Gray was falling for Lizbeth and she really didn't want to. This beautiful, strong, self-confident lesbian woman was afraid of a little ol' straight girl. Lizbeth found that slightly amusing and grinned.

"What are you grinning at?" Gray asked in amusement.

"Nothing," Lizbeth said, barely able to stifle a laugh. "So what's on the agenda today?" She changed the subject to keep Gray from asking any more questions.

Gray, redirected, said, "We need to move your car to higher ground, before all the good spots are taken. It's all about island topography. You have to know where the high spots are and get there first."

"Where should we take it?" Lizbeth asked between bites.

"Over by the lighthouse is the highest ground. We'll start there. I'd hate to see a car like that get salt water in it."

"James loved that car," Lizbeth said with a laugh.

Gray understood the car was one of Lizbeth's spoils of war and laughed with her, adding, "Remind me never to piss you off."

"Hell hath no fury…" Lizbeth giggled.

"Did you let him keep his golf clubs?"

Lizbeth grinned. "Yes, in exchange for my college tuition."

"Ooo, you play dirty," Gray responded, still laughing.

"I had ten years to plan my escape. That's a lot of time to think."

"Like I said, I hope to stay in your good graces. Wouldn't want all that experience taking someone to their knees aimed at me."

Lizbeth swallowed. "It's not a skill I recommend acquiring, but I could probably write a book on how to catch your cheating husband."

The cloud darkened in Gray's eyes. She asked softly, "Did it help, getting even?"

Lizbeth thought for a second, fork poised in mid air. "I wouldn't say I got even. He'll never know the kind of pain he caused me, because I don't think he is capable of loving anyone but himself. Let's just say it was bittersweet."

Gray absorbed this information, but had no comment. Lizbeth finished as much of the food on the platter as she could and then took the platter to the sink, scraping off the leftovers in the trashcan. She washed the platter and returned to the table, handing it to Gray.

"Please tell Fanny thank you. That was delicious."

"I will. I'll run this plate back home while you get dressed, okay?" Gray said, standing up, and holding the plate between them with both hands.

They were face to face and too close together. Lizbeth started to feel the tiny lightning bolts dance across her body. Gray looked down at Lizbeth with blatant desire in her eyes. Up until then Gray had initiated every physical encounter between them, but something took over Lizbeth in that moment. She reached up, putting her arms around Gray's neck.

"Well," Lizbeth said, "You've seen me eat a meal."

Gray, still holding the plate, hesitated for only a second before leaning down to Lizbeth's waiting lips. This time the kiss was hungrier, their tongues seeking each other as a soft moan left Lizbeth's throat. Gray's own tiny moan followed close behind. Shockwaves crashed through Lizbeth's nervous system. Her brain was screaming, "This is fucking fantastic," while pumping all kinds of good chemicals into her body like a drunk running the beer keg.

Gray stopped kissing Lizbeth and took a few staggered steps backward, bumping into the wall. She held the plate up like a shield between them.

"Whoa," she said. "That's enough of that."

The kiss dazzled Lizbeth as well, but the affect it had on Gray thrilled her even more. She giggled and said, "Maybe I should go get dressed."

Gray didn't move. She held the platter in place and rotated, keeping it between them as Lizbeth exited the kitchen. Lizbeth heard Gray leaving after she got upstairs. She could have sworn she heard Gray muttering to herself, "Damn," followed by, "What in the hell have I gotten myself into?"

#

Gray was sitting on Lizbeth's front porch when she came out the front door. She was back to her signature look of board shorts, tank top, and Ray Bans. Lizbeth had thrown a load of laundry in the washer before coming outside. She had only the blue plaid Bermuda shorts and white tee shirt she was wearing left of her clean clothes. She wanted to get things washed and dried before the hurricane knocked out the power.

Lizbeth stopped in the doorway before Gray was aware that she was there. Gray was once again in some far off place. Lizbeth hated that what was happening between them was somehow causing Gray discomfort, but she couldn't help herself. Lizbeth, caught up in the moment, didn't want to think about down the road. She knew that's what was bothering Gray. It worried Lizbeth, too, when she let herself think about it, but she tried hard not to. Lizbeth felt alive inside for the first time in fourteen long and brutally lonely years. This felt like a second chance. She couldn't afford to pass it up. At this point, Lizbeth knew she couldn't if she wanted to.

She made her presence known by tossing the keys into Gray's lap, saying, "You drive."

They drove over to Lighthouse Road, but all the good spots were gone. Lizbeth asked, "Where to now?"

Gray aimed the Mustang back to Harbor Road and took a left, explaining, "We'll go over by the community cemetery. That's the side where the Navy dumped the sand they took out of the natural harbor when they made it bigger. That's when they changed the name from Cockle Creek to Silver Lake. Old folks still call it the Creek."

They locked the car and started back toward home on foot. They were joined, both in front of them and behind, by other people coming back from having moved their vehicles to higher ground. Every few minutes a car or truck would pass, a hand out the window, waving at neighbors. When they would pass Lizbeth and Gray, a loud "Gray!" would emanate from the driver and all passengers. Gray would smile and wave, sometimes calling a name back at the passersby.

Lizbeth admired Gray's apparent magnetism among her fellow natives. She commented, "I see I'm not the only one you've charmed. You have quite the fan club."

"Just islanders," Gray said nonchalantly. "There's barely over seven hundred of us year round, so I guess we gotta get along."

It was calm out, with just a bit of a breeze. The air was warm and smelled heavily of salt spray. They walked around the harbor, down to the Cedar Island ferry dock. The harbor was almost empty. Most of the smaller boats were out of the water and could be seen here and there, lashed to trees and steel poles or some other immovable object. The remaining free-floating boats in the harbor all had extra lines tying them in all directions, creating a bit of a spider web effect on the slick surface of the water.

"Which one's yours?" Lizbeth asked, looking over the small fleet of fishing skiffs.

"That one." Gray pointed at a small white skiff, with its characteristic forward pilothouse. "She's twenty four feet long, not too big, but it'll do."

Lizbeth stepped around Gray to get a better view of the boat. As she did this Lizbeth trailed her hand around Gray's waist, stepped under Gray's pointing arm, and leaned back into her ever so slightly, pretending to be getting a better vantage point. She could feel Gray's breathing quicken against her neck. The wind blew the boat just enough for Lizbeth to read, "Fanny Gray," painted on the stern.

"I like the name," Lizbeth said, not moving, but looking up over her shoulder at Gray.

"Fanny said she told Granddaddy he was a fool for naming a boat after a ship that sank."

Gray was talking to Lizbeth, but Lizbeth could see her mind was churning beneath the surface. Lizbeth had not played this flirting game since she was a teenager. Sure, she flirted with James when their marriage had been good, but this was different, it was exhilarating. She felt emboldened by the power she seemed to wield over Gray. If Gray was having second thoughts, Lizbeth was going to make it as hard as possible for Gray to resist her. Lizbeth, still looking over her shoulder at Gray, leaned back a little harder into Gray's chest.

Gray shook her head, grinned at Lizbeth, and said, "God, you're killin' me."

The loud cry of "Gray!" shattered the moment. Four women, stopped in an SUV just ten feet away, had shouted it. Gray stumbled backward, almost unbalancing Lizbeth, before she stuck a hand in Lizbeth's back to steady her. Then when Gray was sure Lizbeth had gained her feet, she turned to the women in the large black vehicle.

The local lonely women's club had found the island rogue, or that's what went through Lizbeth's mind. Because the blond thirty something hanging out the passenger window, Bloody Mary in hand complete with celery stick and umbrella, was looking at Gray like she was a big piece of candy. This woman was making no attempt to cover her lust for the woman standing beside Lizbeth.

Gray waved. "Mornin' ladies."

Damn, did Gray have to be so charming? Lizbeth was watching Gray smile at these women and a twinge of jealousy pinched her chest.

The Bloody Mary woman said, "Well, there you are. We've been looking for you. We're having a party. Come on. It'll be fun."

The accent and the jewels the woman possessed told Lizbeth two things: she had money, and she was from somewhere near Charlottesville, Virginia. The woman dropped her r's, farm became fahm, car became cah. Lizbeth immediately didn't like her. The way she was undressing Gray with her eyes didn't help.

The two other passengers and the driver started in on Gray for her to join them at their hurricane party.

Lizbeth was happy when Gray said, "Thanks for asking, but I got things to look after. Y'all go on and have fun."

The driver, another thirty something bottle blonde, yelled out, "Gray, you know our girls' week wouldn't be the same without a visit from you."

The one hanging out the window said, "Yeah, we've been looking for you since Monday." She looked at Lizbeth. "Who's your friend?"

Gray was blushing. "This is my neighbor, Lizbeth. Lizbeth, this is Della, Pam, Sarah, and... I'm sorry I forgot your name." Gray indicated each woman, as she called her name. Della was the one hanging out the window.

Della said, "Oh that's Ellen. She dyed her hair."

"It's a pleasure to meet you all," Lizbeth said, smiling at the women. A bit of tigress crept into Lizbeth. She stepped up beside Gray, slid her arm around her waist, and patted her on the stomach. It was a friendly gesture, nothing sexual to the untrained eye, but understanding registered on Della's face. Lizbeth said, "I'm sorry to have kept Gray away from you ladies. She's been helping me get acclimated."

Gray's body froze under Lizbeth's touch.

Della smiled knowingly, saying, "I bet she has." Gray evidently had lost the ability to speak. Della continued, "Well, if you change your mind, you know where we are. Nice to meet you, Lizbeth." Then the SUV pulled away slowly, the women inside laughing loudly.

Lizbeth released Gray from her grasp. Gray's face was still red when Lizbeth looked up at her. "Thought you said all the tourists had to leave."

"Della and her husband own the house. She comes down once a year with her girlfriends for a girls' week. How'd you know she wasn't a local?"

"That accent, pure Virginia, Charlottesville probably." Lizbeth answered.

Gray was impressed. "Very good. You're on the money."

Lizbeth raised an eyebrow, grinning out the side of her mouth. "I suppose you're part of the local wildlife."

"Something like that," Gray said, which Lizbeth was coming to know as Gray's answer when she didn't want to admit something out right.

Lizbeth laughed at Gray, because she seemed so uncomfortable. "Gray, don't be embarrassed. I told you I didn't care how many women you've slept with. I'm not jealous."

Gray chuckled. "You sure staked your claim awful quick."

Lizbeth turned so she was facing Gray, looking up at her, mirroring their positions from the kitchen earlier. Lizbeth was no holds barred into this now. Lizbeth had turned the corner of wondering if she would sleep with Gray, to now wondering how much longer Gray was going to wait to make a move. Waiting didn't feel so much like an option anymore and taking it slow went out the window long ago. She locked eyes with Gray.

"I have now witnessed, with my own eyes, two different women more or less begging for more of whatever it is you do. I've experienced a bit of it myself." Lizbeth's eyelids lowered in a sultry invitation. "I'd be lying if I said I wasn't interested in finding out what all the fuss is about."

Gray raised her eyebrows. Her expression read, "Be careful what you wish for, little girl," but she said, "And I suppose you are going to tease me mercilessly until I give in?"

Lizbeth inched closer, feeling Gray's body heat, watching as Gray's chest began to rise and fall, quickening the longer Lizbeth stayed there. "Yes, Gray, there's no turning back now. You have to finish what you started."

A short laugh left Gray's throat. "What I started? How did I start anything?"

Lizbeth said softly, "You said hello."

This rocked Gray. She searched Lizbeth's face, her eyes darting back and forth. An expression of actual physical pain enveloped her. Lizbeth was afraid of what Gray would say next. Lizbeth didn't give her the opportunity.

"Take a chance, Gray. I don't know where this is going to go either, but I'm willing to find out."

Ever so softly, Gray said, "And what have you got to lose?"

Lizbeth didn't hesitate, when she said only, "My heart."

Another loud "Gray!" from a passing truck broke them out of their solitude. Lizbeth had forgotten they were standing at the docks. Everything had disappeared but the two of them for a few moments. She wondered for an instant what they must have looked like, standing there lost in each other's eyes. Then she realized she didn't care. Lizbeth was passing Molly's test. She was putting what other people thought at the back of her mind and being happy in the forefront.

Gray waved at the man in the truck. There was no further comment about what had just been said. They began to walk again, back toward Howard Street, passing the Community Store. A few locals were gathered there on the porch. Gray and Lizbeth stopped to listen. Everyone on the porch shouted, "Gray!" simultaneously, and greeted them with a smile. She introduced Lizbeth. The porch dwellers had known Aunt Minnie, so Lizbeth was accepted into the fold. Islanders were notorious for their "us and them" attitudes and were not readily accepting of "woodsers" into their circle, until you'd been there good long while. Lizbeth's association with Gray and Aunt Millie offered her a little leeway.

They listened to the old timers' predictions of sixty to seventy miles an hour wind. Not too bad, they thought. The worst winds would be on the northeast face of the hurricane, which would remain out at sea. No one thought the storm would come much closer than a hundred miles, keeping the eye off shore. The storm surge would come from the Sound. There were some side bets made on whether the surge would be closer to four rather than the predicted six feet. Overall, the natives were taking it all in stride. Everyone seemed to be reveling in the quiet, with all the tourists gone.

Gray bought them ice cream cones. They ate them on the way back to Lizbeth's cottage, finishing them on the front porch. Trying to eat the ice cream and not have it melt down their arms prevented them from talking too much. When they were finished with the cones, Gray followed Lizbeth into the kitchen where they threw away the soaked napkins that had been wrapped around the cones and washed their hands. Gray remained very quiet.

Lizbeth started another pot of coffee. She was beginning to think she might have pushed Gray too far, too fast. It was painfully obvious that Gray was struggling with falling for Lizbeth. She had even told Lizbeth she was afraid of her. Maybe it was going to take a lot longer for Gray to trust her. She was lost in these thoughts when she crossed to the refrigerator in front of Gray, who was leaning with her back against the sink.

Lizbeth felt Gray's fingers on her elbow, just an instant before Gray spun Lizbeth to her, wrapped her arms around her, and kissed her passionately. Gray pulled Lizbeth close to her body and Lizbeth melted into her. Lizbeth's hands went to Gray's face. She caressed the smooth skin there and then ran her fingers through Gray's hair and down her neck. There were so many sensations happening at once, Lizbeth could not settle on one before another overwhelmed it.

Want, need, lust, whatever it was called, consumed both women. Gray backed Lizbeth the few steps into the wall of the narrow kitchen. Lizbeth's hands went above her head to the wall, where Gray grabbed them, holding them there, pressing her body into Lizbeth's. Their lips never parted. Desire overcame Lizbeth. She pulled her hands from Gray, and wrapped her arms tightly around Gray's neck. Gray took Lizbeth around the waist and stood up straight, pulling Lizbeth off the floor and into her arms. They banged around in the kitchen for a few minutes, before coming up for air.

Lizbeth, panting against Gray's heaving chest, said under her breath, "Oh, my fucking God."

Gray held Lizbeth, while she tried to catch her own breath. Finally, when Lizbeth felt she could talk again, she looked up at Gray, whose scandalous grin had returned, and said, "I take it you've decided to take a chance."

Gray winked. "Something like that."

"So what happens now?" Lizbeth asked, her head back on Gray's chest.

"In about an hour we're expected across the street for lunch. Fanny is cooking everything that might spoil, before the power goes out."

Lizbeth had not moved. Her eyes were closed and she was breathing in Gray's scent. Her head moved up and down with Gray's now slowing breath. She said dreamily, "Oh, I don't think an hour would be enough."

Gray's laughter rang like sweet music to her ears.

#

After Gray checked that Lizbeth had enough candles and batteries and knew where everything was, she went over to her house to help Fanny with lunch. Lizbeth stayed behind, promising she would follow soon. She kissed Gray on the cheek before she left, knowing that if she kissed her lips again they would probably miss lunch. Lizbeth moved her wet colored clothes from the washer to the dryer and threw her white clothes in to wash. She ran upstairs, brushed her hair again, checked herself in the mirror, and then hurried down the stairs.

The winds had now picked up and were blowing a steady ten to fifteen miles an hour. More clouds filled the sky and the horizon was beginning to darken. The outside edge of Earl was closing in on them. Aside from the wind, everything was eerily quiet when Lizbeth tapped on Fanny's screen door.

The front door was open and soon Gray's beaming face appeared. "Come on in," she said.

The aroma of boiling collards and frying pork overtook Lizbeth. A flashback of Sunday dinner at her grandmother's flooded her mind. She followed Gray to the kitchen where Fanny was busy frying cornbread. A large bowl of chopped collards graced the center of the table. An old ketchup bottle sat beside bowl. Long green and red peppers in vinegar replaced the original contents of the bottle, because no good southern cook would serve collards without homemade pepper vinegar.

A platter of pork chops glistened beside a plate of sliced tomatoes, fresh from Fanny's own vines. Next to that was a small bowl with sliced cucumbers and green onions, bathing in vinegar and sprinkled with black pepper. There were boiled potatoes and green beans, probably the ones Lizbeth saw Fanny snapping that first day, in another large bowl. A fresh pitcher of sweet iced tea, at the end of the table, capped it all off. This was some down home food, a southern soul food delight.

"Oh Miss Fanny, this looks amazing. I haven't had cooking like this in years. Thank you so much for having me," Lizbeth said with true appreciation.

"Go on, sit down. I'll be through with this here bread in a minute," Fanny said, turning back to the cornbread, while she continued to talk. "Gray tells me you had one of them sinkin'

spells again. Thought we ought might to feed you. Get ya'
perked up."

Gray, continuing to grin from ear to ear, pulled out a chair
for Lizbeth. Lizbeth sat down. Gray sat down beside her on the
same side of the table. This left the other side of the table clear
for Fanny to move around and have a place to sit. This also left
Gray and Lizbeth's legs covered under the tablecloth and
within inches of each other. When Gray's leg brushed
Lizbeth's, she shivered. Lizbeth was glad Fanny's back was to
them.

The first time it happened, Lizbeth thought it was an
accident. The second time it happened, Lizbeth had been
looking at Gray, and she saw the corner of Gray's mouth
twitch. Gray glanced at Lizbeth, her blue eyes twinkling with
mischief. Lizbeth, not to be outdone, slid her hand under the
table. Ever so gently, she ran the back of her hand up the side
of Gray's thigh.

Gray jumped. Fanny turned around. Looking at Gray, who
was trying to act like nothing happened, Fanny said, "Good
Lord, Gray. What's got into you? You been jumpin' round
here for days, like a minnow with a bird after it."

Gray moved her chair further from Lizbeth, saying, "Must
have been a rock under the leg."

It was all Lizbeth could do not to burst out laughing. She
drank some tea to cover her smile, while Gray shot daggers at
her with her eyes. Fanny joined them at the table, bringing the
still sizzling cornbread with her. They bowed their heads while
Fanny thanked the Lord for their meal and asked for protection
from the coming storm. They ended the prayer together.
"Amen."

Food was passed and the plates were filled. Lizbeth and
Gray didn't have much to say. Fanny did most of the talking,
with the other two adding to the conversation when she
prodded them. Lizbeth ate as if it was her last meal. If spinach

made Popeye stronger, then these collard greens could be just what she needed. Lizbeth had a feeling she was going to need all of her strength tonight. She and Gray were vibrating with so much sexual tension, Lizbeth didn't know why the whole room wasn't shaking.

Fanny was suspicious. Lizbeth could see her looking back and forth between the two of them. Gray wasn't helping. She had never been so non-talkative. Lizbeth, at least, was trying to stay engaged in the conversation. Gray had just checked out. Lizbeth tried to distract Fanny.

"Miss Fanny," Lizbeth said, "In forty-four, how did you deal with the storm surge? That was an enormous amount of water."

"We all stayed to the lighthouse keeper's quarters. Highest spot on the island. The water just washed on through. Ain't nothin' to keep it here. It can only get so high, then it washes right off the other side." Fanny paused. She looked over the table at Gray, locking eyes with her namesake. "Does the island good to wash off the past now and then. Lets us start fresh. Some folks could learn a lesson from nature. Wash away all that bad stuff from their life, and start over with fresh ground under their feet."

Lizbeth looked at Gray and then at Fanny. Both women held their stare. Gray spoke next. "Yeah, and another lesson they could take from nature is mind their own business, they'll live longer."

"Ornery as a pole cat, always has been," Fanny said, shaking her head from side to side and chuckling under her breath.

"Look at my role model," Gray shot back, but it was playful.

The two women would take each other on, but always end it laughing. It was lighthearted banter between two strong willed women, separated by a whole generation, who had found a way to coexist here in this little cottage. Gray stood to do the dishes. Lizbeth rose to help. Gray motioned for her to sit back down.

"No, you sit. This is my job. She cooks. I clean. That's our deal," Gray said, grabbing the now empty plates.

Fanny sat up taller and pointed at Gray, saying, "That's because all you know how to cook is fish, or somethin' else you brung in here from out the water. Seems to me you'd get tired of fish. Takin' care of 'em all those years and then comin' home and eatin' 'em. Would'a made me quamished. I lived off fish my whole life, but fish ever day, that ain't for me."

Gray's back was turned. She said over her shoulder, "It's good for you. That's how you got to be so old and mean."

"Well, if I start eatin' tuna out of a bag, I want you to go on and put me out of my misery," Fanny said, chuckling.

Gray was quick with her retort. "I'll try to remember to get some the next time I'm up the beach."

"Gray, you're horrible," Lizbeth said, but laughed.

Fanny patted Lizbeth's hand. "I don't pay no attention to 'er. She likes to put up a good front, but she ain't as tough as she makes out to be. Cries like a baby ever time a mention a that dog she left in Texas comes up."

Gray's head snapped around. A pan clanged loudly against the porcelain sink. Gray's eyes were wide with anger. Her voice was lower and took on a tone Lizbeth had not yet heard, and not one Lizbeth wanted directed at her.

"I think that's entirely enough about me for awhile, don't you think?"

Fanny knew she'd crossed a line and backed off. She changed the subject to a game of gin rummy and was able to coax the two younger women into playing with her. Once the table had been cleared, they sat down for a long afternoon of cards and sweet tea.

Gray winked at Lizbeth, apparently over her flash of anger. "Watch her. She might look like an innocent old lady, but she cheats."

"Drime," Fanny said, as she cackled.

#

At five o'clock, after Fanny had beaten them both handily, the card game adjourned. Lizbeth needed to go put her clothes in the dryer. Fanny said she'd warm up some food for supper, while Lizbeth was gone, and made her promise to be back in thirty minutes. The O'Neal women had made it their mission to make sure that Lizbeth ate plenty.

There had been no more footsy under the table. As a matter of fact, Gray had moved her chair to the end of the table, leaving Lizbeth alone on one side and Fanny on the other. She claimed it was so Fanny wouldn't try to see her cards, but Lizbeth knew better. The sweltering looks she caught Gray giving her, from time to time, told her she was at the forefront of Gray's mind.

Gray followed Lizbeth home like a puppy, telling Fanny she was going to help Lizbeth fold her clothes so they could get back in time to eat. Lizbeth wasn't fooled. As soon as they were behind Lizbeth's closed front door, Gray was on her. Gray pressed Lizbeth's back to the door and kissed her hard. Lizbeth reciprocated, her arms around Gray's strong back, pulling her in tighter.

Their breathing was out of control. They were out of control. Lizbeth put her arms around Gray's neck. Gray placed her hands on Lizbeth's hips and lifted her with ease. Lizbeth wrapped her legs around her waist. Gray pressed Lizbeth into the wall behind the door. Lizbeth felt her crotch was going to burst into flames any minute. This was the hottest sex she'd ever had and they hadn't even taken off their clothes, yet.

Gray ran her hands down Lizbeth's sides. Lizbeth wanted Gray to stop taking her time and she meant in a hurry. Usually a bit shy in bed, Lizbeth lost all her inhibitions. She grabbed one of Gray's hands and pulled it onto her breast. Gray's skillful touch sent waves of ecstasy through her entire body. Gray rocked Lizbeth against her hips and the wall. Just their bodies' rubbing against one another was bringing Lizbeth close to climax.

Gray was a wonderful lover from the start. She sensed when Lizbeth could not contain the orgasm any longer. She put one hand in the small of Lizbeth's back and pulled her tightly to her. Gray slid her other hand between Lizbeth's legs and moved her hand up against Lizbeth's thrusting pelvis. It only took two thrusts and Lizbeth came in a rush of seizing muscle. She gripped Gray's shoulders and fell into her with a loud drawn out, "Oh my God!"

Gray held her there pressed into the wall until the muscle spasms subsided and Lizbeth's breathing began to slow. Lizbeth released her legs from Gray's waist and slid down her body. Gray kept her arms around Lizbeth, and she was smiling down at her, when Lizbeth finally reopened her eyes.

Lizbeth smiled weakly, spent from the orgasm still echoing inside her. "Jesus Christ, Gray. That was with my clothes on."

Gray kissed Lizbeth on the forehead. She was proud of herself and it showed in that all too familiar grin. "Well, something had to be done. There was so much sexual tension across the street, I couldn't concentrate on my cards, and lost to Fanny. You know she keeps a running tab on our games. You cost me dearly."

Lizbeth sighed, placing her head on Gray's chest. "Yeah, something had to be done." Suddenly she looked back up at Gray. "What about you?" Lizbeth asked.

Gray chuckled. "It's okay, I'm fine."

Lizbeth was flustered. "But I... You didn't... I mean... I had fun, but you..."

Gray kissed Lizbeth and then whispered in her ear, "Oh honey, believe me, I had fun, too."

Lizbeth said, "Oh," and then really understanding, she repeated, "Oh," emphasizing it with a wicked grin.

Gray loosened her hold on Lizbeth. "Now, where's this laundry we're supposed to be folding, or did you make that up to lure me over here?"

"No, there really is laundry. I have some in the washer and some in the dryer," Lizbeth said, still weak and uninterested in laundry at the moment.

"We better get those in the washer put in the dryer, before the power goes out. You wouldn't want them to get goaty."

"Goaty?" Lizbeth had a new word to learn.

Gray had gotten used to translating for her. She said, "It means foul smelling."

"I guess you're right, but I'd rather stay right here," Lizbeth said, smiling at Gray.

Gray kissed her again, lightly on the lips. "I'd like to stay like this too, but that old woman will come looking for us, if we don't show up on time."

"What do you think Fanny would say if she found us like this?" Lizbeth asked.

"Gray, you're gonna be late for supper."

#

Lizbeth and Gray were not late. They showed up just in time. Fanny had the table set again. They resumed the previous seating arrangement, only Gray didn't sit so far away from Lizbeth this time. Lizbeth was sure Fanny was going to see the "I just had sex" look on her face, but if she did, she made no indication of it.

Gray acted nonchalant as if nothing had happened. She seemed much more relaxed now. Gray was always more relaxed when she was in control. She had regained control because she held Lizbeth in the palm of her hand, literally and figuratively. Once more, the tide had turned in their little sexual game of cat and mouse. Lizbeth was yet again the prey of the "wampus cat."

They listened to the radio while they ate, processing all the latest news of Earl. The maximum velocity winds inside the hurricane had decreased. Still, the storm would bring at least sixty mile an hour winds to the island. Heavy bands of rain were expected along with storm surge. Ocean waves reported on the Diamond Shoals were already approaching twenty feet. Low tide would be around eight p.m. The wind outside had picked up to a steady twenty miles an hour, merely a strong breeze, but the worst was yet to come. Earl was expected to pass Ocracoke in the wee hours of the coming morning, near or at high tide.

After the supper dishes had been cleaned and put away -- this time Lizbeth insisted she help just to keep herself busy -- Gray and Lizbeth closed the storm shutters on Fanny's house. The wooden shutters were pulled closed and then a two by four, cut to fit, was inserted through braces and bolted to the windows with wing nuts and preplaced bolts. It didn't take long and then they all, Fanny included, piled into the Jeep to take a ride "over the beach," as the islanders say. The waves were crashing so fast it was hard to distinguish one from another. The wildness and strength of the waves proved once again nature's awesome power. The foam-crested waves reached up as high as they could before slamming into shore, sending salt spray cascading into the air. The roar was deafening.

Fanny pronounced, "She's angry. She'll spit out some ol' ship parts before she's through."

Gray, in a moment of self-disclosure, confessed, "Even though I barely remember him, I used to walk this beach after every storm, looking for pieces of Dad's boat."

Fanny patted Gray's hand on the gearshift. The O'Neal women knew real pain. Lizbeth realized they got through it together, one strong when the other was weak.

Back home and the Jeep locked safely away again, the three women settled into the parlor. Fanny pulled out some old family albums, and showed Lizbeth pictures of Gray's mother and father. They had been a stunning couple. Lizbeth could see a little bit of Gray in both of them, but mostly Gray looked like her tall, blond mother with the same smooth complexion and laughing eyebrows.

Lizbeth held the family album in her lap. She began to thumb through it. She and Gray were sitting side by side on the floor in front of the couch, so they could both see the pages. Fanny sat behind them on one end of the couch, leaning over to point people out or give a location and time for the photo. Her mind was like a steel trap. She remembered everything and everybody.

Lizbeth turned another page and let out a small gasp. There on the page before her was a baby Gray. She knew because there was no mistaking those eyes. Gray must have been about a year old. She was white headed and tanned as she was now, running around in nothing but a diaper. Even at that age, Gray already had the mischievous grin and twinkling eyes.

"Gray, you were adorable, but even then you looked like trouble," Lizbeth said, chuckling.

Gray grabbed the book from Lizbeth's lap. "Let me see," she said.

When Gray lifted the photo album, a few things fell out of the back. Lizbeth picked them up, while Gray examined her childhood image more closely. Lizbeth looked at the items in her hands. There were five photos and a Christmas card, one of those with the family portrait on the front, and Merry Christmas sprawled above their smiling faces.

Lizbeth looked at the photos first. They were all of Gray, wearing a Sea World shirt in various places in the park. When she got to the Christmas card, Lizbeth's heart skipped a beat. The top of the card read Christmas 2004. Under the heading, a smiling Gray stood with her arm around a beautiful blond woman, a little shorter than Gray, and a Golden Retriever at her feet. The bottom of the card said, "From Gray, Dana, and Coker," as in O'coker, Lizbeth presumed. She was also assuming that was the dog's name.

Lizbeth realized too late that Gray had stopped looking at the photo album and was now focused on the card in Lizbeth's hand. Fanny, seeing what the two were looking at, rectified the situation by unceremoniously reaching down and plucking the card from Lizbeth's hands, before Lizbeth could get a good look at the woman beside Gray in the picture. There was something familiar about her, but Lizbeth hadn't gotten the chance to identify it.

"Been meanin' to go through these and throw out some of this stuff nobody need remember. This is a good place to start as any." With that, Fanny threw the card into the trashcan beside the couch.

Gray had not moved or spoken. Her tan face had gone pale. Whatever that woman did to Gray left her paralyzed for the moment. She stared at the place where the card had been in Lizbeth's hand, lost somewhere in the past. Fanny saw it, too.

As if Lizbeth were not there, Fanny said, in a calm loving tone, "Gray, you got to let that go sometime. If you hold on too tight to the past, darlin', you won't have no hands to grab onto the present."

Gray sat the book down on the floor between her and Lizbeth. She stood up slowly and walked out the front door. Lizbeth started after her, but Fanny put her hand on Lizbeth shoulder, preventing her from getting off the floor.

"Leave her be for a minute. She'll get all right. Gray don't like to lose control of her emotions in front of folks. She's always done that, gone off to cry on her own. Didn't want no one to know when her feelin's got hurt."

Lizbeth looked up at the older woman, torn between believing her and running after Gray. She stood up, smiling at Fanny, saying softly, "Maybe that's what's wrong with her. She's been crying by herself too long."

Fanny reached out and patted Lizbeth's hand. "Honey, if you're what's gonna mend that child's heart, I wish you'd do it. Lord knows I been tryin' for goin' on five years now." She paused, but didn't let go of Lizbeth's hand. She studied Lizbeth for a moment and then continued, "She sure has taken a likin' to you. First one I seen her give a second look to in the time she's been back, but be careful on your own account, Gray's not the easiest person to love. She loves too hard. She's a tough nut to crack, my Gray, but if you can get to her, she'll love you with all her heart and soul. She don't know no other way."

Fanny's candor took Lizbeth aback. Fanny had known all along what was going on between them, and as it turned out, was somewhat of a cheerleader for Lizbeth. Lizbeth leaned down and gave Fanny a big hug, whispering into the old woman's ear, "Thank you, Miss Fanny."

Fanny squeezed Lizbeth tightly. She was deceptively strong for an eighty-five year old. She released her grip on Lizbeth and patted her on the back, saying, "Now, take her over to your house. You young folk 'bout wore me out. I'm going to bed."

Lizbeth helped Fanny to her feet. "You aren't going to stay up and wait for the storm?"

Fanny grinned, a faint hint of Gray flashed on her face. "No, honey. I've seen enough of these to know that this one ain't worth stayin' up for." She winked. "But I bet that storm that's 'bout to hit across the street's gonna be a might size blow."

#

Gray was seated in one of the rocking chairs on the porch. The wind was more agitated now, but still not a gale. Rain had started to fall and was being blown through the screen surrounding the porch. Gray didn't seem to notice. She stared off in the distance.

Lizbeth stepped onto the porch and closed the door behind her. She grabbed Gray's hand and pulled her up out of the chair. "Come on, Fanny's going to bed and you're going with me."

There was no protest from Gray. She held onto Lizbeth's hand and followed her silently across the street. When they got inside, the lights blinked for the first time. Lizbeth led Gray to the couch where, still not speaking, she sat down. Lizbeth went to the kitchen, retrieved a bottle of wine and two glasses, bringing them back to the parlor. She poured a glass of wine for Gray and handed it to her. Gray took it robotically.

Lizbeth set about lighting candles all over the room. She could feel Gray's eyes on her, watching as she moved about the room. She also lit the two oil lamps on the mantel. Then Lizbeth cut off the parlor lights, sat down on the couch beside Gray, and poured herself a glass of wine. Still no words had been spoken.

Lizbeth waited patiently. She had been right where Gray was at one point in her life, unable to speak the truth of how a heart got broken. Lizbeth would wait, because she knew that when the time was right Gray would tell her everything. Lizbeth thought that helping someone with a broken heart was like trying to help an addict. They couldn't be helped until they were ready to move on, re-engage in life.

Gray sipped her wine. The wind had picked up, shaking the plywood on the windows occasionally. Lizbeth hardly noticed.

She was so attuned to Gray's every sound and movement that she had begun to breathe in the same rhythm. The lights flickered one more time and then everything went silent and black except for the parlor. Candlelight danced on the white walls. Lizbeth watched the reflected amber radiance shimmer through the wine in her glass. Gray finally sat forward. She rested her elbows on her knees, holding the wine glass in both hands in front of her. She cleared her throat.

"Dana is a veterinarian. We met when she came to treat one of the animals in the park. I'd been running wild since college. I had quite a few girlfriends and affairs, but nothing serious. I was young and having fun, nothing wrong with that. After I met Dana, things changed. I settled down. I loved her. Hell, I even flew to Canada and married her."

Gray took a sip from her glass and then continued, "Like you said, everything was fine. I had no idea. Ten years into it and boom, it just blew up. One day, my life was perfect, except for the recent death of my mother. The next day, I didn't have a life anymore."

Lizbeth's heart was breaking for Gray, but she remained still, while the tears fell softly on her own cheeks.

Gray swallowed hard. Her voice came out scratchy and dry. "I came home from work and my dog was sick. I didn't call Dana. I just threw Coker in the car and drove to her office. It was after hours, but I knew she'd still be there. She always was at that time of day. I had a key to the back door so I let myself in. I stepped into the hallway. I thought I heard Dana in her office. I went to get her to help me with the dog. I found her on the couch in her office with one of our closest friends."

Lizbeth couldn't help the sharp intake of breath. She was reliving all the pain right along with Gray.

Gray wasn't finished. "They had been having an affair for a year. It began when I came here to watch my mother die. They even came to the funeral together. To top it all off, my dog was really sick and I had to leave him behind so she could take care of him. I packed. I left. I have only talked to her a few times since. The last time she called to tell me my dog died."

Gray hung her head and cried quietly. Lizbeth thought Gray was probably afraid to all out cry, too afraid just to let it all out, too scared she couldn't stop if she did. Lizbeth had been there, too. It had taken her nearly five years to get back on her feet when she first discovered James' infidelity. She spent the next five plotting her revenge and the last four reveling in it. Gray never got any revenge. Lizbeth rubbed her hand gently in circles on Gray's back.

Gray finally raised her tear-streaked face to Lizbeth and said, "I don't want to fall in love with you. What good will it do either of us? You'll go back to Durham and I'll be here."

"Gray, I want you to listen very carefully to what I am about to say. Then you can make your decision. You have two choices. You can continue your life as it has been for the last almost five years, never letting anyone get too close. You can try to kill the loneliness by sleeping with strangers. It hasn't worked, as far as I can tell, but you can keep trying. You can walk out that door right now and I promise you will not see me again."

Gray tried to interrupt, but Lizbeth put up her hand to silence her. Lizbeth continued, "Or, you can give us a shot. It isn't perfect. Granted, there are some logistics to work out, but how will we know if we can work them out, if we don't try?"

Lizbeth took a deep breath, because she was laying all her cards on the table. If she bet wrong, this was all going to backfire miserably. "Gray, if you can walk away and not wonder 'what if' for the rest of your life, then do it. But I'm telling you, if kissing me feels anything to you like kissing you does to me, you're going to wonder."

Lizbeth stood up, placed her wine glass on the table, and went All-In on the river card. "There's the door. You can take it or you can follow me upstairs. That's entirely up to you. Choose wisely."

Lizbeth held her breath as she walked away. She took an oil lamp from the mantel and climbed the stairs. She exhaled loudly, sitting on the edge of the bed to await the outcome of the ultimatum she had just given Gray. The house was deadly quiet except for the occasional creak or rattle caused by the wind. She heard Gray clear her throat and then set the wine glass on the table. Her heart sank when she heard Gray's footsteps heading for the front door. Lizbeth had overplayed her hand.

Lizbeth threw herself back on the bed. Her own tears flowed freely now. She never heard the door open and close, because she was too wrapped up in misery. She would be the one always wondering "what if." Lizbeth would spend the rest of her life reliving the first seven days of knowing Gray and trying to forget them. Lizbeth couldn't understand why this had happened at all. Here she was crying over a woman of all things. This was cruel and unusual punishment and Lizbeth thought that she had already had her fair share.

Lizbeth felt the weight of someone sit down on the bed with her. She bolted upright to see Gray sitting there.

"I heard you go to the door," Lizbeth said in disbelief.

Gray smiled and gently brushed a stray hair from Lizbeth's face. "Lizbeth, I just went to lock the door."

"Then you're not leaving?" Lizbeth asked, still not believing Gray was actually sitting there.

"No, I'm not going anywhere," Gray said.

The amber light from the oil lamp flickered on the walls in the room. Gray's eyes were dry now. The tears had been dried from her face, only a smear of moisture left on one cheek, glistened in the lamplight. Using the fingers of both hands,

Lizbeth wiped her own wet face. Now that Gray was there, Lizbeth didn't know what to do. She hadn't thought beyond getting Gray to give in. They sat beside each other, looking into each other's faces, neither speaking.

There was a lot of soul-searching going on in that little bedroom. The wind had begun to howl against the windows. Rain was being driven sideways into the house and drumming loudly on the roof just above their heads. The cottage creaked around them. Earl was closing in. The storm outside played out in vivid symmetry with the whirling thoughts inside the room. Lizbeth sighed loudly.

Gray smiled. She guessed Lizbeth's quandary. Her mood was lifting and the twinkle was returning to her eyes. She reached again for Lizbeth's face, tucking a stray wave of hair behind Lizbeth's ear. She spoke softly, "Now that you've got me here, you don't know what to with me, do you?"

Lizbeth chuckled. "No, I hadn't really thought it through, before I started talking."

Gray teased her. "What would you normally do in this situation?"

"I've never been in this particular situation."

"What's so unique about this one?" Gray asked, grinning broader now.

Lizbeth blurted out, "Well, you're a woman for one thing."

Gray raised one eyebrow, saying, "And?"

"And... Well, I don't know. I should say that's plenty," Lizbeth shot back.

The island rogue began to pour on the charm. "That didn't seem to bother you this afternoon."

"That was different. I remind you I was fully clothed." Lizbeth's voice raised an octave and her true deeply southern accent revealed itself. It always did when she got excited or stressed. She was both.

Gray let out a sultry laugh, followed by, "Five more minutes and you wouldn't have been."

The warm glow of anticipation once again returned to Lizbeth's body. She was melting under the smoldering look Gray was giving her. Lizbeth's inner Scarlet reappeared, batted her eyes, and said, "Gray O'Neal! My mother warned me about rogues like you."

Gray's eyes bored into Lizbeth with pure lust. Lizbeth had awakened the sleeping beast and it was hungry. Gray turned and leaned into Lizbeth. Lizbeth withdrew, falling back on her elbows, overwhelmed with the full force of a seduction by Gray O'Neal. Gray kept coming, reaching over Lizbeth, which now pinned Lizbeth beneath her.

Gray's eyes were sparkling and behind them were not so veiled intentions. She was inches from Lizbeth's face. In a voice that stopped Lizbeth's heart in mid beat, deeper and dripping sex from each syllable, Gray said, "Your mother never warned you about me."

Not too many minutes later the windows rattled and the house shook, rivaling any noise ol' Earl was making.

Chapter Eight

Lizbeth awoke the next morning enveloped by Gray. She was spooned into Gray's naked body behind her. The memory of last night flooded into her and she blushed warm all over. Gray had been right. No one had ever warned Lizbeth about someone like her.

Lizbeth couldn't believe the places Gray had taken her. She made Lizbeth feel things she had never experienced, let alone knew existed. Gray's lips and hands had explored Lizbeth's body, driving Lizbeth over the edge repeatedly. Gray had begun with a full-fledged ravaging of Lizbeth and ended their night of lovemaking sweet and slow.

Molly had been correct that Lizbeth would know what to do. After a complete and very thorough demonstration, by Gray, of what a woman could do to another woman, Lizbeth had no trouble following her lead. The sight of Gray's naked body had been enough to quash any nervousness. Gray really did look like a Greek statue. Her skin was smooth, tightly sculpted over the surface of a long toned body. Gray's skin under her fingertips was soft and silky, much different from any of Lizbeth's previous lovers. Lizbeth found she couldn't touch her enough.

Gray was breathing deeply, still lost in sleep. Her arm was around Lizbeth, her hand cupping one of Lizbeth's breasts. Lizbeth's thoughts of their night together had heightened her awareness of Gray's nakedness against her. She moved her body in a little closer to Gray's, feeling her entire nervous system go on high alert. The thing that had caused it so much pleasure was close by. Her body began to crave Gray's hands, and that tongue, oh my.

Lizbeth could stand it no longer. She turned over so she was facing Gray. She ran a fingertip down Gray's jaw line and then touched her lips. Gray's eyes fluttered open. She smiled, pulling Lizbeth closer to her.

"Good morning," Gray said softly.

Lizbeth squirmed against Gray's body, running a hand down her side to her hip. In a sexy, hushed voice, Lizbeth said, "I need you to wake up."

Gray slid her hand into the small of Lizbeth's back and pulled Lizbeth's pelvis in contact with hers. In one smooth move, Gray pushed her leg between Lizbeth's, her thigh brushing up against Lizbeth's now throbbing crotch. It had only taken seconds for Gray to turn Lizbeth into putty in her hands.

Lizbeth only said, "Ummm," as she began to move against Gray's body.

The charming grin showed itself, as Gray said, "You need me, huh?"

Lizbeth let out a breathless, "Yes."

Gray laughed, then kissed Lizbeth down her neck and onto her chest, where she found Lizbeth's breasts, who were on the inside screaming, "Pick me! Pick me!" In a matter of moments, Lizbeth was digging her fingernails into Gray's back, repeating, "Oh God! Oh God!"

#

"Come on, Lizbeth. We have to get up." Gray was standing, pulling on the covers that Lizbeth, who was still in the bed, held tightly.

"I don't want to get out of bed. I want to stay here all day," Lizbeth whined.

Gray dropped the covers and started putting on her clothes. Lizbeth reluctantly relented and got up.

"I thought you wanted to stay in bed," Gray teased.

"Not without you and you seem hell bent on getting up, so I guess I have no choice."

Gray, who was only wearing her shorts, took the still naked Lizbeth in her arms. "Okay, here's the deal. I need to check in with Fanny and see about my boats. I'm going to go across the street, take a shower, grab you some breakfast, and then I'll be right back. Unless you want to come with me."

Lizbeth grinned. "No, I don't think I could get this just fucked look off my face. Fanny would know."

"She probably already does," Gray said, laughing.

"I guess she knows you pretty well. She did call you the village tomcat."

"About that," Gray said, suddenly serious. "I'll admit to being... let's just say a little cavalier of late with my love life, but I want you to know this is different."

Lizbeth tightened her arms around Gray's waist. "I could tell."

Gray grinned. "And how's that?"

"Because if I had been one of your conquests you would have slept with me the night you took me to the Sound, but you didn't even try. You kept leaving me at my doorstep." Lizbeth added, giggling, "I was beginning to wonder."

Gray laughed loudly. "Oh, you need not have worried. I had impure thoughts about you from the first moment I saw you."

"What took you so long?" Lizbeth said, squeezing one of the cheeks of Gray's ass.

"I told you, you were different. Fanny knew it, too. She kept dropping hints."

Lizbeth cocked her head to one side. "Why, what did she say?"

"She told me yesterday morning that I could mope around for the rest of my life, or I could open my eyes and see what was right in front of me. Not too subtle, huh?"

Lizbeth thought a second, then asked, "What will she think of me? She won't think I'm one of those women running around here throwing themselves at you, will she?"

"No, she'll know you're special," Gray said, her eyes twinkling.

"How's that?"

"She knows I don't spend the night," Gray answered.

"Ever?" Lizbeth asked.

Gray kissed Lizbeth on the lips and then pulled her into a tight hug, whispering in her ear, "Never."

#

Gray brought over sausage biscuits from Fanny's kitchen. She was wearing her customary board shorts, and added a sweatshirt against the still blowing wind outside. Her hair was wet. Gray had hurried. Lizbeth had also taken a shower, putting on a pair of jeans and a tee shirt, and a light sweater for the chill. With the windows boarded up the cottage was dark and cold.

Lizbeth suggested they eat on the front porch. Luckily, Lizbeth discovered that her kitchen came with a stovetop coffee pot and was equipped with a gas stove. She poured them each a cup and followed Gray to the front door. Gray stopped before opening the door, turning to kiss Lizbeth sweetly on the lips, and then they went out into the tropical storm weather that remained from Earl's passing.

Howard Street was shielded, but Lizbeth could hear the more powerful winds whistling through the treetops. It had rained hard in the night and brief periods of rain were expected all day. Gray had gotten a full report on the storm from Fanny, who was up early this morning, getting a damage report from the locals walking back and forth in front of her house.

Gray was laughing when she said, "Yeah, she made some wisecrack about me being too lazy to see to my own boats, so she had to ask on the street."

"She's quite feisty for her age," Lizbeth commented. "Have you ever known her to miss a sunrise?"

Gray darkened a little, before answering, "Only on the day my granddaddy died. Momma said they weren't up when she came downstairs, so she went to check on them and Fanny was lying there, just holding his hand. He'd passed in the night. That's the only time I know of."

Lizbeth sighed. "She must have really loved him."

Gray's eyes misted over. "Yes, she did, very much. I never heard a cross word between them. There was plenty of teasing and lots of laughter, but never a raised voice."

"That's so sweet." Lizbeth wished for a love like that, a lifetime with the one person you were meant to love. Fanny had been lucky and found hers when she was a teenager. They had lived more than a half a century together and Fanny had loved Laurence until the day he died. It seemed the O'Neal women loved hard and long.

Gray changed the subject. "Fanny says the word is minimal damage. The dock down at the Harbor Inn fell in some. A tree went down on a roof, but didn't punch through. The tide came up in places but it's gone now. We stayed pretty dry here on Howard."

"How hard did the wind blow?"

"Gusted up to near seventy, they say. Knocked the power out for good around four in the morning."

Lizbeth winked over the edge of her coffee cup. "I didn't notice."

Gray chuckled. "We were kinda busy."

Lizbeth blushed, a memory flashing in her mind. She finished her biscuit, thinking about the next memory she was going to make with the sexy blonde seated beside her. Lizbeth ran the back of her hand along Gray's forearm absentmindedly, as her thoughts of Gray pressed against her took on a life of their own.

Gray put her hand over Lizbeth's to stop it from moving. Gray's eyes revealed the thoughts she was having, too. Her voice was smoky when she said, "Just hold that thought. We have to go check the boats and then I plan on spending the rest of this rainy day in bed with you."

Thrilled at the prospects, Lizbeth leapt to her feet. "Well, let's go."

Gray squirmed in the chair. She looked a little distressed. "Give me a minute."

Lizbeth asked, "What's wrong?"

Gray shifted in her seat again. "Nothing's wrong." She grinned up at Lizbeth. "I just need a sec."

It dawned on Lizbeth that Gray couldn't move because she was as horny as Lizbeth. Lizbeth took no pity on her. She moved closer, stepping in between Gray's open legs, touching one of her calves to Gray's. Lizbeth batted her eyes and said, "Is it anything I could help you with?"

Gray swallowed hard. In an instant, she stood up, grabbed Lizbeth's hand, and pulled her back into the cottage. Once inside the cottage, Lizbeth turned into the aggressor. She yanked at Gray's sweatshirt, pushing it up over Gray's chest. Gray obliged by taking it the rest of the way off. They banged down the wall, across the room, and onto the couch.

Lizbeth's fingers made quick work of the little cotton string at the waist of Gray's shorts. Gray slid out of her shorts and underwear with Lizbeth's assistance. Lizbeth stood up, peeled off her sweater, and threw it across the room. Her shirt followed shortly after. Lizbeth's pants and underpants took Gray one swift tug to remove.

Gray, who was sitting on the couch, pulled Lizbeth down onto her lap, Lizbeth's knees straddling Gray. Gray was strong and she moved Lizbeth around like a feather, but she was gentle with her, taking her time, building the tension to a climax of earth shattering proportions. She held Lizbeth with one hand in the small of her back, the other between her legs, as Lizbeth arched backwards in a shuddering orgasm and then fell forward against Gray's chest.

Gray moved her arms to wrap them around Lizbeth while she tried to catch her breath. Little shivers of delight repeatedly cascaded through Lizbeth. She didn't know just how much further Gray could take her before she just keeled over and died from pure pleasure. Gray was a skilled and practiced lover. Lizbeth didn't begrudge her those other women. Gray had honed her skills and Lizbeth was reaping the benefits.

Lizbeth had also discovered that giving was as good as getting. When she had stopped trembling and caught her breath, she pushed Gray down on the couch and had her way with her. Gray groaned loudly when her back arched off the couch, sending shockwaves through Lizbeth. Gray came and Lizbeth with her, falling into Gray's body. They lay there, not speaking, trying to calm their breathing.

Lizbeth's head rested on Gray's chest. Their legs were entwined. Gray ran a hand through Lizbeth's hair. Very few times, Lizbeth had seen into Gray's heart. Gray covered her true emotions with humor and the island rogue persona, but every now and then, she said something that sounded heartfelt. This was one of those times.

"Lizbeth Jackson, you're going to make me fall in love with you and then break my heart."

Lizbeth raised her head and then supported her chin in her hands, in the middle of Gray's chest. "You know that's a two way street, don't you? You could just as easily break mine."

"I wouldn't do that," Gray said, running her fingertips along Lizbeth's back.

Lizbeth squirmed, but held her ground. "And you think I would?"

"You have a whole life waiting for you off this island. A life I am not a part of."

Lizbeth slid her body up, so that their mouths were almost touching. She whispered against Gray's lips, "You could be."

She kissed Gray to keep her from talking anymore. Every time Lizbeth let Gray think, she started stressing about where this was all going to go. Lizbeth didn't want to think. She wanted to fall in love, with all the bells and whistles, and no thought to what happens next. Damn the consequences!

She released Gray from an impassioned kiss long enough to whisper, breathlessly, "Fall in love with me, Gray."

Lizbeth's kiss swallowed Gray's whispered, "I am."

The boats would have to wait.

#

There were a few branches and limbs on the ground, but Howard Street had faired pretty well during the storm. After hunting down all of their clothing, Lizbeth accompanied Gray to check her boats. They were right where she left them. The tour boat was tied down in her back yard and had not even lost its cover. Down in the harbor, the fishing skiff still had all its lines intact.

They walked down to the Community Store, where locals were once again gathered on the porch. This time they were swapping damage reports and mid-storm stories. For the first time Lizbeth felt it. From the moment the porch dwellers turned to them and shouted, "Gray," Lizbeth felt different. It wasn't that anybody looked at her strangely, although she did think the cute young blonde in the corner gave her a knowing smile. My God, had Gray slept with every woman on this island? Now that Lizbeth had seen the full force of Gray's power over women, she thought it was a distinct possibility.

Lizbeth was experiencing being a lesbian, or having at least slept with one, in the public eye for the first time. Gray seemed relaxed, almost subdued. Lizbeth watched her as she laughed and joked with her friends. Gray was comfortable in her skin. She set an example for Lizbeth and Lizbeth took the lesson to heart. Gray didn't pretend to be any more or less than she was. People genuinely liked her and didn't seem particularly to care that she was a lesbian. By God, she was their lesbian and they loved her.

Lizbeth had only slightly jumped when Gray placed her hand in Lizbeth's back and escorted her down the steps of the store. It was a sweet gesture. Gray was letting everyone know that this one had taken. Knowing glances and smiles told Lizbeth it was good news to the natives. Lizbeth belonged to Gray and that was good enough for them. Lizbeth didn't have to worry about homophobia just yet.

Lizbeth started laughing on the way home. Gray asked her, "What's so funny?"

"Well, I came down here to study the language, but I was so preoccupied back there, I didn't even listen. I've totally put my paper out of my head."

"What were you thinking about?" Gray winked.

"I just knew they could tell what we'd been doing. I'm sure the cute little blonde did," Lizbeth said, one eyebrow up, looking for confirmation.

Gray, a little bashful, said, "Jaye, yeah, I think she did."

Lizbeth feigned shock. "Wow, Gray. She's young."

Gray smirked. "She's not as young as she looks and definitely not as innocent."

"Well, she's off limits to you now," Lizbeth said.

"Staking your claim there, are you?" Gray asked, beginning to grin broadly.

"Considering your past, I'd be stupid not to set some rules for you, so there will be no misunderstandings," Lizbeth said, not meaning to sound serious, but she was. She would not be cheated on, never again. Gray needed to know that. She tried to lighten her pronouncement with, "I never have shared my toys well with others."

Gray grabbed Lizbeth's hand and turned her so they were facing each other. Gray was serious. Her grin was gone. "I don't cheat. I never have. I'm not like that. If I tell you I'm with you, then I'm with you, nobody else."

Lizbeth matched Gray in somberness. "It's a deal breaker. So, are you with me?"

"Jesus, Lizbeth, I thought you'd know that by now," Gray answered.

"Gray, I left things unsaid in my last relationship. I won't make the same mistake twice." Gray winced. Lizbeth's remark had a ring of truth for Gray, too. She added, "I need to hear you say it."

"Lizbeth, I am not going to be seeing anyone else. Is that what you want to hear?"

Lizbeth smiled. "Yes, that's exactly what I wanted to hear."

Gray grinned at her. "If you'll move it along, so we can get done with lunch at Fanny's, we can get back to seeing more of each other."

With those prospects at hand, Lizbeth tore away from Gray and ran toward Fanny's porch, Gray hot on her heels, laughing.

#

The power was back on by the time they got home. Gray and Lizbeth opened the storm shutters on Fanny's cottage and got soaked in the process by a short rain shower. Lizbeth had not put on a bra, which was blatantly obvious when they came inside. Gray, unable to stop looking even after she got them towels to dry off, finally asked Lizbeth if she wanted to go up to her room with her, to find something dry to wear. Fanny stifled a laugh just as they left the kitchen.

Lizbeth followed Gray up the stairs and into her room. Paintings of boats and the seashore covered the walls. A picture of Gray and her grandfather mending nets stood on the nightstand. On the dresser was a picture of her mother and father and Gray as a baby, the first corners of that grin just starting to show. Other frames held pictures of Gray and her dog, Coker. There was a tiny frame at the back, leaning on the mirror, almost obscured by the others. It was a small photo of Gray laughing, with her arms around a smiling Dana. They looked so happy. A pang Lizbeth knew was jealousy trickled across her chest. It was silly, yet, it was there.

Gray, however, was not looking around the room. She had retrieved two dry tee shirts from the dresser and was in the process of moving in on Lizbeth, with a glint in her eye. She quickly did away with Lizbeth's thoughts of jealousy by grabbing the bottom of Lizbeth's wet shirt and stripping it over her head in one swift move. Her mouth was headed for one of Lizbeth's breasts when Lizbeth snatched the dry shirt from her hands and jumped back, covering herself.

"Oh no," Lizbeth said, holding her hand out to stop Gray from getting any closer. "You're not doing that to me in here, not with Fanny downstairs."

Gray laughed, pulling off her own wet sweatshirt. "Then cover yourself, woman. I can't be held responsible for my actions if you don't."

Lizbeth, suddenly forgetting Fanny was downstairs, stared at the toned, wet skin in front of her. Her eyes slowly trailed down Gray's chest to the V formed by Gray's sculpted ab muscles, disappearing into the top of her pants. Lizbeth thought Gray had absolutely no idea how gorgeous she was.

Da Vinci's Vitruvian Man had its mate in the body before Lizbeth. She wanted to touch it. She'd have to remember to get Gray in the shower, so she could see those wet glistening muscles up close and personal, but for now, she waved her hand at Gray.

"Gray O'Neal, cover that up, before you get us both in trouble."

Gray grinned, as if challenged. "Oh yeah," she said and started toward Lizbeth. She had Lizbeth on the run and she was enjoying it.

Lizbeth backed around the room, keeping Gray at arm's length. She whispered so Fanny couldn't hear her, "Gray, stop... She'll hear us."

"Only if you make noise," Gray teased, continuing to circle her prey.

Lizbeth tripped on one of Gray's boots, sticking out from under the bed. She fell backwards on the mattress and the hunter pounced. Gray kissed her lustfully and then stood up, leaving Lizbeth breathless on the bed. She put on her dry shirt and laughed at Lizbeth.

"Come on, I have to feed you before you lose your strength." Gray winked and added, "You're gonna need it."

Lizbeth bolted off the bed. "Now who's being a tease?" She slipped the dry shirt on over her head and let it drop. It swallowed her.

"That's good," Gray said. "It covers up the details and there was entirely too much detail in that wet one."

Lizbeth looked down at the tee shirts and picked them up. "Well, now that I'm officially unattractive, let's go eat."

Gray stopped Lizbeth at the door. She put her arms around Lizbeth's waist and said, "Darlin', you'd be attractive in a tow sack." She kissed Lizbeth one more time on the forehead and opened the door.

Gray hung their wet shirts in the bathroom and followed Lizbeth to the kitchen. Fanny had fried up some bacon for BLT's. The vine-ripened tomatoes were so sweet they tasted like candy. Lizbeth was starving again. Gray was using up every calorie Lizbeth could take in. She ate a whole sandwich and then split a second one with Gray. This did not go unnoticed by Fanny.

"I see you two worked up quite an appetite... opening those storm windows." Fanny let the pause hang there long enough to catch Lizbeth and Gray's attention. Then she chuckled to herself at their reaction. "Go on, y'all ain't foolin' nobody. Y'all are buzzing round here like bees after honey."

Gray's mouth hung open as she stared at her grandmother in amazement. Lizbeth froze, watching the exchange.

Fanny slapped her hands on the table, saying, "Bout damn time, too. Thank you, Lizbeth. I thought ol' Gray there'd crawled up and died inside. It's nice to see that ain't so."

Gray's half of the sandwich was poised in her hand, just inches from her still gaping mouth. The pieces started falling out of the bread, but Gray just sat there.

"What?" Fanny said, looking at Gray. "I have watched you mope around for near on five years. I think I've earned the right to speak my mind."

Gray came back to life. She dropped the sandwich on the plate, saying, "Well, I guess you have."

"Spoke my mind or earned the right to?" Fanny asked.

Gray's smile crept into the corners of her lips. She answered, "Both."

Lizbeth breathed a sigh of relief loud enough to turn both of the other women's heads toward her. She had not known what Gray's reaction was going to be. She looked from one O'Neal woman to the other, not sure what to say.

Finally Lizbeth said, "Lord, young'uns, ain't I been mommicked this day."

The tension broke in the little room and sent all three women into peals of laughter.

#

When lunch was finished and everything put away, Gray and Lizbeth walked to get her car and spent the rest of the afternoon across the street. The sun was shining again. They worked together pulling the plywood from the windows on the bottom floor. By the time that was done, it had started to rain again, ending plans for any more work outside.

Gray was a worker; Lizbeth had to give her that. Lizbeth was four years younger and had a difficult time keeping up with her. Gray was also strong as an ox. Lizbeth trailed behind Gray with the tools, while the larger woman grabbed the last piece of plywood they had removed and carried it to the shed out back. Lizbeth watched the muscles in Gray's arms and shoulders as she walked behind, admiring once again how toned she was. Lizbeth thought about her own body and the fact she hadn't done her work out routine in the mornings as she usually did. A grin captured her face when she thought, "I've been working out, just not by myself."

Lizbeth put the bucket of tools down, coming up behind Gray as she lifted the heavy piece of plywood and stored it on the drying shelf above her head. Lizbeth slid her arms around Gray's waist, running her hands across her stomach. She placed her head on Gray's back, hugging her tightly.

"Umm, you feel so good," she purred.

Gray put her hands over Lizbeth's, leaning back into her. "I have created a monster."

"Yes," Lizbeth said, into Gray's back, "and the monster is hungry."

Gray turned, still in Lizbeth's arms, and looked down at her. "Do you need me to fix you something to eat?"

Lizbeth's eyes narrowed. She placed her hand on the back of Gray's neck and pulled her toward her when she said, "Not that kind of hungry."

Gray reached out with one hand and shut the shed door, closing them inside. The old shed hadn't seen anything like that in years, or maybe ever. Lizbeth emerged from the shed a few minutes later, her hair tussled and looking a bit dazed, followed by a grinning Gray. As Lizbeth made her way through the rain to the back door, Gray skipped by, popping her on the butt.

"Go on in. I've got to go home and get something. I'll be right back."

Gray turned and ran toward her house. Lizbeth made no comment. She continued into the house, still vibrating from their last encounter. Gray had left her speechless. James and Lizbeth had a great sex life, or at least she thought they had, until now. Sex with Gray was so much more intense. Lizbeth hadn't known what she had been missing, but she was now on a mission to make up lost time. That was if she could stop trembling from the incident in the shed a minute ago.

Gray was gone a few minutes. It gave Lizbeth time to think while she made a fresh pot of coffee. She would need the caffeine if this kept up. Was it just because Gray was a woman that this all felt so different? Was it because her skin was soft and smooth to the touch, or was it the fullness of her lips? Was it their uncontrollable physical attraction to one another, or was it deeper than that? Lizbeth knew what falling in love felt like and she was falling madly in love with Gray.

It couldn't just be the sex. Lizbeth felt a deep connection with Gray. She had the "I've known you before" feeling about her, as if in another life they had crossed paths. It frightened Lizbeth a bit, because the emotions were very strong. Strong enough to take her down, if this didn't work out. Lizbeth was feeling some of the same things she had begged Gray to ignore. Lizbeth's "throw caution to the wind" statement might come back to haunt her.

The sound of Gray entering the front door drove those thoughts from Lizbeth's mind. She looked up the hallway, where she saw Gray coming towards her with an overnight bag thrown over one shoulder and a laptop case over the other.

"I need to contact my customers for tomorrow and tell them we're up and running for the rest of Labor Day weekend," Gray said, as she sat the laptop down on the kitchen table. She said nothing about the overnight bag, dropping it to the floor, and kicking it over by the wall.

Lizbeth, her eyebrows raised, asked, "And what's in that bag?"

The corners of Gray's mouth crept into a grin. "I told Fanny I wasn't coming back tonight and I have an early day tomorrow, so I just brought a few things for in the morning." She paused and winked at Lizbeth. "I was assuming you wanted me to stay."

"You assumed correctly," Lizbeth said, smiling up at Gray.

"Oh, I almost forgot," Gray said, reaching down and unzipping the bag on the floor. She pulled out a two-quart plastic container that still had frost on the top. "Fanny sent along supper. It's clam chowder, homemade."

"I have to quit letting the O'Neal women feed me. I'll have to cook for you sometime," Lizbeth said, while taking the container and putting it in the refrigerator.

Gray chuckled, taking a seat at the table. "I can't speak for Fanny, but I have ulterior motives."

"I think the spells have passed. I mean I still have to eat, but the fainting was all stress related. The anxiety I was experiencing caused my blood sugar to run lower than usual. It's happened before. It goes away when the stress releases."

Gray cocked her head to one side. "What were you stressing about?"

Lizbeth popped Gray playfully on the shoulder. "You know damn well what."

Gray pulled Lizbeth down on her lap. Lizbeth wrapped her arms around Gray's neck. Gray enjoyed teasing Lizbeth, so she continued her cross-examination.

"Now, Lizbeth, you know I did not do a thing to start this whole affair. It was you."

"I know. That's why I was stressed. I couldn't believe I was attracted to you, a woman. It really freaked me out that I couldn't control what I was feeling."

"I knew," Gray said slyly.

"When did you know?"

"The first time I met you. You were checking me out."

"I was not... Well, what do you mean by that?" Lizbeth wasn't sure. She may very well have been checking Gray out. In fact, she was certain that she had, but she didn't think anyone noticed.

"The first time I shook your hand this look came over your face. Then when I joked we could sleep together, because Fanny said we weren't kin, your face turned about fifty shades of red." Gray was having fun with this. "I could tell you were at least thinking about it."

Lizbeth, not to be outdone, said, "Seems to me you were watching me pretty closely."

Gray's grin grew. "I was. It's not every day that I come home and find someone like you on my front porch."

Now Lizbeth teased Gray. "No, you just have them drop you off there at night."

"Not anymore," Gray said, pulling Lizbeth to her for a kiss.

Lizbeth melted into the kiss and felt something inside shift. Lizbeth knew in that instant that she loved this woman and she wanted to spend the rest of her life in her arms. This was it, the thing a heart looks for, and the thing Lizbeth had longed for. It came in the form of a woman and for that she could not be faulted. Somehow, this woman was what Lizbeth needed and wanted in her life. If she let this chance pass, because it was a woman... she just didn't care anymore. It was done.

When the kiss ended, Gray held tightly to Lizbeth, holding her in a hug. Lizbeth lay her head down on Gray's shoulder, turned her mouth to Gray's ear, and whispered, "I just keep falling harder for you."

Gray responded in a low whisper, "Yeah, me too," and held Lizbeth to her until the emotion of the moment had subsided for both of them.

Lizbeth knew this was a big step for Gray. This was exactly what Gray had not wanted to happen, but it had. It was a huge leap of faith for Lizbeth, as well. It was hard after being burned, as she had been, to be willing to love somebody else. To love Gray meant that she could be setting herself up for another broken heart. Lizbeth couldn't help herself. She was swept up in a wave of emotion. Lizbeth was beyond being able to stop it. Gray was now in possession of Lizbeth's heart and soul.

Gray released the hold she had on Lizbeth and tucking a finger under Lizbeth's chin, lifted her head from her shoulder. She looked into Lizbeth's eyes, once again searching back and forth for something. She cleared her throat.

"Lizbeth, you do realize that not everyone is going to be as happy about your sudden lifestyle change as you are. Have you thought about your family, your friends, how they're going to react?"

Lizbeth was quick with her answer. "The only person's opinion of me that matters is my daughter's. I'm too old to care what my parents or my sister think. I don't have many close friends. I lost them in the divorce, probably because half of them were sleeping with my husband."

"You'll care, Lizbeth. It will hurt and you will lose many of them."

"But no one seems to care about you. You get along just fine," Lizbeth countered.

"That's here, on this island. It's not like this everywhere. I've had my share of distasteful comments."

"So, let's stay here."

Gray smiled, but she wasn't finished. "Honey, I'm trying to tell you that it isn't going to be all a bed of roses. I can't grab you and kiss you in public, even here. I'm careful about my actions in front of the locals, because I know if I don't rub it in their faces, they can deal with it."

Lizbeth had her doubts. "Come on, Gray. Every one of those people knows who and what you are. They love you anyway."

"That's 'cause I don't fuck with their wives and the women know I'm not after their husbands. They can be comfortable with the island lesbian as long as she keeps within the proper boundaries."

Lizbeth tickled one of Gray's nipples playfully. "Well then, they should be ecstatic that you're no longer prowling the streets at night."

Gray squirmed and grabbed Lizbeth's hand, still trying to be serious, but losing ground rapidly. "I just want you to know what you're getting yourself into. It's not going to be as easy as you think."

"Gray, it's not going to matter, trust me. I know there isn't a thing anyone can say or do that will change the way I feel about you."

Gray was not so sure. "We'll see."

"Yes, we will," Lizbeth said, trying to stand.

Gray pulled her back down. "Where are you going?"

Lizbeth batted her eyelashes, which sent a look of thrill across Gray's face. Smiling seductively, Lizbeth said, "I was promised a rainy afternoon in bed. I figured if I got off your lap and let you send your emails then it might happen sooner, rather than later."

Gray pushed Lizbeth off her lap. "You got a point there."

#

Gray finished her emails quickly and then took Lizbeth upstairs for an afternoon of slow lovemaking. There wasn't a whole lot of talking. The windows were still covered upstairs, making the room seem even more secluded from the rest of the world. There, beneath the sheets, unspoken promises were made. They fell asleep entwined in each other's legs and arms. Just before Lizbeth dozed off, she looked at Gray's face on the pillow next to her. Gray had fallen asleep wearing her special grin. She was at peace and it made Lizbeth love her more.

Later they woke and warmed up the clam chowder. As soon as they finished eating, they were back in bed. Lizbeth just could not get enough of Gray. Luckily, the feeling appeared to be mutual. When Lizbeth's eyes closed for the last time, before she drifted off, spooning her body into Gray's, she said a silent prayer.

"Please, God, if this is a dream, do not let me wake up."

Chapter Nine

The next morning, Lizbeth woke to find that she was alone in the bed. She looked at the clock. It was six fifteen. Lizbeth climbed out of bed, throwing on Gray's tee shirt she found on the chair in the corner and went in search of her new love. Lizbeth realized about halfway down the stairs how badly she wished there was a bathroom on the second floor. When she rounded the corner near the bathroom, she heard the water in the shower running.

Lizbeth needed to go to the bathroom. She knocked softly, but didn't get an answer, so she opened the door, saying, "Gray, I have to go to the bathroom. Do you mind?"

Gray stuck her head out from behind the shower curtain. "Hey good lookin'," she said. "Come on in."

Lizbeth took care of business, took off the tee shirt, and pulled the curtain back. Gray grinned, reached out, and pulled Lizbeth into the shower with her. Lizbeth had been accurate in her assumption that a wet, soapy Gray would be sexy, but then a fully clothed Gray nearly took her breath. The wet one sent her to the moon.

After the shower, Gray got dressed quickly. She had to get her boat back in the water and ready for a full day of tour guiding. She promised to come back for Lizbeth in two hours. Gray wanted Lizbeth to spend the day with her on the boat. Lizbeth was left with instructions to get dressed, eat a good breakfast, pack food and water in a cooler, and be ready to go at eight forty-five.

Gray yelled out, over her shoulder, as she jogged toward the back of her house to get the Jeep, "And bring sun screen. Wouldn't want you to get laid-up for days with a bad burn." Her laughter followed her until she disappeared behind the house. A few minutes later, Gray pulled out of her driveway, towing the boat on a trailer. She gave one short beep before she drove away. Lizbeth waved to her from the porch and then noticed Fanny watching her from across the street. Fanny waved a hand, holding a dishtowel, in Lizbeth's direction. Fanny chuckled heartily at the two lovers and then shaking her head, went back in the house.

Lizbeth did as she was told and was waiting on the porch when Gray pulled back into the driveway across the street. She disappeared behind the house and then popped back out, jogging toward Lizbeth's. Lizbeth's heart fluttered at the sight of her. Gray didn't stop at the screen door, but yanked it open and pulled Lizbeth back into her cottage. She started kissing Lizbeth as soon as they crossed the threshold, not even shutting the front door behind them. Gray, it seemed, had missed Lizbeth, a lot.

When they came up for air, Lizbeth said, "Wow, you should go to work more often."

"I'm not going to get to do that for a while, so I thought I had better when I had the chance," Gray said, grinning. "Come on, we can't be late."

Just that quickly, she pulled Lizbeth out of the house and they were on the way to the docks. Gray didn't talk much. She seemed preoccupied. Lizbeth thought it was because she was rushed. She had a hard time keeping up with the longer legged Gray. Lizbeth was glad Gray had picked up the cooler for her by the time they reached the dock. It had been a brisk walk.

Before they made the corner of the Kitty Hawk Kites building, Gray stopped and turned to the trailing Lizbeth. Lizbeth suddenly understood why Gray had been so distant.

"Lizbeth," Gray said, with a cautioning tone. "Now, I couldn't find anybody else that could do it, and I had to go get you, so please don't suspect anything."

Lizbeth's head tilted to one side in question. She raised one eyebrow. Gray stepped to the side. There leaning on its little kickstand was the red moped. Undoubtedly, the blonde that went with it was nearby. Gray was nervous as a cat and the longer Lizbeth stood there, without saying anything, the more excited Gray got.

"I needed someone to stay with these people and the boat. Everybody was gone or busy. I swear there is always someone down here hanging out, but not today. Then she came by and I asked her to stay."

Lizbeth, not putting on the happy face Gray was hoping for, asked, "Where did you tell her you were going?"

"I told her I had to go get my girlfriend."

Lizbeth smirked, but she was playing with Gray now. Gray was in obvious distress. She patted Gray on the chest and then pushed her aside with one hand, saying, "Good answer."

Lizbeth rounded the corner with Gray hot on her heels. Lizbeth recognized the blond head, seated on a piling. Lizbeth could now see that this was a woman about her own age, maybe older, but still quite a looker.

The woman smiled when she saw Gray coming. She was also checking out Lizbeth heading straight for her. Lizbeth could hardly contain herself. She knew Gray was about to burst behind her, not knowing what Lizbeth was about to do.

After all, Gray really barely knew Lizbeth. She could be a crazed maniac when provoked and it would all be a surprise to Gray.

Gray attempted to slow Lizbeth down by saying under her breath, "Lizbeth, this is exactly the kind of behavior I was talking about not having in public."

Lizbeth looked back over her shoulder with a wicked grin. "And what behavior would that be?"

Lizbeth was too close to the other woman for Gray to answer. Lizbeth could have sworn she heard Gray take a deep breath and hold it. Lizbeth smiled at the blonde, extended her hand, and displayed the charm her mother had paid for.

"Hi, my name is Lizbeth. It was so kind of you to help Gray. Thank you. I don't know why she insisted on coming to get me. I could have come on my own."

The woman took Lizbeth's extended hand and shook it, while giving Lizbeth a shrewd smile. "I have a sneaking suspicion I know why she did." Then she laughed.

Gray made the introductions. "Lizbeth Jackson, this is Holly Harris. Holly, Lizbeth." Lizbeth could hear the relief in Gray's voice.

"It's a pleasure to meet you, Holly."

"The pleasure is mine," Holly answered. It had the hint of a pick-up line attached to it.

The situation did a complete one hundred and eighty degree turn on Gray. Lizbeth almost laughed aloud when Gray stepped closer to her, because now Holly was making eyes at Lizbeth, and Gray's own green monster reared its head.

"Thanks, Holly. I appreciate it. We better get going," Gray said, all the while lightly pushing Lizbeth toward the boat with a hand in her back.

"See you later, Gray," Holly said.

Without missing a beat, Lizbeth said in her sweetest southern drawl, "Not if I can help it."

This cracked up both Gray and Lizbeth. Holly took it in the spirit it was intended and laughed along with them.

Holly started away, saying, "Good luck you two. Nice catch, Gray," and then she got on her moped and put-putted away.

Gray loaded the tourists into the boat, one by one, helping each down the ladder to the deck. Lizbeth watched Gray laugh and joke with her customers, making each feel warm and welcome. Gray was a people magnet. Women were at ease with her, men wanted to be near her, and the children thought she was "cool." Gray's smile and trouble-free air put everyone at ease.

Before leaving the dock, Gray gave a speech, her accent a little thicker than usual for the tourists' benefit. "Now, all a y'all are here for the drop off out in the duck blinds, right?"

The tourists looked puzzled, but then the adults noticed the grin. The kids yelled, "Portsmouth Island!"

Gray played with the kids. "Oh, oh that's right. Portsmouth Island. Okay, then before we leave, all the kids under twelve have to wear a life jacket. You never know when a pirate ship will show up and we have to be ready to flee at a moment's notice."

The kids grew quiet and their eyes got big. The adults giggled under their hats and sunglasses. The last time Lizbeth had been on the boat with Gray, she had not given this little bit of information. It must have been because that group didn't appear to understand a word Gray said.

Gray made note of the plastic pirate swords and various wooden weapons, found in the local shops, now attached to the children. "I see some of you have brought along your pirate fighting gear, that's good."

Gray continued, as she walked around making sure all the kids were outfitted correctly. "Now, I've never sunk a boat..."

"There's a first time for everything," a man in the back interrupted.

Gray didn't miss a beat. "Yes sir, that is true, so with that in mind, under your seats are compartments with floatation devices for everyone. The cushions you are sitting on are also floatation devices. And should worse come to worse and the pirates shoot up the boat, then the boat itself will float, even if it's cut in two by a cannon ball."

A little girl, about five, raised her hand. Gray squatted in front of her and said, "Yes, darlin', what can I do for you?"

The girl, with huge brown eyes, said, "What happens if the pirates capture us?"

"Sugar," Gray said, pointing at a Coast Guard cutter moored nearby. "See that big boat over there? That is the United States Coast Guard and they watch over all of us. They'll come rescue us and we'll all have a big party on the pirate ship."

The little boys in the group thought that was a swell idea. Several had plastic pirate swords at the ready. Gray had the youngest kids going. They were watching her every move with hanging mouths and wide eyes. Even the two teenagers thought the kids' reaction was funny.

"Okay, everybody set? Let's take a scud out to sea, shall we." Lizbeth recognized the island word, scud. It meant to take a short trip in a boat or car.

Gray acted conspiratorial with the kids, speaking in a hushed voice. She asked, "Anybody want to see where they cut off Blackbeard's head?"

The kids yelled, "Yes," in unison.

Gray said, "Arrrrg!" and all the kids and some of the adults followed with their own pirate cheer.

Gray was very entertaining. It was clear that she loved her job. The tourists did not irritate her, which was a prevalent attitude toward the woodsers. Gray reveled in sharing her island with these people. She fairly glowed while doing it. The entire boat was laughing and smiling by the time she was ready to leave the dock.

Gray came back to the stern to crank the boat, after assigning the bowline to a gentleman in the front. She was grinning and so was Lizbeth. Lizbeth had ceased swooning in Gray's presence, but she was no less enthralled with her. Gray slid into the seat beside Lizbeth, started the engine, checked her gauges, and decided it was time to go. Lizbeth removed the stern line, feeling useful.

With the engines running, even at the slow speed used to exit the harbor, Lizbeth had to lean in close to Gray's ear to be heard without shouting.

"You're really good with the kids."

Gray smiled. "Yeah, it helps if you still are one."

Lizbeth threw her head back and laughed. That was one thing Lizbeth loved about Gray, her childlike wonder at the magical land she lived in. It was part of her appeal. Gray was forty-four, didn't look a day over thirty-five, usually dressed like a teenage boy, and had the good looks and charisma to pull it off. Definite Peter Pan syndrome, Lizbeth thought to herself, and giggled because that made her Tinkerbelle.

When Gray sped the boat up out in the channel, the little chop they faced sprayed the passengers, sending squeals of delight from some of them. Gray stood, looking out in front of the boat, checking for changes in the channel from the storm. Lizbeth so wanted to put her hand in the small of Gray's back, just to touch her. She didn't. That's when she felt the first twinge of what Gray had told her yesterday; it would be different in public. Lizbeth understood now what it meant to be a homosexual in America. Whom she chose to love would now be somebody else's self-proclaimed right to judge.

Gray piloted the boat, unaware of Lizbeth's sudden realization. It was a twenty-minute ride to Portsmouth Island, but Gray was doing what she called her long tour this morning. She turned the boat toward Ocracoke, slowing in the shallows just beyond Springer Point. The newly changed sandbars beneath the surface kept her vigilant. It wasn't until she had pulled to a stop and cut off the engines that she began to speak.

Gray winked at Lizbeth before moving to the front of the boat. All eyes were on Gray as she sat down at the bow, in between two small boys. She assumed the campfire storyteller's persona and began, "On this very spot, on November the twenty-second, 1718, Edward Teach, otherwise known as the feared pirate Blackbeard, was beheaded by Lieutenant Robert Maynard of the British Navy."

A few "Wows" filled the boat. The adults were into it too. Lizbeth could see a bit of a glint of child in all of them. Everybody loved pirate stories, especially true ones.

Gray went on. "They call this place Teach's Hole. It appears ol' Blackbeard liked it here on Ocracoke and often used the inlet in his travels to and from North Carolina. Lieutenant Maynard had been sent on a mission from the Governor of Virginia to capture or kill the dangerous pirate. He found him here, busy entertaining aboard his ship, Adventure, while half of Blackbeard's crew was on the mainland, in Bath. He had no more than twenty-five men on board."

Gray built the story. "At daybreak, there," she pointed at the inlet. All heads turned to where she indicated. "There, through the inlet, Maynard's two sloops entered the channel. A small boat led the way, dropping a line in the water, sounding for the bottom, guiding the two larger ships. As soon as the little boat came into view, the Adventure fired a cannon shot. It was a warning, 'Don't come any closer, we're pirates,' but the British boats kept coming."

Some of the kids were now in the bottom of the boat, gathered near Gray. Gray made eye contact with each child, assuring that they were all anticipating the coming battle. Lizbeth felt herself physically fall more in love with Gray every minute. It astounded her how fascinating she found this woman.

"Does anybody know what Blackbeard looked like?" Gray asked.

The boy beside her said, "He had a black beard."

Gray laughed. "That's right. One description said he grew it long and bushy and it grew up to his eyes." Gray demonstrated how high that was for them on her own face. "He had long curly black hair to go with it. He would twist ribbons in his beard for decoration and sometimes he would put long wicks under his hat so they stuck out, burning and smoking while he dueled with swords on deck." She took a plastic pirate pistol from one of the children and demonstrated the next part of the description. "He wore a sling over his shoulder, like this, with three of these pistols hanging from holsters and he had daggers and swords." She handed the toy back to the child, who now looked at it as if it were real. "They say he had fierce eyes and with all that smoke and hair, he looked like the devil himself."

Gray brought them all aboard with her as she told the tale. "Now imagine Blackbeard coming out on deck and seeing the two big ships moving into position to fire cannons at the Adventure. He shouted at Maynard's ship, 'Damn ye for Villains, who are ye? And, from whence came ye?' Maynard yelled back that Blackbeard could see from his flag who he was and he intended to board the Adventure. Blackbeard ordered the anchor line cut so he could move into position to fire on Maynard's ships."

Gray used her pirate voice for the next part. "Blackbeard took a glass of liquor and drank a toast to Maynard, saying, 'Damnation seize my soul if I give ye Quarters, or take any from ye.'"

Some of the children gasped. "Now, we don't know exactly what happened, whether the Adventure ran aground or Maynard's ships did. There was lots of cannon firing and small arms fire, but eventually two ships, the Adventure and the Jane, floated free. The Adventure sent a barrage of cannon balls into the broadside of the Jane. Blackbeard closed the distance on the Jane, with Maynard aboard; cannon balls from the Adventure had crippled the other ship. Blackbeard crashed into the side of the Jane, threw over the grappling hooks, and boarded the enemy vessel, his men throwing homemade grenades across the deck. Loud explosions and men clashing with pistols and swords filled the air. Surely Blackbeard's band of experienced pirates could take care of the few men left alive on the British ship, but..."

She let the pause hang in the air, before continuing, "Maynard was smart. He had left half of his crew below decks. Once the pirates were on board, the hatches burst open and the men rushed forward, firing and shouting. The two groups fought back and forth across the deck, slick with blood." The gory details were just what the little boys wanted. They leaned even closer. "Blackbeard's crew was driven back toward the bow, leaving the great pirate surrounded by Maynard and the rest of his men. The two enemies fired flintlock pistols at each other and then threw them aside. Blackbeard drew his cutlass and managed to break Maynard's sword with a smashing blow. Maynard withdrew, grabbing another pistol to fire at Blackbeard. Blackbeard rushed at him, but was slashed across the neck by one of Maynard's men."

"That's not fair," one of the boys said.

Gray grinned at him. "No, I guess it doesn't sound fair, but Blackbeard was a legendary fighter. Everyone was afraid of him. One man could have never taken him down. He was badly wounded this time, though. Several more of Maynard's crew, seeing the great pirate at a disadvantage, pounced on him and killed him. The rest of the pirates were captured and later taken back to Virginia for trial."

"Who cut his head off?" Blackbeard's young defender asked.

"Well, we don't know who actually did the deed, but when Maynard examined Blackbeard's body, he reported the pirate had been shot no fewer than five times and had as many as twenty slashing wounds. They put his head on the bowsprit and threw his body in the ocean. It's said that his body swam around the ship three times, looking for its head, and then sank below the surface."

One of the boys said, "Oh, cool."

"Yeah, that's cool," Gray said, standing and moving back to the console.

She cranked the boat and headed it across the inlet to a small island covered in pelicans. She explained that this was Beacon Island and it was the northern most habitat breeding area for the Brown Pelican. She pointed out the differing colors, explaining the lighter ones were younger. The birds were used to people watching them and paid the boat no mind. The passengers took pictures and then Gray took them to the dock at Portsmouth Island.

As Gray helped the passengers onto the dock, she continued her tour guide speech. "Portsmouth Village was established by North Carolina's Colonial Assembly in 1753. There's about two hundred and fifty acres here. The last permanent residents left in 1971 and the island became part of the Cape Lookout National Seashore in 1976. About twenty of the buildings are preserved and you'll find a visitor center at the end of this path. They'll have maps to help you get around. Just a warning, put the bug spray on before you get off the dock. I'll be back here at one o'clock to pick you up."

Ten of the passengers got off at the dock. The remaining family of six was being dropped off on the beach. They had a day of seashell hunting planned. Gray ran the boat up on the beach, helped the passengers down, and hopped back in the boat. Gray arranged to get them at three, but she would check back periodically when she could, in case they wanted off the island sooner. Little kids didn't always have the same plans for the day as their parents, so she slipped the mom her cell phone number just in case.

Finally alone in the boat, Gray aimed it toward the channel and opened it up. With the passengers gone, she could plane it out above the waves. Once she was sure they were far enough away, Gray slid an arm around Lizbeth's waist and kissed her on the forehead. Lizbeth looked up at Gray, wanting to say so much, but unable to over the roar of the engines. She decided to be content with just spending the day watching and listening, learning all about the islands and more about Gray.

They did the round trip from Portsmouth to Ocracoke four times that day. Each trip Gray told the stories, a little different every time, but the facts remained the same. They caught moments alone on the water when they could, but they were fleeting; between dropping off and picking up, the boat was usually filled with passengers. With only a couple of trips on shore to use the restroom, Lizbeth spent the entire day on the boat. The only time they stopped moving was to load passengers, except for the fifteen-minute floating lunch between pick-ups.

Just off the dock at Portsmouth Island, Gray had dropped the anchor overboard and sat down beside Lizbeth on one of the bench seats. Lizbeth handed Gray a sandwich and a bottle of water, pulling the same out of the cooler for herself. Gray stretched her long legs across the deck of the boat. She went off tour director duty for a few minutes, resuming her true laid-back persona.

"Gray, you have the best job in the world."

"It is a cool job, I'll admit it," Gray said.

"Do you miss Sea World?"

"No, not really. It was something I wanted to do and I did it. I certainly don't miss being on someone else's schedule."

"I don't want to pry, and tell me if it's none of my business, but you seem to do all right financially." Lizbeth was just curious.

Gray smiled at her. "Are you trying to figure out if I can afford you?"

Lizbeth couldn't help but laugh. "No, honey. When I said I got even with my ex-husband, I mean I really got even with him. As a matter of fact, you could be my kept woman."

"I can take care of myself, thank you," Gray said, pretending to be offended. Then she added an afterthought, "What happens if he finds out about me?"

"Nothing, as far as I know. There was no contingency on the money. I have an annuity and the lump sum of cash I dug out of his soul. God, James loves money. I also have a massive house that he was forced to pay off, so I'm good."

"Jesus, what kind of evidence did you have on that guy?"

"The kind where he would never have been able to show his face at the country club again if it got out. I wasn't the only person he was betraying. It would have hurt his reputation and his wallet a whole lot worse to reveal the extent of his sexual conquests."

Gray let that sink in, then answered Lizbeth's original question. "I do really well actually. I paid for the boat a long time ago. I make more money now than I did at Sea World. I do have to pay for my own benefits, but it's still more."

Lizbeth grinned. "Good, then we don't have to worry about money. We can check that off the list of things couples fight about."

"There's a list?" Gray asked, stuffing more sandwich down and checking her watch.

"Yes, there is. We've already discussed the infidelity thing. I think we're both clear on that. We won't be fighting over children, because I'm not having anymore and the one I have is grown. I think if you were going to have a kid, you would have by now. You should have. You're wonderful with them."

"Being a mother wasn't something I saw myself doing. I would have supported Dana, if she wanted to, and I would have been a good parent, but actually being the mother wasn't on my list of things to do."

Lizbeth giggled. "Gray, as hard as I try, I cannot picture you nine months pregnant."

Gray sat up, pulling her legs under her. "I know," she said, laughing. "It just doesn't suit me."

Lizbeth continued with her list. "So, kids we can check off, too. I love Fanny, so in-laws aren't a problem for me and I don't care if my parents like you or not."

Gray was watching Lizbeth intently as she checked off her list.

"Housework, snoring, what to eat, I don't think that those things will be a problem."

Gray chuckled. "Lizbeth, you snore."

"I do not," Lizbeth shot back.

"You did last night."

"I must have been exhausted. That's the only time I think I snore," Lizbeth said, then added quickly, "I'm sorry. Did it keep you up?"

"I found it endearing. I just nudged you and you snuggled up to me and quit," Gray said, sliding an arm around Lizbeth's shoulder. "What else is on the list?"

"Ex's, sex, and careers. The sex I think we've got a good handle on." Lizbeth laughed and winked at Gray. "The ex thing, well, you don't have to worry about dealing with mine. He's completely out of the picture."

"Mine, too," Gray said, but Lizbeth didn't really believe her.

Gray hadn't recovered fully. Dana's betrayal would rear its ugly head, of that she was sure. In that regard, Lizbeth's own conviction never to be taken advantage of again might cause some issues, if she ever suspected Gray of anything. Hell, Lizbeth knew she'd be gone before Gray had a chance to explain, but she'd made that clear, hadn't she?

"That just leaves careers. I think yours is fantastic," Lizbeth said as she put away the wrappers from the lunch. When Lizbeth looked back, Gray had stopped smiling. "What's wrong?"

"What about your career, Lizbeth? You've waited all your life for this."

Lizbeth smiled, sliding up close to Gray. "I've waited all my life for you, too. I don't have to take that job in the library. I don't have to have a job at all."

"But I don't want you to wake up one day and blame me for taking that away from you."

"Gray, if I lived here, I would be living in the middle of my research area. I could write papers, consult, freelance, there are an endless number of possibilities."

Gray brightened. It was obvious to Lizbeth that Gray had not thought about her career in that way. It gave Gray hope and it showed in her big smile.

Lizbeth pecked her on the cheek. "See, I told you not to worry. We'll figure this out."

Gray hugged Lizbeth to her and said, "I guess I'll just leave the logistics up to you. You seem to have put quite a bit of thought into it."

"Honey," Lizbeth began with a wicked grin, "if you think I'm going to let your ass back on the street, you're crazy. Now that I know why all those women wanted more, I don't plan to let them have any."

"Lizbeth, you don't think what went on with those other women compares to what goes on between us, do you?"

"I wouldn't know. You're the only woman I've been with. I did wonder if it was so amazing because you're a woman, or because you're you."

"No, Lizbeth. What's going on between you and me is not just because I'm a woman. This is unique, at least in my experience."

"Well, you're the expert," Lizbeth said, giggling.

"Are you curious about other women?"

"Why would I want another woman when I seem to have stumbled upon the queen lover herself?"

"How would you know all lesbians couldn't do what I do?" Gray grinned.

Lizbeth laughed at Gray. "I'm no expert, but I'd venture to guess you have special talents."

They had been too close, too long. Lizbeth could feel Gray breathing against her. It intensified her already constant craving for Gray. She saw the shift in Gray's eyes as well. If they hadn't been where people could see them, they would have been naked in second. An arm around the shoulder was one thing, butt-ass naked in the bottom of the boat was something else entirely.

Gray stood up suddenly. She dropped her sunglasses on the seat and pulled her tank top over her head, leaving her wearing the board shorts and swim top. She took one big step up on the seat cushion and then dove overboard. The water was calm and clear where they were and Lizbeth could see Gray underwater. She swam under the boat and around to the back, not coming up for air, as Lizbeth walked along the railing watching her. Gray, Lizbeth learned that moment, was an excellent swimmer and very graceful underwater. Gray's blond head popped up behind the motor. She used the stern ladder to enter the boat.

Gray shook her head, showering Lizbeth with the spray, then pulled a towel out from under the console bench and dried off.

"Gray, do you want to explain your sudden need to plunge into the sea?"

"One of us needed a cold shower. That was the closest thing handy and I volunteered."

Gray put the tank top and sunglasses back on. They began their next run of loading and unloading. Lizbeth even got into the action, helping with the tying up at the dock and loading of passengers. By the end of the day, Lizbeth was tired, sunburned, and even more in love with Gray and her island. It really was Gray and the island. They were a package deal. If Gray was plucked from this place, she would wither and die. Lizbeth started working on a plan to stay on Ocracoke, never going back to Durham unless it was to visit. Lizbeth was buying into the whole deal, hook, line, and sinker.

#

That evening, after removal of the final pieces of plywood from the upstairs windows of Lizbeth's cottage, and supper with Fanny, Gray sat on the edge of the bed, gently rubbing aloe on Lizbeth's sunburned skin.

"I guess I shouldn't have kept you out in the sun so long."

Lizbeth smiled into the pillowcase, cool against her burning skin. She was lying face down, sans clothing, as Gray's fingers slid across her shoulders. The aloe immediately cooled the fire engulfing every part of her body that had been exposed to the blazing autumn rays.

Lizbeth, eyes closed, practically glowing inside and out, said, "I loved every minute of it. Thank you." The thank you faded into the pillow, as she drifted between pleasure and sleep.

Gray had brought Lizbeth home after supper and had her way with her in the shower. Lizbeth didn't even notice the sunburn until afterward, when she was completely naked, and the beet red glow of her limbs contrasted so vividly with the paleness of her protected skin. Lizbeth was satiated, satisfied, and sleepy. She felt her body floating between earth and her dreams. Gray kissed Lizbeth on the cheek, still tracing her stinging flesh with aloe on her fingertips.

With Lizbeth's last cognizant breath, she said, "Gray O'Neal, your hands are a gift from God."

Chapter Ten

Gray told Lizbeth that she usually didn't run tours on Sunday mornings, but she had lost so much business from the storm, she had to make it up where she could. The summer season was coming to a close. Tomorrow was Labor Day, the last big weekend of the summer. She left a sleepy Lizbeth in bed at seven and went down to the docks.

Lizbeth roused herself in time to accompany Fanny to church. Small talk about the weather accompanied the walk. The storm left behind clear skies and temperatures in the mid eighties. The wind today would be a bit cooler because it had shifted to the east-northeast. Lizbeth learned this from Fanny as they strolled along. Lizbeth could tell Fanny had something on her mind, but they made it to the church without her finding out what it was.

Without the distraction of Gray, Lizbeth was able to follow the sermon and participate in all the congregational activities fully. She had remembered to eat this time, which she had to explain to numerous people who had witnessed her previous swoon into Gray's arms. She waited patiently as Fanny visited with her friends. Lizbeth listened as the brogue twisted and rolled off the islanders' tongues, relaying their recent experiences with Earl to one another.

She was deep into thoughts concerning her research paper on the way home. Listening today had sparked an idea she wanted to get down on paper before she forgot it. Fanny's remark quickly snapped her back to Howard Street.

"I hope you're prepared for how hard Gray can love a thing."

Lizbeth thought silently for a moment, evaluating Fanny's observation. "Yes, ma'am, I think I am."

"Gray's told me a bit about you. I got a feelin' y'all both got your hearts mommicked. Been hard on Gray. She don't even won't another dog cause she says she don't won't to go through losin' nothin' else, and that child has had a dog taggin' along behind her since she could walk. Damn dogs used to follow her to school and wait on her. School teacher had to let 'em inside in the bad weather or Gray would leave." Fanny chuckled at the memory.

"Fanny, I'm not going to hurt Gray." Lizbeth thought that was what Fanny was getting at.

Fanny stopped walking. She had been a tall woman, like Gray, but time had stooped her. She looked long and hard at Lizbeth, before speaking.

"Gray is tough as nails. She's wild as the sea and smart. That made for quite a chore raisin' her. She's hard headed, but on the inside she's fragile, like a child. Ya' got yer work cut out for ya' that's for sure." Fanny paused to chuckle, and added "But she's mad for ya', so that ought'a be good for something."

"I'm mad about her, too," Lizbeth gushed. She couldn't help herself. "I can't think when I'm around her. She takes my breath away."

Fanny laughed. "Oh, I could tell that last Sunday. At least today you didn't have the hymnal upside down."

#

Lizbeth spent the afternoon cooking supper. She had invited both Gray and Fanny to join her. After dropping Fanny at her friend Marvina's house, Lizbeth walked down to the Community Store. She ran into Jaye there, the blonde from the porch, who seemed to have intimate knowledge of Gray. She eyed Lizbeth suspiciously as she purchased the supplies she needed for spaghetti dinner. When Lizbeth got to the checkout counter, Jaye, who was working the cash register, finally got around to asking the question burning her little brain.

"So, how long ya' stayin'?"

Lizbeth knew why she was asking and made sure Jaye got the message clearly. "You know, I think I'm going to stick around. I've become quite attached to this island and a few of its natives."

"I see," Jaye commented with an eyebrow raised. "You sure keep Gray busy. Hadn't seen her at the pub in a week."

"And that's unusual?" Lizbeth had found a source willing to talk and she dug for information.

Jaye was more than ready to spill the beans. Lizbeth could see the little wheels turning behind the younger woman's eyes. She tried to scare Lizbeth off. "Oh, yeah, Gray's a regular. She's quite the party girl." Jaye winked. "If you know what I mean."

Lizbeth braced herself against the counter as Jaye checked her groceries. "No, I don't know what you mean. I've only known her a week. She didn't strike me as the party type. Too laid-back."

Jaye was enjoying this too much. Her eyes sparkled at the thought of telling Lizbeth something that may upset her. "Yeah, she's laid-back, most of the time, kinda sad actually, but if you catch her with a good buzz on, then that's a different story."

"What does she do, dance naked on the bar?"

"Now that might be worth paying for." Jaye laughed. "No, she don't get naked on the bar, but she's a whole lot easier to get close to, if you know what I'm sayin'."

Lizbeth was growing annoyed and she didn't know why. It was ridiculous for her to be angry over something Gray may have done before she met her. Still, she found Jaye's growing innuendo offensive. Did this little tart believe they shared something in common, just because they obviously both had sex with Gray? Lizbeth refused to let her mind call it making love, because that's what they did, not what Gray had done with the blond young thing in front of her. They were alone in the little store, but Lizbeth wasn't sure if she wouldn't have gone ahead and said it even if they weren't.

"Well, darlin'," Lizbeth began with a smile, "I hope that you have fond memories of your time with Gray. I can imagine an event like that would be hard to forget, but she's not going to be getting drunk and falling for your considerable charms anymore."

Jaye, who was more mature than she appeared, remarked unflustered, "Oh, I can see that as long as you're around, she's preoccupied. Good luck killing that ghost."

Lizbeth was intrigued. "And what ghost would that be?"

"Whoever done that woman wrong did a real number on her head. You can see it in her eyes sometimes, her ghost is still there."

"Wise observations from such a young soul." Lizbeth relaxed. Jaye wasn't an enemy.

"Oh, I been studying Gray ever since she came back. I was eighteen the first time I met her. Took me years to get her to pay attention to me, you know. But I seen that far off look in my momma's eyes and I know what that means. My worthless piece of shit father's memory haunts that woman every day. Gray's hurt bad, don't want nobody close to her."

Lizbeth was overcome with sympathy for the young girl. "Oh, honey, you're not in love with her, are you?"

"In a way, I guess I am, but I'm smart enough to know that isn't going to happen, so if you make her happy, I think that's a good thing. If you don't, she'll still be at the end of the bar when you're gone."

Lizbeth chuckled. "They grow such practical women on this island."

"No need to worry about something you got no control over," Jaye answered with the wisdom of someone four times her age.

Lizbeth marveled at the younger woman. "Jaye, you are going to be a lady to be reckoned with. I'll keep my eye out for that ghost."

Jaye smiled. "If you stay, maybe we can be friends."

Lizbeth took her change from Jaye, but held Jaye's outstretched hand for a moment. She gave the young girl's hand a squeeze and said, "I'd like that very much."

#

Lizbeth made one dish very well, meatballs and spaghetti sauce. She was an okay cook the rest of time and no one ever went hungry, but people raved about her meatballs. Luckily, the Community Store had everything she needed. She rushed around the little kitchen making sure everything would be perfect for the first meal she cooked for the two women who had sustained her for the past week. Gray just kept dragging her to Fanny's for meals. Lizbeth had begun to feel guilty and wanted to repay them.

Lizbeth was waiting on the porch, food ready and table set, when Gray came strolling up just after six thirty. As soon as Gray saw her, her face burst into a wide grin. Her pace picked up. Lizbeth could see by the look on Gray's face that there was no need to remain in the rocking chair. She stood up and walked back into the cottage, stopping just inside the open front door.

Gray came in the through the screen door and right into the house, where she located Lizbeth and wrapped her arms around her waist. She kissed and hugged Lizbeth a few moments, before saying, "I missed you."

It was thrilling to be wanted and missed. Lizbeth hadn't felt that way in years. She could get used to this kind of greeting, each time they came back together after parting. Lizbeth stretched up her hands and ran her fingers through Gray's hair, thick from the salt spray. She pulled Gray's lips to hers and kissed her, letting Gray know she had missed her, too.

Gray lifted her head and sniffed the air. "That smells delicious."

Still with her arms around Gray's neck, Lizbeth said, "Everything's ready. I just need to warm the bread. All we need is Fanny."

"I'm going to take a quick shower and then I'll bring her over, okay?" Gray started to release her hold on Lizbeth and move toward the door.

Lizbeth stopped her with, "Kiss me again." Now that she had Gray in her arms, it was hard for Lizbeth to let her go, even for a quick shower.

Gray obliged Lizbeth's request, kissing her, and then she pried Lizbeth's hands from her neck, saying, "I'll be fast. Hold that thought."

Lizbeth let her go reluctantly and went to warm the bread. Soon Gray returned with Fanny in tow. They ooo-ed and ahh-ed over the meatballs, enough to make Lizbeth blush. She promised to show Fanny how to make them. When they finished eating, Lizbeth made Fanny and Gray stay seated while she cleared the table and loaded the dishwasher. Supper a complete success, Lizbeth felt wonderful as the three women went to the porch for evening sweet tea and a view of the sunset.

The conversations she had with both Fanny and Jaye were not far from Lizbeth's mind all afternoon. Even now, she thought about how Gray brought out the protective streak in each woman. Neither of them wanted to see Gray get hurt and they seemed to hope that Lizbeth was the answer to waking Gray's sleeping heart. No one but Lizbeth appeared to believe it was possible. Both Fanny and Jaye had wished Lizbeth good luck.

Gray and Fanny prattled on about Gray's day and tomorrow's schedule. Gray kept Fanny informed about everything to do with the business. She had explained earlier to Lizbeth that she always wanted Fanny to know where she was and when to expect her, so if something went wrong Fanny would send the men out looking for her. Lizbeth didn't think of Gray's job as dangerous, but then accidents happen at sea all the time. Boats break down and go adrift, sandbars shift, storms erupt. Anything could render a boat inoperable, stranding its occupants in the elements.

Just after the sun finally faded behind the trees, shading Howard Street in darkness, Fanny suggested it was time for her to go home. She was up before the sun every day and generally followed it to bed in the warmer months.

"Well, Gray, will I see ya' at breakfast?" Fanny cut right to the chase.

Gray grinned out one side of her mouth. "Yes, Granfanny, I believe I will have breakfast with you."

"Lizbeth, you come along, too," Fanny said, standing with a little difficulty. Gray noticed and stood to help her. "Old bones are achin' today." It was the first time Lizbeth had noticed Fanny acting her age, but her wit had ripened. She cracked, "Ain't no use t'a ya' playin' meehonkey around me."

Lizbeth raised her eyebrows in question, which Gray saw and translated, "We shouldn't play hide and seek around her. She's fine with it."

"Ain't nothing wrong with two people fallin' in love. It's the hate that ruins the world." Lizbeth thought Fanny to be a very wise woman.

Gray escorted her grandmother into her house and then returned.

"Gray, is she okay with you being gone at night?"

"Yeah, she's fine. I asked her. Said she lived there alone before I came back and I check on her every morning. That's why we have breakfast. She's asleep most of the time I'm over here anyway."

With that settled, Lizbeth launched into the little plan she had been brewing. She wanted to see the island girl in her native habitat, Gaffer's Sports Pub. Gray seemed so uninhibited to Lizbeth naturally, Jaye's description of the loosened up party girl had her curiosity at peak interest. She knew they would have to come home early so Gray could sleep, before her Labor Day crowd tomorrow, but a few hours drinking beer with Gray sounded like fun.

"Gray, let's go to the pub. I want to drink some beer and listen to music." Gray looked a little disappointed, so Lizbeth added quickly, "Who knows, the beer might make me lose the inhibitions I have left... if there are any." Lizbeth gave Gray a look that said, "You don't want to miss this."

Gray was up and out the door, calling over her shoulder, "Let me get some cash, I'll be right back."

Lizbeth laughed. Motivating Gray had been easy.

#

Lizbeth had heard of Gaffer's Sports Pub, one of Ocracoke's few nightspots, but never been there. During the day and into the night the pub would serve food, beer, wine, and cocktails to hungry, thirsty tourists. A typical sports bar,

TV's lined the walls tuned to different sporting events. Live music did battle with big screen TVs and pool tables for the attention of the patrons. People dined on the deck or inside the bar. Lizbeth stood on the deck drinking the pale ale draft Gray had selected for her.

Gray leaned back against the railing on the deck, letting the ocean breeze blow her hair back. The live music was just starting up and some of the people on the deck started heading in to hear the band or refresh their drinks. Mostly locals were left on the deck sipping their beers, so familiar with the band inside they didn't need to look.

Lizbeth turned around from where she had been gazing at the sea oats, and leaned against the railing with Gray. She saw Jaye across the deck and exchanged a smile and wave. Gray saw this and looked down at Lizbeth, who was grinning. It made Gray grin, too.

"So, you've been visiting with some of the locals, I gather."

"We chatted at the store today," Lizbeth said this as nonchalantly as possible, not wanting Gray to discover her ulterior motives for getting her to the pub. "She's a lovely girl and as you said, not as young as she looks."

Gray's eyebrow shot up, intrigued, she asked, "You got all that from a chat at the store? I wonder, what was the topic of conversation?"

"Gray, you know she has a giant crush on you," Lizbeth teased.

Gray looked embarrassed. "Yeah, I know. I shouldn't have gotten involved with her, but..."

Lizbeth bailed her out. "She caught you in a moment of weakness."

Gray let out a big breath. "I was drunk, and Jesus... she was relentless."

"Who can blame her?" Lizbeth said. "She's a young lesbian on this little island and a lesbian role model such as you moves back home. She really couldn't help herself." Lizbeth was enjoying watching Gray squirm.

"I shouldn't have let her think there was a chance. I don't want to hurt her."

Lizbeth saw how honestly Gray did not want to cause Jaye any pain. She let her off the hook, somewhat. "She's fine Gray. She knows she can't have you. I think she's satisfied with what she got."

"That must have been quite a chat."

Lizbeth said, over the top of her beer glass, "Enlightening."

"Hum. I don't know if I like the sound of that."

Lizbeth drained her beer and presented the glass to Gray. "Shall we have another? You are trying to get me drunk and take advantage of me, aren't you?"

Gray turned up her glass and finished its contents. The dashing grin appeared when she walked away, saying, "Yes, yes I am."

Several beers later, the deck had refilled with people. Lizbeth saw Holly across the deck and watched as her eyes traveled up and down Gray's body. Holly realized Lizbeth was looking at her and smiled. Lizbeth smiled back with her best, "Look, but don't touch," smile. Holly nodded receipt of the unspoken message. People danced to the music coming out of the bar. The group of women from the black SUV that wanted Gray to come over appeared in the middle of the deck, drunk and looking for a party.

Della, the one who had made no bones about the lust she had for Gray, spotted the two of them, and led the others straight to the railing. Della paid no attention to Lizbeth. She was drunk and had focused in on her prey. She stumbled up, throwing herself around Gray and hugging her too long, as far as Lizbeth was concerned. Gray smiled and hugged the woman back. Jaye had been right about the booze loosening Gray up. She was more animated and gregarious than usual. This gave Della hope and she continued to paw at Gray, and in Lizbeth's opinion Gray wasn't doing enough to discourage her. She seemed more amused than concerned about what Lizbeth was thinking.

Della finally noticed Lizbeth and announced a little loudly, "Hope you don't mind if I borrow your girlfriend for a minute."

Well, Lizbeth thought, she's not too drunk to have noticed that. She wondered, for a second, how many other people there knew she was with Gray. It didn't matter and it surprised her that she even gave it a thought. The matter at hand regained her attention. Oh, but Lizbeth did mind the other woman touching Gray. Over the years of being cheated on, Lizbeth had acquired quite an aversion to other women touching what was hers alone to have. Even the slightest friendly hug observed had become a suspicion, and this woman was not hugging Gray with friendly intentions.

Some switch in Lizbeth's head flipped. She had brought Gray down here to observe and had ended up in a panic of jealousy. It could have been the alcohol - she would blame it on that later - or it could have been the uncontrolled rage she had built up all those years of saying nothing when women pawed at James. Whatever made her do it, Lizbeth moved quickly and without hesitation, pulling Gray from the clutches of the drunken woman and laying a big ass kiss on her right there in front of God and everybody. She let go of a dazed Gray and turned to Della.

"I'm sorry darlin', but Gray is otherwise engaged, indefinitely."

Holly, Jaye, and a few other men and women, presumably locals, began to clap and cheer. If an outsider was going to have Gray, they evidently had decided they would rather it be

Lizbeth. She had passed some unspoken test. Gray still had an astounded look on her face, as Lizbeth lead her by the hand through the crowd and out of the pub. Lizbeth had staked her claim and now intended to take Gray home and ravish her. The adrenaline from the confrontation fueled her desires. Jealousy, Lizbeth found, was a powerful aphrodisiac.

For the next several hours, Lizbeth lived up to her prediction. She lost the few inhibitions she had left with Gray, all over the little cottage. They had stumbled through the front door with Lizbeth already tearing at Gray's clothes. Lizbeth took complete control for the first time in their lovemaking and Gray gave it up easily. The teacher was pleased with the student's performance and fell asleep on Lizbeth's stomach when they finally made it to the bed, spent and grinning. Lizbeth's claim had been thoroughly staked.

Chapter Eleven

"Lord, have mercy. Look at you two." Fanny's chuckle accompanied her words as she poured the two younger women coffee. "Had a late night, I s'pose?" She giggled, enjoying herself.

Lizbeth was hung-over. Gray didn't look much better. They were both smiling, but weakly. Fanny passed out aspirin and orange juice, even though she continued to harass them.

"You two ain't as spry as you used to be. Cain't be howlin' at the moon like your younger days. It'll catch up with ya'."

"A truer statement has not been spoken," Lizbeth said weakly. She had gotten up with Gray, even though she wasn't going with her today, because she felt guilty for getting her drunk.

Fanny went to the refrigerator and removed a bottle of tomato juice. She began creating a concoction it appeared she was familiar with making for Gray. Lizbeth wondered how many times the older woman had put Gray back together after a night of drowning her sorrows. Lizbeth saw hot sauce and black pepper go in the mix and decided not to watch the rest. Fanny talked, or rather teased them, as she worked.

"I guess y'all been getting reacquainted. Been a long time since Gray tied you up to that tree." Fanny was finding herself exceedingly funny and prodded her granddaughter for a response. "I ain't seen you this drug up in some time. That little old girl there too much for ya'?"

Lizbeth blushed. She guessed they deserved it. They did look like they had been in a drunken orgy all night. Gray's hair was sticking out in ten different directions. They had slept as late as possible and Gray had not taken a shower before they crossed the street for breakfast. Lizbeth had no idea how she looked. She had not cared enough to look in the mirror earlier. The orange juice was kicking her sugar levels back up, and though she still felt like shit, she became extremely amused by Gray's appearance. She was sure she had no room to laugh, considering what her own hair must look like.

Lizbeth began to giggle, staring down at the eggs and bacon on her plate. She felt like a teenager that had been caught necking behind the barn. There wasn't enough upset at being caught to overwhelm the pure joy and excitement the event had brought her. She couldn't look at Gray or Fanny for fear of breaking into all out convulsive laughter. Gray began to giggle, too.

Fanny placed a juice glass full of her tomato juice blend in front of both of them. "Here, if this don't kill ya', it'll help ya' wake up." Neither woman moved to take the glass. They were both trying so hard not to laugh they couldn't move. "Good Lord. You two act like young'uns that just found out what all the fuss was with the birds and the bees. I don't reckon passion is anything to be shy about."

Lizbeth lost it first, but Gray followed close behind. Yep, they looked like passion personified this morning and the old lady was getting her kicks tormenting them with this knowledge. Lizbeth *had* just discovered what all the fuss was about. She found this observation, on Fanny's part, extraordinarily funny. Lizbeth had yet to find an end to the places Gray took her. Each sexual experience with Gray had unlocked another pinnacle she had never known before. It was like finally being let in on a secret. It thrilled her and was currently making her laugh until she cried. She kept her head down, unable to look at Gray, because every time she did they both laughed harder. Lizbeth laughed until her sides ached, and then slowly regained her composure, wiping the tears away with her napkin.

A short laugh escaped occasionally, but she was finally able to drink Fanny's magic elixir. The mixture burned her stomach and she began to sweat, but it was working. She did feel better. Gray also drank the juice laced with hot sauce and pepper and Lord knows what else. Her face began to flush and she started in on her eggs, seized occasionally by a giggle in between bites. Lizbeth joined her.

Fanny laughed along with them and at them. Fanny took delight in making Gray squirm and in the change in Gray since Lizbeth had come into her life. Fanny had the disadvantage of being able to see through Gray's devil may care attitude and grinning persona. Fanny knew the depth of Gray's pain, having lived with her for the last five years. It appeared to be a relief to Fanny that Gray was coming back to the land of the living.

The phone on the kitchen wall rang. It startled all of them. Fanny, still chuckling, got up to answer it.

"Hello... Yes it is..." Fanny's smile disappeared from her face as she listened to whoever was on the other end. "Yes, she is." Gray's ears perked up. "Let me ask." Fanny took the phone from her ear and held it out to Gray.

Gray looked completely surprised that someone would be calling her on that line. She used her cell phone, not the house phone. "Who is it?" She asked Fanny.

Fanny's eyes darted from Gray to Lizbeth and back again. She sighed and said, "Dana."

Lizbeth saw the light go out of Gray's eyes and the color drain from her face. She felt a pain shoot across her chest as Gray rose to take the receiver. Lizbeth could only imagine what Dana wanted and none of it sounded good bouncing around in her brain. She felt like she was intruding. She heard the uneasiness in Gray's voice when she said hello. Gray didn't look at Lizbeth. She faced the wall and listened to what Dana was saying. Lizbeth held her breath. Fanny reached across the table and patted Lizbeth's hand. She was trying to reassure Lizbeth that everything would be okay, but Lizbeth wasn't so sure. The mere mentioning of Dana's name had brought a cloud into the room that hung over Lizbeth, waiting to dump its contents at a moment's notice.

Lizbeth's heart nearly stopped beating when Gray said, "No. Don't come to the house. I'll meet you somewhere."

Lizbeth must have had fear in her eyes, because Fanny now squeezed the hand that she had been patting, and mouthed the words, "It'll be all right."

Lizbeth was paralyzed with terror. All of the other women she knew about meant nothing to Gray. Lizbeth could deal with that and them, but she didn't know what to expect from Dana. Hadn't Gray said they had not spoken in years?

"Okay, seven o'clock, Harbor Inn... Yeah, see you then." Gray hung up the phone slowly. She didn't turn around right away. Lizbeth could see Gray visibly get control of herself, sighing heavily, before she turned around. She had the look of someone who had just had just seen a ghost. Lizbeth let go of Fanny's hand, stood up, left the room and the cottage without another word.

She heard Gray say behind her, "Lizbeth, wait."

Lizbeth couldn't stop. She saw the future with Gray vanish before her eyes. She couldn't see anything in front of her; it had all gone fuzzy. She mechanically made her way across the street and shut the door on Gray's footsteps closing in on her. She locked the door and ignored the knocking. She climbed the stairs and fell face down into the bed they had occupied less than an hour ago. Gray's pounding on the door and calling her name made no difference. Lizbeth could not fight the panic that struck her.

The pounding stopped on the door downstairs. The tightening in her chest released enough for Lizbeth to take a gasping breath and then the sobbing started. Lizbeth had finally let herself love someone again and it was going to kill her this time when her heart broke. She knew it. This was only the beginning of the pain she was going to feel. She couldn't get control of herself if she wanted to.

Gray had done nothing to make her feel this way. All that Lizbeth had witnessed was a phone call from Gray's old girlfriend, wife, whatever. Still it rocked her to her core, because she never thought, in a million years, that not only would she be fighting the ghost responsible for Gray's broken heart, she was now up against Dana in the flesh. Lizbeth simply assumed she would lose.

Lizbeth was crying so hard she didn't hear the footsteps coming up the stairs. She didn't realize Gray was there until she heard her voice, close up behind her, and felt Gray's weight lie down on the bed beside her. Gray covered Lizbeth's body, racked with sobs, with her own and hugged her to her.

Gray attempted humor first. "If you're going to try and keep people out, you should lock the back door, too." Lizbeth didn't laugh. Gray tried again. "Lizbeth, honey, her coming here doesn't change anything... stop crying and listen to me."

Lizbeth had turned into a ball of mush. She couldn't catch her breath, let alone talk. She gasped out between sobs, "I...can't...do...this."

"Nothing's going to happen." Gray waited for a response from Lizbeth. When she got none, she tried again. "Baby, please don't cry. There's no reason for you to be upset. I'll meet her, find out what she wants, and send her on her way."

Lizbeth tried to believe her. She wanted to so badly, but she'd been down this road before, the "trust me, honey," road. It had not worked out in her best interest the last time. How could she set herself up for that fall again?

Gray was becoming exasperated. She pleaded one last time, "Really, Lizbeth, don't you know I'm in love with you?'

Lizbeth spoke, more clearly this time, "I've heard...that before." Gray was paying for somebody else's mistakes.

Her voice more commanding this time, Gray said, "I'm not James, Lizbeth."

Lizbeth just couldn't deal with Gray right now. It really didn't matter what she said. Lizbeth was lost in her sorrow. It had besieged her. She wasn't prepared for it and it had sliced her legs right out from under her. She had not experienced a panic attack like this since the first time she caught James cheating. Panic, that's what this was. "Lizbeth, you are having a panic attack," she heard a calm inner voice say. The mere fear of experiencing that pain again had shut her ears to Gray's pleadings.

The panic attacks began when she found James on the beach that night in Hilton Head, the final one culminating in her taking to the bed for months. Lizbeth knew her psyche was fragile. As hard as she tried to be strong, sometimes her mind and body simply took over, bringing Lizbeth to her knees. Lizbeth hated the loss of control. It was a long time before Lizbeth's doctor could convince her that she really had no say in the matter.

Lizbeth managed to say, "Please Gray, just leave me alone."

Lizbeth's gasping cries and frequent attempts to get a complete breath into her lungs were the only sounds in the room. Complete seizure of her diaphragm muscles met each attempt for air, stopping it cold.

"Okay, Lizbeth, I'll leave, whatever you want."

Lizbeth nodded her head yes, she wanted Gray to leave. At this point Lizbeth was more worried about her own sanity than anything Gray had to say. Her panic had now exceeded any rationality, because logically this breakdown made no sense. Gray just told Lizbeth she was in love with her. It was the terror of giving in and being wrong that crushed her chest. Her mind and body sensed danger the moment Fanny said Dana's name, and it had gone into full alarm and flight mode, with no notice to or assistance from Lizbeth.

Her heart remembered the agonizing pain from all those years ago. It had taken Lizbeth down for weeks. She couldn't function well enough to take care of herself, much less an eight-year-old daughter. Her sister had come to stay with her. Lizbeth's catatonic state had scared James so badly, he had called Lizbeth's sister and confessed what he had done. It was the one and only time he ever acknowledged betraying Lizbeth, right up to the bitter end. It had taken two weeks for Lizbeth to regain her feet; more weeks went by before she gained her resolve. In the end, the pain had been so unbearable, it was many years later before she could recall most of that two-week period. Her mind would not let Lizbeth feel the pain until she could process it. Lizbeth thought her mind might be letting her feel some of it now, as a caution. It was gripping Lizbeth around the throat, screaming, "You will not do that to us again."

Gray let out a heavy sigh. She let go of Lizbeth, stood up, and walked to the top of the stairs. "Lizbeth, when you get yourself together, call me. I'll try to get back as soon as I can." Gray's voice was shaky and betrayed her own fear of what was happening to Lizbeth. "I do love you." She paused there for a moment longer. Lizbeth heard her descend the stairs, and leave through the front door.

They had opened the windows last night. Lizbeth heard Fanny's voice, from the porch below, "How's she farin', Gray?"

"I don't know. She sure as hell has had a fit and fell in it. I tried to tell her it didn't make any difference, but she won't listen."

"It does make a difference, Gray. She saw the same thing I did. You lost your color when I said that girl's name. You got unfinished business there and you damn well better get it done, or you'll lose the one person that might have been what you've been pinin' for all this time."

"I didn't ask Dana to come here. I haven't talked to her in years. I don't know why she's here. You, of all people, should know I've been done with her for a long time."

"No, you ain't been done with her by a long shot. Fanny Gray O'Neal, I know you better than you know yourself. You got wronged. You got fooled. You got lied to. Ain't never taken to that in yer life."

Gray defended herself. "Who would?"

"But you took it this time. You took it to heart and you brought it home with you."

"What else was I supposed to do? You're not suggesting I should have stayed with her, after..."

"The Gray I raised gets revenge. Like that dye you put in that girl's shampoo up to the campground. My Gray gets even."

"I don't think coloring Dana's hair blue would have solved anything."

Fanny chuckled. "No, Gray, I don't 'magine it would have."

Gray's voice dropped lower. "How do you get even for betrayal? I couldn't betray her back. There wasn't any point to it."

"Darlin', the best revenge for betrayal is to live your life and be happy without 'em. Gray, I'm gonna say it plain. You ain't used the brains God gave you on this one. Sleep walkin' through the days. Hard headed enough to think you couldn't be hurt again, if you just never loved anybody else."

"But Fanny, I'm trying. I let myself fall in love with Lizbeth and look what's happening. She's upstairs balling her eyes out, won't talk to me, and I haven't done anything wrong."

"Neither one of you has a lick of courage when it comes to broken hearts. You both had one and vowed never to have one again. Now, you let yourselves fall in love and it scares the hell out of you both. You go on to work. I'll watch out for Lizbeth."

Lizbeth listened in silence. During the conversation her sobbing had subsided. She was concentrating so hard on hearing what the O'Neal women were saying, she forgot to be lost in her misery. She heard Gray clear her throat. When Gray began to speak, her voice was hoarse with emotion.

"I do love her, you know."

"Which one?" Fanny asked. Lizbeth thought it was a fair question.

Gray reacted to the question angrily. "Dammit Fanny, Lizbeth! I'm in love with Lizbeth."

Fanny out right laughed this time. "Lord child, I believe you."

Gray added, solemnly, "Now, if you can just convince her of that."

Still laughing, Fanny said, "Oh, I'm gonna leave you to your own convincin'. I'll just try to put her back together before you get home."

Lizbeth heard Gray say, "Thank you. I love you, old woman." She knew Gray was hugging her grandmother.

Lizbeth heard the screen door open and shut and Gray was gone. In a few seconds the front door creaked as Fanny entered the cottage downstairs. She closed the door quietly behind her. Fanny's house shoes made shuffling sounds across the floor below. The noise stopped at the bottom of the stairs. After a moment of eerie silence, Lizbeth heard Fanny speaking softly.

"Minnie, I sure do miss you."

A moment later, Fanny stood before Lizbeth with her hands on her hips. Lizbeth, upon hearing Fanny's approach, sat up against the headboard and clutched the sheet to her chest, like a security blanket. Still sniffling and trying not to all out sob again, Lizbeth looked to Fanny for the answer.

"Miss Fanny, what am I going to do?"

Fanny's approach was straightforward. "You panicked, Lizbeth. Sure as yer born."

"It overwhelmed me. I couldn't control it. I treated Gray horribly." More sniffles followed.

Fanny smiled at Lizbeth. "No, darlin', I think you scared some sense into her. It's piss or get off the pot time for Gray."

Lizbeth didn't smile. "I think I scared myself." She was still unable fully to comprehend why she had acted so emotionally to Dana's call.

Fanny came over and sat on the edge of the bed. She reached out and took one of Lizbeth's hands. "You and Gray. Such beautiful and smart women and you let your hearts lead you 'round by the nose hairs. You both got knocked down pretty hard, but that's life. To lose your child would have been worse. There are so many things that could have been worse. You survived it. You put your life back together and you're better for it. You are much stronger than you give yourself credit for. You're just like Gray, lettin' the fear of the unknown paralyze you. Darlin', the unknown is what makes life exciting, worth living. Hell, if I knew what the rest of my days had in store for me I'd rather go now."

Lizbeth managed a weak smile. "You can never go, Miss Fanny. What would Gray do without you?"

"Live happily ever after, I hope. I was thinking you were going to help her out with that and I could go to God knowin' Gray's gonna be all right, but if you're gonna fall apart every time Gray O'Neal is faced with temptation, you're right to give up now."

Lizbeth laughed a little. "I've had a ringside seat to quite a few of Gray's temptations. Women flock to her like geese on a cornfield. Last night I saw men checking her out. Everyone falls in love with Gray. I knew I was wrestling with Dana's ghost, too. I thought I could handle it. I wasn't prepared for this."

Fanny's chuckling accompanied her next pronouncement. "The Lord works in mysterious ways. He brought you here. Put you here for a reason. He put Dana here, too. Gonna bring this boil to a head and be done with it."

Lizbeth couldn't help but be amused at Fanny's practical way of stating the facts. "You do have a wonderful insight, Miss Fanny. Gray's lucky to have grown up with such a wise woman."

"Darlin', when I was y'all's age, I was crazy as you. Age made me wise; my youthful follies gave me that wisdom."

Sometimes Lizbeth wished she were recording Fanny. Pearls of profoundness spilled from her mouth endlessly and Lizbeth was worried she wouldn't be able to remember them all.

"Do you think Gray will forgive me for behaving so badly?" Lizbeth asked.

"I think I'll leave the forgivin' and makin' up to you two. I've stuck my nose in as far as I plan to. If I was you, I would get up, fix myself up, and go and make my peace with her, but

I ain't you." Lizbeth started getting out of the bed, before Fanny finished. Fanny chuckled, adding, "She'll be back at the dock around ten."

Just before Lizbeth stepped into the bathroom for a shower, she watched Fanny leave the cottage. Fanny shook her head and laughed, looking up to the heavens. "Lord Minnie, these young'uns is blind with love and lust."

#

Lizbeth showered, put on her clothes, and got herself together. She still had a few minutes to grab another cup of coffee. Lizbeth made up her mind to find Gray and apologize for her meltdown. She was embarrassed and afraid she might have scared Gray off. How could she explain it had all been a panic attack? She had them infrequently, but when she did, she had no control over her emotions. She heard Gray say she loved her. She knew the whole reaction was over the top and irrational. Now, she had to apologize and fix the mess she'd made.

She double-checked in the bathroom mirror, making sure her eyes did not look like she'd been on a crying jag. The little make-up she wore helped and the redness had almost gone. Lizbeth left the cottage resolved to trust Gray to handle the Dana business. It was a big decision and a hard one to make, but Fanny had said Lizbeth needed to put it in the hands of the higher power, and that, Lizbeth had decided, was a wise choice.

When Lizbeth left the cottage, Fanny was waiting on her porch. She had Gray's little cooler and a small wicker basket, its contents covered by a red and white checked dishtowel.

"Gray left without taking any food or water with her. I thought I'd pack you two a lunch and maybe she can find the time to eat it with you."

Lizbeth hugged Fanny. "Miss Fanny, you are the true jewel in the sea."

"I don't know about all that, but I've seen what happens to you if you get stressed and don't eat, so I thought somebody ought to feed you. Now, go on get. Relieve her mind, 'cause she don't need to be worried about you out on that water."

Lizbeth made it down to the dock, but Gray's boat wasn't tied up. She had not come back yet from her first run. Her next tour was gathering on the boardwalk. Lizbeth made her way through them and walked to the end of the dock. She put the cooler and basket down and peered out over the water. No sign of Gray.

Lizbeth stood at the end of the dock and looked back toward the boardwalk. There were quite a few children in the next group preparing for Gray's ride to Portsmouth Island. She smiled to herself, thinking how much these kids were going to enjoy Gray's storytelling. There were several young couples, still in love and enchanted with each other. An older white haired couple held hands and smiled at each other. They had a lifetime of love together. Lizbeth thought you could see it in their eyes, hers still twinkling when she looked at him, his forever on her. Lizbeth wondered if she'd ever have a love like that. They were so rare. Lizbeth imagined it could be that way with Gray, if they could work out their trust issues.

Lizbeth heard a motor slowing down as it approached the mouth of the harbor. She turned to see Gray's boat make the turn into the "creek." At the sight of Gray, Lizbeth's heart began to beat faster. She was so ashamed of her breakdown this morning. Lizbeth hoped she would be able to convince Gray that she didn't know what happened and she would do her damnedest never to let it happen again. She would make no promises, because promises got broken, but she would make a commitment to work on healing her own hurts and insecurities. She would, however, like Gray to do the same. Lizbeth had come to this realization after her talk with Fanny.

Other people began to join her on the dock. The tour group grew antsy. Lizbeth kept her eyes on Gray, waiting for Gray to see her, hoping for a favorable reaction. Someone stepped up beside her. Out of the corner of her eye, Lizbeth noticed it was a blond woman, but nothing more. Her eyes were glued to Gray.

Gray approached the dock, slowly coming closer and closer. She stood up behind the wheel, readying for the approach. She cut the engine back and idled toward the end of the dock. Lizbeth smiled at Gray's look of concentration. She still had not noticed Lizbeth on the end of the dock. Once the boat was lined up correctly, Gray took her eyes off the landing and let them travel up to where Lizbeth was standing. Gray's mouth fell open. Even though the ever-present Ray Bans shielded her eyes, a look of shock and dismay was clear on her face.

Lizbeth realized Gray wasn't looking just at her in a flash of conscious awareness of the woman beside her. The blonde was almost as tall as Gray. She had a definite Charlize Theron resemblance, almost uncanny. Not the Charlize from "Monster," by any means, but one of those roles where she oozed sophistication and sex appeal. This woman was drop dead gorgeous. If she walked in a room, heads most definitely would turn. Some necks would be sore in the morning. She certainly stunned Gray.

The recognition came slowly at first. The trickle became a raging river as the memories, of the picture on Gray's dresser and the Christmas card, rushed into Lizbeth's head. She had only glanced at the photos and had been mostly looking at Gray. This was *the* "Dana" in the flesh, and Lizbeth suddenly realized what she was up against. The ghost of this woman had been one thing, but the magnitude of her presence hit Lizbeth like a ton of bricks.

Dana smiled down at Gray, who was still stricken, frozen with the look of panic on her face. The only movement she made was when her head followed her eyes slightly, as they darted back and forth between the two women on the dock. Dana saw this too and turned to Lizbeth for the first time. The full effect of Dana's beauty became all too clear when she smiled at Lizbeth.

She extended her hand and said, "Hello, my name is Dana." Lizbeth noted the sophisticated accent of a well-educated and aristocratic Texan. Dana continued, "You must know Gray. I'm an old friend."

Lizbeth reached for Dana's hand. She knew she had to overcome her awe and say something. The first thing that popped into her head came out of her mouth. "I'm Lizbeth. I'm a... the new friend."

Dana smiled and let out a little laugh. Both of their heads turned when they heard the boat engine go back into gear. Gray looked at the dock just once more, before plopping down on the console seat, whipping the wheel to the left, and driving the boat away from the end of the dock as fast as she could, pushing the No Wake rules to the limit.

#

"She never was good at confrontation," Dana said, as she and Lizbeth stood side-by-side, hands on hips, watching Gray make a huge sweeping arc around the harbor.

"I'm learning that," Lizbeth said.

"How long have you known her?" Dana asked, not taking her eyes off the circling boat.

"Ten days, if you don't count her tying me up to a tree when I was four."

For some reason, Lizbeth felt comfortable answering Dana's question. She had somehow rationalized that it wasn't Dana that posed the threat. It was Gray's remaining feelings for Dana that she would have to battle. Lizbeth's husband

James was as much of a Greek statue as Gray. He was extremely handsome with dark good looks that made women of all ages swoon, but she wouldn't go back to him. Gray wasn't fighting James' ghost. If anything, Gray was fighting to get to Lizbeth through the scars he left behind. Lizbeth in turn was competing with the love of Gray's life, and paying for Dana's betrayal. It occurred to Lizbeth that people who betray trusts and cheat seldom, if ever, understand the magnitude of the damage they leave in their wakes. The next lover the broken soul becomes involved with pays so much more of the price than the actual cheater.

Dana looked down at Lizbeth and chuckled. "Somehow that doesn't surprise me."

"Which part?"

"Gray tying you up. I've heard stories. Quite the wild thing, isn't she?"

"Yes, quite." Dana intrigued Lizbeth. Of course, she had no idea why she was here, but Lizbeth felt no need to be guarded against her. Dana didn't appear phased at all by Lizbeth's presence. Her voice gave no indication that she felt the need to be competitive with Lizbeth.

Gray was still out on the harbor, having made no move to return to the dock. The tourists began to grumble in confusion, looking at their watches and watching the boat circle around again. Lizbeth looked over at Dana. "How long do you think she'll stay out there? These people are getting restless."

Dana laughed and shook her head. "I don't know. I guess I should go, so she'll come in. I wouldn't want to be detrimental to business." She stuck out her hand again. "It was nice to meet you, Lizbeth. Maybe we'll see each other again."

Lizbeth shook Dana's hand. Smiling, she said, "I think I'll go, too. She still might not come in, if I stay. Like you said, afraid of confrontation."

Dana's eyebrows raised above her sunglasses. "And would there be a confrontation?"

"Only between Gray's need to not let anyone know what she's really thinking and feeling and the fact that she's wired up tighter than a drum. She's bound to explode sooner or later."

"You really do know her. All that insight in ten days. Must have been an intense week," Dana said, as they moved toward the boardwalk together.

Lizbeth grinned up at the taller woman. "I've had a crash course on Gray O'Neal and becoming a lesbian." With a touch of sarcasm, she added, "and now that you're here, it just keeps getting better."

Dana stopped at the end of the dock, where it connected with the boardwalk. She said what could have been a veiled threat, but sounded genuine, "Let's hope this all ends amicably, shall we?"

The corner of Lizbeth's mouth slipped into a wicked grin. "Yes, let's."

They exchanged polite smiles and went their separate ways. As Lizbeth left the dock, she heard Gray's boat starting to make the approach again to the dock. She didn't turn around. Lizbeth walked back down Howard Street to await the outcome of Dana's arrival.

#

Lizbeth approached the cottage and had almost reached it before she saw the rear end of the familiar car in her driveway. She stopped. The absurdity of the levels of anxiety Lizbeth faced struck her. There was just the fact that she had become a lesbian seemingly overnight to deal with, the fact that she was in a complicated relationship with Gray, Gray's ex lover arriving, and now this. She looked to the sky, seeking an answer to how much more she was going to have to handle. Mazie was waiting on Lizbeth's porch.

Lizbeth dearly loved her daughter, but she didn't really need this today. She planned to tell Mazie everything, when she knew what to tell her. Everything was so up in the air right now, she had no idea what she was going to say. Mazie was a very intuitive person. She had sniffed something out and come to see for herself. Lizbeth knew her well enough to know she wasn't going home without an answer.

Mazie was rocking in a chair, grinning from ear-to-ear when she saw her mother. She ran off the porch and hugged her.

Lizbeth was happy to see her, even with the anxiety she brought with her. "Hey darlin', what are you doing here?"

Mazie took her mother's hand and walked back up on the porch with her. Her eyes were twinkling with childish delight. "I had to come, Mother. You were being so mysterious and then I ran into Molly."

"What did Molly say?"

"She just asked if I'd heard from you, yet. Sounded like I should be expecting a call. When the storm passed and you didn't call, I knew you were up to something. My curiosity got the best of me and here I am."

Lizbeth had not opened the front door. In her mind, she was cataloguing all the clothing that had been thrown around downstairs last night. She had been too preoccupied this morning to notice and now she was faced with opening the door onto the unknown. She had forgotten that Fanny walked through the house this morning. Surely, she would have said something, if there were undergarments just lying around.

Mazie noticed Lizbeth's hesitation. She started giggling.

Lizbeth wrinkled up her brow, and asked, "What?"

Mazie could contain herself no longer. She burst into peals of laughter. "I've already been inside, Mom. Who have you been having sex with all over the house?"

Lizbeth tried to play innocent. "What are you talking about?"

"Mom! You know exactly what I'm talking about." More seizures of laughter followed. "I found your underwear under the kitchen table. There was a bra sticking out of the couch cushions, and I know that tee shirt on the floor behind the front door is not yours." Mazie was whipping herself now. "And if that wasn't enough, I went upstairs and saw your bed. If somebody wasn't having wild sex in that bed, I'll kiss your ass on Main Street and give you an hour to draw a crowd."

Lizbeth had to laugh at Mazie and the predicament in which she found herself. Between giggles, she said, "I don't guess trying to convince you I'm a terrible housekeeper is going to work, is it?"

Mazie, who could barely breathe now, gasped out, "Hell no!"

Lizbeth slid her arm around her daughter. "Come on in," she said, still giggling, "I guess the cat's out of the bag."

Mazie took several deep breaths to recover her powers of speech. She followed her mother into the house. "Thank you, Mom."

"For what?"

"For letting me know there is life after forty."

Lizbeth threw her head back and laughed. "Oh, Mazie there is so much more to life than you can ever imagine."

Lizbeth kissed her daughter on the cheek and then left her by the door, as she went around the parlor collecting items of hers and Gray's clothing. When she picked up Gray's Calvin Klein underwear from under the coffee table, she glanced up to see Mazie watching her. She was no longer laughing. She stood there with an expression that told Lizbeth her intelligent, intuitive daughter was deriving a conclusion rather quickly.

"Mom, those aren't your underwear."

Lizbeth knew not to lie. She was caught. Might as well tell her now. "No, they're not." Lizbeth grinned from nervousness and because she really did want to tell Mazie how amazing Gray was.

"Those are women's briefs," Mazie declared.

"Yes, they are."

"Mother! Are you... Is the person you're... What's going on here?" Mazie was dumbfounded.

"Honey, come sit down on the couch." Lizbeth sat down and patted the cushion beside her.

Mazie moved in slow motion toward the couch. She hesitated before sitting down on the scene of the crime. Once seated, she stared at her mother, waiting for an answer.

"Mazie, a lot of things have happened in the last ten days. I was going to tell you. I was just waiting for everything to settle down so I'd know what to tell you." Lizbeth paused, taking a big breath and letting it out before continuing, "Honey, I'm involved in a relationship with a woman."

"Oh, from the looks of this place, you're more than just involved."

Lizbeth had to laugh. "Yes, last night was a little intense."

"I'd say. It looks like somebody's clothes got ripped off just inside the door."

Lizbeth grinned and said, "Hers."

"Mom, you're awful." Mazie started to laugh again. "Well, tell me about her."

Lizbeth eyed Mazie. "You're not freaked out, because it's a woman?"

"No, I mean it was the last thing I suspected, but no, I'm not freaked out. Of course, I haven't seen her yet, so I reserve judgment. If she's a big burly dyke on a Harley, I may have to have a minute."

Lizbeth beamed. "No, she doesn't have a bike that I know of. She does have a couple of boats."

"What's her name? How did you meet her?"

"Her name is Gray O'Neal and she lives across the street with her adorable grandmother. She's a native islander."

"Did you know her before, when you were younger?"

"I don't remember, but I've been told she tied me to a tree when I was four."

"Is she... I mean, did she seduce you?" Mazie was still trying to wrap her head around Lizbeth's sudden departure from the heterosexual world.

"Yes, she is a lesbian and no, I pursued her more, I think." Lizbeth paused to ponder that for a second. "Well, there was lots of mutual pursuit in play, but I started it."

"Wow." Mazie was truly dismayed at Lizbeth. "You know, I just never saw this coming."

"Believe me, neither did I."

Mazie was inquisitive. "So, are you a lesbian now?"

Lizbeth thought about the question before answering. "I really don't know, Mazie. I'm very new at this. I have noticed that I look at women differently, but Gray's the only one I want. I'll have to ask Molly if that qualifies."

Mazie clapped her hands. "I knew that grin on Molly's face meant she was keeping a secret. I could tell she knew something was going on down here."

"And you didn't think a phone call would have sufficed?" Lizbeth cracked.

"You would have dodged me. I knew you couldn't lie to me to my face." Mazie laughed, slapping her mother on the knee.

"I have never lied to you, on the phone or otherwise," Lizbeth defended herself.

"No, but you hide things from me until you're ready to tell. I was so excited that you finally might be getting on with your life after Dad, I had to come see for myself."

"You know curiosity killed the cat," Lizbeth quipped.

Mazie was quick to add, "And satisfaction brought him back."

Lizbeth squeezed Mazie's shoulder playfully. "How did I raise such a smart ass?"

Mazie grinned at her mother. "I learned at the feet of the master. Some of the things you used to say to Dad would just crack me up."

Lizbeth smirked. "Most of it went right over his head."

Mazie slapped her thigh. "Ha! That was the funny part."

"Oh God, I hope I didn't do that too often around you. I never wanted you not to like him. He's a good father, just a lousy husband."

Mazie said, sincerely, "No, Mom. I made up my own mind. You're right. He's a good father, but even I know not to trust him. He's always doing something or someone he shouldn't. I think he's an adrenaline junkie."

Lizbeth warmed with pride, looking at her grown, wise beyond her years, daughter. "Mazie, you are still a wonder to me. How you got to be so smart with parents like us, I'll never know."

"Don't sell yourself short, Mom. You taught me two very valuable lessons as a woman. First, if you get the breath knocked out of you, you will breathe again and second, take notes. If you're patient, vengeance is ever so much sweeter."

Lizbeth grinned. "I did do that, didn't I? Have I told you lately that you're my favorite?"

"You stole that from Reba."

Lizbeth pulled Mazie into a bear hug, whispering in her ear, "Doesn't make it any less true. I love you, Mazie."

"I love you, too, Mom. I'm starving. Let's make some lunch and you can tell me all about Gray. I want to know everything."

"Okay, how about leftover meatballs made into sandwiches?"

Mazie stood up. "That sounds great. Do you have any wine? I think I'm going to need a drink."

"Yes, there's a bottle open in the fridge and another on the counter. I don't think I'll be joining you though. I had a bit much last night." Lizbeth still felt a little hung-over even after Fanny's magic formula.

"I could tell," Mazie said.

Lizbeth thought she had done a decent job fixing herself up before she left to go to the docks. How could Mazie tell? "What, do I look bad?"

"No, you look absolutely sparkling," Mazie said, then began to giggle again. "But it was obvious the way the clothes were strewn around that there was a large quantity of alcohol involved."

Lizbeth flashed on a scene from last night. She was thankful Mazie couldn't read minds. She giggled herself and said, "Yes, yes there was."

#

It was six o'clock that evening before Lizbeth finished filling Mazie in on all that had happened in the last ten days. She told her everything, how she felt, what was going through her head. Lizbeth left out the details of her sexual encounters with Gray, just leaving it at "fan-fucking-tastic." She included the fact that Dana was now here on the island and that Mazie's timing couldn't have been worse, but she was glad she had come.

"Her ex is here?" Mazie was aghast.

"Yes, and she's a dead ringer for Charlize Theron."

"Not 'Monster'…"

Lizbeth cut her off. "No, think 'Bagger Vance' or 'Hancock."

Mazie's eyebrows went up. "Holy shit!"

Lizbeth nodded in agreement. "Exactly."

"Where is Gray now? Are you going to see her before she sees this Dana?"

Mazie was formulating a plan of action. Lizbeth could see it. She'd seen that little plotting expression before. Maybe she should let Mazie help. Lizbeth hadn't been doing a very good job with the Dana thing so far.

Gray calling her name as she came through the front door interrupted Lizbeth's thoughts. She stood up and looked at Mazie.

"Speak of the devil, here she is now." Lizbeth stepped into the archway. "I'm back here, Gray." She turned back to Mazie. "Wait here."

Lizbeth met Gray in the hallway, out of sight of Mazie. She walked right up to Gray, placed her hands on Gray's chest, stood on her tiptoes, and kissed her. Gray wrapped her in her arms. Lizbeth could feel Gray's relief in the kiss. Gray pulled back and looked into Lizbeth's eyes. She started to speak.

"Lizbeth, I..."

Lizbeth put a finger over Gray's lips to silence her. "Shh. You can tell me later. Right now I have company."

"I saw the car. Who is it?"

They both heard Mazie clear her throat at the end of the hall. Still wrapped in Gray's arms, Lizbeth turned her head toward her daughter.

"Gray O'Neal, this is my daughter, Mazie."

Gray dropped Lizbeth from her arms in a flat second. She took a step back, gathering her composure. Lizbeth found it amusing and started giggling again.

"It's okay, Gray. Mazie and I have already talked."

Mazie came toward the two lovers, wearing a smile to match her mother's. She extended her hand. "It's a pleasure to meet you, Gray. My mother has just been filling me in on the recent changes in her lifestyle. You can relax, I approve."

Gray shook Mazie's hand. "It's a pleasure to meet you, too, Mazie. I've heard a lot about you, as well."

Lizbeth was beaming, looking from Gray to her daughter and back. This, at least, was going well. Mazie smiled at Gray. Lizbeth could see Mazie checking out her mom's taste in women and approving. The Gray charm hit Mazie, too. Lizbeth saw it creep across her face. First impressions had been well made.

Gray said, "You look like your mom."

"I'll take that as a compliment, since you seem to be so enamored with her," Mazie replied.

Gray grinned. "It was."

"Okay," Lizbeth said, before it got awkward, "Mazie, I need to talk to Gray for a minute. She has an appointment to keep."

"Yeah, about that," Mazie started.

Lizbeth raised her hand, cutting her off. "Mazie, don't. Let me deal with this."

Mazie was not deterred and quite a bit sassier than her mother. She had no problem saying what she felt. "Damned if someone I was seeing would be meeting up with the former love of his life, especially if she looked like what you said."

Gray chuckled. "Shy little thing, isn't she?"

Lizbeth chuckled, too. "Yes, I don't know what I'd do if she ever really spoke her mind."

Mazie looked at her mother. "Well, are you going to let her go alone?"

Lizbeth stopped smiling and turned serious. "Mazie, Gray is a grown woman. I won't be 'letting' her do anything. This is something she has to do and I have to trust that she'll be back. I can't do anything beyond that."

"Mom, you'll kick yourself all the way back to Durham if this backfires."

Lizbeth put her hands on her hips. "So be it."

Mazie waved her hands in the air in defeat and started back down the hallway to the kitchen, slinging, "I'm just sayin'," over her shoulder, as she went.

Gray had watched the exchange between mother and daughter silently. She took Lizbeth by the hand and led her back into the parlor for the little privacy the tiny cottage provided. Once they were alone, Gray kissed Lizbeth again and then held her tight for a moment, not speaking, just clinging to Lizbeth with her face buried in Lizbeth's hair.

When Lizbeth was finally able to peel Gray off her, she could see tears in Gray's eyes. "What's the matter, baby?" Lizbeth whispered.

"I'll be back, Lizbeth. I promise."

Lizbeth wanted so much to believe her, but Gray had not met with Dana, yet. Lizbeth surprised even herself when her voice came out strong and certain. "Gray, don't make promises. Go listen to what she has to say. I'll be here, if it's really over with her. If it isn't, don't come back. Don't come to explain, don't come to apologize, just don't come back. If you do return, I expect you to fall madly in love with me. I love you, Gray, but if I can't have all of you, I don't want any of you. Do you understand what I'm saying? All or nothing. You have until morning."

Gray looked deeply into Lizbeth's eyes and said with resolve, "I'll be back, Lizbeth."

"I'm betting on it," Lizbeth whispered, "but just in case you don't make it back, would you kiss me again?"

Gray enveloped Lizbeth. She smothered Lizbeth into her arms and kissed her zealously. Then without another word, Gray left Lizbeth standing in the parlor, and exited the cottage. Lizbeth watched her walk across the street and then returned to the kitchen where Mazie waited. Lizbeth didn't cry. She was done with crying for a while. She'd cry enough if Gray didn't come back. Right now, all Lizbeth could do was wait and pray.

Mazie was smiling at her when Lizbeth stepped into the kitchen. "I heard what you said, well, most of it. This is a very small house." Mazie stood up and crossed to Lizbeth. Hugging her, she said, "That took a lot of courage. I'm proud of you."

"We'll see how proud you are of me when I'm face down in a pillow blubbering because she didn't come back."

Mazie patted her mother on the back, comforting her. "She'll be back, Mom."

"How do you know? You didn't see Charlize."

Mazie pulled away, holding her mom out at arm's length. "You're kidding, right? Don't you see the way Gray looks at you? Mom, she's in love with you."

"She thinks she is, Mazie, but I want her to be sure. No doubts."

"How did you get to be so wise?" Mazie teased.

Lizbeth quipped, "By making the same mistake twice. I won't do it a third time."

Mazie wrinkled her brow. "What mistake was that?"

"I trusted your father," Lizbeth said flatly.

"Are you afraid you can't trust Gray?"

"If I can't trust her completely, then I won't be involved with her at all. I can't think of a bigger test than this. Not where Gray is concerned, anyway. Dana's memory has been in the middle of this since the beginning. It's like Fanny said, time for it to come to a head."

"When do I get to meet this Miss Fanny?"

Lizbeth looked back down the hall and then over at the clock on the stove. "Let's give Gray a few more minutes to get gone and then I'll take you over there."

Mazie took Lizbeth by the shoulders. She squared her up and looked into Lizbeth's face with all seriousness, "Hey, if she doesn't come back, I'm here for you." Then she giggled, saying, "If she does come back, do you think Fanny would let me sleep at her house? Like I said, noise travels in this little place."

Mother and daughter's laughter filled the air.

#

At seven fifteen, Lizbeth walked Mazie across the street. Fanny, as usual was having iced tea on the porch and they joined her. Mazie was immediately taken with Fanny. Fanny entertained them for an hour with stories from her past. All the while, a clock was ticking away in Lizbeth's head. She could barely concentrate on the conversation. Lizbeth was glad Mazie was there, or she would be holed up in the bed, watching the digital numbers flash and change. Instead, she was here on the porch with Fanny and Mazie, and this was keeping her from losing her mind. Except for the fidgeting. She could not sit still.

"Lizbeth, you're jumpy as a mullet. Stop frettin', it won't help none," Fanny said, unexpectedly.

Mazie, ever practical, said, "Mom, you gave her until morning. Are you going to twist yourself in a knot all night waiting for her?"

Lizbeth looked at the other two women on the porch. The statement shot out of her mouth, before she had time to stop it. "That was too long. I shouldn't have given her that much time. Anything could happen."

Fanny and Mazie became very amused at Lizbeth's wound tight state. Mazie was enjoying this all too much, as far as Lizbeth was concerned.

"Mom, you were so courageous a few hours ago. Where's that tenacity now?"

Lizbeth's anxiety showed clearly in her voice when she blurted out, "You've never been around Gray with other women. They're like heat seeking missiles and her track record isn't the greatest at beating them off. If that woman is pouring it on, I don't know if Gray can say no. You didn't see her. Dana is an extraordinarily beautiful woman."

Fanny piped in, "Gray's as loyal as a dog. She'll come home. Besides, she also hain't forgot what Dana did to her. Looks don't mount to squat, if you're a bad person on the inside."

Lizbeth sat down from her most recent pacing attack. "Fanny, I met her. She was wonderful, so poised and kind. I can see why Gray fell for her, besides the fact that she looks like she stepped off a movie set."

Mazie tried to make Lizbeth feel better, seeming to have thought better of teasing her mother. "You are beautiful, too."

Lizbeth argued, "Not in her league. Tell her Fanny."

Fanny harrumphed, "Yes, and sometimes you bite into a beautiful apple and get a worm."

"Maybe she just made a mistake. Maybe she's sorry," Lizbeth heard the words and couldn't believe they had come out of her mouth.

Mazie couldn't either. "Lizbeth Jackson, I am stunned that you would say that. There is no excuse for betrayal. You taught me that... and as far as being sorry, well, Dad was sorry too, but it didn't stop him. If you were Gray, would you forgive Dana?"

"I did, the first time, and that's what scares the hell out of me. I know how easy it is to make that mistake."

Fanny chuckled, causing both Lizbeth and Mazie to look at her. "I don't know a lot, but I do know Gray. She don't usually make the same mistake twice. I ain't never known her, in all her days, forgive anybody that wronged her. She'd even pretend to be over it sometimes, but I knew she was just biding her time. In the end, Gray always got even. She's been waitin' a long time to get square this time."

Lizbeth knew what Fanny was saying, but she added her own comment, "Yeah, but she's got to get over her first."

"Come on, Mom. Let's go for a walk." Mazie was lifting Lizbeth out of the chair by the arm. "I think we need to wear you out, or you will never sleep."

"Sleep? Who's going to sleep?" Lizbeth let out a helpless titter.

Fanny called after them, "Make sure she eats!"

#

Mazie and Lizbeth walked down Howard Street, toward the docks. They bought ice cream cones at Kitty Hawk Kites and ate them standing on the porch, looking out over the harbor. They walked by Gray's boat, rocking with the slow rise and fall of the waves. It was a warm night and many people were milling about. Down the boardwalk, an impromptu jam session was taking place near the large yachts and sailboats moored by the ferry dock.

Lizbeth had her arm around Mazie's waist and Mazie's arm was thrown over her mother's shoulders. They stood there, leaning on each other, listening to the man with the clarinet send out his song over the open water. The Blues took on a whole other haunting ache, its echo across the slick surface bouncing back from the other side.

Lizbeth grew nervous that Gray would come back and she wouldn't be there. She told Mazie she needed to go home and eat. The ice cream cone was not the kind of food she needed to settle her spinning head. Mazie, remembering Fanny's warning and having witnessed her mother's spells herself, agreed that it was a good idea. It was after nine and Lizbeth had usually eaten by then. Once again, she had let Gray occupy her thoughts so much she had forgotten. It was also a great excuse to hurry home.

They had to walk by Gray's boat again on the way. As they neared the slip, Lizbeth heard Gray's laughter. She froze. Mazie ran into her from behind.

"Geeze, Mom. A little warning on the brakes," Mazie protested.

Lizbeth said nothing. She raised her hand to quiet her daughter and concentrated on the voices coming from the dock. She crept as close as she dared. She knew it was wrong to eavesdrop, but she couldn't help herself. She maneuvered into a position where she could see Gray in the boat, but still remain in the shadows. She could feel Mazie's breath on her neck. Mazie had figured out what was happening very quickly and was playing wingman on the mission.

Dana's voice came from above Gray. She was still on the dock. She giggled and said, "Here, hold my beer. I'm a little buzzed to be crawling down this ladder."

Gray laughed, reached up, and took the beer from Dana's hand. Gray moved over in front of the ladder, poised to help Dana if she fell. Of course she did. Lizbeth saw through that move easily. Dana, instead of turning around and backing down the ladder, faced Gray and attempted a descent. She made two rungs before falling into Gray and sliding down her body. Gray caught her without dropping the beer and held her just a little too long for Lizbeth's taste. She heard a sharp intake of breath behind her ear, as Mazie must have seen it too.

Gray released Dana and went to the bow. She untied the bowline, started the engine, released the stern line, and sat down on the seat at the console with Dana. The running lights on the boat flicked on. In the glow from the console, Lizbeth could see Dana smile over at Gray as she backed the boat into the harbor. Dana slid her arm around Gray's waist and Gray's arm went around Dana, pulling her close into her side. Gray turned the boat toward the mouth of the harbor and slowly pulled away.

Lizbeth's hands went to her face. They tried to rub the image of what she had just seen away, but it didn't help. She clasped her hands below her chin in a sign of prayer, pursed her lips, and sighed heavily. Mazie put her arm around her mother's shoulder.

"I am so sorry, Mom. I would have never bet on that happening. I was sure she was in love with you."

Lizbeth bit her lip so she wouldn't cry. Her mind raced away from her for a moment. Everything around her disappeared. She could only see flashes of the last ten days, much as she imagined her life would flash by her in the end. When the last images faded and her surroundings became real again, Lizbeth blinked her eyes and focused. The task was daunting, but Lizbeth was determined to be packed and off this island, before the last ferry left at midnight. Gray wasn't coming back.

Lizbeth started walking quickly without a word to Mazie, who was trying to keep in step beside her. Mazie was reasoning the situation aloud. "You don't know what that was all about. Maybe they're just taking a ride. Maybe Gray's just taking her time, waiting for the right moment. You heard what Fanny said, she might be taking her out to dump the body."

"You saw her. I don't think dumping Dana's body is what's on Gray's mind. More like fucking her out there on the high seas is my guess." Lizbeth had made up her mind that Gray couldn't resist Dana. She hadn't thought Gray was strong enough and she had been right. Gray might have thought she was in love with Lizbeth, but when she was presented with Dana in the flesh, Gray had been forced to face the truth. She would always be in love with Dana and Lizbeth couldn't and wouldn't compete with that.

Mazie was having a hard time staying up with Lizbeth without breaking into an all out run. "Slow down. Where are we going? What are we doing?"

Self-preservation mode kicked in. Lizbeth remembered it well. It had gotten her through some of the worst times. Lizbeth allowed it to guide her. She trusted it to make all the decisions. Lizbeth had been making the decisions herself up to now, and look what a mess she'd made.

Lizbeth's voice was scary calm, even to her. "Mazie, I know you've had a long day, so you can stay, but I'm leaving."

"Where are you going?"

"I'm going back to Durham, where I belong," Lizbeth answered.

Mazie didn't think that was a good idea. "You should wait until morning. You did give her that long."

Lizbeth was determined. "I don't need to wait. I saw enough."

Mazie grabbed Lizbeth and brought her to a halt. "Stop! Just stop! Listen to me."

Lizbeth stopped, but she didn't care what Mazie had to say, she was leaving.

"I saw the same thing you saw, Mother, and granted I'm not in love with her, but I think you're letting jealousy cloud your judgment. I still think there's room to hope here. You did tell her to make sure. Maybe that's what she's doing, what you asked of her."

Lizbeth's glare took Mazie aback. She released her grip on her mother's shoulders when Lizbeth said, "Mazie, I love you, but get out of my way."

Mazie gave it one more try. "There won't be a hotel with an empty room all the way to Durham. We'll leave on the first ferry tomorrow morning."

Lizbeth had turned her fear and hurt into anger. "You stay. I am getting the fuck off this island!"

Mazie saw no reason to argue. While her mother went to pack, Mazie crossed the street to where Fanny was still sitting on the porch. Lizbeth could see them talking through the upstairs windows as she packed her suitcases. Packing was much quicker this time than when she had done it for the trip down. She didn't care how the stuff went into the bags.

Lizbeth balled up clothes and crammed belongings into every opening in the suitcases.

Mazie came in from Fanny's just in time to help pack up the spare bedroom. She began putting research materials and pads containing notes for Lizbeth's paper into boxes and hauling them to the car. They worked quietly, barely speaking. Mazie, it appeared, had decided to go along. Lizbeth ran through the downstairs, grabbing personal items and throwing them into her big canvas shoulder bag. The food she would leave. Someone would come to clean and throw away anything she left behind. Double-checking the washer and dryer, Lizbeth then turned the lights off in the kitchen and prepared to leave for the last time.

She looked around the little kitchen while she stood there in the dark. There was a lifetime of memories in this house, old and new ones. The new ones she hoped in time would fade. Having this short-lived affair with the tall, tanned, blonde across the street had hopefully not marred the old memories. Lizbeth would have to worry about that later. Right now, she had to get away, because she never wanted to see Gray O'Neal again.

Lizbeth walked out the front door, shutting it for the last time. She turned the key in the lock and heard the bolt latch. The loud thud shook her, but she held it together. Lizbeth kept telling herself if she could just get home, then she could fall apart. She turned to leave and discovered Fanny standing by Mazie in the front yard. Lizbeth made her way over to the old woman and hugged her.

"Thank you, Fanny, for everything. You've been really good to me, I'll never forget you."

Fanny, who always had something wise to say, was speechless. Disappointment creased her already leather lined face even more. She held out a card in her hand, finally managing to say, "Mazie gave me your phone number. I'm listed in the book. Call me sometime, Lizbeth. Gray never answers my phone."

"I will, but let me have a little while. I won't forget to call you, I promise. Just give me some time." Lizbeth said, feeling the tears begin to burn through the barrier she had erected against them.

Mazie hugged Fanny and her mother and then got into her car, pulling it out onto the street so Lizbeth could back out in the Mustang. When Lizbeth had her car facing School Road, away from the docks, she paused in the street. She looked around and felt the first tear trickle down her check. Fanny tapped on Lizbeth's partially opened window. She had walked toward her house and stopped to wave goodbye to Lizbeth. Now, she leaned down, peering into the car. Lizbeth rolled down the window all the way.

Fanny put both hands on the car door. "Lizbeth, she's a damn fool and I intend to tell her that. Do you want me to tell her somethin' for you?"

There were a million things going through Lizbeth's head that she would like to say to Gray. The only thing that she could grab onto, as the thoughts whirled in her head, was, "Tell her, I hope she'll be happy."

Lizbeth hit the accelerator, because she could no longer control the flow of the tears that began to pour down her face. Through blurry, water filled eyes, she looked in the side mirror and saw Fanny waving, still standing in the street. Lizbeth looked away, determined not to look back.

Chapter Twelve

It was after four in the morning when Lizbeth pulled her car into the garage at her home in Durham. Lizbeth's home was a monstrosity her husband had insisted they build. He was sorry now. With its five bedrooms and over eleven thousand square feet on five acres, it was much too much house for Lizbeth. Lizbeth had grown accustomed to the finer things in life, but her time in the little cottage on Ocracoke had convinced her she would be happy in a smaller home with much less stuff. She had thought about getting a loft apartment downtown, but wanted to wait until she graduated before making the move.

The soaring ceilings and spiraling stairway were impressive. It was a beautiful home. The property contained a theatre, fitness and sauna room, stone fire pit on the patio, full guesthouse, pool, and spa. The master suite on the second floor was of royal proportions. Lizbeth had worked with a designer on the kitchen layout and loved to supervise huge meals, cooked with the help of a professional chef, and throw parties for guests. That's how she had survived her marriage. She threw herself into being the best wife and mother she could be. Hosting parties for James' clients or baking cookies with Mazie and her friends had seen her through the worst of times.

Lizbeth didn't entertain anymore. She only took the house because James had loved it so. It was an important part of his grandiose self-image. She wanted him to know what it felt like to have to start over, build your life again. Lizbeth hurt James where she could, in his wallet and his ego. It was obvious he had no heart. The house would go on the market soon, and if he wanted it back, she'd make sure he paid top dollar. That was one way to get her money out of the deal in the current housing market. Lizbeth's house appraised at nearly four million dollars.

Behind the gates of her exclusive neighborhood, locked tightly in her mansion, Lizbeth fell apart. She had refused to let Mazie stay with her, saying she needed to just cry it out and get it over with. Mazie had her doubts that it would be that easy. She wanted to stay with Lizbeth and watch over her. Lizbeth refused her company, unplugged all the house phones, and turned her cell phone off. Lizbeth didn't want to see or talk to anyone for a few days. She preferred to wallow in her misery alone.

Lizbeth did not unpack the car when she arrived. She went straight upstairs, took off her clothes, and crawled into bed. She had cried off and on the whole trip. She was spent emotionally and physically. It did not take Lizbeth long to cry herself to sleep. Six hours later, her eyes popped open.

Lizbeth was awakened from a dream of Gray, coming for her as she stood on the shore waiting. Gray was on a boat, but every time she tried to clear the breakers to reach Lizbeth, the wind and rain drove her back, the waves pounding her hull. Lizbeth ran up and down the beach, waving her arms, calling to Gray to rescue her from the unknown island. Each attempt pushed the boat further out to sea. Finally, the boat was just a dot on the horizon and Lizbeth screamed for Gray not to leave her behind. The scream had escaped the land of dreams and reverberated around Lizbeth's cavernous bedroom.

Lizbeth blinked her eyes. It took only that long for the full force of where she was and what had happened to seize her with misery again. Sleep had been a respite from the gnawing agony in her gut. Once more, the pain of loss invaded her every thought and nerve ending in her body. It wasn't just heartbreak. It was a smack down from a mind that would not be led astray again. She was going to remember this pain for a long while. There would be no next time.

Lizbeth threw her body over on its side, trying to force the sleep to return. She buried her face in the pillows, pulling the covers up tightly around her neck. She was naked and the air conditioning was doing its job very well. Lizbeth had lacked the energy to put on clothes to sleep in after removing the ones she had on when she arrived this morning. She normally did not sleep naked. She never had. Mazie came so soon after their marriage, she and James had just never slept without clothes on. She never knew when she would have to get up or when Mazie would join them. In the last ten days, Lizbeth had gotten used to not having anything on in bed, well, except for Gray's body draped across hers.

Her mind lost control of her memory and allowed it to share once again the thrill of Gray holding her while she slept. Gray's lean, smooth muscles pressing into her back, her small round breasts warm and soft against Lizbeth's skin. Gray's legs entwined in hers, those strong arms around her, it all came rushing back. Lizbeth gasped into sobs and stayed that way for some time.

Later, when she was able to climb out of bed and make it downstairs to the kitchen, she sat drinking a cup of coffee, and shoving oatmeal down her throat. She didn't want the food, nor could she taste it. She was simply eating because she had to, or go into shock. She had only a housecoat covering her body. Even her skin hurt. She didn't think she could tolerate clothing yet; maybe after a shower if she could muster the energy. She thought about just getting in the hot tub and letting it do the work. It would help with the tension in her overloaded muscles. She could take a bottle of wine with her. At least if she got drunk, she might pass out. Aching dreams and nightmares would be welcome in comparison to her current state.

Lizbeth's cell phone sat on the kitchen table beside her purse, where she had dropped it upon entering the house. She picked it up and turned it back on. She needed to let Mazie know she was all right, or her darling daughter would be over there pestering her. The phone buzzed and rang with different tones, alerting Lizbeth to missed texts and calls. She had programmed Gray's cell phone info into it days before. When she flipped it open and pressed the missed calls button, she saw Gray's name fill up the screen. As she scrolled down the screen, she saw that Gray had called nearly every fifteen minutes since seven o'clock that morning.

All it meant to Lizbeth was that it had taken that long for Gray to discover she was gone. That was all she needed to know. Although she had told Gray that she had until morning to make up her mind, if it had been an all-nighter, it proved to Lizbeth that she wasn't the one. The only one that made Gray's heart beat faster. The only one that Gray truly loved. Lizbeth had been "not the only one" before. That wasn't what she wanted from Gray. Lizbeth needed to be somebody's "only one."

Lizbeth wished that she had not fallen for Gray. What started as flirting and curiosity turned so quickly into total infatuation. If it had just stayed that way, Lizbeth could have let Gray bed her, notch her bedpost, and move on. Lizbeth fell hard for Gray and there was no way she could be around her, talk to her, or even be on the same island with her if she couldn't love her. Lizbeth could not let herself love Gray if she was not the one that Gray wanted without question or doubt. Last night clearly showed that doubt existed, so there really wasn't anything left to say.

Lizbeth set the phone down, rising to get a refill of coffee. Before she had taken a step, it began to ring and vibrate across the surface of the table. Lizbeth picked it up. She saw Gray's name on the caller ID. She held the phone, staring down at the screen. Something began to boil inside her.

Along with the pain of heartbreak came the rage. Rage was the emotion Lizbeth most feared. It left her unable to control what she said and did. Rage was like a child lashing out in pain, wanting to inflict the hurt it feels on everyone around it. Lizbeth had let rage loose a time or two on James, but wound up horrified by her behavior and the hateful, awful things she had said. Although he deserved her wrath, threatening to prevent him from ever speaking to Mazie again and physically attacking him with various objects from the shelves and walls in the den had not been her finest hour. She was always grateful his golf clubs had still been in the car.

Rage was bubbling just below the surface, telling Lizbeth to answer the phone. She did, but only pushed the receive button, followed immediately by shutting the phone. The phone was connected just long enough for Lizbeth to hear Gray say her name. Rage flashed when the phone immediately rang again. Lizbeth's eyes narrowed as she focused on the name, flashing on the caller I.D. Rage won out. She flipped the phone to her ear. She did not give Gray time to speak.

"I told you not to try to explain. Fuck you, Gray. Leave me the hell alone."

Lizbeth slammed the phone shut. Rage had its say, but was not appeased. To make sure her rage was satisfied, Lizbeth hurled the phone against the wall, shattering it into pieces. She forgot all about calling her daughter. She snatched open the wine cooler, grabbed two bottles, the opener and a glass, and headed for the hot tub.

#

They found her naked, passed out in the corner of the shower, three hours later. She had an empty bottle of wine gripped tightly in her hands and clutched to her chest. The first thing Lizbeth heard and recognized as not a dream was Molly Kincaid's voice.

"Oh, honey…look at you. Come on Lizbeth. Let's get you out of there."

Hands grasped her body and she let them lift her off the wet tile. She crumpled to the bathroom floor as Mazie and Molly wrapped her in towels, speaking softly in turn to Lizbeth, who had lost the drive to function. Lizbeth had not wanted this to happen. She had tried to stop the relationship before it got this far. She didn't want to go down as hard as before, but down she went into the blackness of not feeling anything. Unable to care for herself in this state, Mazie and Molly fussed around trying to revive her.

Mazie's voice was shaky with tears. "Mom… Mom… I'm so sorry. I shouldn't have left you alone… I'm so sorry."

Molly took control of the situation. "Mazie, go get your mother some dry clothes. Let me talk to her."

Mazie left. Lizbeth was aware of what was happening. She could see and hear everything, but it felt like she was inside a fish tank looking out at the world swimming around her. Molly wasn't much bigger than Lizbeth, but she had been an athlete and stayed in shape. She pulled Lizbeth to her feet. Lizbeth was limp as a noodle and offered not much help. Molly put Lizbeth's arm around her shoulder and lifted her enough to be able to get Lizbeth onto a nearby couch, in the dressing room.

Molly covered Lizbeth in the thick terry cloth robe she found hanging on the wall. With Lizbeth now sitting up, Molly got on her knees in front of her, so she could look into Lizbeth's down turned face. The wine had done its job. Lizbeth was drunk and numb.

"Lizbeth, we have to get you dry and sober. Are you hearing me? When did you eat last?"

Without notice, Lizbeth jerked to the side and vomited all over the floor. Molly jumped out of the way, but chuckled. "Good. That'll help." She hunted around and found a trashcan, holding it for Lizbeth while she retched, and keeping Lizbeth's hair out of her face. "Lizbeth, we have just crossed a new threshold in our friendship. You know you have a true friend if they'll hold your hair while you puke."

Mazic came back with clothes in her hands. Seeing the situation, she said, "Oh God, Mom." She looked at Molly. "Is she okay?"

Molly tried to ease Mazie's concern. "She's going to be fine. Just got the wind knocked out of her." Molly looked at the floor and grinned. "I guess she's paying you back for all the times she had to clean up after you."

#

Molly sent Mazie to the store because Lizbeth really had no food in the house. She had planned to be gone until December and removed all the perishables before she left. Mazie returned with stuff to make sandwiches she knew her mother would eat, and chicken soup, because that's what she thought you gave someone who was sick. Carolinians swear by the healing powers of Coke, so she brought a two-liter and a six-pack of little bottles because they were the best.

Now, Molly sat feeding Lizbeth bite sized pieces of toast and forcing her to drink the Coke to get her sugar levels up. Mazie buzzed around the kitchen cutting up vegetables for the deli sandwiches that she intended to force her mother to eat. Molly spoke softly to Lizbeth.

"Honey, you have to eat. If you don't come back soon, I'm taking you to Duke Hospital."

Molly knew Lizbeth well enough to know that would get a rise out of her. Lizbeth had eaten half the piece of toast very slowly and had a few gulps of Coke, so she was coming around, but barely. She rolled her eyes at Molly and snatched the bread from her hand. She bit a piece and chewed the dry bread forcefully to appease Molly.

Molly laughed. "Okay, I see you in there. Eat both pieces of your toast and I'll leave you alone."

Lizbeth remained silent, but set about the business of getting the food and Coke down. Slowly her senses began to return. She no longer had the inside the fish bowl feeling. She once again felt a part of the same world occupied by the rest of humanity. Lizbeth finished the last bite and chased it with the remainder of the Coke in her glass. Molly refilled the glass, sat back, and waited. She was patient and gave Lizbeth the time to gather her scattered thoughts back into some kind of order.

Lizbeth finally managed a whispered, "Thank you."

Molly leaned in and looked Lizbeth in the eyes. "Are you with me now?"

Lizbeth nodded yes.

"Good, then listen to me. Mazie told me what happened. Lizbeth, I think you overreacted." Lizbeth started to protest. Molly wouldn't let her. "No, you need to listen to me on this one. Lizbeth, lesbian relationships don't often end as neatly as heterosexual ones. From what Mazie said and how much she thinks this Gray really loves you, I think you made a mistake taking off like you did. I did notice you closed the lines of communication rather permanently." Molly pointed at the pieces of Lizbeth's cell phone, now neatly piled on the table.

Mazie piped in, "That's why I called Molly. You unplugged the house phones and you obviously couldn't answer that." She pointed at the phone pile on the table. "I was afraid of what I'd find when I got here."

Lizbeth said, hoarsely, "I'm sorry if I scared you."

"It's okay, Mom. Are you feeling better?"

"Yes," Lizbeth answered, unable yet to have a full-blown conversation.

Molly took one of Lizbeth's hands in hers, getting her attention again. "Lizbeth, I know what happened here, or at least I think I do. This Dana person made the same pilgrimage a lot of people do, when they realize how incredibly badly they have behaved and what they lost by doing so. In some cases, it is simply to acknowledge the pain they caused and apologize. In others, it is a last ditch effort to reclaim a lost love, believing the fantasy that once they tell the ex-lover how sorry they are for letting them go, all the pain will go away and they will live happily ever after. It seldom, if ever, works out that way, but people continue to try."

Lizbeth rallied somewhat. "But Molly, I was right. She didn't know I was even gone until seven o'clock this morning. She spent the night with her."

This was news to Molly. She sat back against the kitchen chair, silently assessing this new information.

Mazie asked, "How do you know when she found out? Did you talk to her?"

"When I turned the phone back on there were all these missed calls from her that started right after seven."

Molly became more interested; leaning forward, she asked, "Did you listen to the messages?"

Lizbeth drank some more Coke, feeling her wits start to sharpen. She snapped back, "No, I don't want to hear her try to explain. I've listened to speeches like that before. I don't want to hear her lie."

Mazie walked over and picked up a piece of Lizbeth's phone. "Well, I don't guess that's a problem now."

Molly wasn't finished. "So you haven't talked to her?"

Lizbeth answered sharply, "I talked. I did not listen."

Mazie wanted to know, "What did you say to her?"

"I told her to fuck off and leave me alone, and then I hung up on her. That's when I disabled the phone."

"Disabled, yeah." Molly laughed. "Guess there's no doubt in her mind where you stand, is there?"

"Mom, I want to know what she said." Mazie left the kitchen, calling back over her shoulder, "What's your voicemail password?"

Lizbeth shouted after her, "I'm not telling you."

Mazie returned from having retrieved her own cell phone from the foyer, where she had left her purse. She smiled sweetly at her mother. "That's okay, Mom, you use the same password for everything. I got it." Mazie hit the speed dial button for her mother's cell and listened. She pulled the receiver away from her head and punched in four digits. Returning the phone to her ear, she listened again and then smiled. "Predictable," she said to her mother.

"Mazie, I don't want to know."

Mazie responded with, "Then I won't tell you." She walked away when she pressed the number one, to start the message playback.

Lizbeth drank more Coke and stared straight ahead, as if ignoring Mazie on the phone could save her from reality. It was a valiant effort, but Molly's expression of intrigue while she watched Mazie's reaction to the messages did nothing to keep Lizbeth from wondering what excuse Gray had offered. It took a few minutes for Mazie to go through all the messages, but when she turned back around, she had tears in her eyes. Lizbeth felt worse immediately. Mazie was about to confirm what Lizbeth already suspected. Gray had decided to go back to Dana.

Mazie put her phone down on the table. She came over to her mother, pulling a chair up to sit in front of her. She shook her head from side to side. This was all very dramatic and Molly couldn't take it anymore.

"What in God's name did she say, Mazie?"

"Mom, I'm sorry, but you went through all of this for absolutely no reason."

Lizbeth shuddered. She knew she had put herself through so much heartache because she was stupid enough to fall for a total stranger, a woman at that, without having all the facts first. She said, "I know, I was such an idiot."

"No, Mom. You shouldn't have left."

Lizbeth was doubly shaken. "What in the hell are you talking about? Why are you crying?"

Mazie's tears rose again. "Because Gray loves you and you're breaking her heart. I could hear it in her voice."

Lizbeth shot up out of the chair. "What! I'm breaking her heart?"

Mazie started to smile. "Molly was right. Gray was ending it with Dana for good. They just took a boat ride because Dana wanted to for old time's sake. Somebody stole the gas out of Gray's boat. She didn't look at the gauges because she said she had just filled the boat that afternoon. She was stranded out in the inlet till sunrise, when someone came to get her. Her cell phone was dead or she would have called you."

Molly started laughing. Lizbeth couldn't believe it. She stared at her daughter for a second, and then said, "You have got to be fucking kidding me."

Mazie began to laugh as well. "No, Mom, you had your breakdown a little prematurely this time. I told you, you should have waited for her."

"Don't be a smartass," Lizbeth shot at Mazie and then turning on Molly she said, "And what in the hell are you laughing about?"

Molly shook her head from side to side. "Nothing, just good ol' fashioned lesbian drama."

The doorbell rang at that moment, startling all three women. Lizbeth recovered first. "It's got to be a neighbor. I haven't left anyone's name at the gate and besides, no one knows I am home but you two. Get rid of them for me Mazie, please."

Mazie left to deal with the visitor, still giggling at her mother. Molly looked at Lizbeth and said, "I have to say it, Lizbeth. I think you owe this Gray an apology."

"I do, too," the voice behind her said, snapping Lizbeth's head around.

Molly stood up. Lizbeth caught the look on Molly's face. Molly was stunned. Charlize Theron was in Lizbeth's kitchen and heading straight for them.

Mazie was all smiles behind Dana. She said to Lizbeth, "Mom, Miss Fox has something to tell you."

Of course, her name would be Fox. What else could it be? Lizbeth was standing in her kitchen, wet hair drying in mats on her head, only a robe between her and complete nudity. She pulled the robe closed tighter. She motioned for Dana to take Mazie's vacated seat. All the while, Molly stood there with an odd expression of awe as Dana approached them.

"Dana, won't you sit down," Lizbeth said, casting a questioning look at Molly. "Molly, are you going to sit back down?"

Molly fumbled with her chair. "Yes," was all she could manage to say.

Lizbeth got tickled at Molly. Molly was always so sure of herself. Lizbeth had never seen her literally gush over anything, especially not a woman. It was usually the other way around, with Molly inundated with women seeking to get a piece of the extremely successful, very rich, lesbian lawyer.

Lizbeth introduced them. "Dana, this is my good friend Molly Kincaid."

Dana extended her hand to shake Molly's, saying, "It's a pleasure to meet you Molly. I'm sorry it isn't under different circumstances."

The usually confident Molly blushed and only replied, "Me too."

Lizbeth smiled at Mazie, who had noticed Molly's captivation with the stunning Miss Fox. Mazie giggled. Molly finally released Dana's hand. Lizbeth thought she saw a twinge of blush on Dana's face, too, but she let it go. She was really more interested in why Dana was at her house and even better, how did Dana find her?

"Dana, why are you here?" Lizbeth asked.

Before turning away from Molly, Dana said to her, "Molly, has anyone ever told you, you look just like Jodie Foster?"

Molly blushed even redder. "Yes."

Dana continued, "It's uncanny really. She's one of my favorites. I would know."

Molly gushed, "Well, you look like Charlize Theron, no kidding."

Lizbeth was entertained, but growing impatient. "As much as I'm enjoying this little celebrity lookalike contest, I would much prefer to discuss my life, which I appear to have fucked up royally."

Dana pulled herself away from Molly's stare. "I'm sorry, Lizbeth. You want to know why I'm here. It's because Gray doesn't deserve what you did to her."

Lizbeth took offense. "What I did to her?"

"Yes. She is heartbroken and inconsolable. She did right by you, Lizbeth. I'll be honest with you."

"Please do," Lizbeth interjected.

"I went to Ocracoke to tell Gray how wrong I had been and beg her to take me back. I survived a cancer scare last year and it got me thinking about how I had screwed up the best thing that ever happened to me. I didn't want it to be easy for her to tell me no. I knew it would be harder in person."

Mazie sat a cup of coffee down in front of Dana. Dana said, "Thank you," and then returned her attention to Lizbeth. "She never gave me a chance to ask her. Lizbeth, the first words out of her mouth were, 'I don't care what you've come here to say. I'm in love with someone else,' and she is... with you."

Molly clapped her hands together. "See, I told you."

Dana laughed at Molly. Lizbeth stared in disbelief. She still wasn't sure she understood; after all, she saw the way Gray looked at Dana on the boat.

"Dana, I saw you on the boat. Gray didn't act like she was in love with someone else, the way she was looking at you."

"We were together a long time, Lizbeth. Those were just memories in her eyes, nothing more." Dana leaned forward just a little. "I didn't give up as easily as it sounds, but Gray stood her ground. I even tried to get her drunk, but it didn't work. All she talked about was you."

"Oh no! What have I done?" Lizbeth said, her hands flying to cover her mouth.

"I'll tell you, if I hadn't been on that boat, she would have swum to shore. She couldn't leave me out there alone, in case the weather changed or something. She was crazed with worry about what you must have been thinking. If she finds out who stole the gas, she's liable to kill them."

"Does she know you were coming here?"

Dana shook her head from side to side. "No, actually the last thing she said to me was, and I quote, 'Get the fuck off my island and don't come back.' She was extremely angry and I really don't blame her. I screwed this up for her and for that, I truly wanted to apologize. I knew she wouldn't listen to me, so I got your phone number from Fanny and when you wouldn't answer, I did a reverse look-up and got your address. I had a rental car and GPS so here I am."

"How did you get past the gate?" Lizbeth asked and then answered her own question. "With looks like that, I imagine it wasn't that hard."

Dana grinned. "It comes in handy sometimes."

"Well, Mom, what are you going to do now, call and apologize?" Mazie held out her cell phone.

"I don't know her number. It was on my cell." All heads turned and looked at the pile of phone parts on the table.

Dana shrugged her shoulders. "I don't have it either. She got a new one when she left and I never knew it. I always just called Fanny's number. I have that right here."

Dana dug around in her purse for her cell and wrote the number down on a napkin. Lizbeth took the phone from Mazie with trembling hands. She was scared at how angry Gray was going to be with her. Dana must have sensed her hesitation.

"Go on. She won't be as mad as she is glad to hear from you. She really is in love with you, Lizbeth. Don't leave her twisting any longer."

All eyes were on Lizbeth as she dialed the phone. She put the receiver to her ear and waited as the ringing began. Lizbeth's heart was racing by the time she heard Fanny say hello.

"Fanny, this is Lizbeth."

"Lord child, did you finally find a phone that worked? I've been calling the number Mazie left me, but it went straight to voicemail."

Lizbeth was confused. "You were calling me?"

"Yes, after you told Gray off she stormed out of here and I haven't seen her since. Lizbeth, you've got to come back. I never seen Gray like this."

The alarm in Fanny's voice frightened Lizbeth. "I'll leave right now. Keep looking for her. I'll be there as soon as I can."

"Lizbeth," Fanny paused. "She tried to get back to you."

"I know. Tell her I'm sorry and I'm coming, okay?"

Lizbeth hung up the phone and looked into the expectant eyes around her. She stood up suddenly. "I have to go back. Gray's run off and no one can find her. Fanny's worried." She started out of the room.

Molly said, "Wait, Lizbeth. I can help you."

"I can't wait, Molly. I have to go now. I've got to get there as soon as I can."

Mazie interrupted. "Mom, you just recovered from being drunk and passed out an hour ago. You haven't had any sleep. That's a long drive."

Lizbeth was insistent. "I don't care. I'll drink two pots of coffee, if I have to, but I'm leaving here in fifteen minutes. Lock up when you go."

"Lizbeth, stop," it was Molly. "I can help you get there faster."

"Molly, I appreciate it, but I don't need you to drive me."

Molly grinned. "I don't plan on driving you," she paused for effect, "I have a jet."

#

"Molly, I knew you were well off, but a jet?" Mazie asked from the backseat of Molly's car.

Molly laughed. "I got it after a big case. It was part of the deal."

Lizbeth, sitting with Mazie in the back, tried to remember. "Which case?"

Molly made eye contact in the rearview mirror with Lizbeth and grinned. "I'll never tell."

Molly invited Dana, to Lizbeth's dismay, along for the ride to the airport. Molly seemed to intrigue the Texan. She asked, "And this jet is just waiting for whenever you need it?"

Lizbeth noticed Molly's eyes twinkle when she looked over at Dana. Molly answered, her Jodie Foster grin and dimples showing more than usual, "I'm set up through a charter company and rent it to other business associates when I don't need it. It's an extravagance, but I can go where I want pretty easily."

"Planning any trips to Texas?" Lizbeth quipped, while at the same time goosing Molly under the seat with her foot. She couldn't resist.

Molly's eyes flicked back to Lizbeth's in the mirror. Guilty! It was written all over her face. Molly was smitten with the charming Miss Fox. They were riding in Molly's Lexus, on the way to Raleigh Durham Airport's private hangers. An hour and a half had passed since Lizbeth talked to Fanny. In that time she had taken the suitcases out of the car and repacked them, showered and redressed, eaten a sandwich Mazie insisted on, and put her fate in Molly's hands.

Molly got on the phone, arranging for her pilots to ready the jet for the flight to Manteo. She knew they were available, because she had cancelled a trip to come to Lizbeth's rescue. The tiny Ocracoke airport's three thousand foot runway was not long enough for the jet to land there. From Manteo, Molly chartered a small plane for the rest of the way. Someone would meet Lizbeth at the airport and deliver her to Gray's door by six thirty or seven, just before the airport on Ocracoke closed for the night. Lizbeth offered to pay Molly, but Molly waved her off, saying, "Consider it my welcome to the family gift."

Before leaving the house, Molly had come up to Lizbeth's room to tell Lizbeth the plan was in play. Molly stood in the dressing room door, while Lizbeth applied her make-up and tried to repair the damage the last twenty-four hours had done. Dana was still downstairs because, Molly informed Lizbeth, she was staying for dinner.

Molly was defending her actions. "She did do a really nice thing, I mean, she didn't have to drive all the way here and tell you what an idiot you are. She doesn't have a flight out until the morning. She's here alone and..."

Lizbeth put her hands up in defeat. "Okay, okay, Molly. I get it. She's pretty."

Molly gushed, "No fucking kidding."

Lizbeth laughed. "You know, you and Gray are a lot alike. She can't think around a pretty girl either."

"Then she must have been walking around the last few days in a stupor. You're a beautiful woman, Lizbeth."

"Thank you, Molly... for everything." Lizbeth stood and gave Molly a hug.

"It was my pleasure," Molly said, patting Lizbeth on the back. "Now, go find your lady love and get on with being happy."

Lizbeth walked over and checked herself in the mirror. Maybe if she took a nap on the plane, she wouldn't look so tired. She had on a summer weight white cotton, sweater/shell combination. Her newly tanned skin glowed in stark contrast. She wore navy blue Capri pants and looked every bit the southern upper class housewife that she was. It was the first time she noticed the stark contrast between her and Gray, but she smiled because they complimented each other. Gray's charming tomboy played well against Lizbeth's feminine curves.

Lizbeth stood peering at her reflection long enough to compel Molly to say, "Lizbeth, you look great. She's not going to care if you show up in a tow sack."

Lizbeth laughed, remembering Gray's comment about her looking good in a tow sack. "Well, it'll have to do," she said, "I just hope I know what to say. How do you say, I'm so sorry, I'm an idiot?"

Molly chuckled. "That sounds about right."

Lizbeth turned to Molly. She began to grin. "How did you keep this a secret so long? I feel like running around telling everyone that they have no idea what they are missing. The sex is mind blowing."

Molly laughed and clapped her hands together. "Lizbeth, you are a trip. I am so glad you have discovered your destiny. In defense of the rest of the world, I must say that I am sure the sex in many different kinds of relationships is mind blowing to the individuals participating. I think it has more to do with finding the one person who takes you there, male or female."

Lizbeth smiled broadly. "I think I found her."

"I think you did, too." Molly put her arm around Lizbeth's shoulder and escorted her from the room. "So, about this Dana..."

"Oh no, Molly, you can't be serious."

"Lizbeth, she's hot, I mean really hot."

Lizbeth looked at Molly and recognized the symptoms. "It's been a while, huh, Molly."

Molly's lips twitched into a grin. "Yes, it has. Hey, it's just dinner. She'll be back in Texas tomorrow. She's just lost the love of her life..."

Lizbeth giggled. "Shooting for some sympathy sex there, Molly?"

"Something like that," Molly said, grinning from ear to ear.

Lizbeth stopped before they exited the bedroom. Molly was so much like Gray in her charm and wit. A thought crossed her mind. She asked the still grinning Molly, "What if Dana falls madly in love with you, what then?"

"No, Lizbeth. They always go home. That's my policy."

"I heard something exactly like that from another lesbian this week. I cannot wait for you to meet Gray. I think she's your clone."

"She'll be gone before you get back, I promise," Molly assured her.

"Don't make promises, Molly. Stranger things have happened. Besides, I don't want to come back. I have a plan and it requires your help."

Molly winked at Lizbeth. "Oh, I love plans"

#

They were all standing in the hanger, waiting for Lizbeth to board. Hugs went all around. Lizbeth even hugged Dana and thanked her for coming to straighten things out. Mazie gave Lizbeth her cell phone since she had destroyed hers, and promised to box up and mail all the research materials Lizbeth had left in the Mustang.

"Well, Lizbeth, good luck," Molly said, giving Lizbeth a kiss on the cheek.

"She's mad right now, but she'll be glad to see you," Dana said, adding, "I wish the both of you many happy years together."

Molly turned to Mazie. Out of politeness, Lizbeth was sure, Molly asked, "Mazie, would you like to join us for dinner?"

"No, thank you. Just drop me at the house. I've had quite enough lesbian drama for one twenty-four hour period. I'm going home to my simple little life and my simple little man. Women are complicated."

The laughter of the four women rang through the hanger.

Chapter Thirteen

The trip itself was uneventful. The Cessna Citation jet was sleek and fast and made the trip from Raleigh-Durham to Manteo in less than an hour of flying time. While on the ground, as her bags were being transferred from the jet to the plane, Lizbeth attempted to reach Fanny, but no one answered, which she thought was odd.

Lizbeth caught a nap on the jet, just a short one, but it helped. She had been consuming water as if she had been lost in a desert for days. Luckily, the Citation had a fully stocked kitchenette. She nibbled on snacks because she wanted to have it all together when she faced Gray.

It wasn't just that Lizbeth left without talking to Gray. Gray was going to be angry that Lizbeth didn't trust her, didn't believe her when Gray said she loved her. Lizbeth had hurt Gray and, like Fanny said, Gray didn't like to be hurt. She would lash out at Lizbeth and Lizbeth had to be strong enough to weather the storm, because she deserved it. When the wind blew through, Lizbeth hoped it wouldn't be too bad. Maybe

Gray's anger would just be a tropical depression and not a full-blown hurricane.

On the way across the Pamlico Sound to Ocracoke, Lizbeth looked out the windows at the boats leaving trails across the water. The Sound was dark blue in its few deep channels, interspersed with shallower greens and sandbar tans and whites. Lizbeth imagined that it would be easy to hit one of those sandbars if you didn't know the water very well. Gray had told her stories of fishing on the Fanny Gray with her grandfather. Her friends Cora Mae and Jane ran the boat on a daily basis and Gray pitched in when the tourists went home. They had planned to go out fishing with Cora Mae and Jane on Gray's next day off, before all this happened. Lizbeth wondered if one of the little specks below was the Fanny Gray.

True to her word, Molly had a guest services Hummer pick her up and drop her off in front of Gray and Fanny's cottage. The driver put her suitcases on Lizbeth's porch, but she went straight to Fanny's door and knocked. She held her breath, hoping Gray would answer the door. She did not. It was a very worried looking Fanny, who flung the door open and hugged Lizbeth tightly.

"My Lord, child. Did you fly?"

Lizbeth smiled at Fanny. "As a matter of fact, I just discovered I have a friend with a jet."

"Must be a very good friend." Fanny finally smiled.

"Yes, Miss Fanny, the best kind of friend." Lizbeth looked around, hoping for signs of Gray. "I called, but got no answer. Have you heard from Gray?"

"You must have called when I walked down to the docks to look for her."

"You still don't know anything?" Lizbeth was disappointed.

"Sun's going down. She ought'a be showing up soon," Fanny said. "She won't stay on the Fanny Gray in the dark.

She's been working on the electrical system and half the lights is out."

"So you know where she is?" Lizbeth was relieved. At least she had a location for Gray.

They sat down on the porch. That's when Lizbeth noticed the phone clutched in Fanny's hand and the marine band radio crackling with communications occasionally from inside the house. The look of worry returned to Fanny's face.

"Cora Mae called. Gray ended up over there with a jar of moonshine she bought off one of them Swan Quarter boys. Lizbeth, Gray don't drink hard liquor much. It's always a sign she's about to blow when the bottle comes out."

Lizbeth pursed her lips. "Oooo... she must really be mad."

"She got accused of somethin' she didn't do and then couldn't convince you of it. Gray was as mad as I've ever seen her. She sure as hell wasn't in no frame a mind to listen to me when she left. Blamed me for not makin' you stay, for not believin' in her."

"Then she ought to be thrilled with me," Lizbeth threw out.

"I think she will be happy to see you, but don't expect her to jump up and down. Her pride is wounded. She'll hide how she really feels to spite herself."

"I really don't blame her for being mad. I did jump to conclusions," Lizbeth admitted. "Dana came to see me."

Fanny looked surprised. "She did?"

"She said Gray didn't deserve this and it was her fault, well, and the asshole who stole the gas. What I saw at the dock was just Gray saying goodbye. I misread everything."

Fanny let a thin smile creep onto her face, not replacing the worry, only taking her mind away for a second. "Well now, maybe I misjudged that girl. When she asked for your number, I saw no harm in it. You weren't answerin' anyway."

"I'm glad you did. She found me and that's why I called you." Lizbeth reached out and patted Fanny's knee. "So,

Gray's drunk somewhere out on a boat with Cora Mae and Jane."

Fanny's facial expression darkened. "Not exactly. Gray is drunk, but she's out on the boat alone. She got in a shoutin' match with Jane, who is trash from down east and should never let alcohol cross her lips. Cora Mae has had a time with that one. I don't know how many times Gray has gone with Cora Mae a lookin' her, when she gets on a drunk."

Lizbeth interrupted Fanny, "I'll learn about Jane's drinking habits later. What happened to Gray?"

Fanny understood the need to hurry along, and did so with no further straying from the main plot. "Cora Mae said Jane hit a nerve, telling Gray she didn't blame you for runnin'. With all the tail Gray's chased, why would anyone trust her?"

Lizbeth gasped. "Oh my God. I'm sure that didn't go over well."

"Not by a long shot," Fanny said, stopping the rocker and growing more serious. "Gray don't never go on the water drunk. Learned that from her granddaddy. I can't call her cell, 'cause she threw her phone at Jane when she took off from the dock behind Cora Mae's. They watched her with binoculars until she disappeared, heading straight northeast toward the mainland."

"I hope she has gas this time," Lizbeth said, not meaning it to sound flippant.

"It ain't the gas that worries me. Jane had the toolbox off the boat working on something. All the safety flares and flashlights were in there, too. If she does get in trouble, she's got nothing to signal with. Her cell phone is in the Sound and the radio has been givin' her fits for months. That's why she was rewirin' it."

"Fanny, you're not really worried about Gray making it back, are you? She's an expert waterman. She'll come back when she sobers up a little."

Fanny looked hard at Lizbeth. "I've knowed a lot of experts ain't come back from the water. That water out there is mean and unforgivin', and she'll make you pay for your mistakes."

Lizbeth was now comforting the old woman, trying to ignore her own growing anxiety. "She'll come dragging up here in a little bit, I'm sure. Don't worry, Fanny."

Fanny looked up toward the sky, peering through the treetops and branches swaying in the light easterly breeze. "No moon tonight they say. Gonna be real dark soon."

Lizbeth patted the old woman's hand. "She'll be back in a minute, you'll see."

The two women waited on the porch in silence for some time. Lizbeth caught herself listening to the traffic on the marine radio inside. She had no idea so many people were out there working on the water or pleasure cruising. The night air was filled with communications, as the unseen world of the nocturnal sea went on unbeknownst to most. Down the street, the sound of music filtered through the trees. There was a banjo and guitar, accompanied by the high-pitched wail of a fiddle singing out the melody of some lonesome Appalachian tune. The tourists had almost all gone home. The end of a summer season was at hand. Although most of the businesses would stay open into November, the tourists would not flock back in droves until next spring. It was still seventy degrees, beautiful weather for sitting on the porch.

It would have been perfect if Fanny and Lizbeth were not growing more apprehensive with each passing moment. The sky turned an inky blue and faded into blackness in a slow dimming into night. There was still no word from Gray. Fanny dialed Cora Mae's number to see if there had been any sign of her. Cora Mae had not seen hide or hair of her, but they had the big lights on the dock pointed out on the Sound, so Gray could find her way back. Lizbeth could tell by Fanny's reaction that Cora Mae was worried, too.

The radio crackled from the parlor. It began to emit a series of loud pops and hisses. Fanny perked up, listening. It clued Lizbeth in that she too should pay attention to the noises. Lizbeth leaned toward the door, listening intently. Her heart leapt to her throat at the first sound of the human voice.

"Mayday, mayday, mayday. This is fishing skiff Fanny Gray, I require immediate assistance. Mayday, mayday, mayday. This is fishing skiff Fanny Gray, calling United States Coast Guard Ocracoke. "

Fanny was on her feet and in the house before Lizbeth could recover from the shock and follow her. The radio crackled again.

"Station calling, this is the United States Coast Guard Ocracoke communications station, over?"

The next part of Gray's message was filled with gaps and garbled information. Her radio was going in and out.

"…for the United States Coast Guard, this is the Fanny Gray. I need…" followed by garbled noise. Then her voice was clear for a second, "My position is," dropping out again, with only the word "west" distinguishable in the static. Gray came back strong again, this time the fear clearly present in her voice. "I am taking on water – engine out – bilge pump dead – electrical failing – radio in and out. I am flooding by the bow. Over?"

The Coast Guard man replied, "Fanny Gray, this is Com Stat Ocracoke, roger. Understand you are taking on water, flooding by the bow. Repeat your position. Say again, repeat your position, over?"

The radio spat and hissed. They waited for Gray's response. After much clicking and popping, they heard, "…northwest of Ocracoke, Pamlico Sound. Exact position unknown... deep water..." The rest was too garbled to comprehend.

"Fanny Gray, this is Com Stat Ocracoke, roger, understand exact position unknown. Request vessel description. Request number of persons on board, over?"

This time Gray's voice was clear. "White, twenty-four foot, Carolina fishing skiff, no running lights now... One soul onboard, over?"

When Gray said she was alone, Lizbeth could hear the anguish in her voice. Gray was scared, on her own out there in the dark, and she was sinking. Although Gray was a strong swimmer, any number of things could happen before the Coast Guard found her. Finding a single swimmer in the wide Pamlico Sound in the middle of the night was going to be difficult without a clue as to where she was.

"Read you loud and clear, Fanny Gray, this is Com Stat Ocracoke, roger. Understand vessel white, twenty-four foot, Carolina fishing skiff, no running lights. One soul on board. Hang tight there Fanny Gray, rescue boat has been dispatched from Ocracoke, over?"

"United States Coast Guard, this is the Fanny Gray. She's going down, boys," the radio crackled and hissed, then Gray came back, "... see lighthouse beam to my southeast... swimming... try to make it to Howard's Reef."

The cracking stopped.

"Fanny Gray, this is Com Stat Ocracoke, over?" Nothing. No popping and hissing. Nothing.

"Fanny Gray, this is Communication Station Ocracoke, over?" The operator paused and added, "Fanny Gray if you can hear me, confirming vessel sinking, swimming southeast. Search and rescue ops under way. Choppers in the air. Stay afloat. We're coming, over?"

Another pause. Then a final communication. "All stations, this is United States Coast Guard Ocracoke. We have a vessel in distress, sinking in Pamlico Sound, northwest of Ocracoke. Exact position unknown. Vessels in the area, be on the lookout for survivor in the water. Repeat, survivor in the water. Assist if possible."

White noise filled the room. Lizbeth was frozen in place. Fanny stood in front of her staring at the little marine radio on the mantel. She didn't move or say anything for a few moments, then she turned the phone she had been holding over in her hand. She started punching buttons then put the receiver to her ear. In a moment, someone picked up on the other end.

"Austin, it's Fanny. Gray's in trouble. The boat sunk out in the Sound, she's swimmin' in." She listened, then answered, "Northwest of the island. She said she was headin' toward Howard's Reef. Coast Guard's on the way." Fanny waited and then added, "All right. I'll be right here," before hanging up.

Fanny turned to Lizbeth, who was still frozen in stunned silence. "They'll find her."

Lizbeth, although quite still, was running a hundred miles an hour in her brain. She was trying to figure out how a drunken Gray was going to swim to shore in the dark. How would she know which way was east? She could use the stars. Gray would know how to do that. Surely she had a floatation device. How cold was the water? How long could she stay afloat? Were there sharks out there? The questions flew by in rapid succession. Lizbeth didn't know the answers to many of them and it frightened her even more.

The radio came alive again as the Coast Guard cutter from Hatteras Inlet joined the rescue boat in the search. Two helicopters, dispatched from Elizabeth City, called out grid assignments. Gray had waxed poetic about the Coast Guard and how much respect she had for them. Her father's best friend had taken a cutter out in thirty-foot seas that no one else would risk. Against orders, he set out to rescue a crew from a sinking fishing vessel. He was unable to get out of Oregon

Inlet, because the sea kept throwing them back into the Sound, so he drove the cutter as fast as he could down the backside of Hatteras Island and out the inlet at Ocracoke, saving all hands. He received the highest award possible for an enlisted man from the President of the United States. In order to receive The Coast Guard Medal an individual must have performed a voluntary act of heroism in the face of great personal danger. The men and women of the Coast Guard were brave and took their mission to help a sailor in distress to heart. Lizbeth prayed they would be up to their best performance tonight.

They spent the next few hours pacing the floor. The news traveled quickly through the village. Friends and neighbors started pouring into the little cottage, spilling out onto the porch. Platters and bowls of food trailed through the door. Cora Mae showed up without the offending Jane. Concern creased their brows, even as the gatherers told funny Gray stories to ease their minds. It reminded Lizbeth of the way people acted at a funeral, the food, the stories, hushed voices, and questioning glances. Gray wasn't dead, she couldn't be. Lizbeth had to get away from these people. When Jaye showed up, she offered to go for a walk with Lizbeth. Lizbeth gave Fanny her daughter's cell phone number, so she could call if she heard anything.

Fanny seemed to understand Lizbeth's need to get out of the house. She kissed her on the cheek and whispered, "You just keep prayin'."

Jaye and Lizbeth found themselves standing by the Swan Quarter ferry dock, staring out into the black water. They could see the lights from some of the boats out looking for Gray. The villagers had rallied to form their own search party, running a line of boats on the backside of the island, moving west into the Sound, hoping to intercept Gray swimming in. Occasionally, the sound of helicopter blades echoed through the air.

"How cold is that water, Jaye? How long can she swim?" Lizbeth asked, peering over the water.

Jaye answered with an islander's certainty. "Sound water's usually about the same as the air temperature, so it's close to seventy in the shallow places, gets colder out deep. Gray can swim in, if she's smart."

Lizbeth argued, "But she's at least ten miles out. I heard what those men in the yard were saying. They said if she was in the deep water, then she was at least that far and she's drunk."

Jaye tried to reassure Lizbeth. "I guarantee you when that boat started sinking she sobered up pretty damn quick. If she keeps moving, the alcohol will burn off, anyway."

"I just hope she can keep moving. Did you hear Cora Mae say they had taken all the lifejackets off the boat to clean them this afternoon, so she doesn't even have one."

Jaye sniffed the air, observing, "Wind's pushing against her, but it's not strong. She can swim from sandbar to sandbar. She can wait a while between swimming. Water's flat so she should be able to see the beacon from the lighthouse even if she's swimming."

"If anything happens to her, I'll never forgive myself. This is my fault."

Lizbeth started to cry for the first time since she knew Gray was in trouble. She had not let herself cry in front of Fanny. Fanny had enough to worry about. Fanny was strong and showed faith that all would be well and they'd all have a good laugh over it later, but Lizbeth knew Fanny was desperately worried for Gray.

Jaye continued to impress Lizbeth with her insight. "I don't 'magine it was you that told her to get on that boat like a damn fool, drunk. From what I gathered, you weren't even on the island at the time."

"How do you know where I was?"

Jaye laughed. "Well, after the scene down at the docks this morning, I kinda figured it out."

Lizbeth's brow creased in question. "What scene?"

Jaye started laughing harder, and her words were interrupted repeatedly by all out guffaws, as she relayed the story of what happened after Gray found out she was gone.

"Gray got hauled in this morning around seven and she was pissed. She stormed down the dock telling anyone that would listen that she was going to find out who stole the gas and kick some ass. She did pull back on that when she found out it was Billy, and he meant to put it back this morning when the store opened. He didn't know she was going out again. She didn't kill him, but she made his ass sorry, that's for sure."

"So all this started because some guy named Billy borrowed her gas." Lizbeth was shaking her head at all the little things that had brought them to this moment. Gray might have been in time to stop Lizbeth from going to Durham, if she had not run out of gas.

Jaye continued, "I overheard Gray tell that pretty blond lady that this was all her fault and that you had left because of her. Gray told her to get the fuck off the island, right there in front of the Community Store."

"Yeah, the pretty blonde told me that part."

"So, you met her. Is that the one?" Jaye asked.

"Yeah, Jaye, she was the one, but it's over, for good. Now, if Gray will just come out of that water, we can go on with our lives."

Jaye threw an arm around Lizbeth's shoulder. "She'll be back. Little bit of water won't stop Gray. If she knew you were on the island again, she'd be here already."

"Do you really think so?"

Jaye smiled. "I've watched Gray real close. I think I know her pretty well and she is head over heels in love with you.

She's probably out there swimming in, thinking about you, and what she's going to say to you if she gets the chance."

"I know what I'm going to say to her, if I get the chance," Lizbeth said. "She's not to take anymore nighttime boat rides with other women. It leads to trouble."

Jaye snickered. "You got that right."

#

Lizbeth woke up on Fanny's parlor couch, with an afghan tossed over her by someone in the night. She had waited until the wee hours of the morning before shutting her eyes against the sheer exhaustion of not knowing. The sun was just coming up and Lizbeth could hear hushed speech in the back of the house. The radio was gone from the mantel, moved into the kitchen, where Lizbeth could hear an occasional crackle of voices from the searchers.

There was still no word from the rescue party. Lizbeth stood and stretched the sore muscles in her neck back into place. She had fallen asleep awkwardly positioned and her body was fighting back with pain. Lizbeth tiptoed to the bathroom in the hall. She relieved her screaming bladder and then stood washing her hands in the sink. She caught her reflection in the mirror. Dark circles from lack of sleep and worry had formed under her eyes. Lizbeth took a shuddering breath and then sat down on the edge of the tub.

Gray had been missing for more than nine hours now. The Coast Guard helicopters had located an oil slick and debris field where they believed the Fanny Gray went down, approximately ten miles off the coast. There was no sign of Gray. The grids had tightened and the search was underway still, with more Coast Guard resources now engaged. They hoped that at daylight they would be able to spot her. Lizbeth couldn't let herself lose hope. It was the only thing keeping her from going over the edge.

In the bleakest of times, even the most staunchly anti-religious person will seek a higher power. Lizbeth realized she could not do this alone. She needed a hand this time. Lizbeth wasn't an extremely religious person, but she believed in God. She knew she was at the end of her rope. She slipped off the edge of the bathtub and dropped to her knees, folded her hands and prayed.

A soft tap on the door startled her. Fanny's voice came through the door. "Lizbeth, are you all right?"

Lizbeth stood and opened the door. She managed a weak smile for Fanny, whose own anxiousness shrouded her face. "I'm fine Miss Fanny."

"Come on, let's feed you." It was just like Fanny to be more worried about Lizbeth than herself.

Lizbeth followed Fanny to the kitchen, where to her surprise they were alone. "Where did everybody go?"

Fanny bustled around cracking eggs and placing bacon on the griddle. "I sent them to the porch for a while. Give me some time to collect my thoughts."

"You and Gray have a lot of friends."

Fanny dropped an egg in the frying pan, where it sizzled. "Kin to most of 'em, but we're all like family here. What happens to one affects us all."

"Fanny, Gray's still out there. I can feel her. I know she's trying to get back to us."

"You hang on to that feeling. I believe Gray's out there, too. Gray's got too much life in her to go down without a fight."

Lizbeth laughed under her breath. "When I do get my hands on her we're going to have a talk about going off drunk and half cocked."

Fanny chuckled. "Get in line. I'm gonna beat her within an inch of her life with a boat paddle, after I hug the tar out of her."

Lizbeth nibbled on the edge of the toast Fanny sat in front of her while she waited on the eggs. "You know, that Sound is shallow. She could swim up on a sandbar out there real easy."

Fanny looked back over her shoulder at Lizbeth from her duties at the frying pan. "How'd you go to know so much about that Sound?"

"I looked up nautical charts on Gray's laptop in her room. She said Howard's Reef and I figure she could have made it there and just be sitting in the shallow water waiting to be picked up."

Fanny turned back to the eggs, but continued talking. "That's a long swim from where they found the slick, 'tween seven an' eight miles, 'magine it would've taken awhile, but God knows as stubborn as that girl is, she will swim that water."

"Yes ma'am, I do believe you're right about that."

The cell phone in Lizbeth's pocket rang. Lizbeth looked at the caller I.D. and saw it was Molly. Evidently, Mazie and Molly had exchanged numbers during Lizbeth's recent downfall. She answered.

Before she could get beyond hello, Molly started talking fast. "Lizbeth, oh my God, I just saw it on the news. Are you okay?"

Lizbeth hadn't thought about anyone but the people on the island knowing about Gray. "Yes, worried sick, but okay." Lizbeth glanced at Fanny and took the phone out onto the back deck to finish the call. The sun was just beginning to dawn.

Lizbeth heard a voice in the background, and then Molly said, "Is there anything I can do?"

"No, just pray, I guess. We're just waiting to hear something, anything. You could call Mazie for me. Tell her I'll call as soon as I know something."

"Okay, I'll do that. Is there anything else?" Molly paused and Lizbeth heard the voice again. "We can be there in a couple of hours if you need us."

Lizbeth was worried, but she wasn't so preoccupied that she couldn't figure out what was going on. "Molly, when you say we, are you referring to you and Mazie, or the other woman there with you?"

Molly chuckled. "Yeah, you're all right. You still have your sense of humor."

"I take it dinner went well," Lizbeth teased.

"Very well," Molly said, and Lizbeth could visualize the smile on her face.

"Then why are you up so early?"

"I was just getting ready to take Dana to the airport. She has an early flight, but she just called and cancelled it. Said she couldn't leave till she knew Gray was all right."

"Molly, keep her in Durham. Whatever you do, do not let her come down here. When I do get my hands on Gray, Dana is the last thing I want to see or discuss. You keep her busy."

Molly laughed loudly. "That, Lizbeth, would be my pleasure."

"God, I'm dying out here and you're getting laid," Lizbeth said, but she was laughing, too.

Molly's tone changed as she said, sincerely, "Lizbeth, I'm praying for you and Gray. She'll be all right. From what I gather, she's quite tough. Dana said she'd make it."

"And yet, Dana is staying because she's afraid she won't," Lizbeth said, gravely.

Molly tried to cheer her, whispering so Dana wouldn't hear, "I'd like to think she used it as an excuse to stay with me just a little longer."

Lizbeth smiled into the phone. "One woman's trash is another woman's treasure, 'ey Molly?"

"You just never know, Lizbeth. You just never know."

"Well, if you do hook up with her, Ocracoke is off limits. I understand lesbians have a tendency to become lifelong friends with their exes. I'm going to hang onto my heterosexual roots here and say I'm not comfortable with that. Not for awhile anyway."

"All right," Molly said. "I'll keep her away from Ocracoke. I haven't spent much time in Texas. I think I'd like to see some of the Wild West."

Lizbeth quipped, "Remember the Alamo."

"Is that a warning?" Molly asked playfully.

"Well, I've seen her take one woman to her knees, shall you be next? Don't forget she professed her undying love for Gray just days ago."

"Hang on a sec," Molly said, and Lizbeth could tell that she was on the move. She heard a door close, and when Molly started talking Lizbeth could tell she had gone in a smaller room, probably the bathroom. Molly asked, "Lizbeth?"

Lizbeth answered, "I'm here."

"Hey, does this Dana thing really bother you?"

Lizbeth took a second to answer. She had to search her soul. If Gray was really done with Dana, then it shouldn't matter to Lizbeth what Dana did or with whom she did it. "Molly, Dana isn't my problem anymore. I believe Gray is finished with her. My concern is with you. Be careful. 'Things are not always what they seem; the first appearance deceives many; the intelligence of a few perceives what has been carefully hidden.'"

"You know your Plato," Molly said, adding, "I'm a big girl, Lizbeth. I see it for what it is and frankly, it doesn't bother me. Women attach too much meaning to sex. It doesn't always have to be about love. It could just be a mutual sexual attraction. I think I've been through enough women to tell the difference."

Lizbeth sighed. "Oh my God, you are just like Gray. Dana is going to fall in love with you and I'm going to have to learn to live with it. I see it coming."

Molly laughed. "Let's hope not. I'm not looking for a relationship. The last one wasn't a pleasant experience."

"I'm so sorry I never talked to you about any of that. I knew when Ann wasn't around anymore, but I just never asked you why."

"Long story," Molly answered, quietly. "We'll talk about it sometime. Just don't worry about me. I can handle Miss Fox."

Lizbeth got it. "You'd know already if she was the one, wouldn't you?"

"Yep. Pretty much like you knew with Gray. I don't get that connection here, but the sex is great and I've had a dry spell, so forgive me my indulgence."

Lizbeth laughed. "Okay, indulge away. Have a good time. I'll call you when I know something. And thanks again, Molly. I love you."

They exchanged goodbyes and Lizbeth went back in the kitchen, where Fanny had filled their plates and was waiting. Lizbeth pulled her chair out and sat down.

"That was Molly, the friend that arranged for the jet. She saw the story on the news."

"Technology sure has made this a small world," Fanny commented.

Lizbeth added, "And yet they can't find a woman swimming in the water less than ten miles from here."

Fanny said grace and then they proceeded to eat in silence. The marine radio squawked out positions. One search block after another was checked off. The sun had completely risen and the sky was bright and clear when they finished breakfast and stepped out on the porch. Fanny made Lizbeth leave the dishes in the sink, because that was Gray's job and she would be home to do them. Lizbeth understood. Fanny had to hang on to what was normal for now. If she swayed in her belief, Gray could perish. Gray was the only thing Fanny had left. She'd buried everybody else. She'd outlived her entire family, except for Gray. Fanny was a strong woman and Lizbeth benefitted from that strength.

An old man Lizbeth recognized from the Community Store stepped up to Fanny on the porch. "Daylight now, Fanny. Slick ca'm out there." Slick ca'm meant the surface of the water was smooth. "Ought to find her anytime, now."

At least that is what Lizbeth thought he said. His brogue was so thick he was hard to understand. Any other time, Lizbeth would have been fascinated, but she couldn't listen for sounds, she wanted information. She remembered the marine radio and went to move it back into the parlor, so they could monitor it from the porch. Just as she plugged it in, a voice rang out over the air.

"Coast Guard rescue vessel in the area. Coast Guard rescue vessel in the area. I am vessel to your right, the blue one, see me, over?"

"This is Coast Guard rescue vessel. We see you."

"I see something floating in the water, off my starboard bow, about a hundred yards, over?"

People started pouring into the house, Fanny in the lead. Lizbeth was still holding the radio, squatted down by the plug she had just placed in the wall. Her hand was still on the plug. Lizbeth held her breath.

"This is Coast Guard rescue vessel. Roger. We see it, blue vessel. Will investigate."

A hand touched Lizbeth's shoulder and helped her to her feet. It was Jaye. She took the radio and placed it on the mantle, while Lizbeth fell up against Fanny. She wrapped her arms around Fanny's waist. Fanny hugged Lizbeth to her. No one made a sound as they waited.

The time ticked by in slow motion. Lizbeth could hear Fanny's heart beating as her head lay against Fanny's shoulder. She could hear breathing around her, all ears trained on the white noise coming from the black box with the flashing red lights.

A crackle was followed by, "Hey, Will, what they pullin' out over there?"

Another crackle. "Stay off the air, jackass. Family's listening."

The radio went silent again. The warning to stay off the air had made Lizbeth more afraid. Fanny had tightened her grip on Lizbeth at those words. The radio came to life again.

"U. S. Coast Guard Comm Stat Ocracoke, this is rescue vessel niner five, over?"

"This is Comm Stat Ocracoke. Roger rescue vessel niner five, over?"

"Comm Stat Ocracoke, we have located a floating object. Launch is in the water. Approaching object now, over?"

"Roger that, rescue vessel. Comm Stat Ocracoke standing by."

The way they referred to the thing in the water as an object made Lizbeth's skin crawl.

"Uh, Comm Stat Ocracoke, rescue vessel niner-five. Object appears to be a windbreaker or jacket, possibly yellow. Do we know what the survivor was wearing, over?"

Lizbeth looked up at Fanny. Fanny nodded her head, acknowledging that it was Gray's.

"Comm Stat Ocracoke to rescue vessel, that is a negative, no clothing description. Will check with the family and get back to you, over?"

"Roger, Comm Stat Ocracoke, recue vessel niner-five standing by."

One of the men flipped open a phone and hit a speed dial number. He said into the receiver, "Chuck, go in there and tell them boys, that yellow windbreaker is Gray's... Thank you, bud." He flipped the phone shut.

A few minutes later the radio relayed the news to the rescue vessel that they had indeed found Gray's windbreaker. After a period of no more news, the crowded parlor began to empty back outside. Neither Fanny nor Lizbeth would leave. They sat together on the couch holding hands, listening. The rescue team had to be close now. If Gray was alive, she had to hear them looking for her.

The radio once again began to chatter about an hour later. Lizbeth and Fanny had not moved. Jaye brought them iced tea, but neither woman drank it. It sat on the coffee table in front of them. Lizbeth was caught up in watching the condensation drops slide down the glass and onto the coaster, when the radio came to life.

"U. S. Coast Guard rescue vessel niner-five. This is rescue helo one. Do you copy, over?"

"Roger, rescue helo one. This is rescue vessel niner-five, over?"

"U. S. Coast Guard rescue vessel niner-five. This is rescue helo one. We see something in that duck blind, three hundred yards to your port, over?"

"Roger, helo one. Duck blind, three hundred yards to port. We'll check it out, over?"

"Roger that rescue vessel. Helo one will hover over position." The voice on the air suddenly became excited. "Rescue vessel, we see movement. Yes, one survivor in the duck blind, rescue vessel. U. S. Coast Guard Ocracoke, this is Rescue helo one. The survivor has been located! She's waving. Survivor located!"

"Rescue helo one, this is U. S. Coast Guard Comm Stat Ocracoke. Roger that! Survivor located."

There was so much hooting and hollering, Lizbeth couldn't hear anymore of the transmissions. Gray was alive and that was all that mattered. Now, how would she get to her? Where would they take her? She found herself standing in the middle of the room being hugged and hugging everyone else, but all she could think about was getting to Gray.

Lizbeth found Fanny on the porch grinning just like Gray, from ear to ear. "Fanny, where will they take her? I have to go to her."

Fanny patted Lizbeth's hand. "I don't know darlin', but she'll call when she can."

On cue, the phone rang. The whole house and yard grew quiet when Jaye handed the still ringing phone to Fanny. Fanny took it and pushed the answer button. She stuck the receiver to her ear, and as if there was nothing going on said, "Hello," very calmly into the phone.

Her smile told everyone it was Gray. Fanny held the phone away from her ear and said to the gathered throng, "Gray wants to know if one of y'all could pick her up at the Coast Guard base? She's a little tired."

A loud and raucous cheer erupted in the room. Fanny put the phone back to her ear and said, "I believe somebody'll be there to pick you up. I'll go on and fix up somethin' to eat, 'cause I know you must be starvin'... I love you too, darlin'." Then she hung up.

The giddiness of the rescue spread through the crowd. Fanny decided she would stay behind with some other women, to cook and prepare for Gray's arrival. She would be tired, water logged, and in much need of food and rest. The rest of the crowd decided to all walk in mass down to the Coast Guard station. Marvina's husband followed in an old Jeep, so that Gray wouldn't have to walk home.

Lizbeth went right along with everyone else, so happy she almost floated down Howard Street. Jaye walked beside her, almost as happy as Lizbeth. Jaye really did care about Gray. Lizbeth reached over, wrapping one arm around Jaye as they walked. There was now an unspoken bond between them. They both loved Gray and Lizbeth realized that was okay.

They heard the helicopter before they could see it. Lizbeth finally spotted it coming in low across the water. The orange and white copter did a wide circle and then hovered over them before landing on the pad. First, the back door slid open and a rescue swimmer stepped out. He reached back into the doorway and helped a wobbly Gray, wrapped in a blanket and clutching a water bottle, down to the ground. She looked up at the crowd of well-wishers and smiled the patented Gray grin. The cheers echoed across the harbor.

Gray took two shaky steps, her feet in obvious distress. Several Coast Guard guys ran over to prop her up under her shoulders and moved her out from underneath the copter and over to her waiting friends. When they deposited her on the ground, several villagers took over the propping up by lifting her off her feet and carrying her to the waiting Jeep. There were so many people, Gray never saw Lizbeth, and Lizbeth couldn't get close to Gray.

Once seated in the Jeep, Gray shook hands and accepted hugs, as everyone passed by her. Lizbeth fell in at the back of the line. She slowly made her way forward, watching Gray and about to burst. She wanted to throw these people out of the way and get to Gray, but she was patient, moving closer one painstaking step at a time.

She was next in line when Gray finally saw her. Gray's facial expression gave away her complete shock. People around them started to fade back as the realization of who Lizbeth was fluttered through the crowd. A hush fell over them as they watched Lizbeth and Gray. Lizbeth stepped up in front of Gray, close enough to touch her, but she didn't.

Lizbeth said, "So, you went for a swim?"

Gray grinned. "Something like that."

Lizbeth could control it no longer. She threw herself into Gray's arms and didn't care who was looking. Gray wrapped her tightly in her grasp and whispered in her ear, "I came back, Lizbeth."

"I know, baby. I'm so sorry," Lizbeth whispered back, the tears she had held in for so long now raining down her cheeks.

Gray started crying, too. She was still holding Lizbeth tightly to her and Lizbeth could feel Gray's body begin to shake with her tears. Gray gasped into Lizbeth's neck, "I thought I wasn't going to get to tell you that I loved you."

Lizbeth pulled back and looked into Gray's eyes. "Gray O'Neal, I intend for you to tell me that every day for the rest of my life."

Gray smiled through her tears. "I will, I promise."

The crowd erupted into cheers and laughter that followed them all the way down Howard Street.

#

Fanny tried to play it cool when Gray was deposited on her doorstep.

"Well, I recon you're too tired to do the dishes."

Gray smiled at her, knowing this was Fanny's way of saying she was glad to see her. "Just leave 'em. I'll get to them after awhile."

Gray's feet and hands were shriveled from soaking up the water she was immersed in for hours. When she had reached water she could walk in, oyster and clamshells strewn along the bottom had ripped up the skin on the bottom of her feet. She stood on shaky legs for just a moment, before being the one to give in, and hugged her grandmother tightly.

Lizbeth heard Gray whisper, "I'm sorry."

Nothing else was said. Lizbeth was sure Fanny would have her say with Gray later, but right now, they were all just so glad she was home. Fanny decided it was time for some peace and quiet around there, so she shooed all the well-wishers home, thanking them for the vigil and the safe return of her granddaughter.

Lizbeth was instructed to take Gray in the house and put her in the shower. As crazy as it sounded, the water logged Gray needed the salt washed from her body by warm water. Even though the water temperature was not that low, the prolonged exposure had taken its toll. Gray followed instructions like a tired child and followed Lizbeth into the bathroom. Lizbeth undressed Gray, turned on the water, and gently guided her over the edge of the tub and under the showerhead.

Lizbeth spoke softly to Gray, "Honey, I'm going to go up to your room and get you some dry clothes."

Gray's hand darted out from behind the shower curtain, grabbing Lizbeth's arm. "No, wait. Stay here."

Lizbeth could sense Gray's need not to be alone. She had been on her own on that water all night. She patted Gray's hand, and said, "Okay, I'll wait. I'm not leaving."

Gray slowly released her grip on Lizbeth's arm and returned to washing her hair. In a few minutes, she was finished. Lizbeth helped her get out of the tub and dried her off. She folded a towel and sat it on the toilet so Gray could sit down. There really wasn't very much room to maneuver around and they ended up standing face to face, inches apart. Lizbeth wrapped a towel around Gray's shoulders. Gray wrapped her arms around Lizbeth, pulling her into her naked body. Gray kissed Lizbeth with the desperation of a woman who thought she'd never kiss those lips again. How close they came to losing each other held them there until Fanny knocked on the door.

"I got some dry clothes here for Gray."

Gray let Lizbeth go and sat down on the toilet, covering herself with the towel from her shoulders. Lizbeth opened the door.

"Thanks, Granfanny," Gray said.

"I need to do something about her feet," Lizbeth said to Fanny.

Fanny pointed to the little cabinet built into the wall behind the door. "All kinds of bandages and salves in there. I put some socks on top to wear over 'em."

Gray spoke up, "I hate socks."

Lizbeth and Fanny looked at each other and laughed. Gray was going to be just fine.

Fanny poked a finger at her, "Well, ornery as ever, you're going to wear 'em."

Gray understood not to argue. Lizbeth was sure Gray knew Fanny could light into her any minute for getting drunk and sinking the boat. Therefore, Gray cowered and promised to wear the socks. Fanny left them alone to go back to the kitchen. Lizbeth found the Band-Aids and first aid ointment and proceeded to doctor Gray's torn feet.

Gray was being a baby about it. Lizbeth understood how tired she was and didn't take the bait when she grumbled. Instead, she talked to Gray in soothing tones and tried to make the best of it, until Gray snatched her foot away, yelping.

"Jesus, that hurts!"

Lizbeth stood up from where she had been squatted on the floor, tending to the wounds. She held out the Band-Aids and ointment in her hand to Gray. "Do it yourself then."

"I'm sorry," Gray said. "They're tender. I know you're just trying to help."

"Yes, I am and you're being a baby."

"I'm tired, Lizbeth. I'm teetering here. I don't know whether to laugh or cry."

Lizbeth got over her bit of irritation, seeing how close to the edge Gray was. "Let me finish this. We'll get you dressed, feed you, and put you to bed. Then you can fall apart if you need to. I know you haven't yet or you wouldn't have made it back."

"Okay," Gray replied weakly, her energy level dipping again.

Lizbeth hurried with the rest of the bandaging and then dressed the exhausted Gray. She led her by the hand to the kitchen, where Gray plopped down heavily in the first chair she reached. Fanny sat a large platter piled high with eggs, bacon, and fried potatoes. A bowl of grits and large glasses of orange juice and milk joined the plate. If Gray consumed it all she would burst, but Fanny was making sure she had plenty.

Gray approached the plate slowly, but once she got started, she ate ravenously. Lizbeth and Fanny watched her, not saying anything. With a good portion of the plate gone, Gray finally looked up at them, while she chugged half the glass of milk.

Fanny saw her chance to speak. "I talked to Bud. He and Charles will do your tours for the rest of the week."

Gray nodded, but didn't make eye contact.

Fanny wasn't finished. "Gray, you 'bout ready to tell me what happened? You don't have to tell me the part where you got drunk and took off in the boat like a damn fool. I got that much from Cora Mae." Fanny was wasting no time taking the gloves off; she was angry with Gray, even though she was happy she was safe. "By the way, what's she gonna make a living on now?"

Gray put down her fork. She hesitated before saying, "I reckon I'll have to let her use the tour boat."

"No, you won't," Fanny snapped. "Ain't gonna tear that new boat up with fishin' nets and crab pots. Elbert's done told her she could use his old one."

Gray still had not looked at Fanny. Her tactic was obviously to try to avoid a direct blow. She took a drink of juice, then said, "That'll work, at least until I can figure out how to get the Fanny Gray out of the Sound."

"Do you think they can salvage her?" Fanny asked.

"Yeah, it's probably only fifteen or twenty feet where she went down."

Lizbeth was on the edge of her seat. "What happened?"

Gray looked down at the floor, the knuckle of her right index finger rested against her lips. Lizbeth took Gray's other hand, squeezing it tight. She could see Gray's eyes darting back and forth, watching an unseen movie unfold before her. She was remembering, or at least trying to order the events in her brain. A lot had happened in the last twenty-four hours.

Gray took a deep breath and let it out slowly. "When I left Cora Mae's I went out the channel and tooled around some. I was mad. I can remember that, but not much else. I'm not proud of it, but I'll admit I drank way too much. I anchored the boat and jumped in the water. I sobered up some, but when I got back in the boat, I got sick. I slept for a while, but I was still drunk. I know that because I got up and started for Swan Quarter. I guess I changed my mind after I sobered up some more."

"Your granddaddy always said, you don't mix liquor and water, not even in a glass," Fanny reminded her.

Gray ignored the remark and continued her recollection. "I was coming back across, got about halfway. It was getting dark. I turned the running lights on and poof, everything started frying. The generator shut down, the engine went off, and the bilge pump quit working. I didn't notice it was leaking because I was trying to get the radio to work. By the time I saw the water in the bow, it was too late. I knew I was going to have to swim, so I just kept at the radio until I got the message out. Just in the nick of time too, because she went down fast after that."

Fanny asked, "Why was she leaking? That boat is tight as a tick."

Gray shrugged her shoulders. "Jane said they hit one of those old submerged duck blinds the other day, maybe the hole just finally opened up."

Fanny flashed angry. "And you knew this and went out anyway?"

"I wasn't really thinking about it at the time," Gray said, only slightly defending her actions.

Lizbeth wanted to tell Fanny it wasn't all Gray's fault. Lizbeth had made her angry. She should shoulder some of the burden. She started to speak, "I had a hand in…"

Gray cut her off. "No, what I did was asinine and inexcusable. Fanny has a right to be mad."

How refreshing to find a grown-up willing to take responsibility for her actions. Lizbeth's admiration for Gray grew in leaps and bounds. Her lifting up of Gray to more than goddess status was interrupted by Fanny's remark.

"Your granddaddy'd tan your hide if he were here. I'd whup you myself, but the price on this little pissin' fit ought to be punishment enough, not to mention comin' near to dyin'."

Gray looked down at her plate. The first tear trickled from her eye. Fanny looked at Lizbeth. "Go on, take her upstairs. She needs to sleep."

Lizbeth took Gray's elbow gently and stood her up. She let Gray lean on her so she wouldn't have to put so much weight on her feet. They made slow progress up the stairs. Once in the room, Lizbeth helped Gray take her pants off and crawl beneath the sheets. Gray had not said a word since the kitchen. She cried softly into the pillow while Lizbeth stood beside the bed, not knowing what to do to help her.

Lizbeth leaned down, kissed Gray on the cheek, and started to leave. Gray grabbed her hand, whispering, "Stay with me."

Lizbeth wondered about Fanny for a second, and then realized Fanny knew and would expect her to stay with Gray.

She crawled in the bed behind Gray and spooned into her. Gray cried harder now that Lizbeth was in the bed.

Lizbeth whispered, "Go ahead and cry, baby. I'll hold you. I'm not going anywhere."

Gray rolled over, her face now streaked with tears. "Why did you leave?"

"I'm so sorry, Gray. I saw you at the dock with her and I panicked. I came back as soon as I found out what happened."

"I called you and told you at seven, when I got off the boat. You didn't listen to the messages, did you?"

"No, Mazie did. She told me and then Dana came to my house."

Gray's face showed her surprise. "Dana did what?"

"She came to my house in Durham and told me I was an idiot and you didn't deserve what I had done to you."

Gray tried a weak grin. Her tears had almost stopped. She said, "I didn't deserve it. I came back as soon as I could."

Lizbeth became a bit defensive. "What would you have thought was happening if you saw me getting into a boat for an evening cruise with my ex, who appeared to be trying to seduce me?"

"I hope I would have trusted you," Gray answered.

This was Gray's vindictive streak showing. Lizbeth had hurt her and now she was having a hard time letting it go. Lizbeth thought she might help her along with it. In some ways, Gray was so much like a child. "Okay Gray, I hurt you. I am sorry, but then you went and made me wonder if you were dead or not, so I think we're even."

Gray reached over and put a stray curl behind Lizbeth's ear. "I made that swim because I had to. I had to come back. I made my mind that if I made it, the first thing I was going to do was go and find you."

Lizbeth knew what Gray was saying and she was flattered. "You would have left this island to come find me?"

"Well, that's where I was going in the boat, until I sobered up some."

Their mood began to lighten a little. Lizbeth even smiled. "How in the hell were you planning on getting to Durham in that boat?"

"That's the thing about being drunk, no planning." Gray grinned.

"Gray," Lizbeth said, and then, suddenly overwhelmed with all the emotion of the past three days, began to cry. "Can we love each other now? Is all that other stuff out of the way? Can we both just give in and let the past go?"

Gray kissed her softly on the lips. "Yes, Lizbeth, and if I have to move off this island to keep you, I will. I made up my mind about that, too, while I was out there on the water."

"I would never take you away from here. It's where you belong."

Gray slid her arms around Lizbeth, pulling her in closer. "I want to be where we belong, not just me."

Lizbeth smiled. "I belong with you, wherever that is and I would just as soon it be here as any other place."

Gray sealed the deal with a kiss and then fell deeply to sleep. She was exhausted. Lizbeth snuggled under the covers with Gray and followed her happily into dreamland.

Chapter Fourteen

Lizbeth woke to Gray nuzzling up to her neck and pulling her into her body from behind. Lizbeth didn't open her eyes. She just snuggled up tighter and tried to go back to sleep. She had gotten up around seven the previous evening, fed Gray the sandwiches Fanny had prepared, and then held Gray until they both went back to sleep. They slept all night.

While she was up, Lizbeth called Molly and Mazic to let them know Gray was okay. Molly was still entertaining the lovely Ms. Fox and working on Lizbeth's plan. Of all the lesbians in the world, Molly had to pick Gray's ex with whom to start an affair. Lizbeth didn't tell Gray that little bit of information. She'd save that for later because it occurred to Lizbeth that, even though Molly was herself irresistibly cute, Dana sure got over wanting Gray back pretty quickly. She would hope the information wouldn't affect Gray one way or another, but just in the off chance it would, Lizbeth would wait until Gray was stronger.

Gray was awake. She ran her hand down Lizbeth's side then back up to her breasts, kissing Lizbeth's neck. Lizbeth remained as still as possible under Gray's growing attempts to rouse her. Gray was determined and within minutes, Lizbeth lost her resolve, rolling over to see the sparkle had returned to Gray's crystal blue eyes.

Lizbeth teased her, "I suppose this means you have completely recovered."

"Well, I haven't tried walking yet, but the rest of my parts seem to be in working order."

Lizbeth slid her knee between Gray's thighs. Gray threw her muscular leg over Lizbeth. Lizbeth pressed her breasts into Gray's chest. "Yeah, and what parts would those be?"

Gray grinned. "The ones that woke up and realized you were in my bed, half clothed."

"If you can make it across the street, I'll get completely unclothed," Lizbeth said, tracing her index finger around Gray's lips.

Gray couldn't seem to get Lizbeth close enough. She pulled Lizbeth tighter into her grasp. Her voice raspy with lust, she whispered against Lizbeth's lips, "What about right here, right now?"

Lizbeth shook her head no, but didn't try to move away. Instead, she ground her hips into Gray's. "No, because I'm not going to be able to control myself."

Gray's breathing was growing more rapid. She kissed Lizbeth hard and deep, a kiss filled with want. She pulled away, catching her breath before saying, "Honey, I don't think I can wait till after breakfast and you know Fanny will make us eat before we go."

Lizbeth pushed off Gray and slid out of the bed, leaving Gray staring in astonishment. "Then you'll be motivated to eat quickly," she said, beginning to dress.

Gray flopped back hard on the pillows. "That's so not fair."

"What's not fair?" Lizbeth was almost finished dressing and Gray was still in the bed.

"Doing that to me and then getting out of bed."

Lizbeth crawled like a tiger up Gray's long body, pinning her beneath the covers. She hovered inches from Gray's face. "I believe this will be the first time we've been together since you thought I had left you and I thought you had drowned, so I'm sure it's going to be intense. I don't intend to subject Fanny to that. These walls are thin."

"You got a point there. You do get pretty loud." Gray giggled.

Lizbeth popped her playfully on the shoulder. "Shhh, or I'll cut you off." An idle threat, Lizbeth knew. She wasn't about to cut Gray off anytime soon. In fact, she would have conceded right there if she didn't know for a fact that yes, she was going to make noise. They'd better keep the windows closed across the street or Fanny might hear her anyway.

Gray knew it was an idle threat. Lizbeth could tell by the confident look on Gray's face and the wicked grin that twitched in the corners of her mouth. "Cut me off, huh? Well, I guess I better do as you say then."

Lizbeth gave her a quick kiss on the lips and then let Gray up from under the covers. When Gray stood up gingerly on her injured feet, she teetered for just a second and then gained her balance.

Lizbeth asked, wincing for Gray, "Do they hurt?"

"Yes, but not all that bad. I've had worse. It's just that first step is a killer."

"We should dress them again after breakfast."

Gray stepped over to Lizbeth, walking softly on the spots on her feet that hurt the least. She wrapped Lizbeth in her arms and said, "Yes, and then can we pleeeeease go to your house?" She drug the please out like a child begging for a toy.

"Only if you're a good girl," Lizbeth teased.

Gray took her hand and led Lizbeth toward the door. She grinned over a shoulder at Lizbeth. "Oh, I'll be on my best behavior."

#

Fanny, true to form, had breakfast waiting downstairs. Lizbeth noticed that the dishes in the sink had been washed. Fanny was glad to have Gray home, safe and sound. After breakfast, Lizbeth washed the dishes while Fanny doctored Gray's feet and put fresh bandages on them.

When Gray winced at a particularly tender spot, Fanny said, "Ya' gone soft in your old age. I pulled cactus thorns out of you when you were five and not a whimper."

"That's 'cause Billy was cuttin' such a fuss," Gray answered.

Fanny chuckled. "Yes, he was a'squallin' weren't he? Learned his lesson 'bout pushing you into cactus, I reckon." Fanny continued to chuckle.

Gray joined her, the two women lost in the memory. Lizbeth loved watching them together. There was such a bond between them, a bond of mutual respect and love. The angry words from yesterday morning had been forgotten.

Lizbeth asked, "Why, Fanny? What did she do?"

Fanny, now in full belly laughs, gathered herself and told Lizbeth, "Billy pushed Gray into a cactus bed. She got stuck up pretty good on her feet, but she walked out of that patch and punched Billy in the jaw, which sent him ass over tea kettle into the cactus bed."

Gray interrupted, through her own guffaws, "He had cactus thorns all over his back and butt. He cried like a baby."

"Is this the same Billy who took your gas?" Lizbeth asked.

Gray shook her head back and forth, saying, "The very same. He's still a pain in the ass."

Fanny quipped, with a chuckle, "I 'magine he's sorry, now."

Gray's eyes twinkled. She said, sheepishly, "Yeah, I 'magine so."

Lizbeth knew that look. Gray had done something. "Gray, what did you do to Billy down at the docks yesterday? Jaye said you made Billy sorry, but she didn't elaborate."

Fanny and Gray exchanged mischievous looks. They were so much alike, their grins exactly mirroring each other. Gray looked down at the floor, unable to respond to Lizbeth's question. She looked as if she were going to burst, trying to hold back the laughter. Fanny answered for her, through her own giggles.

"Way I hear tell it, somebody down there told Gray it was Billy who took her gas and he was hiding behind the Community Store. She found 'im, chased 'im till she caught 'im, and threw his butt off the end of the dock into the harbor."

Lizbeth feigned shock. "Gray, you didn't?"

Fanny wasn't finished. "Well, that ain't the end of it. Gray wouldn't let him up out of the water, and she kept pelting him with rocks and shells from the shore, so he swam out further. Billy ain't never been accused of havin' much sense. Why he didn't get in his truck and leave when he knew Gray was a lookin' 'im, I don't know. What he did do was leave the keys in his truck."

Gray interjected, "Dumbass."

Fanny started whipping herself with laughter. "Gray drove that boy's truck right down the boat ramp and into the water, got out, and threw the keys at him."

Lizbeth gasped. "Oh no, Gray, you didn't."

Gray grinned at Lizbeth like a ten year old that won a playground fight. "Hell yeah, I did it. Teach him to mess with my stuff."

"But Gray, his truck! I mean... are you going to have to pay for his truck?"

Gray laughed when she said, "Probably, but it was worth it."

Lizbeth giggled at Gray. "That was quite an expensive day for you. That temper of yours is going to write a check your butt can't pay for, one of these days."

Gray didn't miss a beat. "Yeah, well, I have a rich girlfriend and it was partly her fault."

Fanny got into the mix. "A rich girlfriend with rich friends, sounds like to me. Did she tell you her friend flew her back down here in a private jet?"

Gray looked surprised. "No, she didn't."

"Molly is an old dear friend. Since, as you say, it was partly my fault, I was trying to get back here as quickly as possible before you did something stupid, but alas I was much too late."

"So you called Molly to fly you back down here?" Gray asked, knowing that meant Lizbeth had to have told someone other than her daughter about them, and that was a big step.

"No, actually, Molly was at my house sobering me up when Dana came over and we found out what really happened."

Fanny seemed to fade to the background. Lizbeth was aware of her presence, but had grown comfortable speaking openly around her. It was impossible not to. Gray was so upfront about who she was, it helped Lizbeth relax.

Gray didn't seem to care that Fanny was there either. She asked, "This Molly knows who I am?"

"Yes, as a matter of fact, she knew before you did."

Gray grinned. "You told her about me?"

"Molly has some expertise in that area. The use of the jet I believe she called my welcome to the family gift." Lizbeth winked at Gray.

Gray understood. "So you freaked out and called your lesbian friend, huh?"

Lizbeth laughed. "Yeah, something like that."

Fanny finally broke their little bubble by standing and saying, "Lawd, y'all go on get out of my kitchen, forc ya' start makin' googoo eyes at each other."

During all those hours waiting to find out if Gray was all right, Lizbeth had gone over to the cottage, unpacked her things, and turned on the air conditioning. Lizbeth helped Gray hobble across the street and put her in the bed upstairs. Explaining she needed a shower, she went back downstairs, under protest from Gray. By the time she returned, Gray had fallen asleep. She may have been feeling better, but she was far from recovered from her ordeal in the Sound.

Lizbeth dressed quietly and then went back downstairs. Gray needed the rest and she would have probably awoke if Lizbeth got into the bed with her. As much as Lizbeth wanted to do just that, she resisted and went in search of her cell phone. If her plan was going to work, she had to make a few phone calls. She dreaded the first one, but she made it anyway and got the results she wanted. The second call went without a hitch, as well. When she hung up, Lizbeth immediately called Molly with the news.

"I did it, Molly," she exclaimed.

Molly knew how hard that first call had been to make. She tried to make light of it, for Lizbeth's sake. "How is James these days?"

"I don't know. I didn't ask him. I got straight to the point and he jumped at the deal. He's waiting for you to call him." Lizbeth felt like she needed another shower after talking with her ex-husband, but it had been worth it.

Molly was nothing if not efficient. "I drew up the papers already. He agreed to the exact numbers we discussed?"

"Yes, exactly what we talked about."

"All right then, I'll call him as soon as we hang up. You're going to need to sign some things to make it official." She paused, and then added, "Lizbeth, you're sure about this? I mean this is much more of a commitment than the usual lesbian U-Haul routine."

Lizbeth giggled. "Enlighten me, Molly. What is the usual lesbian U-Haul routine?"

"It's an old joke. What does a lesbian bring on the second date? A U-Haul."

"So, I guess this makes it official. I'm a lesbian," Lizbeth declared.

"Welcome, sister," Molly said, followed by a laugh. She asked after a moment, "Did you tell James?"

"No, let him figure it out on his own. It'll be more shocking that way."

Both women laughed.

Lizbeth continued, "My cousins are willing to sell. They both have kids in college and the money in a lump sum would really help them out."

"That's great, Lizbeth. I'll call you when the papers are ready for you to sign. How's Gray?"

"Gray is exhausted, but she's going to be fine. She's asleep upstairs." Lizbeth paused, but couldn't resist the dig. "And how is the lovely Miss Fox?"

Molly hesitated. Lizbeth heard Molly sigh, accompanied by a little nervous laugh. "Lizbeth, I... well, uh..."

"She's still there, isn't she?"

"Yes, she doesn't have to be back at the vet clinic until next Monday, so... I talked her into staying. I'm going to fly back to Texas with her Saturday."

"Oh, Lord, Molly. Is it that good?" Lizbeth wasn't angry. She found the whole thing funny, but she couldn't let Molly off the hook that easily.

Molly shot back, "I could ask you the same thing."

"Touché!"

"You know this is all your fault anyway," Molly said, adding, "If you had stayed on the other side of the heterosexual fence, I would be blissfully unaware of the existence of the lovely Miss Fox, as you called her."

"Okay," Lizbeth said, with a sigh of contrition. "I'll stop complaining. I just hope this plays itself out soon. I'm not sure I'm up for a lifetime of lesbian inter-connectivity."

Molly let out a laugh. "Oh, Lizbeth, you know being a lesbian is like that game Six Degrees of Kevin Bacon, only ours is called Six Degrees of Martina."

Lizbeth followed Molly into peals of laughter. After catching her breath, Lizbeth managed to say, "And the web grows larger every day. With Gray's track record, I'm probably now connected up and down the eastern seaboard and part of the southwest."

Molly's laughter subsided only enough for her to gasp out, "Well, I never imagined we'd be connected this way."

"Not in my wildest dreams," Lizbeth said, trying to calm her breathing. She thought she heard Gray stirring upstairs. "I think I hear Gray moving around. I better go. Just call me after you get those papers signed. Maybe Gray and I can drive up next week and you can meet her."

Molly, still catching her breath, said, "Okay, I'll call... and Lizbeth, I'm really happy for you."

"Thanks for everything. See you soon."

Lizbeth hung up. She was in the kitchen, so she started up the hallway and ran into a limping, sleepy-eyed Gray, holding onto the walls.

"What are you doing up?" Lizbeth went to her.

Gray wasn't fully awake. She mumbled, "Bathroom," and headed for the door.

"Are you hungry?" Lizbeth let Gray pass and followed her to the bathroom door.

Gray nodded her head yes, but didn't speak. The exhaustion had really set in during her most recent nap. Lizbeth left Gray in the bathroom and went to the kitchen. Luckily, she hadn't thrown out the food when she left. She managed to put together clam chowder and grilled cheese sandwiches for them. While she worked on the menu, Gray joined her in the kitchen, sitting with her head lying on her crossed arms on the table. Lizbeth glanced at her occasionally. She could see how much the ordeal with the boat had taken out of Gray. She was emotionally and physically drained. Her spurt of energy this morning had been false bravado.

Lizbeth set out the lunch and sat down across from Gray, who had raised her head and sat staring at the food in front of her.

"Gray, honey, eat something."

Gray answered in a voice husky with fatigue, "I will. I just can't seem to wake up."

"If you don't want to eat now, I'll just put this away. You can go back to sleep."

Lizbeth reached for Gray's plate. Gray reached out and took her hand. "No, just give me a minute." She didn't let go of Lizbeth.

Lizbeth waited silently while Gray gathered her energy. She watched Gray's eyes slowly brighten and when she eventually grinned, Lizbeth relaxed her worry and started to eat.

Gray shook her head, as if shaking off the cobwebs that clouded her brain. "Wow, I was really out of it. Thanks for lunch," she said, releasing Lizbeth's hand and diving into her plate.

"After lunch, you should go lie back down. You're exhausted."

Gray swallowed, chasing the grill cheese down with water. "I will, if you come with me." She winked.

Lizbeth scoffed at her, "You are so full of it. You barely have the energy to lift that sandwich to your mouth."

"I'm sorry I fell asleep when you were in the shower." Gray sounded as if she was afraid Lizbeth was disappointed.

Lizbeth reassured her, "Gray, I'll be here when you feel better. I'm not going anywhere. In fact, we need to talk about that."

Gray raised an eyebrow, her sandwich hanging out of her mouth as she froze for a second.

Lizbeth grinned at the expression on Gray's face. She was so childlike it was constantly endearing. "Honey, swallow," Lizbeth said, chuckling at her big baby. "I just got off the phone with Molly, the friend that flew me back here. She's not only a friend, she's my attorney." Lizbeth let that sink in, then went on. "I'm about to make a blind leap of faith here and I hope it's what you want, too." She hesitated, because she and Gray had never gotten around to talking about the future.

Gray, who had finally swallowed, spoke up. "Why do you need an attorney? Are you going to make me sign a pre-nup? Exactly how much money do you have, anyway?"

"As of today," Lizbeth smiled. "Enough so that neither one of us ever has to work another day in our lives, and is that some backhanded way of asking me to marry you?"

Gray looked stunned. "What?"

"Asking me if I wanted you to sign a pre-nup. You don't need a pre-nup if there are no nuptials. Get my drift?"

Gray's countenance darkened. "We've both been married before and it meant nothing to them. Is it necessary to go through a ceremony that in the end had no bearing on the future?"

"Gray, I'm not that old fashioned. It doesn't matter to me. What does matter is a commitment to each other. Do you want me to move down here?"

Gray smiled. The darkness dissipated. "Yes, I want you to move down here."

"Then we need to talk about it," Lizbeth said, still leading Gray through the conversation. She was beginning to understand that this was the way it was going to be with Gray. Gray wouldn't talk about what she wanted unless Lizbeth pulled it out of her.

Gray took a drink of water, then leaned her elbows on the table and concentrated on Lizbeth's eyes. "I still don't understand why you need an attorney."

Lizbeth explained, "She's handling the sale of my house in Durham. I just sold it back to my ex-husband this morning."

"You sold your house this morning?"

"Yes, I'm not going to be living in it and I was planning to sell it anyway, next year, so it worked out for both of us. He wanted it, that's the only reason I took it in the first place. I don't need that feeling of vindication anymore."

"I know what you mean. I spent five years hating Dana, but then when she came here, I didn't feel a thing."

"Oh, you felt a thing, I saw you," Lizbeth said before she could stop herself.

Gray, defensive, said, "Lizbeth, it wasn't like that. I came back to you, didn't I?"

Lizbeth stood up and stepped over to Gray. She leaned down close to her and said, "Yes, you did. I'm sorry. Residual jealousy. Just know that I can't bear the sight of another woman touching you." She kissed Gray on the lips lightly and then looked into her eyes. "Gray, I need to know if I should buy this cottage from my cousins. If I do, will you live with me?"

"Why don't you move in with me and Fanny?"

"Because I have to have somewhere for my stuff and a place my daughter can come visit. I just think three women in the same house would be pushing it, don't you?"

Gray thought about it. "It would give us more privacy and I know you'd never have sex with me over there."

Lizbeth chuckled. "Always thinking about the important things, aren't you?"

Gray pulled Lizbeth down on her lap. She was recovering her strength. Lizbeth could feel it in her grip and see it in her sparkling eyes. Gray kissed her and then said, "I think that's very important. It's growing more important by the second." She pulled Lizbeth to her for a long kiss.

She released a breathless Lizbeth, who tried to continue their conversation, but Gray's insistent lips kept interrupting. "How's... Fanny going... to feel... about this?"

Gray stopped kissing Lizbeth long enough to say, "If I take my meals with her for the most part, she'll be fine. We can spend time with her and when she's asleep, I'll be over here."

Before Gray could kiss her again, Lizbeth suggested, "We could put in a wireless com system and she could reach us anytime she needed us."

Gray stopped being focused on Lizbeth's lips. "That would make me feel better," she said, and then she paused. Lizbeth saw Gray's brow knit. Whatever she was thinking expressed itself in her solemn eyes. "Lizbeth, are you sure you know what you're doing?"

Lizbeth knew exactly what she was doing. She was following her heart. It didn't matter that she'd known Gray only two weeks. She knew that coming here had been her second chance. She no longer carried the heavy heart of the scorned woman, sworn never to take that chance again. Lizbeth felt alive and young, with a world of possibilities in front of her. She wanted to face that future with Gray.

Gray, whom she had found asleep at the wheel, was herself awakening from years of dormant emotions. Lizbeth could be patient as Gray learned to trust her. Even now, she could hear it in Gray's voice. She was still afraid that Lizbeth would change her mind. Gray hadn't quite given in, but she was close to believing Lizbeth was really hers to have. All she had to do was take it.

Lizbeth placed the palm of her hand over Gray's heart. She could feel the steady thumps against her skin. "I know that I want to spend the rest of my life with you. Is that what you're asking? Is that what you want, too?"

Lizbeth saw Gray physically gulp. She was witnessing from the outside the argument between Gray's brain and her heart. Lizbeth wanted to laugh, but she didn't. Gray was suffering with a last minute flurry of what ifs. She had the stricken look of a scared groom, just before he said, "I do." Lizbeth knew Gray was fighting a losing battle. Gray was already in love with her. Lizbeth decided to help Gray with her struggle. She pressed her chest into Gray's, wrapping her arms around her neck, and kissed Gray's breath away.

Gray's eyes were wide and blinking when Lizbeth released her. A grin crept into the corner of her mouth. "Have you been holding out on me?"

"No, I was just trying to encourage you to make the right decision." Lizbeth returned the grin.

Gray sighed. "You got me, all of me, as you requested. I can't resist you. I tried, but it's just no use."

"Okay. Then I believe I am following proper lesbian protocol," Lizbeth said with a sly grin.

"Oh," Gray asked, laughing. "And what would that be?"

"I'm bringing the U-Haul," Lizbeth said, bursting into laughter at her cleverness.

Gray laughed at her and rose from her chair, forcing Lizbeth to stand. She took Lizbeth by the hand and led her, limping only slightly now, toward the bedroom. She said, as she skillfully maneuvered Lizbeth into her lair, "And where did you acquire your newfound knowledge of the lesbian lifestyle?"

Lizbeth, following blissfully along, answered, "Molly. We've also discussed the uncanny way all lesbians seemed to be connected."

Gray's eyes were smoldering. There was no sign of the sleepy baby from a few minutes ago. She casually asked, "What's her theory on that?"

They were climbing the stairs and Lizbeth thought this probably wasn't the best time to spring the news on Gray that Molly was now connected to both of them through Dana. She simply said, "We'll talk about that later."

When they reached the bedroom, Gray let go of Lizbeth's hand and hugged her close to her body. She looked into Lizbeth's upturned face, while her hands began slowly to undress her. Lizbeth's body trembled with each touch. Gray led Lizbeth to the bed, sat her down on the edge, and then stood in front of her, shedding her own clothing. Again, the pure awe of Gray warmed Lizbeth with lust, but she didn't move to touch her. Gray had her paralyzed, bearing down on her with those desire-filled eyes. Lizbeth may have been in control of their earlier conversation, but this nonverbal language was Gray's specialty, and Lizbeth was content just to listen.

She listened. Lizbeth listened for several hours while Gray made love to her. This was their commitment ceremony. There was no doubt when they finally collapsed in each other's arms that, sanctioned by the state or not, the commitment had thoroughly been celebrated.

Chapter Fifteen

The remainder of Thursday and into the wee hours of Friday morning, Gray and Lizbeth alternately slept, talked, consumed food, and then each other. They slept in Friday morning, not bothering to tell Fanny they weren't coming to breakfast. She must have known. Lizbeth had gotten up before Gray and made coffee. Deciding to let Gray sleep some more, she went out on the front porch where Fanny had left a basket containing fresh biscuits and homemade jam.

Gray joined Lizbeth a half an hour later. They ate the biscuits sitting on the porch. Gray needed to go do her mea culpa to Cora Mae about the boat. Even if it was hers, she still owed Cora Mae an apology for causing her grief. Lizbeth didn't want to go. She thought the two old friends had things to be said that she shouldn't be a party to.

Gray had explained that Cora Mae was ten years older and the original island lesbian. She had taken a young Gray under her wing, but not to bed. She was the person who had recognized the symptoms in the fledgling lesbian and helped Gray get through the difficult coming out process. She had been Gray's rock for years. Giving Cora Mae the boat to use, because the bank took hers, had been Gray's way of paying some of the kindness back.

To Gray's credit she was taking all the blame for her recent escapade. She didn't blame Lizbeth or Jane for making her mad. She could fault no one but herself for drinking moonshine, of all things. 198 proof, pure grain alcohol has caused black outs, hallucinations, and in the worse cases death. Luckily, Gray had thrown up or she may not have made that swim, but she did, and she was now facing the consequences head on.

One of those consequences sauntered up to the front of Gray's house and knocked on the screen door. Lizbeth could tell by Gray's body language that she wasn't happy to see the man at her door. Gray rose out of the rocking chair and called out to him.

"Billy, over here."

Billy had the look of a man who had lived in a bottle. Even though he had to be Gray's age, he looked much older. The alcohol had dried up his skin. His gaunt face was unshaven. He dressed like Gray, but somehow his attempt to hang onto his youth didn't wear as well on him as it did his female nemesis. He had the same blond hair as Gray did, but that was where the similarities stopped.

Billy approached cautiously. Lizbeth thought he looked genuinely frightened. Gray stood, holding the screen door open, staring down at the man she would have towered over anyway. This gave them the appearance of the serf coming to pay respects to the queen. He bobbed his head, in a gesture of greeting, in Lizbeth's direction. He didn't know her, but he was raised to acknowledge a lady when present. He didn't nod at Gray.

Lizbeth watched the two old enemies square off from her front row seat. Fanny must have heard the knocking, because she came to the door. When she saw what was happening, she sat down in her rocker, the rhythm of the chair reflecting her anticipation of something exciting. Lizbeth figured Fanny had been watching these two go at it since they were in diapers. The grin on her face said she had probably enjoyed most of it.

Billy kicked at the ground; not looking up, he said, "I'm glad they found you, Gray."

Gray chuckled. "You're just glad I'm alive so I can pay for your truck."

"Yeah, about that. What are you going to do?" Billy asked this with trepidation.

Gray had been leaning with one arm against the screen door and the other stretched across the opening, clasping the door jam with her hand. She straightened suddenly and dropped her hand to her side. This caused Billy to jump back a few steps in anticipation of another pummeling. Gray laughed at him.

"It's okay, Billy. I'm not mad anymore. Have it hauled over to Manteo and I'll put a new engine in it and fix anything else the water damaged. If you can find one for whatever that costs, then I'll give you that amount in cash, but don't try to milk this deal, Billy. You just remember I'm a lot smarter than you."

Billy whined, "What am I supposed to do in the meantime?"

Not missing a beat, Gray said, "Walk. Consider it my gift to the rest of the island. It'll keep your drunk ass off the road for awhile."

"You shouldn't a done that to my truck," Billy said, trying to show a little backbone.

"And you should learn to keep your hands off other people's stuff, asshole."

Lizbeth giggled. The confrontation was quickly being reduced to eighth grade name-calling.

"Dammit, Gray. I was going to put it back." Now, if Billy had stopped there everything would have been fine, but he didn't. Instead, he added, "How was I to know you were going muff diving in the middle of the night?"

It was Billy's good fortune that Gray's feet were in such bad shape, but it didn't stop her from trying to tackle him in Lizbeth's front yard. Due to her injuries, Billy was able to scamper just out of her reach and tear ass down Howard Street.

Gray looked around for something to throw at him. Not finding anything, she yelled after him, "Oh yeah! Well, at least I can get some, you little piss ant."

Fanny and Lizbeth were whipping themselves with convulsive laughter. After a few more rapid breaths and a long stare down Howard Street, Gray became aware of the other two women and the enjoyment they were having at her expense.

"I'm glad you two are having fun." She was feigning anger, but it didn't last long. She joined in the laughter and hobbled back to the porch.

Fanny hollered across the shady lane, "Did she tell you he was her first boyfriend?"

Lizbeth lost it. She doubled over and gasped for air. That was just a jewel of information.

Gray shot back at Fanny, "Yeah, and look at me now. He's probably the reason I like girls."

#

Gray's feet did not look as bad as the day before, but they were still tender. The antibiotic ointment had taken the redness away, but the cuts were still painful. She grumbled about having to wear socks and shoes. After Lizbeth convinced her that two pairs of socks would cushion the bottoms of her feet inside the shoes, she finally gave in and was surprised that she could actually walk without much pain. She kissed Lizbeth and headed off down the lane to Cora Mae's.

Lizbeth spent the rest of her morning cleaning the cottage and making a list of things she needed from the store. Since she was staying, the list grew longer as the morning progressed. She began to think about all the things in her house in Durham. What would she do with all that furniture? She wasn't going to leave it to James. He would probably get rid of it anyway. His new trophy wife wouldn't want Lizbeth's old things. That was assuming she had a brain. Lizbeth wasn't sure. After all, she did marry a man that was cheating on his wife with her when they met. Lizbeth thought they deserved each other. It was like that line from a country song. "If she wants a man, who'll take the ring off of his hand and then turn around and say that he'll be true, then she deserves you."

Now, Lizbeth was faced with cleaning out that huge house and making a home here in this little cottage. Although it was a daunting task, Lizbeth was happy to make it happen. She already felt more for Gray than she ever had for James, now that she thought about it. The prospects of a life with Gray held endless possibilities and Lizbeth was more than happy to divest herself of her old life and begin anew.

The first thing she had to do was get her car. Although she loved Gray's old Jeep, the prospects of driving all the way to Durham in it did not appeal to Lizbeth. She didn't know if Gray even had a top for the thing. Lizbeth needed to call Mazie. Maybe she could help.

She dialed Mazie at home, because she still had her cell phone. Mazie answered after two rings.

Mazie started speaking as if they had been in mid-conversation. "I tell you, it's weird looking down and seeing your own name on caller I.D."

"Thank you for letting me use your phone. I need to get a new one."

"Already done. You should get the new one any day now. I had it shipped to you down there and I retrieved your SIM card from the pile of phone parts on the table."

"God, I love you. Is this the part of life where you start taking care of me, instead of the other way around?"

"I guess so. I thought you had a few more years before that started, but you do appear to need a bit of help right now. I assume you are calling to tell me you sold the house back to Dad."

"Did he call you?" Lizbeth asked.

Mazie giggled. "Yes, he couldn't wait to tell me. He was curious as to why you were doing it and thought I might talk. Silly man, he hasn't learned anything about either of us, has he?"

"No, I don't guess he has. I'm sorry I didn't get to you first. It's all happening so fast and I've been taking care of Gray. Time got away from me."

"How is Gray? Did she survive the ordeal intact?"

Lizbeth couldn't help the dreamy sound in her voice when she said, "She's going to be fine. A little sore on her feet from the oyster beds, but other than that she's feeling herself today."

"You're really going to do this, aren't you?"

The question caught Lizbeth off guard. Was Mazie having second thoughts about having a lesbian mother? "Mazie, are you okay with this? I don't want to embarrass you or anything."

"Mom, I'm not embarrassed. I think it's great that you've found someone, male or female. I'm just worried that you rushed into this and now you're selling off your life to be with her. I just want you to be sure, that's all."

Lizbeth answered without hesitation, "Mazie, I've never been more positive about anything in my life."

"Okay then. How can I help?"

"You need to go through the house and take what you want. If you don't have room for it now, I'll pay storage on it till you do."

"Oh goodie. It'll be like antique shopping without having to pay for anything. Anything I should leave for you?"

"I want my grandmother's dressing table, that's it. I'll pick from what you leave to bring down here and Mazie, I'm adding some of the money from the sale of the house to the trust your grandparents left you."

"Does that leave you enough to live off of? You're only forty," Mazie said, concerned for her mother, which Lizbeth thought was so sweet.

"I had enough before I sold the house, so I'm good. You know I never liked running in the old money crowd. This island and this little cottage are more my speed. Besides, Molly hooked me up with a great accountant when I left your father. I'm set."

"I can't wait to tell Dad. He'll have to do something fantastic to try and out do you on this one."

"Your father wouldn't have a dime to his name if it wasn't for his family. You better get it while the gettin's good. I'm sure he'll blow through it all before the end. He just paid full price for the same house again. How stupid is that?" Lizbeth giggled.

"I wanted to tell him he got played," Mazie said, stifling a laugh, "but it's just too good to let him walk around with his chest poked out, reveling in his victory. He has his house back, whoopee!"

"He loves that house as much as his dick," Lizbeth said. "I knew he'd buy it back."

"Oh my God, mom, that's too funny." Mazie paused, and then asked, "Are you ever going to tell me what all he did that gave you so much power in the divorce?"

"No, but you can ask him. I doubt he'll tell you. He paid a high price for those secrets."

Mazie, undaunted, continued, "Just tell me he didn't rape anybody or fool around with little girls."

Lizbeth chuckled. "No, nothing like that. I'll just say he slept with the wrong men's wives and a few of their daughters, of age, but still very young. If those men knew, your father would be ruined."

Mazie understood. She added, "It's like Grandma said, 'You don't crap where you eat.'"

"Yeah, something like that." Lizbeth had taken to saying Gray's line.

Mazie was satisfied with the answer and moved on. "Okay, well, I'll go over this weekend and start marking things for the movers. Is there anything else I can do?"

"I hate to ask you this, but I seem to have come off without a vehicle."

Mazie laughed. "Yes, you did sort of just leave the other day."

"I wasn't thinking past getting here, at the time," Lizbeth agreed.

"Let me figure it out and I'll get the car to you. I might just drive it down tomorrow, if that's okay?"

"Mazie, that would be fantastic and you can spend some time getting to know Gray." Lizbeth was excited for Mazie and Gray to get acquainted. They were the two most important people in her life and she wanted them to like each other.

"I would like that, too. Oh, and by the way, for your first time out you picked an incredibly handsome woman."

Lizbeth blushed. "She is, isn't she?"

Mazie said, with all sincerity, "You make a stunning couple."

Love for her daughter overcame Lizbeth. She really was a wonderful young woman. "Thank you, sweetheart. You don't know how much it means to me that you've taken all this so well."

"I just want you to be happy, Mom. I know what you gave up to stay in that marriage for me. You deserve to be loved and Gray really does love you. When I saw the way she looked at you, I knew."

"You should have tied me to a tree and made me wait for her."

Mazie chuckled. "I think you would have probably hit me if I tried that, so I thought it was best to just let things play out."

"You're right. I probably would have hit you. I can be so stupid sometimes, but it all worked out in the end, so now we turn the page and start working on the rest of the story."

Mazie giggled. "I can't wait to see what you two do next. It'll have to be a hell of a story to top your beginning."

"I can do without the excitement. I'm shooting for a nice relaxed life here on this little island. No more drama."

"Mom, if what you say is true about women throwing themselves at Gray all the time, there is going to be drama."

Lizbeth surprised herself by saying, "Only if they touch her."

Mazie's laughter filled Lizbeth's ear. She said between guffaws, "Jealous much?"

Lizbeth joined her daughter in laughter. "I have discovered that I have quite the jealous streak when it comes to Gray, and I have no control over what I'll do or say. I kissed her in front of the whole bar the other night when some wench tried to hang all over her."

"You're not worried that she'll cheat on you?" Mazie's protective nature had returned.

"Nope," Lizbeth said, assuredly, "when Gray loves somebody, she doesn't cheat. That's why she and Dana split up after ten years. Dana cheated on Gray."

"You two have a lot in common, don't you?" Mazie asked.

"Yes, as far as relationships go, yes we do. We're both very monogamous."

"That's good. You certainly have had your share of being cheated on. I never could understand it. Dad loved you. He still does. You're beautiful and smart. I just didn't get why he had to fool around."

Lizbeth had thought about that long and hard for many years. She had finally come to the following conclusion. "It took me a while to figure it out myself, but I do believe your father loved me. He's addicted to the excitement of an affair. His new wife won't fare much better than I did, I'm sure."

"Oh, Candy is too stupid to know what's going on. She'll go along blissfully spending his money, totally unaware. He's already up to his old tricks. I saw him myself, the other day, with Robert Harris' wife."

Lizbeth gossiped, even though she knew she shouldn't. After all, this was Mazie's father. "That's old news, Mazie. They've been on and off for years."

"Jesus, does he shoot Viagra in his veins? How does he keep up with all of them?"

A chuckling Lizbeth responded, "I'm just glad I made it out of that marriage without an STD. At least he picks healthy women."

Mazie finally let Lizbeth hang up, promising to call after she talked to her husband about coming down on Saturday. Lizbeth would have to drive her back, but they would visit a few days first. Mazie was making Lizbeth's transition from hetero to homo life so much easier than she had expected it to be. So many people have a hard time being who they really are. The recent rash of suicides among gay teens bore that out. Lizbeth was blessed and she knew it.

Lizbeth had yet to confront her other family members. She really didn't care what they had to say and she would love to be a fly on the wall when James found out. He'd probably think it meant he was the only man she could love, but that wasn't it at all. If Gray had been exactly the same, only male, she would have fallen for her no matter what. James would never understand that. He was too wrapped up in his maleness ever to consider a woman didn't need a man to be happy.

Lizbeth shook off her thoughts of James and proceeded on her next mission. She needed to talk to Fanny.

#

Lizbeth was waiting on the porch when Gray came limping up a little after noon. The walk had not been kind to her feet. She flopped down in the rocker next to Lizbeth. She had a worried look on her face, but managed a smile for Lizbeth when she sat down.

"That bad, huh?" Lizbeth asked.

"She wasn't mad, just disappointed. I scared her and I knew better," Gray said, as she began untying her shoes.

"You two have quite a history. This is just a bump in the road," Lizbeth reassured her.

"I hate that I did that to her, to Fanny, to you. I'm sorry I worried you all so much. That's not all of it, though. Besides the money this is going to cost me, I have to show my face after showing my ass. I got nobody to blame but myself for this mess."

Lizbeth was sympathetic. "Honey, I helped."

"You didn't force that liquor down my throat. I know what happens when I drink that shit. I knew I was gonna blow. I just couldn't stop myself. I hadn't counted on being devastated when you told me to fuck off. I totally lost control and I don't like doing that."

Gray had come back from Cora Mae's in a very reflective mood. Lizbeth wondered what else might have been in the topic of conversation. She tried to lighten Gray up a little.

"Okay, we're checking moonshine off the list of things you're allowed to drink."

Gray did laugh a little. She had gotten her shoes and socks off and stretched her legs out, exposing the bottoms of her feet to the air. She still had a far off look in her eyes.

Lizbeth asked her, "Honey, are you worried about the money?"

"It's going to put a dent in my savings, that's for sure."

Lizbeth took Gray's hand in hers and turned to her, so Gray could see all of her face. She grinned until Gray finally said, "What?"

"Remember when you asked me how much money I had?"

Gray shook her head no. "I'm not taking money from you. I have a job. I make good money. I'll just have to add some more tours to make up what I've lost. The insurance will pay part of what the Fanny Gray will cost, anyway."

"Gray, listen to me. I know you're proud, but if we're in this together, then we're in this together. I don't want you to quit your job, because it is so much a part of who you are, but you don't have to take on more tours. I just sold my house."

"So. You'll need that money if you don't take that library job."

Lizbeth giggled a little. "Honey, you don't understand. Minus the money I am giving Mazie, I'm about to get three million dollars."

Gray sat up straight from her lounging position. A look of total shock seized her face. "Jesus, Lizbeth. What, did you live in a mansion?"

"Yes, I guess you could call it that," Lizbeth answered.

"Are you sure you want to come slumming down here with me? I'm sure this is quite different from the circles you travelled in. It's funny, but you don't act like someone with that much money."

"I never cared about it. Oh sure, it was convenient, but it didn't make me happy, did it?" Lizbeth let that sink in, then added, "You make me happy, Gray. Let me help you. I don't want you to worry."

"I like to carry my own weight," Gray said, seriously, but then she grinned and said, "But that's really sweet of you. I'll tell you what, I won't worry and you keep your checkbook in your purse. If a time comes when I need something I can't pay for, then you can help me. Okay?"

Lizbeth had made one other phone call that morning. She got the salvage company name from Fanny and arranged for Gray's boat to be taken to a boat yard, where it was to be repaired and modernized. Lizbeth could have just bought Gray a new one, but she knew how much her grandfather's boat meant to her. Now, she was afraid she'd overstepped her bounds.

"Gray, I have to tell you something. Now, don't be mad. I did it because I wanted to. It's the least I could do, since I was the source of all that out of control emotion."

Gray's eyebrows shot up. Her imagination was running wild, so Lizbeth thought she should just tell her before she thought up something worse.

"I got Fanny to give me the number of the salvage company and arranged for the Fanny Gray to be taken to a shipyard for refitting."

Gray cocked her head to one side and stared at Lizbeth. Lizbeth couldn't tell if she was mad or just stunned. She stayed like that a few seconds and then slowly a grin formed in the corners of her mouth, before she smiled widely, saying, "Did I tell you I loved you today?"

Lizbeth relaxed. "I can't remember. Maybe you should tell me again."

Gray stood up on tender feet. She pulled Lizbeth into a standing position in front of her. Her eyes twinkled and the raffish grin had returned. She bent down to Lizbeth's ear and whispered, "How 'bout I show you, instead?"

#

When Gray finished explaining to Lizbeth that she loved her in no uncertain terms, they got dressed again and headed over to Fanny's. Sweet iced tea washed down bacon, lettuce, and tomato sandwiches. Lizbeth was going to miss these fresh tomatoes, but luckily, Fanny had canned some for the winter months. Lizbeth planned to use them the next time she made meatballs.

Mazie called back and said she was bringing the Mustang down on Saturday morning. Mazie asked if she could bring anything and Lizbeth gave her a list of groceries, so she and Gray wouldn't have to drive up the beach to Avon. Fanny and Gray were glad Mazie was going to stay a few days. It made Lizbeth proud that both women appeared to like her daughter.

That afternoon, the three women took Gray's Jeep "over the beach." They scoured the shoreline for the sea's treasures. Most of the good stuff had already been picked through, but Lizbeth did find an intact sea dollar. Fanny convinced Gray to put her feet in the salt water.

"Old folks swear by the healin' power of the ocean," Fanny said.

Gray grinned at her from behind the steering wheel. "You are old folk. Not many left much older than you."

"Elmira's ninety-five, so I'm not the oldest yet," Fanny shot back, "Go on, be a hard head, but if my feet looked like that, I'd have 'em in that there water."

Lizbeth observed the discussion from the back seat.

Gray turned to Fanny. "There's all kinds of bacteria in that water. No tellin' what that storm stirred up."

Fanny harrumphed, "I'm eight-five years old and been curin' ails with seawater my whole life, but what the hell could I know?"

Gray stopped the Jeep. She got out, mumbling under her breath, "Might as well do it. You're going to harp on me till I do."

Lizbeth hopped out of the back and joined Gray in the edge of the water. Gray lifted one flip-flopped foot and then the other, letting the seawater flow on the bottoms of her feet.

"I can't take the flip-flops off cause the sand will tear open the cuts, but there is no use arguing with that stubborn old woman," Gray said, when Lizbeth slid her arm around her waist.

Lizbeth smiled up at Gray, saying, "It's an endearing family trait."

Back at Fanny's cottage, they cleaned Gray's wounds and then played cards with Fanny. This time Gray concentrated more, but Lizbeth defeated both the O'Neal women, much to their displeasure and Lizbeth's delight. They had supper with Fanny, another round of BLT's because that's what Lizbeth requested and then sat with Fanny on the porch until she retired to bed.

Later that night, while Gray and Lizbeth held each other, Gray said softly, "Thank you for spending time with Fanny." Her voice cracked slightly. "I don't know how much time I have left."

Lizbeth patted her hand on Gray's chest. "Honey, she's healthy as a horse, but we'll spend all the time you want with her. We can sleep over there sometimes, if you want, but not until I get over this uncontrollable need for you to screw my brains out. I have never been this sex crazed in my life." Lizbeth giggled at herself.

Gray rolled onto her side, pulling Lizbeth underneath her in one smooth move. She bore down on Lizbeth with an expression that did nothing to quell the fire that was growing between Lizbeth's legs. Lizbeth's breath caught in her chest.

This woman consumed the air around Lizbeth and gave it back in a warm cloud of desire that engulfed her.

Gray nuzzled into Lizbeth's thick hair covering her neck. She began to move against Lizbeth's body, slowly sliding over her skin, melding into one. She whispered into Lizbeth's ear, "What makes you think you're gonna get over this uncontrollable need?"

Lizbeth's answer came in the form of an arched back and a deep moan.

Chapter Sixteen

Sitting at Fanny's table the next morning having another home cooked breakfast, Lizbeth was all smiles, inside and out. All of the anxiousness of the two of them just getting it together had dissipated. She and Gray were relaxing into each other, learning each other's quirks and habits. They were settling in to the newlywed stage rather nicely.

Lizbeth was jarred from her thoughts by her cell phone ringing in her pocket. It was Molly.

"Hey, Molly. You're up early."

"I'm at the airport. Look, I'm going to fly to Manteo and rent a car. I'll be there in a few hours, if that's okay. I'm going to be out of town for a couple of weeks, so we need to get these papers signed."

"Sure, it's fine. I hate for you to go out of your way like that, though," Lizbeth said.

"It's no problem. I'm looking forward to the drive. The scenery is breathtaking."

Lizbeth giggled. "Would that be inside or outside of the car?"

"I won't bring her to the cottage, I promise."

"Do you know where I live? I'm sure she could show you." Lizbeth was careful to use pronouns, because she hadn't told Gray about Dana and Molly, yet.

"Relax, Lizbeth. I'm only going to be there a few hours. Then we're off to Texas."

"Do they make U-Hauls for jets?" Lizbeth said, laughing.

When she hung up, Gray questioned her with her eyes. Lizbeth explained that Molly was coming down with papers for Lizbeth to sign. Gray's feet were better this morning. Fanny's prediction that the salt water would help had been correct. She wasn't ready to run a marathon yet, but Gray was moving around with no perceptible limp. Still, when they went back across the street, Lizbeth made Gray lie on the couch while she cleaned the cottage. She gave Gray a copy of the rough draft of her paper to read, to keep her busy.

Lizbeth enjoyed being domestic. She had a maid service in Durham, but this life suited her better. It may wear off over time, she told herself, but right now making a home with Gray was fulfilling. The simple act of finding Gray's tee shirt thrown across the back of the chair in the bedroom made her smile. She remembered how it got there. Little things, like making up the bed where they had just been, filled her with a glowing warmth. It was more than sex, or love even. Lizbeth felt whole. This is where she was meant to be. This is what she was meant to do. This is whom she was meant to love.

A little over an hour later, she stopped on the way through the parlor to grab a quick kiss from Gray. She was just finishing the last page of the paper when Lizbeth walked up.

Gray looked up at Lizbeth. "That was really interesting. I grew up here and I didn't know half of that stuff. You write very well."

"It's still a draft, but I'm glad you approve." Lizbeth leaned down and kissed Gray lightly on the lips.

Gray pulled Lizbeth down on her lap and wrapped her in a bear hug. Then she began to kiss Lizbeth's neck. It was just getting good to Lizbeth when they heard a car pull up and a door slam in the driveway, followed shortly by another car door closing. Lizbeth thought, "Oh God, Molly brought Dana to the house." She hadn't had time to tell Gray about Molly and Dana. Well, to be honest, she had the time; she just hadn't wanted to do it. Then a second car stopped and two more car doors shut loudly, interrupting her thoughts. Now, she was confused. Four doors closing didn't make sense.

Lizbeth disentangled herself from Gray and went to the front door. Before she could get the door open, the approaching woman saw her through the glass and began screeching at her, loudly.

"Mary Elizabeth Jackson, have you lost your damn mind!"

Lizbeth froze, her hand on the doorknob. She wasn't sure if she should open it or not. She looked back at Gray, who now was standing by the couch. Gray was white faced. She had no idea who was on the other side of that door, but she knew whoever it was wasn't happy. Lizbeth swallowed hard and turned back to the door. Gray was going to be no help. This was going to be a confrontation and Gray would probably sneak out the backdoor when Lizbeth's back was turned.

The porch on the other side of the door had now filled up with Jackson women. Lizbeth's mother, Mary Grace Jackson, sixty-six, a gray haired, carbon copy of Lizbeth, was leading the charge. Lizbeth's sister, Annie, taller than the other three and the only blonde, not natural Lizbeth knew, stood behind her mother, wearing a silly grin. Annie loved this. Annie had always been the troublemaker, Lizbeth the good little sister. Except for the pregnancy, Lizbeth had been perfect in her sister's eyes. Even the pregnancy had landed Lizbeth a man her mother approved of and the marriage had lasted longer than anyone expected. Annie flew through men like used cars and most of them were not acceptable to their mother. Lizbeth had finally done something worse than Annie had and she was eating it up. Lizbeth glowered at her through the glass.

Next to her sister was Sharon, her cousin, who had somehow been roped into all this. She looked like she'd rather be anywhere but there on that porch. Her eyes pleaded with Lizbeth to understand. She had no choice. When Mary Grace got on the warpath, you either got on board or got run over. In the back, looking sheepish, was Mazie. When they made eye contact, Mazie shrugged, as if to say, "I couldn't stop her." Lizbeth narrowed her eyes at Mazie. She knew she'd let the cat out of the bag. Someone had said something and Mazie had dropped the bomb on them just to see the reaction. Lizbeth would deal with her later. Right now, she was holding the door handle so her mother couldn't turn it.

Mary Grace glared at her through the glass. "Open the damn door this instant, Lizbeth!"

Lizbeth had no choice. Her mother would rant and rave on the porch until she got her way. She wasn't above throwing a chair through the window, so Lizbeth let go of the handle. She turned her back on the door and walked to the couch, where she was surprised to still find Gray. Although she looked stricken with panic, she had stayed behind to stand with Lizbeth. How long she would remain was the question.

Mary Grace charged into the room, followed by the rest of the Jackson women. Lizbeth's mother was in a rage. Her wide eyes searched the room for a place to vent and settled on Gray.

"What have you done to my daughter? Did you drug her or something?"

A strange calm fell over Lizbeth. She had avoided confrontations with her mother by always doing what Mary Grace thought was best. She had allowed her mother to dictate her choices, but not anymore. She wasn't angry or scared. She was amused. It was such a freeing feeling not to care what her mother thought of her. She smiled and stepped in front of Gray, shielding her from the oncoming fury that was Mary Grace Jackson.

"Mother, I believe you know Gray O'Neal. She's the girl who tied Annie and me to the tree out back."

"I know who she is and I know what she is. Wipe that smile off your face. This isn't funny, Lizbeth. What in the hell is wrong with you?"

Lizbeth couldn't help it. She giggled. Gray pinched her in the back. Trying desperately not to laugh, Lizbeth said, "There's nothing wrong with me, Mother. I've simply discovered what I've been missing all these years and I gotta tell ya'..." She lost it. She could control the laughter no longer. She finished her statement through streams of giggles. "... It's fucking fantastic."

Sharon and Mazie got caught up in Lizbeth's giggles and joined in. Annie was shocked, her mouth hung open, but a tiny hint of a grin was creeping onto the corners of her lips. Mary Grace turned twenty shades of red, before settling on a bright beet color. Gray wasn't amused and said, "Shit," under her breath.

"You watch your language, young lady," Mary Grace spat.

Lizbeth, still giggling, replied, "That's just it, Mother, I'm not a young lady. I am a grown woman. I'm not sure what you thought you were going to accomplish by sounding the alarm and gathering the troops, but I assure you, nothing you say will have any bearing on how I live the rest of my life. I love you, Mom, but I don't have to listen to you."

Mary Grace wasn't to be deterred from her mission. She growled at Lizbeth, "James did something to your brain. You're sick. I've got enough signatures in this room to lock your ass in the psych ward until you straighten up."

"That's funny," Lizbeth said, not intimidated by her mother's threats. "Till I straighten up, that's quite clever."

Mary Grace stepped closer, glaring at her youngest daughter. "Lizbeth, I will not let you embarrass this family."

When Lizbeth heard Gray's big sigh behind her, she knew Gray was thinking she had told Lizbeth this was going to happen. Lizbeth didn't want Gray to think for one moment any of this made a difference in Lizbeth's feelings about their relationship.

Lizbeth looked at Mazie. "Mazie, am I embarrassing you?"

Mazie smiled. She'd been waiting for her chance to speak up and now she had it. "No, Mom. I am not the least embarrassed by this. Dad has done so many embarrassing things, there's no way you could compete with that. I'm glad you found someone that makes you happy. That's all that's important to me."

Mary Grace scoffed at her. "She's young. She doesn't know what she's talking about."

Mazie didn't like that at all. She shot back, "I may be young, but I know the difference in Mom now and before she met Gray is phenomenal. Look at her. She's standing up to your bossy crap for once."

A slight chuckle from Gray, behind her, set Lizbeth to giggling again. Mary Grace's mouth hung open. Annie's eyes flew back and forth between Mazie and her grandmother. She appeared to believe there was going to be physical contact any moment.

Lizbeth drew the attention back to herself. "Well, there, you see. The only person whose opinion I do value is okay with it, so I guess the rest of you can just go away, if that's what you want." Lizbeth stopped giggling and leveled her eyes on her mother. "If you can't accept me for whom I am and accept Gray as part of my life, then to hell with you."

To Lizbeth's great surprise, Annie began to clap. Sharon joined her. Mazie ran to Lizbeth and hugged her. Mary Grace was frozen in place. Lizbeth still held her with her gaze, waiting for the next explosion, but there wasn't one. The air slowly went out of her sails and she began to accept defeat, which totally caught Lizbeth by surprise. She released Mazie from the hug and went to her mother.

"Mom, I don't want you out of my life."

Mary Grace looked at Lizbeth; a tear hung in the corner of her eye. "I just don't understand, Lizbeth."

Lizbeth answered her softly, "I don't understand it either, but I know I love her and she loves me and that's all that really matters. Gray makes me happy and I deserve that."

"Yes, you do," Mary Grace answered, "but are you sure this is going to make you happy in the long run? Do these things last?"

"These things, as you call it, are just like any relationship. Some last. Some don't..."

Gray, who had been nearly silent through the whole ordeal, interrupted Lizbeth, "This one will."

Lizbeth smiled back at Gray. "See, Mom. She really loves me. That's all I've ever wanted. Somebody who would love only me. Be happy for me, please. I'm not shutting the door on you, but I'm not going to listen to your opinion on this. It's going to take some time for you to come to grips with it, I know, but in the end, I think you'll come around. After all, you did introduce us."

A knock on the open door startled everyone. It was Molly.

"Sorry, I hope I'm not interrupting."

Lizbeth went to greet her. "No, Molly. Come on in. We were just having a little family discussion. You know my mother."

Molly stuck out her hand to shake Mary Grace's. "Yes, how lovely to see you, Mrs. Jackson, and of course I know Annie."

Annie smiled and nodded. Lizbeth suddenly wondered how well Molly did know Annie, but she moved on.

"And this is my cousin, Sharon." Molly shook Sharon's hand. Then Lizbeth led her to Gray. "Molly Kincaid, I'd like for you to meet Gray O'Neal."

Molly shook Gray's hand. "It's a pleasure to finally meet you, Gray. I've heard a lot about you. It was all good."

"Nice to meet you, too," Gray said.

Lizbeth could tell all the attention overwhelmed Gray a bit. She slid over close to her and took her hand. Lizbeth looked around the room and decided the best thing to do was to try to get Gray alone for a minute, so she could make sure she would make it through this impromptu Jackson family reunion.

"Mazie, why don't you take everybody back to the kitchen and make some coffee? I'll be right there."

Mazie got the rest of the women to follow her to the back of the house and Lizbeth pulled Gray by the hand upstairs. When they were alone, Lizbeth kissed Gray and then looked up into those scared blue eyes.

"Honey, I told you I didn't care what they thought. I know that was uncomfortable for you, and I would have headed her off if I had known she was coming. I'm sorry, but it's over now. Are you okay?"

Gray grinned at her. "Yeah, I'm a big girl. I can take it. I was just surprised, that's all."

Lizbeth laughed. "I thought you were going to run there for a second."

"I thought about it," Gray said, chuckling.

"So, you're okay? Do you want to go to Fanny's while I deal with this?"

"No, I'll stay. How would it look if I went and hid across the street after you just told your mom she could go to hell if she didn't like it?"

Lizbeth giggled. "I did, didn't I?"

"Yes, you did." Gray hugged her, saying, "I love you, Lizbeth."

"Good, because I need to tell you something about Dana and Mo…."

Her sentence was cut short by Fanny's, "Yoo Hoo!" at the front door.

"I guess it'll have to wait," Gray said. "This should be good. Your mom and Fanny go back a ways."

They hurried down the stairs. Lizbeth ran into the back of Gray when she abruptly stopped at the bottom of the steps. Lizbeth peeked around her to see Fanny standing there with Dana.

Fanny said, "Look who I found walking down at the end of Howard Street."

Dana smiled, but Lizbeth could tell Fanny had made her come. Dana didn't want to be there any more than Lizbeth wanted her there. She made eye contact with Lizbeth.

"Hey, Lizbeth. Glad to see everything worked out okay," Dana said weakly.

Lizbeth stepped around Gray and turned to look at her. Gray was definitely confused.

"Honey, that's what I was going to tell you," Lizbeth said, distracting Gray from staring at Dana. "Dana and Molly are… well, seeing each other. They met at my house."

By this time, the women from the back of the house had flooded the room again. Molly looked at Lizbeth.

"I swear I told her not to come here," Molly offered in her defense.

"It's okay, Molly. I think Miss Fanny here had a lot to do with it."

Mary Grace broke across the room to hug Fanny. "Oh, Fanny! It's so good to see you."

Fanny laughed. "I guess we're related a bit now, with these two."

Mary Grace was taken aback. "You know about them and you approve?"

"Yep, I think my Gray there finally got her head on right. Lizbeth's a fine woman and I'm proud to call her family."

Mary Grace then turned her attention to Dana. "And who is this beautiful creature?"

Lizbeth answered, "Dr. Dana Fox, this is my mother Mary Grace Jackson and that's my sister Annie and my cousin Sharon. Mother, Dana is Gray's ex and Molly's new friend."

"Oh my God, are you swapping?" She directed her next question at Lizbeth. "Were you and Molly….involved….before this?"

Molly laughed and then covered her mouth. Lizbeth grinned at her and shook her head. "No, Mother. Molly and I are just friends and nobody's swapping. Dana and Gray split up years ago. She was just visiting."

Mary Grace was still having a hard time. She shook her head, looking around the room. "All these beautiful women and they all like girls. Was there something in the water? What happened? Are there just no good men left out there?"

Fanny saved the day. "Oh hell, Mary Grace. They don't need a man to make 'em happy. They're takin' care of each other, not fallin' round behind some man that don't appreciate 'em. Let 'em be. They love each other."

"But Fanny, the Bible…"

Fanny raised her hand to silence Mary Grace. "Don't come at me with what the Bible says, Mary Grace Jackson. I 'magine I know most every word in it. Some I take as the gospel and some I got sense enough to know was put there by man and ain't got squat to do with the word of God. It says, 'Judge not, lest ye be judged.' I try to live by that. And I seen with my own eyes how God brought these two together and he had to have a reason. They were meant for each other like two peas in a pod, ain't my place to argue with that."

Gray slid her arm around Lizbeth and said, "Amen."

Others in the room followed with their own, "Amen." Even Annie and Sharon added their affirmation. Mary Grace was outnumbered.

"Well, I guess if she's going to carry on with some woman, I'd rather it be Gray than anyone else. I always liked you, kid."

The room erupted in laughter. Lizbeth was so happy she started crying. She looked up at Gray, who was looking down at her. It was done. She had given herself over to Lizbeth, all of her, even the places she had sworn never to allow to see the light of day. When Lizbeth first met Gray, she wondered if she'd ever really know what she was thinking. Looking in her eyes now, she knew without a doubt Gray loved her. Waking up Gray had been a challenge, but from the look in those crystal blue eyes, it was most definitely going to pay off.

Epilogue

Lizbeth graduated in December with honors. Gray met her with a wide grin when she stepped out of the mass of graduates being rushed by proud families. Lizbeth took a research job with the North Carolina Language and Life Project, working to preserve the Carolina Brogue, allowing her to work from home. Shortly after graduation, on an unusually warm day in January, Lizbeth and Gray took the recently restored Fanny Gray out on the Sound. Gray made a promise to Lizbeth just as the sun began to set over the slick calm water.

Six months later, standing on the white sands of Portsmouth Island, a small group of people gathered before a preacher. Mary Grace and Lizbeth's father David, Annie and her squeeze of the month, Sharon and her husband were all mingled in with islanders. Along with other friends and family members, all dressed in white and barefooted, as requested by the brides, they listened as the preacher read the story of Ruth from the bible. Molly and Mazie stood beside Lizbeth. Dana was back in Texas, but Molly still made occasional, what Lizbeth referred to as, bootie calls. Mazie's handsome husband beamed at his wife. Lizbeth loved the way he cared for her daughter. Fanny stood with Gray. Jaye was in the front of the congregation, smiling from ear to ear.

Lizbeth had smiled so much her face hurt. No one cared that this ceremony had no legal standing. It was a commitment they were making in front of their family and friends and the government had nothing to do with it, which is what marriage was meant to be in the first place. When it was time for their vows, they turned to each other. They had agreed to make them short, because Gray wasn't really good at expressing her emotions in public and she didn't want to screw it up. Lizbeth went first.

"Gray, I've loved you since the first time I ever laid eyes on you and when I close my eyes for the last time on this earth, I will still be in love with you."

Gray grinned that raffish grin that still made Lizbeth weak in the knees. The grin slipped into a big smile when she said, "Yeah, something like that."

It wasn't much, but it was all Lizbeth needed to hear. She smiled up at Gray and laughed. The onlookers laughed as well.

When the rings came out, Gray had no clue what to expect. Lizbeth had the rings custom made and kept them a secret. Gray held out her left hand for Lizbeth to slide the ring on her finger. When Lizbeth let go, Gray looked down and started laughing. She took Lizbeth's matching ring and slid it on her hand. They held them up together to show the well-wishers.

On the ring fingers of each woman were three tiny bands of gold rope shaped as if they were tied around a tree.

About the Author

R. E. "Decky" Bradshaw is a native of the Outer Banks of North Carolina, now living in Oklahoma. A former university and high school theatre instructor, Bradshaw worked both on stage and backstage, as well as directing and designing during her twenty-five year Theatrical career. Now writing full-time, Bradshaw debuted her first four lesbian fiction novels in the fall of 2010. Proud of her Tar Heel roots, all of R. E. Bradshaw's books, thus far, have been set in her beloved home state of North Carolina. Her love of the Outer Banks, southern traditions, and Carolina women rings throughout her works. Bradshaw and her partner will celebrate their Twenty-fourth anniversary in June 2011 and have a son they are both very proud of.

Made in the USA
Lexington, KY
17 June 2011